A CANDLE
IN
DARKNESS

June Livesay

A CANDLE IN DARKNESS

June Livesay

STARBURST PUBLISHERS™

P.O. Box 4123, Lancaster, Pennsylvania 17604

To schedule Author appearances write:
Author Appearances, Starburst Promotions, P. O. Box 4123, Lancaster, PA 17604 or call (717) 293-0939.

Cover art by Dave Ivey

We, the Publisher and Author, declare that to the best of our knowledge all material (quoted or not) contained herein is accurate; and we shall not be held liable for the same.

First Printing, June 1990

ISBN: 0-914984-22-5
Library of Congress Catalog Number 90-70126

Printed in the United States of America

Dedicated to
My Mother
Who Loved Ecuador
As I Do.

Pronunciation

adiós
buenos días
capitán
cariña
corazón
mamá
mañana
niñita
niños
papá
¿quién
señor
señora
señorita
señores
Jermán
Joél
José
Luís Peréz
Ramón
Yaruquí

Contents

Preface

In the early 1970's my mother and I drove a packed Volkswagen from Portland, Oregon to Panama City where we boarded a freighter. Five days later we disembarked in Ecuador.

When my mother flew back home I remained in Ecuador where I would live for the next nine years. Without knowing a word of Spanish or understanding the Ecuadorian culture, I found myself living in an Indian village several miles east of Quito. During the first years, I worked with an American and a jungle Indian in an orphange and maternity clinic. I later lived in a 200 years-old mud house—among the people.

After my return to America, it was the prodding of my friends that led me to put the account of my experiences down on paper. Many of the experiences recorded in this book were actually mine. However, I have given them to friends and acquaintances and placed them in settings very familiar to me. Read this book and go with me as I relive my life in the country of Ecuador.

June Livesay

Book 1   *Rolando*

Chapter 1

I t was the incessant talking outside his bedroom window that pulled Rolando from a sleep filled with dark, oppressive dreams. Two fat, black flies buzzed against the pane hoping for escape. A ray of sunlight streamed from a gap between the two uneven, faded cotton curtains and glanced off a small mirror hanging on the flaking, whitewashed wall and glared in his eyes. Heavy, humid air left him breathless and nauseated. The pillow and bed felt clammy as he turned his sweat-soaked body. His mouth was dry and bitter tasting, his head and heart pounded. Lifting himself on one elbow, he groaned as his eyes focused on his two brothers still in the bonds of sleep. Geoff's mouth hung open, a muscle in his cheek twitched and his eyes fluttered as if involved in a dream of pursuit and fleeing. Roberto lay with his arm across his eyes in an unconscious attempt to keep out the light. The talking outside paused a moment and Geoff snored softly.

Rolando passed his hand over his face and tried to sit up. The nausea and dizziness increased so he sat for a moment until he felt safe to stand. It took a minute to remember today was Sunday. Market day. That explained the noise outside.

The Martinez house lay directly across from the open market. Only on Sunday could the residents of the village and neighboring hills and valleys buy fresh meat and produce. Hours before dawn, merchants laid out their wares on long, rickety wooden tables. Ripened tomatoes, carrots, potatoes, beets and green beans placed side by side with rows of oranges, lemons, chirimoyas and taxos added color to the simplicity and poverty. Along the walls women with sleepy-eyed children laid combs, batteries, threads and colorful yarns on woolen blankets. Trucks filled with thin pigs, sheep and cows backed into a makeshift corral and husky ranchers prepared to slaughter.

At dawn the market filled with people who had walked throughout the night, descending from the mountains that surrounded the town of Pachuca. As the sun spread over the sleepy village, the excitement of friends meeting, the clanging of church bells, the squealing of helpless pigs being led to slaughter and the motors of several buses and trucks brought life to an otherwise lethargic people. This eagerness would by afternoon change into a drowsiness brought on by drinking beer in local saloons or by the droning of lengthy church mass. One day a week, the Indians attempted to forget the dreadful toil of grubbing an existence out of the thousands of steep hillsides that make up the Andes Mountains in Ecuador.

Yawning, Rolando pulled on his pants and buttoned them. Yanking a towel from the bedpost, he searched a drawer in the scarred bureau for a clean T-shirt and padded through the door, down the hallway to the back entrance which led to a small patio. Directly in line with the house sat a small, squat one-room dwelling built of large, dried mud blocks crumbling with age. A deep oven had been built into the wall which now was stacked with old mattresses, tires and sacks of rags. The roof was layered with chipped, weatherbeaten mud tile in a futile attempt to keep out the heavy rains. Hamsters, part of the Indian diet, scurried about among the stored debris nosing for grass and corn stalks tossed in for their feeding.

Rolando plodded by as hens scratched in the dust between rows of corn stalks, clucking in contentment while keeping a watchful eye on their baby chicks. A thin cat looked up from licking his paw and made a move toward Rolando, then changed his mind and returned to the sunny spot by the weather-worn rabbit hutches lining the wall.

Moving to the back side of the patio where water was running into a cement vat from a faucet, he pushed a tub of soaking clothes to one side and placed the towel and shirt on an extended branch growing from the hardened mud wall which divided the Martinez property from their neighbors.

He was oblivious to the beautiful morning. A bright sun was almost overhead now, the dark blue sky to the west was starting to lighten, while white, lazy, puffy clouds gathered in the east throwing shadows on the rolling green mountains that towered above the drowsy town of Pachuca. A patchwork quilt of tiny farms rose to the summit, a day's journey away.

Rolando dipped a metal cup into the vat of water and filled a bowl. Finding a bar of soap behind the tub of clothes, he wet his face and lathered the bar.

"Rolando, oh, I'm so glad you're awake. Mama said if you come, I can give you breakfast."

A twelve-year-old girl burst through the door leading from the house and ran across the patio, long black braids dancing on her back. She threw her arms around his waist.

"Watch out, Elena, or you'll have soap all over you." He winced in pain at his throbbing head.

"I don't care. I'm just glad you're up. Mama said I can go to the party with you this afternoon."

His heart warmed as he watched her. Even with a tendency toward stoutness, she was quick moving, her large dark eyes always sparkling with either anger or excitement. He adored her.

She was his only sister in a family with four older brothers. From the day of her birth, she had a lively charm that had won his heart completely. He could deny her nothing.

He leaned down and kissed her lightly. "You know what happens when I take you to parties. You capture all the attention and the other girls are ignored."

"Oh, silly. Hurry, come and eat."

She vanished through the door.

Rolando shaved, stripped to the waist and washed, trying to push a nagging thought from his mind. He was drinking too much. It was the curse of this downtrodden town. Liquor held it in a tight vise and Rolando knew of no one who had escaped the degradation either directly or indirectly. It destroyed families, sent young men to early graves, turned beautiful girls into old women. Only the fittest of children survived the poor diet they were forced to eat day after day because money went to quench the thirst of their fathers and mothers. Half of the infants in the village would die before their first birthday. This Rolando knew as, of the ten children his mother had delivered, only five had survived.

He was weak in character. Only his unusual height and fair complexion had set him apart from others his age and allowed him the honor of leadership among his friends. He cringed at the thought of his lack of will power. It resulted in his drinking himself into a stupor each weekend. He hated how he felt the next morning. Well, tonight had to be different, he reasoned. Uplifted with the thought that he would stay away from liquor, breakfast began to sound good. Perhaps he could still try to keep Elena home. There was no sense in exposing her to that kind of entertainment. It was bad enough having an alcoholic father.

He pulled on the clean shirt, combed his light brown hair absently, unaware of his masculinity. His large, brown eyes, soft mouth and straight nose, combined with a perfectly curved chin and jaw, brought more than his share of attention from females and males alike. At times he took advantage of this, but basically he loved his family and friends and when sober took heed to show care and concern.

Grabbing the towel and bending to pet the cat who had casually wandered close, he sighed, wary of the argument that would ensue when he would have to tell Elena she should not go to the party.

She had a cup of hot milk waiting and pushed a jar of instant coffee to him as he seated himself at the old wooden table placed in the middle of the small, dimly lit kitchen. He reached for the sugar bowl as she quickly cut fresh buns bought at the bakery that morning, spreading them thick with butter and chunks of white cheese.

"Where's Pablo?" He asked wondering at the whereabouts of his youngest brother.

"He left with his friends hours ago. They're probably playing soccer." "She placed the food before him.

He slowly stirred the hot coffee mixture, watching her movements.

"Elena, if I take you with me, you'll only be able to stay for an hour. Tomorrow is school."

Her reaction startled him, as she spun on her heels, hands on hips.

"Oh!" She yelled, her eyes flashing with anger. "That's not fair. Pablo is going to stay with you."

"Carina, Pablo is fifteen. He is old enough to stay out late. Anyway, he usually ends up sleeping through much of the evening."

"I don't care," she snapped. "I hav...er...I want to go and stay the whole party."

He stared at her, mystified, wondering why she was so insistent.

"Anyway," she continued, eyes now sparkling with tears, "I don't want to stay home tonight. Papa is always worse on Sundays."

Sighing inwardly, he started to relent, hating confrontations with his sister.

"Go talk to Mama. Maybe I can take you to Aunt Mariana's house later. You can go to school from there tomorrow."

Jumping with delight, tears still bright in her eyes, she kissed his cheek and ran from the room.

He sighed audibly, knowing she was right. Papa was always worse on Sundays. But he was convinced Elena was too eager to attend the party this evening and instinctively knew her desire to go was more than her fear of their father.

He had long ago determined Elena would never grow up in Pachuca without being educated. Rolando looked on the ruin in his town with dismay, girls married at age fifteen to boys so young they knew nothing more than to work as peons. Most of the time they had to marry. Many couples had six living babies before they were married ten years, more if all the children conceived had lived. Tiny white, wooden coffins were sold daily at the local carpenter's front door. Couples lived in mud huts, cooking and sleeping on floors, the only escape being liquor. That would never happen to Elena, his darling sister.

From the day of her birth, Elena's future had been his obsession. He had been age eleven at the time his mother's labor pains began. Unfortunately, it was late Sunday afternoon and as his mother had been under the care of a doctor in Quito, it became Rolando's responsibility to find transportation. All of his mother's previous deliveries had occurred in their home, assisted by a neighbor, but Pablo's delivery had been so difficult, Senora Martinez had realized she'd not be able to complete this one without medical attention. She had sent Rolando to find his father, however he had had little hope of finding him sober.

As expected, the boy was informed in the plaza that his father had walked up the mountain to visit with a second cousin who had invited him for lunch. Late that evening Rolando found him, too drunk to accompany his wife to Quito, therefore the boy hurriedly descended the mountain alone running through the plaza and home to find his mother groaning in bed, her face wet with sweat. She had sent Geoff to find a car or bus, but none were available as almost all the men in town were drunk.

Rolando suddenly thought of a foreign nurse who had a maternity clinic a few blocks from the house. She resisted his suggestion. Strange stories circulated about the nurse and her Ecuadorian helper. And too, it was understood that unless a patient received pre-natal care in the clinic, service was refused.

As the labor pains intensified, his mother finally relented and decided perhaps the nurse would admit them if she could see the need and closeness of delivery.

Rolando ordered Roberto to find a midwife in case the foreign nurse refused them and sent them away.

The small boy ran for the door.

"It's raining, Rolando. It's raining hard," he yelled.

"Just go. Don't worry about something like a little rain now. Go!"

Roberto dashed into the street as Rolando brought a poncho to his mother and pulled her from the bed to her feet, wrapping her warmly. She swayed and reached for him as he attempted to embrace her thick body while fighting to keep his balance. Contractions gripped her as she screamed in agony. He allowed her to crouch until they subsided. Panic clutched his heart as he realized the pains were coming closer. The delivery could occur before reaching the clinic. Rearranging her poncho, he tugged at her arm. Hurrying to the door, he discovered the rain that had been threatening all day had indeed arrived. As they stepped out, stinging pellets of windswept water soaked them before they had crossed the road and darkness settled around, hiding the familiar scenes. His mother walked slowly, stumbling, head bent against the pelting drops. Guiding her arm, he attempted to wipe her face with the palm of his hand and felt a warm substance. Puzzled, he brushed his hand across her mouth again and asked her if she was having a nosebleed.

"My head hurts so, Hijo. If only I could deliver this baby. My nose bleeds when my head aches, and I'm sure it is because of the child."

Rolando trembled, aware of his mother's problems with high blood pressure during her pregnancies. Rage toward his father engulfed him. His father seemed to consider nothing but himself and his own needs.

Stopping a moment to let his mother rest, he felt her sway against the wind and his small frame.

"Please, Mama. We must go on."

"I can't," she wept in despair. "I can't go on. Please, a pain is coming and I must rest."

"But, Mama, it's too cold and wet in the rain," he pleaded. "Please try to go on. It's not far now."

"I can't. You find the nurse. Ask if she will come and help me."

"I'm afraid to leave you," he sobbed. "Where will you stay? There is nothing but mud and rivers of water."

"Please, dear, leave me. There is so little time. We can't worry about the weather," she urged, "you must find help soon. Hurry!"

Hot tears ran down his face, mixing with the cold rain. Shaking with fear, he fell on his knees and felt with his hands until he reached the edge of the uneven rock road and found a patch of wet grass. Pulling off his thin sweater, he laid it out.

"Mama," he called. "I found a spot for you. Stay here until I return. Please don't move. If you go further onto the road harm may come to you."

His chattering teeth made talking difficult and his body shivered uncontrollably as he helped her down, wrapping the poncho around her, tucking the edges under. Then, as though shackles had been cut free, he ran with all his might. Rain ran off his head in streams and down the short-sleeved shirt he wore, water sloshed in his shoes. Dogs barked from a hut behind the high-walled barriers as he sought a moment's shelter beside a gate. He strayed into the oozing mud at the side of the road, but his fear and weariness were put aside with the thought of his mother lying helpless, vulnerable to untold dangers.

"Oh, God, please help me. It's so dark," he cried aloud.

Suddenly he saw a bright light through a large crack in the ever present mud wall that surrounded all properties close to the plaza. Feeling his way closer, he ran his hand over the steep side until he found a branch growing from the structure. Praying it would hold, he pulled himself up to the crack, where clods of dirt had worn away. Relief spread through him. He was close to the entrance of the clinic. Running with renewed strength, he fought the deep pools of water gathering on the sides of the road and arrived at the metal gate that stood at the top of a steep entrance between two high, dried mud walls. The doors were thick and heavy, but were always left unlocked for patients seeking help, and now he hurriedly opened them, gasping for breath.

The white two-story building had a dim light turned on in the recovery room and he knew someone should be there. A long wire fence divided the width of the clinic, barring access to a clump of buildings several meters in the distance. The inner entrance to the maternity hospital was used only by the American nurse and her helpers and was off limits to the town's population.

Rolando yelled with all his might, pounding on the windows. Dogs barked in the distance and he saw movement in the clinic. After a long, agonizing wait, the door slowly opened.

A woman, aged forty, more or less, appeared, stern and disapproving. The boy fought rising panic and dislike as he viewed Lucia. Her small, cold, black eyes held no expression but contempt, her slender hooked nose accentuated large lips. Short black hair, combed back, wide shoulders and small breasts gave her a masculine look.

"What do you want?" She squinted at him.

"Please come with me. My Mama is having a baby." He hated the anxiety in his voice.

"Well, I'm not going out in the rain to see your Mama." She slammed the door.

Rolando beat on the closed door causing the dogs to bark again. In a state of panic, he ran to the end of the clinic and yelled. It seemed to be raining less, but growing colder. With an effort, he tried to control his shaking, but just as he gave up, he saw the door of a house at the end of the long sidewalk open. The light behind revealed the shape of a woman and he caught his breath with hope as he realized she was going to the clinic. Time stood still as the shadow moved under the field lights hanging on poles along the sidewalk. He then ran back to the patient's door as he heard the far entrance open and close. Heavy footsteps approached and the door opened quickly.

He had always wondered at the strangeness of the woman standing above him. Tales circulated far and wide about Margaret Brewer. Leaning toward a masculine look with a neglected brush of hair above her mouth and signs of shaving on her chin, she still appeared more feminine than Lucia. She was an American nurse who had arrived in Ecuador twelve years earlier and had decided to make it her permanent home. No one had been able to become more than an acquaintance. She remained aloof and mysterious. Stories were passed from hut to hut that she was wealthy, due to connections in the United States, and this caused her to be a subject of awe. Rolando felt he could trust her more than Lucia and sensed the nurse had more compassion for people. Margaret had soft brown eyes which could look kind at times. Her eyes and competent hands caused women to continue delivering babies at the clinic, as it was widely expressed that, if nothing else, Margaret Brewer loved nursing.

Now, with great hope, Rolando greeted her.

"Buenas noches, senorita. Please, come with me. My Mama is on the road in labor. She needs your help."

The woman hesitated a moment contemplating the situation.

"I can't help you. It's raining and I must not catch cold. One of my patients is ill with a throat infection. What if I become ill? Anyway, I understand your mother has been seeing a doctor in Quito. Why doesn't she go there?"

"Because there are no cars." He felt his throat choke with tears and fought them, blinking hard.

Lucia peered over Margaret's shoulder and snickered. The nurse turned and stared at the Indian without a word until Lucia shrugged her shoulders and walked away, stung.

"I'm sorry, but I just don't go out on clinic calls and I don't like to deliver a baby when I haven't checked a woman previously. This and because it is rainy and cold. My goodness, child, there you stand without a coat. Don't your parents care for you? Sometimes I believe you people would rather live like animals."

He couldn't believe his ears.

"But my Mama. She's close to delivery and she's ill. Her nose is bleeding and she said her blood pressure is up."

"All the more reason why I can't help you. Now please leave me alone. I have my patients to care for."

The door shut and Rolando sprang to life ramming his fists onto the clinic wall.

"I hate you! Oh, how I hate you! The great American who leaves her country to help us."

Spitting on the door, he screamed. "Thank you. I'll never forget you."

Turning, he ran down the soggy pathway. Upset from his encounter, he no longer realized how cold it was. Out of breath, he moved up the road, slipping and falling until he finally reached the spot where he'd left his mother. He called her name softly, then more loudly. Falling on the road, he felt with his hands.

"I must not be in the right place." Moving further, he called again. "Mama, Mama, where are you?" He returned several meters, calling her name.

"Mama, please answer me. Mama!"

Dread filled his heart. Thinking he might faint, he rested against the mud wall a moment. From deep within, large sobs rose to rack his body. Knowing he was close to the spot where he had left her, panic overcame him and he screamed in hysteria. Dogs barked as he moved to the road on his hands and knees, crawling the length of a block. He was soaked, cold and distraught. His head swam with exhaustion.

Sitting a moment he was able to relax. "Perhaps she returned home?" he asked himself aloud. No. She was too weak. It was impossible.

But the thought gave him hope, and rising to his feet he started back to his house. He burst through the front door and into his mother's bedroom. It was empty. Yelling through each room, he found no one. Fear gripped his heart and bile rose in his throat. Without thinking of a coat, he ran from the house and up the block to the main plaza and the home of the town's nurse's aide. The large, aged two-story dwelling built of dried mud blocks and wood stood in a central location directly in front of the main plaza. It leaned at a comical angle where it had settled after being buffeted by two hundred years of fierce winds, rainstorms and occasional earthquakes. Rolando beat on the door, yelling. After a long wait, it was slowly opened by an elderly, heavyset man wearing a wide grin that revealed two remaining teeth. Don Eduardo went through all the maddening greeting formalities. Anxious to ask if the man's daughter, Olivia, was home, Rolando was almost rude.

"Why no, Rolando, she's not here," he replied, pursing his mouth thoughtfully. "Now, where did she go? Let me see. Yes, she was here for awhile today. You know, I think she decided to go to Quito tonight. Or, was that last night? No, wait. She might be up at my son, Cesar's house." The old man spoke slowly, squinting his eyes and scratching his chin.

Rolando wanted to scream. He pressed his hand to his face and, breathing deeply, he said. "Actually, I'm looking for my mother. She's ill and I thought perhaps Senorita Olivia knew where she had gone."

Shifting his weight from one foot to the other, Don Eduardo suddenly clapped his hands together.

"You know, I think I saw your mother go to the church tonight. Was that your mother? But, there again, maybe that was...."

But Rolando was gone. Don Eduardo stared after him, shrugged and yawned.

Rolando knew of one place he could ask. Someone was always present at the corner store and much of the town's activities were discussed over beers and bottled sodas. He ran the half block to the corner.

Chapter 2

One naked lightbulb hung from the store's ceiling, making a vain effort to light the room. Shadows darkened the crowded, uneven shelves which held meager staples of the Indian diet along with rows of liquor bottles in various shapes and sizes. On the floor, barrels of rice, flour, sugar and salt stood open as if in invitation to the scores of flies that seemed to light on every exposed surface. A large cupboard set in the dried mud wall held several round chunks of soft, white, salty cheese made from soured milk, each decorated with specks of dirt and sand that had been carelessly added in the separation of curd from whey. Tall cabinets of wood and glass set on the floor with assorted buns and rolls available for customers. Two thin dogs watched from the doorstep hoping the cabinet doors would be left open.

The store owner had recently bought a small black-and-white television set, something the villagers had never heard of. As Rolando ran through the door, he started with fright at the sound of a siren. Realizing it was coming from the television, he almost laughed out loud from nervousness.

Several children sat on the filthy floor staring at an American program dubbed in Spanish. He pushed past the group and approached a girl standing behind the counter.

"Buenos noches. Is your papa here?"

Grudgingly she acknowledged him. "Si. Wait here and I'll see." Her eyes remained riveted to the television set as she moved away.

"Please hurry and call him. It's very important," urged Rolando.

She looked at him resentfully and walked to the back of the room, while he glanced around the familiar room impatiently, not actually seeing the patches of plaster and mud, or the shelves in disarray. The uneven wood floors were worn and muddied from heavy traffic that had frequented the store all that day. He looked at the television and couldn't help forgetting for a moment why he was there. Two American actors were toting guns and sneaking into a building somewhere in a far off country called, he thought, the United States of America. Snapping to attention, he saw the girl return.

"I don't know where Papa is, but my Mama is coming."

She returned to her spot behind the counter and leaned on her elbows. Through a narrow opening in the wall covered by a thin blanket, a pleasant-faced woman emerged. Her hair was pulled back and caught with a rubber band at the base of her neck, a sweater wrapped around the typically stocky build of a woman who had borne several children. Her kindly face broke into a wide smile.

"Buenas noches, Rolando. What are you doing out on a night like this without a coat? You must be cold. I will get a poncho for you." She started to turn and Rolando grabbed her arm.

"Buenas noches, senora. Please, I'm not really cold. I'm looking for my Mama and wondered if you had seen her tonight."

"Your Mama? No. She's not at home?"

He shook his head, fear renewed. "No, she started her labor pains tonight and I don't know where she went. I hoped maybe you had seen her pass."

"Would she have gone to your uncle's house?"

"No, they would have sent a messenger. Anyway, she was too weak to walk up there."

The woman thought for a moment and finally brightened. "Why don't we go up to the saloon? Maybe someone there knows something. First, I'm going to get you a poncho and we'll walk together."

She stepped behind the counter, walked to a shadowy corner and stooped. Up into view came a dingy, faded poncho.

"Take this. I was going to have my daughter wash the clothes tomorrow, but you might as well use it tonight. Come chiquito." She wrapped the poncho around him and turning to her daughter said, "Watch the store a little longer. I'll be right back."

Without looking at her, the girl grunted.

Glancing at the sky, Rolando noticed the rain had passed, but the sky remained cloudy. He moved swiftly beside Ernestina as they passed the bakery, a small restaurant, and then turned into the saloon.

Blaring music greeted them as they climbed the broken cement steps leading to the surprisingly bright interior. Stale air and the smell of beer assaulted the boy, causing him to long for the out-of-doors.

He followed Ernestina, picking his way between the rows of littered tables surrounded by bleary-eyed Indians. Some had fallen asleep, sprawling backwards on their chairs and others had slipped to the muddy floor in drunken stupors. One young man staggered to a battered record player in the corner to replay the only available record. The mournful tune blared as the young man returned to his table to drag his wife to her feet. They danced halfheartedly in the corner, leaning on one another's shoulders, the woman's baby strapped to her back in deep sleep.

Ernestina walked directly to the kitchen in the back of the large room. She pushed aside a curtain blocking the doorway and yelled out a greeting. Rolando followed reluctantly, longing to return to the street. Only the hope of finding his mother pushed him on. He poked his head through the doorway and looked around.

There was a movement at the back of the dimly lit room and a woman turned to notice them. She was thin and wiry, her face a network of wrinkles from years of harsh exposure to the fierce rays of the equatorial sun. She looked aged and yet Rolando knew her youngest daughter was about to enter grade school.

A huge pot of new potatoes bubbled on a small kerosene stove. Plates of chicken necks, heads and feet, along with ropes of intestines, set ready for cooking over an open fire on the back patio. Indians awakening from drunken stupors would soon have to face the long journey home and many thoughtful wives would purchase food to provide strength.

The kitchen was narrow and long, stretching into darkness. A lopsided table, one leg shorter than the others, precariously balanced a pile of dishes, several pots and pans and a large bowl of cold, greasy water, which dripped onto the dirt floor forming a mud puddle.

The woman stood under the only light wiping her hands on a dirty sweater. She greeted them with a handshake.

"Buenas noches. This is a pleasure. What brings you to our home?"

Returning the greeting, Ernestina replied, "Rolando is looking for his Mama and wondered if perhaps one of your family had seen her. Her labor pains started tonight, but no one knows where she is."

Wiping the sweat from her face with a filthy apron tied at her waist, she replied slowly, "No, I don't remember seeing her tonight, but come to think of it, about fifteen minutes ago, someone came here asking for water. You know the old lady who lives below the plaza and gives out cures? Her son came running for a bucket of water saying they had an emergency."

Ernestina bit her lip thoughtfully. "We might go down there and just peek in. What do you think, Rolando?"

He shrugged and sighed, "I guess we might as well because I don't know what else to do." Looking up hopefully, he asked, "You will go with me?"

"Of course, dear," she smiled, patting his shoulder.

Pushing through the crowd in the saloon, they quickly reached the entrance and walked back past the corner store and across the street, through the plaza and into the darkness of the neighborhood beyond. It was cold, black and silent, a direct contrast from a few hours earlier when the streets had held throngs of people buying, selling, drinking and dancing. Terror struck him afresh as he remembered his mother alone.

Ernestina, sensing his fear, walked confidently beside him, reaching for his hand in an effort to calm him.

"Do you remember what house she lives in?" he asked, comforted.

"I think it sets behind her daughter's house about a block from the plaza. We must be here now, I'd guess. It's difficult to see clearly. Wait a moment and I'll call out. Let's hope they don't have a dog."

They left the muddy road and walked toward the wall that separated the property from the roadside. Ernestina felt along the bumpy surface until she came to a small gate. Yelling a greeting, they waited for an answer. Twice. Three times. A menacing growl sounded from the direction of the house and a dog barked. Eventually the door of the house opened and a man walked onto a cement step, a candle in his hand.

"Quien es?"

"Buenas noches. La Senora Ernestina from the corner grocery store and Rolando Martinez. We're sorry to disturb you, but can you tell us if you know Rolando's mother? We are hoping she may have been brought here tonight because she is about to deliver a baby. Can you tell us anything?"

With a small grunt he turned to go back into the house. They waited impatiently until the old man finally returned to open the gate and told them to step in. The smell of beer was present and Rolando wondered if the man was drunk and if so, had he understood their request.

Cupping his hands around the candle flame, the elderly man mumbled an order to follow and turning, led them around the house and down an uneven pathway that led to another small building directly behind. There was no step, as the floor of the house became an extension of the dirt pathway.

Stepping inside, Rolando noticed the room was almost filled with burlap bags containing grains of corn ready for sale. The old man held the candle high and walked to the door in the opposite wall. He slowly opened it, motioning them to follow. Flickering candles brought a shadowy light to the inner room and revealed several chairs lining the walls. Rolando realized, as he slowly glanced around that there were two elderly women sitting together, each holding a bottle of beer. It was a typical hut, with one small window. Thick walls made from dried mud were constructed around a mud floor. There was no ceiling, but wood beams held the dried mud tile in place to form a roof. Repeated cooking had blackened the beams. Long cobwebs streamed from the tiles.

Ernestina moved to the two Indian women while the old man silently walked out the door.

"Buenas noches, senoras. Can you tell me if Senora Martinez is here tonight?"

The two elderly women merely pointed their chins in the direction of a room that lay beyond.

Rolando ran to the door, but Ernestina held him back.

"No, dear. Let me go in. I'll see first if she is here and what condition she's in. Wait just a moment."

Ernestina paused at the door, slowly pushing on it, and poked her head inside.

Rolando peeked from behind her arm. More candles flickered, dimly lighting the room to reveal three beds, a bureau, and a bedstand. A small shelf on the wall held yet another candle beneath a picture of the Madonna. Two women knelt by one of the beds and Rolando saw his mother resting there quietly.

Walking to the bed, Ernestina stooped slightly as the two midwives looked up without curiosity.

"Buenas noches, senoras. I have been looking for Senora Martinez," explained Ernestina.

The two women rose to make room for Ernestina as she knelt to put her mouth close to Senora Martinez' ear. "Buenas noches. Your son has been very worried."

At that moment, Rolando's mother gasped and screamed out, arching her back to push down. One of the attending women grabbed a feather and thrust it in her hand. "Blow on the feather. Blow on it. Blow, blow," she crooned.

Senora Martinez grabbed it and blew, relaxing as the pain eased. "It's taking longer than I expected." She attempted a smile.

Rolando tried to ignore the strong smell of sweat and childbirth and considered returning to the outer room. However, his attention was drawn back to the bedroom when he heard Ernestina questioning his mother.

"How did you get here? Rolando has been looking everywhere for you."

Attempting to rise on her elbow, his mother glanced toward the doorway and spoke with effort. "He left me close to the American nurse's clinic. I was lying on the side of the road when a small car passed. I didn't move, but the car returned. A nice man from Tababela told me he was going to look for someone in the plaza. He almost passed me by, but his son noticed something by the side of the road. He was so insistent the man returned to look. I directed the man to my house, told him to send the children up to my brother-in-law's house and then he brought me here. I remembered that sometimes the senoras can help with deliveries."

Rolando's desire to be close to his mother overcame his revulsion at the strange sights and smells. Creeping forward timidly, he observed the bedside table. On it sat a candle, several bottles, chicken feathers, a basin, knife and thread. Pondering on these items, he realized Ernestina had noticed him. She patted his mother's raised arm as she reached out to him. As he eased forward, Ernestina rose and put her arm around his shoulders. "Rolando, come with me. Your mother needs her rest. You can either go to your uncle's house, where your brothers are staying, or go to the outer room."

Just then, another scream rang out and Rolando grabbed at Ernestina's arm, terror in his eyes. "I'll stay in the other room, but please warn them that the last delivery was difficult and please tell them she has not been feeling well. Her headaches have been very painful."

"I'm sure she has already told them, carino. I'll go back in to keep an eye on her while you wait out here."

Rolando seated himself, wrapping his arms tightly around his chest to warm himself as the poncho did little to ward off the chill of the room and the dampness of his clothes. He fought to keep his teeth from chattering as the tension of the long evening overcame him. Looking at the two elderly women he noticed they were asleep, chins drooping on heavy woolen ponchos. Several empty bottles and glasses lay scattered on the dirt floor.

Why don't they go home and go to bed? he thought. "It's always that way in Pachuca," he muttered softly, resenting their intrusion. "They have to come out and just sit, hoping for some little excitement."

Despite the chill, he soon found himself becoming drowsy. A scream from his mother jerked him awake and set his teeth to chattering again. An hour passed, the screams occurring closer together until he finally heard loud and frantic talking and a cry. A baby's cry. In a short time Ernestina came to the door, smiling, and called him. Rushing to the door, he tiptoed into the room. Plastic pails sat at one side of the room, rags piled beside them. The smell of blood and other unfamiliar scents were strong and sickening.

Greeting the ancient midwife and her daughter, he approached the bed where his mother lay with her eyes closed. With fear in his heart, he knelt and sought her hand.

"How is she?" he asked Ernestina, not taking his eye from his mother's face.

"Fine," she smiled. "She seems fine now. Outside of suffering a lot of pain and a terrible nosebleed, it was a good delivery."

He reached out and patted the sleeping woman's face and watched as she slowly opened her eyes, smiling up at him.

"You are such a good boy, my darling son." She squeezed his hand and slept.

"Now, Rolando, would you like to see your new sister?" asked Ernestina.

He turned, eyes wide. "A sister? You mean I have a sister?"

"Why are you so surprised?"

"I never thought of having a sister."

"Come with me." She took his hand to help him rise and led him to a basket on the floor. Holding a candle for him to see, she smiled. "There she is."

Rolando knelt by the basket. Looking down, he turned his head quickly as tears rushed to his eyes. What was wrong with him? Embarrassment burned his cheeks. The women were watching him. But this was his sister and even in the red and wrinkled state of new birth she was beautiful to him. A love clutched his heart that he had never before felt, a powerful blending of emotions. A surge of possessiveness and joy caused him to feel lightheaded and he laughed.

Ernestina laughed with him, relieved the ordeal had ended.

"Come," said Ernestina, "We must be getting back. Your mother will stay here tonight, but she wants you to get home and see that all is well there."

He looked again at his sister. Rising, he returned to his mother and leaning over, he kissed her cheek. Then, thanking the two women heartily, he promised to pay them as soon as he could speak with his papa.

Ernestina and Rolando walked to the front of the property and out onto the road, moving as if in a dream.

A sister. It had never occurred to him he would have a sister. Emotion and excitement shook him to the bone as they crossed the plaza and Ernestina explained to him the events of the night and his mother's experience.

The streets were deserted and dark, only a dim light glowed above the entrance to the store. Ernestina banged heavily on the door until at last the same girl who had been watching the store earlier irritably peered through a crack and then opened the door.

Ernestina pushed her way through, escorting Rolando as the girl turned without a word and shuffled behind the curtained opening to the back. Ernestina lifted the curtain aside and they entered a small room. A sagging green sofa and matching chair sat in the center with a few straight-backed chairs along the painted mud wall. A large dish cabinet, scarred and aged, completed the living room setting. One small light hung from the fly-specked ceiling and Rolando noticed there were no windows. She invited him to sit on the sofa as she disappeared into an adjoining room, that he imagined to be a kitchen.

Ernestina's chatter sifted back to him. When she returned to the room, she brought two cups of steaming liquid, and a platter of cheese. She spooned sugar into both cups and handed one to him. Sipping his, he realized how hungry and tired he was. The cheese was strong and salty, the milk rich and sweet and drowsiness overtook him. He fought the temptation to close his eyes for a moment. She noticed this and invited him to stay the night, but he declined the offer.

"I must see if Papa is home. He should know about the baby."

Anxious to leave, he thanked Ernestina and as he left her at the door, he felt embarrassed and uncomfortable knowing he couldn't reimburse her properly. She sensed his discomfort and waved him on. He turned and started running home, barely missing a dark object on the sidewalk. Opening his eyes wide, he looked carefully into the darkness and saw a woman lying on the dirty curb. A small, weeping boy with a baby wrapped in a linen blanket tied to his back, was sitting alongside the woman.

Stooping, he recognized the child. "Carlos, is that you? What is wrong?"

"I can't get her home," the boy sobbed.

Rolando went to the woman and shook her shoulder until she muttered for him to leave her alone. How well he understood this predicament, children late at night responsible for their siblings and parents. He had labored to guide his drunken papa home many times.

"Carlos, all I can tell you is you must take your sister home and put her in bed or she'll be ill. Here, let me see if I can find the key to the padlock on your door."

He felt in the pockets of the mother's skirt, fighting revulsion, until he heard the sounds of keys. Pulling them out, he thrust them into the boy's hand.

"Here they are. Go home. I'll tell Senora Ernestina to send someone to take your Mama home."

Walking away reluctantly, the boy thanked Rolando. After he returned to the store, the motherly Ernestina sent him on his way and began to coax Carlos' mother inside. Rolando ran for home, thinking of a beautiful little sister and a poor Indian boy.

Chapter 3

"**R**olando, Mama said it's okay. I can go with you to the party and then to Aunt Mariana's house for the night."

Elena danced a jig in the kitchen. He shook his head and picked up his coffee cup. It was cold. He had been daydreaming. Rising, he felt better for the breakfast he had eaten and he reached over to mess his sister's hair, smiling his approval.

That hadn't been the end of the experience for Rolando those many years ago. During the night while he dreamed of his new sister, his mother had had a stroke which left her entire right side paralyzed. Nothing had been the same since that day.

"Come on, let's go." Elena's excitement was contagious.

Laughing, they walked out of the kitchen, arm in arm.

Book 2   *Elena*

Chapter 4

A t age sixteen, Elena Martinez was lovely. Having lost her childish stoutness, she was slim and small. Her black hair pulled back, revealed an oval face with large black eyes and a sensual mouth. Her abundance of energy often exploded in laughter, joy, affection, tears, frustration and temper tantrums at a moment's notice, and Rolando delighted in her. In one year she would complete high school, his dream for her of a university education coming closer to reality. At an early age, Rolando learned he could not depend on his father, who was now in a continual state of drunkenness. Despite this, Rolando and his brothers had managed to buy a flatbed truck. They had built up the sides of the rear bed, placing a sign on the side advertising the use of the truck for hauling materials such as cement blocks, bricks, tiles, sand and topsoil. Rolando's own schooling had been sorely neglected since the family depended on his financial support. He was determined that, following the graduation of each of his siblings, he would finish school and then find work in Quito. But now, his obsession to see Elena settled was as severe as ever and, until that time, he would not consider leaving Pachuca. As for marriage, there was no time. His days were filled with seeking work and delivering materials in the truck.

He could no longer turn to his mother. She was unable to leave her room. After the birth of Elena, she had not regained her strength, and from the day they had brought the baby home, Rolando, with help from his Aunt Mariana, had cared for the child. His mother had at first joined them for meals and evenings in the living room, but the time between these visits became lengthy and she took to sitting by her bedroom window facing the green mountains. It seemed she never tired of watching the little brown huts on the hillsides. She remembered the people who lived in these homes and, through memories, they became the center of her existence. Rolando could hardly believe the change in his mother. He remembered her before his sister's birth as a vivacious woman on whom he was dependent. She had been a rare person in the small village, one active in school affairs and civic duties. From her garden she took vegetables to the market to sell each Sunday. Her household had been run with pride and enthusiasm and in turn a great amount of love and respect from her children gave her a sense of contentment and security.

One ambition Rolando's mother held stood out from the rest. She wanted all her children to graduate from the university in Quito. In the years of her youth, before the highway to Quito had been laid with concrete, she traveled by truck with her two brothers and one sister along deep rutted roads to attend high school. Her parents were ridiculed for the value they placed on their girls in a culture where women were only worthy to bear children. As if in defiance, the two girls graduated with honors in a class dominated by men.

Rolando grieved for his mother and wondered whether her life would have been different if the American nurse had helped her. She was almost a vegetable, a destroyed human being incapable of caring for herself. His mother's illness was the despair of his life as he helplessly watched her dying before his eyes. He longed to share his pride in Elena as the girl proved herself a deserving, intelligent and attractive young lady.

Chapter 5

The most important day of Elena's sixteenth year had arrived. Her saint's day, which would be celebrated with greater festivities than her birthday.

For weeks, the party had been in the planning stages. Aunt Mariana and Uncle Hector had offered the use of their home for the occasion and would host a dinner and dance.

Having returned home early from school, Elena was nervous with excitement, willing the hours to pass quickly. A local seamstress had completed a new dress, a knee-length green velveteen creation which had been copied from a borrowed European magazine. Unable to wait another moment, Elena washed at the tap behind the house, scrubbing her face in the cold water until it was glowing. Brushing her strong, white teeth, she rinsed her mouth and dropped the toothbrush in an old plastic cup on the corner of the cement counter. Running to her bedroom, Elena took the green dress from a hanger, pulled it over her head, and belted it at the waist. She brushed her hair, tying it back with a dark green ribbon. Rolando had purchased a pair of poorly made shoes in a Quito dress shop and Aunt Mariana had given her a pair of earrings and a necklace. Glancing in the small mirror on her dresser, she smiled at her reflection and bounced to the door.

She found Rolando in back of the house combing his hair, squinting his eyes in an attempt to see himself in a small cracked mirror hanging on a pole.

"Aren't you ready, Rolando? I can't wait for you. Do you mind if I go ahead?"

He turned his face in an effort to see the back of his head in the mirror. "Will you please be patient? Why do you want to arrive early? Your brothers and guests aren't coming for an hour or so. They won't begin without you."

"I just can't wait. Anyway, you are too proper. What's wrong with being a little early? Oh! Someone is at the door." She disappeared to the front of the house and found her two cousins on the doorstep.

"We came by for you, Elena. You look so nice," they exclaimed.

She twirled in a circle, showing her pleasure, and they each grabbed one of her arms, pulling her to the door.

"Come with us. We want to show you the preparations."

Clapping her hands, she cried, "Yes, I'll go, but I must tell Rolando first." She skipped to the back patio. "Susana and Miriam are here. I'm going with them now."

Rolando sighed. "Okay, but be sure to stop and see your mother before you leave."

Rolando completed dressing for the party without enthusiasm. He had hoped it could be a small family affair instead of a gathering of Elena's school companions, but since it was her sixteenth saint's day, the family let Elena choose her own guests. Rolando put off his departure until he felt sure his brothers would have arrived. He looked in on his mother and the young neighbor girl he had asked to watch her for the evening. He glanced at his father sleeping on the sofa in the living room and shook his head. The elder Martinez had stumbled in earlier that morning, collapsing in a stupor. Rolando could see little chance of his father attending the party and wondered if his absence would bother Elena. He shook his head again and walked out into the blazing afternoon sun. The grade schools dismissed at noon and now the streets were almost deserted. Everyone was indoors eating the main meal of the day before siesta time. Slowly walking toward the plaza, he waved to a few stragglers playing basketball in the schoolyard. Passing Don Eduardo's house, he glanced in the open door and saw the heavy, elderly man spooning hot soup into his mouth. Waving to Ernestina, at the corner store, she greeted him with a wave in return. The saloon was silent and empty, the variety store had its doors closed and the few mud huts along the roadway were quiet and sleepy looking, shut tight against the heat of the day as the occupants relaxed through the siesta hour.

Pachuca had survived centuries of the hot suns, hurricane-force winds and torrential rains of the equator. A small community of one thousand residents, Pachuca nestled at the nine thousand foot level in the Andes Mountains. Rolando was unaware of the town's ugliness and decay. Deterioration touched everything, the houses, roads, vehicles, people. He had heard things were better beyond the mountains, but his limited imagination allowed few fantasies. On one or two occasions, he had felt panic about the sleeping culture and wondered if he was being sucked into a way of life from which he'd not be able to break.

But this day, he paid no more attention to the poverty and filth than he did the breathtaking beauty of the mountain ranges surrounding the town on three sides, or the vast valley lying before Quito in the distance.

As he drew close to his aunt and uncle's house, he glanced at his watch, realizing it was still early. The house had been built fifty years earlier of oven-baked brick, then plastered and painted now a fading blue. More recently, indoor plumbing and a toilet had been installed, adding to the prestige of the family. Two acres behind the house boasted chickens, pigs, fruit trees and corn.

Rolando walked through the front door without knocking. "Buenas tardes. Where is everyone?" he yelled.

"In here, in the kitchen." A small dark-haired boy ran into the living room.

"Hi, Rolando. Mama is in the kitchen. We're going to have a party." Rolando swept his cousin up in a hug and kissed his cheek. "Hi, Francisco. How's my boy?"

"Fine. Mama is cooking for the party."

Rolando lowered him to the floor. The boy grabbed his hand, pulling him to the kitchen.

"I wasn't sure you would make it on time." A middle-aged, slender woman with graying black hair cut short and curled, beamed up at him as he planted a kiss on her cheek.

"It looks like I'm early." He smiled after Francisco as the boy ran out the back door. He turned to watch his aunt stir chunks of potatoes in a large skillet on a four-burner gas stove, an appliance rare in these parts. The kitchen was bright and airy. Green plants lined the sills and climbed the window frames. The floor was laid with blue tile blocks and the counters were covered with thick linoleum. Cabinets and drawers had been built by a local carpenter, then painted a blue that did not match well with the floor. One of the more modern homes, it was envied by the townspeople.

Mariana pinched salt from a bowl and scattered it over the potatoes as she chattered about the party. The maid, a young Indian girl, walked in from the back patio carrying a bowl of toasted corn. Rolando greeted her and grabbed a handful of the corn, putting the grains in his mouth.

"Rolando, will you do me a favor and go out behind the house and find Carlos? I need his help," requested his aunt.

"Right now," he replied, his mouth full. Stretching, he swallowed and reached out to pull his aunt's hair with affection. Outside, he went to look in the chicken house.

"Carlos, where are you?"

"Here I am."

Rolando swung around and saw him carrying a large gunny sack filled with ears of corn. Behind Carlos walked his two cousins and sister. Rolando greeted Miriam and Susana and turned to Carlos.

"Buenas tardes. Will you be able to go into the house and see my aunt? She needs your help."

"Fine. I'll first put this corn in the chicken house." The boy adjusted the bag on his back and walked away.

"What are you girls doing out here? I thought you'd be in the house looking over the preparations."

"Oh, we were just walking under the trees and happened to see Carlos in the field," smiled Elena. "You arrived early after all."

"I thought dinner would be ready and everyone would be here. Francisco's yelling. The bus must be coming."

"Yes, he's been waiting all afternoon for it." Susana called as she and the other girls ran for the house.

Rolando arrived in the living room as the bus pulled up before the gate. Several girls, along with Elena's brothers, spilled out the door, through the gate and into the house. There was much excitement with greetings, hugs and waves. Rolando met his brothers with a smile and look of relief.

"I'm so glad you're here."

"Do you mean you aren't going to join the girls in their games and dances?" Pablo teased with mock surprise.

"No, because it's obvious it's you they want." Rolando chuckled at his brother's discomfort. Pablo's shyness was a delight to the girls.

"Are you ready? Dinner is served." Uncle Hector yelled in an effort to get everyone's attention. He started guiding the children into the dining room as Mariana and the Indian helper made several trips from the kitchen to the table bearing plates piled high with fried pork strips, fried potatoes, roasted corn, cooked hominy and pieces of cheese.

"Come to the table," Mariana called over the noise. "Take a napkin and fill it with food. Come, form a line." She directed them into a single line and then returned to the head of the table, face rosy from effort and pleasure. No one used plates or utensils, as food was placed in paper and popped into the mouth with fingers. The living room soon filled again, every chair taken, some of the girls spreading their napkins on the floor.

Hector and the maid passed cola, along with a few glasses which would be shared from friend to friend. Rolando, Geoff, Roberto and Pablo stood along the wall, eating great amounts and tolerating the noisy chatter. Mariana stood by the table snacking, but also keeping an eye on her guests. When she saw they were eating slower, she filled two napkins to overflowing and called the maid.

"This is for you and Carlos," said Mariana. "He can sit with you in the kitchen if he would like. Later we will clean this table."

She stood and clapped her hands, motioning to Miriam and Susana. They jumped to their feet and ran from the room, returning with a small pile of gifts. Color rose in Elena's face as the girls placed the packages in front of her.

Rolando leaned against the wall, watching her as she opened the presents. Her cries of pleasure over a trinket, sweater, ribbon, doll and record by Julio Iglesias brought laughter and clapping of hands. He thought Elena was more attractive than he had ever seen her.

Mariana gathered up the wrapping papers and asked the children to move the chairs back so they could begin the dancing.

Rolando had no desire to stay longer and he motioned his brothers to the door. "Why don't we walk to the plaza to see what's happening. Maybe we can play some basketball." In agreement, they left by the front door.

Chapter 6

Minutes before sundown, Rolando returned alone, his brothers departing for home. The children were gone, having caught the bus back to Quito. The house was quiet and cluttered and he noticed his uncle slumped down in an overstuffed chair sipping a cola. Rolando patted him on the shoulder affectionately, again thinking how different his father was from this man. How could brothers be so different?

"There you are, Rolando. I didn't see you leave. Elena? No, I've not seen her for a while. Perhaps she's in the kitchen, or better yet, maybe in the girl's bedroom."

Rolando walked into the kitchen and found the maid washing the dishes.

"Hola. Have you seen my sister?"

The girl wiped the greasy counter absently and shrugged her shoulders. "About an hour ago, I guess. Senora Mariana sent me to your mother with dinner and I haven't seen Elena since."

He thanked her and walked to his cousin's bedroom, knocked and waited. Receiving no answer, he opened the door and peeked in. No one was there. Noticing a light under his aunt's door, he tapped lightly.

A soft voice invited him in. His aunt and Francisco were sitting on the bed, pillows propping them up, watching a television program on a small black and white set.

"Why, Rolando, I thought you had left for home. Are you all right?"

"I'm fine. The boys went home to their studies, but I need to check with you about Elena staying here tonight and going to school with her cousins tomorrow. You don't happen to know where she is, do you?"

"I thought she was with the girls in their room. Don't I hear them now?" She looked toward the door.

Susana and Miriam walked into the room and stopped, surprised looks on their faces when they noticed Rolando.

"Oh!" gasped Susana, coloring. "When did you get back? We thought you had gone home."

"Dear, whatever is the matter?" her mother asked with concern.

"Nothing at all," snapped Miriam, glaring at Susana.

"No, nothing at all, Mama," replied Susana, glancing at Rolando, then away.

Rolando frowned. "Where is Elena?"

"Elena? She's no doubt in the kitchen or in the bedroom looking at her gifts. She did say she wasn't feeling well. Perhaps she is lying down, or perhaps she has left for home. The party was very tiring for her." Miriam spoke rapidly as she looked from Susana to her mother and to Rolando.

He watched her with curiosity, then gently pushed the girls aside and returned to the girl's bedroom. No one was there. Momentarily a small fear gripped him, but he shrugged it off with a smile. Without a glance backward, he went through the kitchen.

Equatorial dusk was fast approaching with darkness on its heels. Moving quickly to the chicken house, he found it filled with roosting fowl who cackled their displeasure and shifted positions nervously. No one else was there. Turning, he looked out over the cornfield.

Carlos would have left for home by now, so I can't question him, he thought idly. "Perhaps Elena did decide to return home thinking I had gone on," he said to himself.

He turned his attention to the restfulness of the hour. The winds which blew each afternoon had died and as he walked under the taxo tree, he inhaled deeply the fresh-scented air. He loved the combined smells of animals, topsoil and fruit trees and wished for a moment he could capture these few short minutes and live in them forever. Reaching high to grab a taxo, he bounced the orange fruit in his hand, then pocketed it, thinking of the delicious drink it would make later in the evening.

Yawning, he stretched, realizing the last minutes of daylight were quickly running out. He glanced over the fields and yard again, and held his breath as a movement caught his eye. Along the mud wall at the end of the property a small bodega had been built to store an old tractor and other discarded objects. He squinted, waiting for the movement to reappear, but all was still.

"Must have been a cat or opossum."

Turning, he started for the house, but paused, unable to push aside the nagging thought he had seen someone. Walking to the hut, he stopped when he heard whispering. Creeping closer, he looked around the corner and caught his breath in shock and disbelief. Dizziness swept over him as he leaned against the small building, certain his knees would give out.

Elena was sitting on the ground, her head on Carlos' shoulder. The young man was kissing her forehead. Smiling, he raised his head and spotted Rolando. In a flash, Carlos was on his feet, but before anyone realized what was happening, Rolando had grabbed Elena and slapped her hard, then, pushing her behind him, he reached for Carlos in a blind fury. Elena screamed and held the side of her face while the boy tried to reach her. Rolando hit him, the force of the blow knocking Carlos to the ground. Rolando bent over and grabbed Carlos up by the shirt, holding him close to his face. Speaking coldly and softly, he gritted his teeth.

"If you ever touch my sister again, or if I ever see you near her, I will kill you. Do you understand?" He pushed the boy to the ground again as Elena, crying and trembling, tried to reach his side. Rolando turned to her and grabbed her arm, squeezing so hard she cried out in pain.

"And you, young lady. We're going home."

He pushed her past the house with little concern who saw him, and led her home, not once releasing her arm nor speaking. Arriving at the house, Elena jerked herself free and lunged in the direction of her bedroom, slamming the door after her. Rolando glanced around, knowing his famiy had already settled for the night. There was no movement.

Now reality set in. He felt crushed, betrayed, confused and angry. His cousins had known where Elena was and had covered her secret. Marching out to street, he wandered for an hour. He needed to think, to calm himself before speaking with his sister. Sitting in the darkness of the plaza, his anger turned to remorse and he decided that surely this problem could be resolved. Returning home he thought suddenly of his father with a flicker of hope, then snorted in disgust.

"He's either asleep or gone. There's no sense talking with him anyway. How could he understand?"

Chapter 7

nocking at Elena's bedroom door, he spoke softly. "Let me in."

After a moment's hesitation, she opened the door. Her party dress was crumpled and dirty and it was obvious she had been crying. All anger and feeling for himself disappeared as Rolando watched her wipe her hands on the dress, a lost look on her face.

"Elena, come sit down. I want to explain to you how I feel and why I did what I did."

She sat beside him, her eyes red and swollen, hands folded in her lap. He felt a sharp stab of pain, combined with a wave of love and compassion. She looked so young and confused.

"I don't know how to explain this. You see, you just can't get involved with a boy like Carlos. Don't you know what kind of a family he comes from? He doesn't know who his father is! I'll never forget the night you were born. I found him on the street with a baby tied to his back. It was close to midnight. What was he doing there? Trying to drag his drunken mother home. I helped him because he was so desperate. Elena, I've known Carlos all his life and I've never known his mother to be married. Oh yes, she has four children and no telling how many times she has been pregnant. She picked up each of their fathers at street festivals or parties. I don't believe she's ever gotten pregnant while sober, so she probably doesn't remember who the fathers are. And you want to get involved with a boy like this? What are you thinking of, Elena? Haven't I taught you better?"

He felt alarm at the look she gave him. Instead of anger or confusion, he saw maturity and steadiness. In a flash, he saw she was no longer a child, but a woman.

Speaking evenly, she looked him in the eyes. "I love Carlos. I have loved him since I was twelve years old. Do you remember the day I went with you to that party at your friend's house one Sunday afternoon? Remember when you weren't going to let me go with you and I begged so? I cared for him then and he told me he would try to be outside, waiting. I met him and on that day four years ago, we declared our love. Yes, when I was twelve years old. He is the man, the man I say, as he is not a boy, but he's the man I'm going to marry. It doesn't matter to me that his mother lives as she does. Carlos is the most gentle, fine, honest and upright man I know except for you, Rolando. I know I always said I would wait to marry, but that was because you have been so good to me. You've stayed home and even refused to date so I would finish high school. I will finish. I promise you we don't plan to marry until I graduate."

Surprise and fear were building in him so fast he felt his head and heart would burst from the pressure.

"Elena, you can't possibly think of marriage. Have you considered what he does for a living? He works for our aunt. He's a peon. What does he earn each day? Not enough to put proper food on the table."

The pressure was dissolving into a mixture of disbelief, frustration and fear. Standing he walked to the door.

"You'll not marry him. If I ever see you near Carlos, I'll kill him. He means nothing to me. My life means nothing to me if you choose to ruin yours. Now, get in bed."

Chapter 8

H e didn't sleep until dawn. The fact he had been unaware of something of this importance going on for so long left him shaking his head in wonder. How long had his cousins known? Surely Aunt Mariana hadn't been in on this deception. And why Carlos of all people? He didn't mind Elena marrying. In fact he hoped she would, didn't he? Someone educated and influential from Quito. Perhaps if he were truthful, he could admit he didn't want things to change. Time was moving too quickly. But what hurt the most was that Elena had kept a secret from him and for such a length of time. He had been an outsider.

He finally slept, but woke feeling a sense of dread and with a headache that caused his head to reel with pain. Elena stood at the counter in the kitchen, her back to him as he picked at the breakfast she had prepared. No words were spoken and he played with his coffee cup while trying to think of something to say. Finally, with a sigh he rose and walked to her, putting his arm around her. With a sob, she turned and wept on his chest.

"I see you decided not to go to school."

She nodded her head, nestling in his arms.

"Come on, Elena, let's go to Quito together. We'll spend the day in town, buy lunch and have time to ourselves. Okay?" He searched for a napkin to wipe her eyes as she attempted a small smile.

"You'll have to wait until I change my clothes," she spoke softly.

"Take the time you need. I have some unfinished business I must take care of first. It will be about an hour and then I'll return."

Nodding, she left the kitchen while he watched. As she disappeared from view, his face softened with love, then turned dark and hard as he clenched his fists. Looking at his watch, he grabbed a sweater and left the house.

Chapter 9

Rolando was having difficulty sleeping again and there was no way of telling what time it was, so he carefully pushed back the covers so not to wake his brothers. He tiptoed out the door. Feeling along the wall, he found the kitchen entrance and, pushing a stool aside, he felt on the shelf for a match. It was three o'clock. His head was groggy, as he had been drinking that afternoon and now needed another drink. Prepared for emergencies, two pints of liquor sat in the old unused kitchen. Creeping into the night, he slowly pulled on the big wooden door, wincing at the protesting squeaks. Hamsters stirred in their sleeping places as he lit the candle he had carried with him from the kitchen and set it on a stack of burlap bags. Behind a pile of broken pottery, he found the whiskey.

Sitting on the floor, he blew out the candle and put the bottle to his lips. Hearing a noise, he looked up and saw a figure in the doorway, a flashlight in hand. Rolando shielded his eyes against the blinding light.

"Who's there? Will you put out that stupid light?"

"It's Geoff. What are you doing in here?" The boy doused the light as hamsters began to scurry.

"How did you know where I am?"

"You left the door open. If you don't be careful all the hamsters will get out."

"Well, shut it then."

He pushed it shut and stood above Rolando. "Why are you sitting here in the middle of the night?"

Rolando pulled the matches from the band of his shorts and fumbled for the candle. Lighting it, he again placed it on the bags.

"Madre mia! What are you doing sitting here in your underwear and drinking?

"Why are you bothering me, Geoff?" he questioned with a mixture of disgust and embarrassment.

"I heard you were to drive the truck for someone today and didn't show up. Were you ill?"

"Yes, I was ill. Very ill. I spent the entire afternoon in the saloon drinking myself ill."

"Rolando, how can I help you? If only you would tell me what's bothering you." Geoff touched his arm hesitantly.

"How can I tell you what's wrong if I'm not sure myself." He rubbed his face and sighed. "Thank you, Geoff. Maybe I'll be able to talk with you when I get my own mind straightened out. Sometimes I feel my emotions are greater than my body can contain and I'll explode. Drinking helps, and for a short time I forget."

Geoff sat for a moment, then patted his brother's arm again. "Let's go back to bed. You're cold. Leave the whiskey here."

"No, you go. I'm all right. I'll stay here for a while. I've got to think a little. Please."

"Then I'll bring your clothes and a blanket." Geoff reluctantly returned to the house.

Rolando watched daylight peek through the cracks in the roof. He remained sober.

Chapter 10

Later that day, he combed his hair and shaved. Walking to his Aunt Mariana's house, he knew he must speak with her. After his mother's illness and depression had left her helpless and liquor had turned his father into a sodden drunk, Rolando had relied more and more on his aunt and uncle. Of all his relatives, he trusted them as parents.

Mariana was behind the house feeding the chickens. A look of delight lit her face as he approached. "Why, Rolando, I'm so glad to see you." She reached up to kiss his cheek. "Please come in the house. I have coffee, bread and cheese left from breakfast. Are you hungry?"

He smiled, nodding as she tossed the rest of the corn and grass to the chickens. Wandering toward the house, she took his arm.

"Are things all right at your house today? I must go to see your mother this week. To be truthful though, I almost worry more about your father than your mother. At least she seems content."

"Oh, things are the same, I guess. I had to hire a girl from the village to care for Mama as she's in her room all the time now. Papa is here and there. Sometimes he doesn't come home. I wonder how we make ends meet. I've had to put another piece of property up for sale to keep Elena and the boys in school. Gracias a dios we have those acres of land in the family, though I feel bad about selling them."

She motioned him to the table. "You still have several acres in the mountains, don't you?"

He pulled out a chair and sat. "Yes, but they have been in our family for years and I hate parting with each plot. If only the time would come for Elena to graduate so I'll be able to work at a real profession. There is no way I can stop what I'm doing until then."

Mariana prepared coffee and bread, then seated herself across from him.

"Dear, what's really the matter? These problems have been with you for years, but lately you've changed and I don't know why."

He ran his hands over his face. "It's Elena. These past eight months have been difficult for us. I don't know what to do with her. The principal from the colegio sent me a note yesterday saying she is failing her subjects. I couldn't believe it. She's never had problems in school. In fact she has worked harder than her brothers."

She reached out to take his hand as his head drooped in despair. "My dear boy, you will never know how much I admire you. Why, you have raised that girl from birth, plus cared for your brothers. You've put them through school without help from your parents. I think you have done a wonderful job."

Lifting his head, he looked at her. "I could never have done it without you, Tia. We did it together. I've turned to you hundreds of times over the years. But all of this would have been done without a moment's regret, if only I could understand what has happened to Elena."

Mariana bit her lip, hesitating a minute. "I think she still loves Carlos."

Rolando sprang to his feet. "No, that's impossible. That happened over eight months ago. How could she think she still loves him? In the first place, she doesn't know about love and in the second place, he isn't worthy to look at her, let alone touch her." In anger, he set his jaw.

"Sit down a moment. Dear, you may have raised Elena and again I'll say you did a beautiful job, but frankly you don't understand anything about a girl in love and I believe the problem with Elena is exactly that. She loves Carlos and she's suffering. Have you noticed her eyes? They're sunken and she's lost weight. She looks ill and quite honestly, I'm concerned. I had been thinking of talking with you, hoping we might be able to help her in some way."

"She is ill, but I am too. It's affecting my whole life. Do you think I did the wrong thing in separating them?"

"No, you did the correct thing. Class distinction in our society is important and even though we are all Indians, we live on a higher level. We are landowners and in the town of Pachuca, we are a principal family. Our relatives own homes throughout the plaza area; we all have cattle and crops. People like Carlos work for us. We have superior blood flowing in our veins. There is no way we could have approved of a marriage between Carlos and Elena, but as I say, when a girl is in love she doesn't see any difference in people, or classes. She loves Carlos because of who he is, a handsome, well-mannered man. Hector and I were impressed with him and his work while he was with us. It's a shame he hasn't returned to work since the day of Elena's party. He disappeared and when I became concerned, I was told he is working on an hacienda further up the mountain. Perhaps he's afraid of seeing Elena," she smiled at him, "or perhaps he understands the differences in our families. Knowing Carlos, I don't think it's out of fear of you, but out of love for Elena that he hasn't come back."

Rising again, Rolando walked to the window and stared at the mountains above Pachuca. For a fleeting moment an overwhelming longing to escape to the hills, to hide in the brush and canyons, to lie along springs of water, to never have to face the hurts and problems of life swept over him. He was sick of the burden on his shoulders. Sighing, he remained with his back to Mariana.

"Then you really believe Elena is still in love with him? And at her age. You'll never know how this surprises me. It came so quickly and is something I never considered."

Mariana carried the plates to the sink and looked up at him. "Dear, are you drinking more than usual?"

Caught off guard, he managed to control the jerk of alarm. "No, not really. Sometimes I can't sleep and I drink a little to make me sleepy. You can understand that, can't you?"

"Geoff told me he had to carry you home the other night. He came here looking for you and when I told him I hadn't seen you, he searched until he found you in the saloon. Oh, Rolando, be careful. This is what happened to your father."

He laughed and pinched her cheek. "Don't worry, Tia Mia.

I'm taking care of myself. It's Elena I worry about. You know, maybe I'll approach her differently. Maybe I can persuade her to do some things with me socially so she'll forget that boy. Surely in time all of this will pass."

Mariana gave him a hint of a smile with a negative shake of her head. "You don't understand women, do you? Perhaps it's possible for men to forget or leave their loves and emotions behind and look for other relationships, but it's a great deal harder for women, I believe. Especially if they are really in love. Elena won't forget Carlos quickly."

"Say, that's an idea." He snapped his fingers. "I have a friend in Quito. I'll ask him to throw a small party, just a small fiesta and I'll take Elena. He has a couple of nice brothers. Do you think I could get her interested in another fellow?"

"It's worth trying."

"Thanks, Tia. I do love you," he grinned.

She wrapped her arms around his waist. "I love you, too. Very much."

He returned home, took the truck on two runs and waited for Elena's return from school. Time passed slowly. He visited with his mother, but found her uncommunicative. He left after only a few minutes. Making a cup of coffee for himself, he slowly sipped it at the kitchen table, deep in thought. "I'll not drink today and maybe not tomorrow. Never will I become like Papa."

Hearing Elena in the doorway, his heart quickened. They would have an hour alone before their brothers arrived from school, as he had sent the young maid home early. Noticing him, Elena stepped into the kitchen, and with a start he realized how hollow her eyes looked and how listless she acted. Why hadn't he noticed this before his aunt had spoken with him? Elena's school uniform seemed to hang on her. Seeing her every day, the change was less obvious, but what bothered him the most was her quietness.

"Elena, sit down. I'll get you a cola."

She dropped her books on a chair. "No, I can get my own. You stay there and I'll bring you one."

He smiled at her. "How was school today?"

"Okay, I guess," she shrugged.

Rubbing his hands together, he took a deep breath. "I have a good idea. Do you remember the friend of mine who lives on the south side of Quito? Remember when we went to visit him on his saint's day two years ago? Well, I thought maybe we could visit him again. He has two brothers you got along well with, remember? I thought perhaps you'd enjoy going with me. We can have dinner and maybe dance a little afterwards. What do you think?"

Turning from the small counter, she placed a glass of cola beside his cup and looked down at him.

"No. I know what you are doing and I have no desire to go with you."

She started to leave the kitchen and he got up from his chair, taking her arm. She jerked it away, eyes flashing. "Rolando, you'll not choose my friends for me. I'm old enough to know who I want for a friend. Now if you'll excuse me, I want to visit Mama."

He stood, stunned, then slumped in his chair. I'm losing her, he thought. What am I going to do? Perhaps I've already lost her. I did what was right for her, I know it.

The familiar depression settled on him and he pushed the cola away, rising to his feet. Then a wave of anger swept through him and he stomped to the old abandoned kitchen.

Chapter 11

They found him two days later, sprawled on an old bed in a small hut a mile up the mountainside. Vaguely, he remembered being with a woman. Geoff and his uncle half dragged, half carried Rolando as he fought to resist them. They were able to bring him under control and, not wanting the townspeople to see his condition, they sat him beside an irrigation ditch and washed him as best they could. They guided him to Hector's house where Mariana gave him a little to eat and put him to bed. Geoff walked home and returned with clean clothes for his brother.

The next morning, Rolando woke with a terrible headache, but felt hungry. "I'm sorry," he winced with embarrassment. "I guess I have no excuse."

His aunt fried an egg and cut bread for his breakfast. Placing the food on the table, she laid her hand on his hair and brushed it back affectionately. "Yes you do, Rolando. You have never had a chance to live a normal life. You've cared for others more than for yourself. I think one solution to all of this is that you find a girl, get married and settle down. Stop sacrificing yourself for others." She placed her hands on her hips, frowning down on him.

"Sometimes I think you like to live a life of sacrifice. Look at all your friends. They're married and have children and what are you doing? You're living like a monk just to care for your sister. You can't do that any longer. Rolando, Elena loves you. I know that, but she was willing to leave you to marry Carlos. Did you really believe she would remain single for you? Not a chance. She'd still desert you for Carlos if she had the opportunity. And as I say, it's not because she doesn't love you. She's just more selfish than you are, or shall I say, perhaps willing to be a little more human, just as we all are."

"I'd like to be married," he said, spreading butter on his bread. "Do you think I don't wonder what it would be like to have children? It's just that everytime I meet a girl I think I could love, the responsibilities at home pile up, and I put off my own happiness for another year. How could I possibly think of marriage? I'm doing what I must for Elena and Mama. Elena will graduate someday from the university and then I will have my own life."

Mariana dropped beside him and took his arm. "By that time you will be in your thirties. Where will you find a girl who will wait that long? Who is the woman you were with yesterday? Do I know her?"

"I guess so. She means nothing to me," he scowled, embarrassed. "I don't even remember much." He buried his head in his palms. "What's happening to me and my life?"

"Everything will be all right. I spoke with Elena."

His head jerked up and he stared at her.

"You did?"

She stood, patting his shoulder. "Yes. Last night. She feels bad about the way she treated you. I have an idea she stayed home from school today and will be waiting for you. Why don't you run along and see if I'm not correct."

He crammed bread in his mouth, stood and hugged her.

"Thanks, Tia. I'll see you later."

Mariana was right. Elena was waiting and without a word, she walked into his arms.

He held her face in his hands. "Are you okay?"

"Yes, and I'll go to Quito with you to the party."

"No, that wasn't a very good idea," he smiled.

"Do you think I'm ill? Aunt Mariana thinks something is wrong. I don't want to treat you the way I did the other day. I love you and I appreciate all you've done for me. It's just that I have no desire to get up in the morning. I honestly don't know what is wrong."

"Could it be that you still care for Carlos?" he asked gently.

It was the first time since Elena's saint's day that Carlos' name had been mentioned between them. Looking at him for a moment, she left his side and sat down. Suddenly she burst into tears.

"I don't know. I haven't seen Carlos since the day you found us. Perhaps that's part of the problem. If he loved me as I love him, why didn't he try to see me? No matter what you told him, if his love was as deep as he declared, surely he would have tried, wouldn't he?" She wiped her eyes with the back of her hand.

With a surge of relief, he began to understand.

"Is that what's bothering you, Elena?"

"Yes, of course. We were going to get married. He had such grand plans. How could someone tell me they love me with their whole heart one day and just disappear the next. I know he is in the area."

"Perhaps he didn't love you as you loved him. I guess there are different degrees of love." He was having a hard time controlling his joy. "Just remember this. I love you. We all do, your brothers, our aunt and uncle, cousins and our mother. Perhaps in time you'll forget what has happened. I don't expect your feelings to change overnight, but please, Elena, try. Don't let it affect your schooling. For your sake and mine. You've come so far and done so well."

She smiled through her tears. "Thank you for your patience. I'll try. Perhaps you're right. He just wasn't worth my faithfulness all these months, but it hurts so much." Another rush of tears choked her and she turned for her bedroom.

The relief he felt was tremendous. Walking out the back door, he stood in the sunshine and thrust his arms upward. All was well. Out of sheer joy, he found two bottles of whiskey and emptied them. "I'll not be needing you, I guess."

He threw back his head and laughed out loud, causing the maid to leave the hanging of the wash to stare at him in amazement.

Chapter 12

T hree months before Elena's graduation from high school, the young maid knocked on Elena's door to awaken her for school. There was no answer. The Indian girl opened the door and stared at the empty bed and open window. She ran to waken Rolando.

By that evening they realized Elena had disappeared and was nowhere to be found.

Book 3 — *Carlos*

Chapter 13

Carlos pulled on his boots and slipped his arms into an old jacket. He grabbed a freshly baked bun from the table, poured coffee into a tin mug and carried both outside to a bench leaning against the front of the house. Shivering in the chilly air, he dipped water from a bucket and poured it into a bowl to wash his face, splashing a little on his hair. From a window ledge high in the mud-walled house, he took a bar of soap wrapped in newspaper and a razor. After shaving and combing his hair, he ate the bread and drank the coffee, letting the warmth spread through his chilled body. It was cold, the sun still hanging low behind the mountains, but it promised to be a beautiful morning. He looked down on the road from the rise where his two-room house sat. Indian women wrapped in ponchos from the top of their heads to their ankles and heavy burdens strapped to their backs, moved rapidly toward the plaza a mile from his home. Men hunched in smaller ponchos or jackets, hats low on their heads, rushed to their respective positions as peons, thankful they were able to earn a few sucres each day for many hours of grueling labor.

Carlos carried the bowl around the side of the house and threw the dirty water on the onion patch. After replacing the bowl, soap and razor, he took his cup and returned to the house.

He shook his two brothers and sister awake. His mother Laura had left for work two hours before daylight, joining a group of Indians harvesting potatoes in a field several miles north of Pachuca.

"Wake up. I've got to leave for work. Joel, Jerman, get up. There's coffee on the fire and I bought bread. Be sure to eat before you leave for school. And you boys had better collect water from the road faucet. Perhaps you should bring three buckets. Yolanda, you can peel potatoes for lunch. I'll run home before you boys return from school and light the fire. I don't want you to touch the matches. Mama will be home around 3 o'clock, so try to have your homework finished and the dinner ready. Okay?"

He checked the boy's clothes and hurried out the door. Carlos, like so many poor Ecuadorian Indians, had acted as a mother to his siblings all of their lives. The baby girl who had been strapped to his back the night of Elena's birth had died. In the wee hours of the morning she had awakened, whimpering with a high fever. Two days later she was dead. For some time it had an effect on his mother and she worked hard caring for Carlos; however when he was nine years of age she arrived home late one night, drinking heavily, in the company of a young man. Carlos had buried his head in the blankets and tried to sleep while his brother was conceived. Since the father was still studying at the university in Quito, he failed to return and claim his child. Carlos was forced to quit school to care for the baby. His mother had to return to the fields for work.

Two years later, his brother Jerman was born. Jerman was followed a year later by an infant girl who died after the life span of one week. Yolanda arrived close to Carlos' fifteenth birthday. The small room which made up their home was becoming crowded and one day Carlos decided he must look for a larger space or perhaps a house to rent. After a few weeks search he found a two-room mud hut on a small rise above the road leading to Pachuca. In this area wealthy residents from Quito invested in land and crops. To protect their interests, huts were built in full view of the property and families were hired to live on the land to guard against thievery. In a matter of days he had his family settled in larger quarters. They could live there rent free with the stipulation that someone would always be home. There was no electricity or plumbing, but he was pleased to see the property had an irrigation ditch that could be used for laundering and bathing. One Sunday he found a man selling straw mats in the market. Until the family was able to afford a larger bed, he and his brothers slept on the floor and Yolanda slept with her mother. There was one small window in each room, but candles supplied the majority of light for homework. They cooked on the floor and every two or three days gathered firesticks.

As Carlos left the house, he checked the amount of potatoes left for dinner and pondered what else they could eat. It was Friday and there would be no meat in the stores. Inadequate refrigeration limited the supplies of perishables and until the weekly slaughter of animals on market day, the poverty-stricken Indians lived on starches. Carlos decided they could eat soup flavored with bouillon, fried potatoes and boiled rice.

He had taken another bun and, withdrawing it from his pocket, he started munching. His throat closed in anger and he already felt tired from lack of sleep. How dare Rolando humiliate him in front of Elena? It was no secret among the townspeople that Rolando and his father were alcoholics and had low morals. Mixed with the rage, he was concerned that Elena might have been abused upon arriving home. What had Rolando told her? He wasn't sure how much Elena knew about his family life and his heart ached with pain at the thought of her negative reaction. Sometimes he could hardly bear the fact that his mother brought young men home when she was intoxicated. Sometimes he hated her, but sometimes he could see the intolerable burdens she bore and he pitied her. It was the love he felt for his brothers and sister that kept him home, although more and more he recognized the strength they possessed. They scarcely needed him any longer. His dream was to make a new life for himself, to live deep in the country area, to farm, maybe someday to own an acre or two.

When his mother was pregnant with Joel, and Carlos had been forced to leave school, he was able to find work with Elena's uncle. After the baby was born, he cared for the child until his mother returned home from her job in the early afternoon. He would then work until dark tending the crops and animals belonging to the Hector Martinez family. He had worked hard and developed into a fine-looking young man, dark of color, medium height, and strong in build. He didn't smile often and seemed to be alert to potential problems. However, when he was able to relax with someone, he showed compassion and a wonderful sense of humor. His smile was his greatest asset, lighting his black eyes, crinkling his entire face. His laughter rang loud and true, compelling his companions to join in.

Carlos had known Elena all of her life. He first developed an interest in her when he was fourteen and she only ten, and from that time on she became an important individual in his life. She weaved her way through his dreams and he knew he wanted her. When she was twelve, he realized she cared for him and they fell in love. They made grand plans for the future. But Rolando had taken care of that. Elena often spoke of her brother's obsession for her and Carlos had expected opposition to their union, but nothing like Rolando had demonstrated the previous evening. He felt his only chance for a life with Elena pivoted in speaking with Rolando and laying out his plans for their future. He hoped he would be able to do that in the next few days.

The shortest distance to his work was a path which ran alongside an irrigation ditch between two mud walls. It was always his hope to arrive early for a glimpse of Elena in case she had slept over at her cousins' house. Chewing the last of the bread, he knelt to dip a drink of water from the ditch. Refreshed, he rose, wiping his hand on his jacket and began to run. Perhaps all was well. She may have already explained to Rolando that he would love and provide for her. Perhaps she would be waiting at her aunt's house for him. These thoughts drove away all anger and anxiety.

Rounding a bend, he spotted Rolando and one of his cousins leaning against the wall. He stopped suddenly, his heart lurching with fear. There was a possibility he could fight Rolando alone, but not both men. In order to save face, he decided against turning back. He walked ahead, trying not to show concern. Approaching them, he nodded good morning and proceeded to pass. Rolando thrust out a hand and grabbed Carlos' shoulder.

"Where do you think you are going?"

Carlos shook himself free and glared into Rolando's face.

"I'm going to work. Where do you think?"

"Not to my aunt's house. You're through there."

"Don't you think it is your aunt's place to fire me, not you? I'll go and talk with her." Carlos moved to walk away.

Rolando grabbed Carlos' shoulder again and pulled him back, sneering.

"If I ever see you on the street in front of my aunt's house, I'll beat you. Stay away from that house and my house. Do you understand?"

"What will your uncle think if I don't show up for work? They'll be expecting me."

"I don't think it will be too hard for them to figure it out. I'll speak with them about your 'relationship' with my sister. You know they would be against something like that as much as I am. I could vomit when I think of you touching my sister. How do you dare think she could love scum like you?"

Again Carlos shook himself free. "Why am I scum? You can't put your finger on one thing I do that isn't upright and honest. I don't drink liquor. I don't come home drunk. I pay my bills. I don't have girlfriends all over town and that's more than I can say about you and your friends. Why am I beneath you?"

They stood like angry bulls ready to charge. Ricardo left his position and stepped up to Carlos.

"Well, for one thing, you smell. Where do you take baths? In sewer water, huh? Your mother lives like the rats among garbage. Tell me, who is your father?" He laughed. "It's funny. Do you know the fathers of your sister and brothers?" Snickering, his eyes lit with delight, knowing he had hit a raw nerve.

Anger drained from Carlos' face to be replaced with despair.

"Carlos, you've got the wrong kind of blood. You're too dark for my sister." Rolando spoke with less force, but his voice still held authority. "Stay away from Elena, or anyone else in my family. Better yet, stay away from the main plaza. There are several little stores in this area where you can buy food. I don't want to see you anywhere near our house. Do you understand?"

"Have you spoken to Elena about this? Has she expressed her desire never to see me again? I love her and she loves me. She's told me so and I want to marry her."

Unprepared, Rolando's fist caught him against the mouth knocking him down. Blood flowed freely from his lip and automatically, he checked for broken teeth.

"I don't care if you kill me. I won't stay away from her. I love her."

Rolando grabbed at his hair and jerked him to his feet. Pushing back Carlos' head, he stood over him. "If you show up in town, I will not only ruin you, I'll ruin your mother. You don't realize what a family like mine can do to you. Think of all the relatives I have in Pachuca. They work in the schools, in the government of our town, they own the fields where your mother works. I could go on and on. You'll never survive. In the first place, your mother would lose her job. Second, you'll never find another job. Your brothers will suffer in school. Not only will they find it impossible to pass a day without someone causing them trouble, but they will never graduate from one class to the next. Oh, we can do a lot of things. That's just a beginning."

Rolando pushed him again and he lost his balance, falling backward. He watched, then turned to Ricardo. "Let's get out of here before I get sick," Carlos heard him say.

In humiliation, Carlos turned face down on the grass for several minutes. He heard a pig grunting on the other side of the wall. Birds sang and he felt the sun warming his back. Carefully, he sat up and put his head in his hands, swallowed hard against a knot in his throat and struggled to breathe. Then he cried, not so much for the humiliation, or the unfairness of being a poor Indian, or for having a mother who cared little about her reputation, or even for the frustration of knowing there was no way out. He cried for Elena. He knew she had no idea Rolando had met him this morning. In his heart he knew she still loved him and he could do nothing about it. An hour passed and finally he got to his feet and returned to the house to sit in the dark front room. Yolanda was behind the house caring for the chickens. What a life for his sister. At five years of age she carried water, cared for the animals, washed dishes and swept the dirt floor. She was learning to cook and wash the smaller articles of clothing in the ditch. There was no money for toys. She was fortunate to have shoes.

He couldn't think straight. His emotions were so raw, he wanted to scream. He had to see Elena. But how? Rolando would not change his position, he was sure. Part of what the man had threatened was true, part exaggerated. His family was large, but not that influential. Faced with this predicament, Carlos could not involve his own family. That would be taking a big risk to satisfy his own needs. He'd have to explain to his mother he had decided to look for a better-paying job, perhaps on an hacienda somewhere. He'd start looking tomorrow higher in the mountains.

"Carlos, what happened? Why are you home? What happened to your face?"

Yolanda ran to him, breaking into his thoughts and sat on the bench, staring at him.

"Nothing, sweet. Just a problem that shouldn't concern a pretty little girl like you. Anyway, I thought I'd come back home. We'll fix a nice dinner and have something hot and ready for you, Mama and our brothers. Okay? Why don't we go out to gather wood so Mama won't have to worry about doing it."

A sudden emotion ran through him and he threw his arms around her, hugging her tight. "I'm proud of you. You work so hard and don't have a chance to play."

"When I go to school, I'll play. Jerman told me there are toys at school. There are even swings and a slide. Think of that. A slide. I'm not sure I know what that is, but Jerman tried to explain. I don't think I'd be scared, but he says I will be. What do you think?" She looked at him eagerly.

"I think you'll be able to handle almost anything that life sends your way, little one."

"I peeled the potatoes. They're setting in water. What else shall I fix?"

"Here's a little money. Why don't you run down to the store and buy garlic? Also, some of those flavored cubes for the soup. Let's see, do we have rice? You know what we can do? Let's make popcorn. That's what we'll do for a surprise tonight. Now, get along."

She danced out the door, and he followed, walking behind the house, absently passing the chickens and pigs. The family was allowed a small plot of land in front of the house and a section behind, large enough to grow a few crops and raise animals for meat. Rabbit cages lined the mud wall which served as a boundary.

Descending the rise where the house set, he walked through a field of corn until he reached the end of the property where a stream of water ran from east to west. It was shady and cool, sheltered from the sun by tall eucalyptus trees that arched like umbrellas, casting refreshing scents and long shadows. Sitting on the large rock the family used for scrubbing laundry, he sighed a deep sob. It was no use. There was no way to see Elena, unless she came to him. That seemed improbable now.

Rolando would either watch her too carefully or he would convince her she could not be happy married to him. Perhaps he would have to let a few months pass and then when Rolando turned his attention to other interests, he would set up a chance meeting. But how could he wait to see the girl? His heart felt like lead in his chest. When Rolando had found them last night, they had been planning their future together. She had been in the process of preparing the speech she would present to her mother and brothers informing them of their engagement. He had intended to with talk to Elena's uncle, in hopes of persuading the man to hire him as foreman on his harvesting crew. The family had a great deal of land, not only in Pachuca, but high in the mountains several miles inland. He had planned to ask if he could oversee the work, not only at harvest time, but during the planting season. Now that dream was dead. With the extra money he would have earned he could have given Elena the home and attention to which she was accustomed. If only Rolando hadn't stepped in.

"Oh, God, help me." He held his head and wept. It was useless. What if Elena didn't love him? Would she find someone else? Perhaps by the time he could marry her without her parents' consent, she wouldn't care for him. After all, she was only sixteen. And what chances were there that Rolando would feel any different when she came of age? Well, tomorrow he would look for another job. He'd make money, enough to care for her. He'd buy her a home that would be more comfortable than the house she lived in now.

Chapter 14

He was tired. Unsaddling the horse, he led her to the railing and secured the rope. He wiped her flank and brushed her, pausing a moment to pet the big head. Untying the mare, he led her to the gate to unlatch the heavy corral door. The horse trotted to her companions, nuzzling them before settling down to chomp on the sweet pasture grasses.

Discovering the water in the trough was low, Carlos brought several buckets of water from the well beside the barn. Fatigue made him weak and he wondered if he could walk the distance home.

During the weekend two horses had escaped from the pasture below the hacienda, and he had been tracking them all day. This morning, he had questioned people on the roads and nearby homes, but no one had seen the stray horses. Carlos could only presume the animals had traveled southeast along the sides of a canyon and up into the mountains.

Departing early, he wrapped himself in a poncho and pulled his hat low.

An hour later sunbeams reached the top of the canyon and warmth spread through his chilled limbs. He stopped to remove his wraps and eat the bread he had stuffed in his pockets. He drank from the ditch beside the road. The way had been laid with smooth rocks, making travel easy; however an hour from Pachuca, the road became a path of hardened ruts, rocks and tufts of grass. Billowing clouds of dust, a testament to the lack of rain, compelled him to tie a handkerchief around the lower part of his face.

He rode down into a small canyon, crossed a wooden bridge and emerged on the other side, enjoying the cool shade. Turning away from the canyon, the road widened, a surface of smooth rocks proved Hacienda Palugo was near. Two men on horseback passed, nodding their greetings.

"Please wait," called Carlos turning to approach them again. Buenos dias. Have you, by chance seen two stallions without riders in these parts? One is brown with a white patch on his face and two white front legs, the other all brown with black mane and tail."

The two men cordially told him no and continued on.

The rock-laid road ended abruptly and took a direct right turn narrowing to a trail alongside a deep canyon with a drop of two thousand feet. To the right stood a sheer mountainside, rising hundreds of feet to the sky. Peons had labored throughout the years constructing the pathway connecting haciendas and towns, despite the mountains, the huge rocks, and the rains that caused mudslides to cascade thousands of feet to the river below.

Carlos dismounted to lead his timid horse along the narrow, treacherous area. He picked his way around sections of path that had disappeared into the abyss below. Beyond, the road remained intact and he sighed in relief when they reached it safely. He traveled several miles before cobblestone appeared once again, indicating he was close to another hacienda. Stretching high in the saddle, he saw a group of houses. With a yelp of delight, he nudged his horse into a fast trot that took him into the yard. He dismounted and embraced the shady coolness offered by the trees.

Several Indian women sat working on a long porch that ran the length of the main house. Piles of golden corn seemed to fill every vacant spot. Leaning their backs against the wall of the house, they husked the corn cobs, dividing bad grain from good. The good grain would be taken to Quito and sold for seed or roasting corn, the bad used as animal feed.

Carlos tied his horse to a railing on the porch and glanced at the women, hoping for someone to call him forward. The women grew silent as he approached. With relief, he spotted a woman in the foreground who looked familiar.

"Buenos dias," he said with a slight bow.

The woman looked at him carefully, wondering from where he had come.

"Buenos dias."

"My name is Carlos Tapia. Perhaps you know my mother, the Senora Maria Laura Tapia from Pachuca." He smiled hopefully.

A smile lighted the woman's face and she stood, wiping her roughened, dirty hands on her apron. Corn kernels flew in every direction. She held out her hand as her smile widened into a grin that revealed a mouth with few teeth.

"Of course. We call her Laura. We have worked together often. I do hope all is well with your family."

Carlos opened his mouth to reply just as a baby began to cry. For the first time he noticed an infant behind the stool wrapped in a dirty, white cotton blanket and as the mother glanced to see if all was well, she seemed to forget her visitor. Lifting the baby, she sat on the stool, and proceeded to draw out a breast, placing the nipple in the infant's mouth. Satisfied, the small bundle settled into a relaxed position, sucking noisily.

The woman smiled again. "You're a long way from home. What brings you to us?"

Carlos pointed over his shoulder. "I'm looking for two horses. Did you by chance see any strays in the last two days?"

"I haven't." She raised her voice so all could hear. "Have any of you seen two stray horses pass by?"

All muttered negatively, the girls whispering with giggles among themselves, eyeing the uncomfortable young man.

The woman turned back. "Perhaps you should find the hacienda owner. He knows almost everything that goes on in these parts. Maybe one of the hired men saw your horses." She coughed without covering her mouth and Carlos looked away.

"Thank you for your help. I'll look for the owner." He turned as the woman tucked her heavy breast into the stained blouse and carefully placed the baby behind the stool again. He knew the poor little creature would lie all day wearing the same soiled rag for a diaper until the mother could get home to remove and wash it.

He walked the length of the patio looking for someone to help him. The large hacienda sprawled beside the road. Giant eucalyptus trees formed a canopy over the principal buildings, small corrals, pig sties, barn, chicken coops, rabbit hutches, and a new stone dairy.

Pasture land extended as far as the eye could see up the high, rolling mountains behind the complex. Herds of cattle and caretaker huts dotted the hillside. In front of the grand house there was a crossroad, the right branch leading to the Pan American highway and Quito, and the left to the high summits of the Andes range. Eventually the latter would end in the jungles of Ecuador. If the horses had wandered that far, he would never find them. Directly ahead was the dangerous road to Pachuca. He dreaded the return home and knew he must not be caught on the ledges of the canyons after dark.

To the right of the house he found a large mud-walled barn. Looking into the shadowy light he saw mounds of corncobs, sacks of husked corn, an old abandoned plow and a new pickup. A noise made him turn his head to see a battered tractor move slowly into the yard. A small, dark peon edged the machine close to a tall tree, turned off the motor, removed his hat and yawned. Jumping down, he stretched, then noticed Carlos.

"Buenos dias, or rather, buenas tardes. What can I do for you?"

"My name is Carlos Tapia. I work for the Hacienda Hermosa in Pachuca. We've lost two horses. Have you seen them by chance?"

"No, not me. I've been out with this tractor for the past two days, plowing the field on the east ridge. If any horses passed by up there, it would have been impossible to see." He yawned again. "The owner will be coming for lunch. Maybe he can help you, but I doubt it. He's been very busy overseeing the wheat planting. Sorry I can't help you." He walked off, yawning again. Two little girls yelled with delight and ran towards him. Carlos smiled as the children darted into their father's arms.

He pondered what to do next. Wait for the owner? Travel to the hacienda further east, or perhaps return to Pachuca? He decided to find a spot to eat his lunch. He had turned toward his horse when a large brown stallion galloped into the yard and stopped alongside the tractor. A tall man dismounted and walked toward him, smiling. Striking blue eyes peered out from beneath a wide-brimmed hat. Thick grey hair curled around his neck. He spoke with an educated dialect and walked with a confidence that heralded him as owner of the hacienda.

"May I help you?" He held out his hand and stared at Carlos. "Have we met? My name is Luis Perez, owner of the Hacienda Tulcachi."

"No, sir." Carlos took his hand and introduced himself. "I work as acting foreman of Hacienda Hermosa in Pachuca. I regret I haven't had a chance to visit with you before, however I am very impressed with your hacienda. My family has eaten your cheeses. They are the best in these parts."

"Gracias. His blue eyes twinkled. Now what may I offer you? A drink or perhaps a bit of lunch? The cook will have it completed I am sure. Please stay for an hour before your return to Pachuca."

"Gracias."

Luis Perez ushered him into the main house and took the lead, motioning him to follow. The entrance was a narrow passage leading to a lengthy hallway that ran along the four sides of the house. Several arched openings revealed a large outdoor patio surrounded by the house. An old stone fountain stood in the center, a few broken benches were placed at random among wild flowers, tall weeds and green bushes flourishing in abundance. Towering trees cast shadows lending the area a gloomy, unkempt look. A balcony decorated with arches and a simple railing ran along the four sides of the house on the second floor. At the end of the hallway stood a staircase and it was up these steps Luis Perez led Carlos. The upper floor was lined with doors and at one he stopped. Pushing the double doors open, he stepped inside and flipped on a switch.

Carlos followed, entering the cold room, its faded green walls climbing to a high, chipped plaster ceiling. A simple wooden-backed divan sat along one side with two matching chairs against the adjoining wall. A single light bulb hanging from a long electrical wire and a bright sunbeam from the doorway provided the only lighting. It took a moment for Carlos to realize the room was larger than it appeared because the majority of it lay in shadow.

Carlos sat on one of the chairs while Luis tossed his hat on a squat, scarred coffee table, and plopped down on the divan.

A small girl appeared in the doorway smiling shyly. "Buenas tardes, senores. May I bring you something to drink before lunch?"

Luis motioned to the girl and she ducked quickly out of sight leaving the men sitting in uncomfortable silence. Carlos was hungry as he had eaten little more than bread that morning. He tried to put the thoughts of lunch out of his mind as he turned his attention to the host.

He noticed Luis observing him. As the young man's black eyes met the bright blue eyes, Carlos felt an unfamiliar stirring as if something passed between the two men. Admiration? Love? Destiny?

Carlos looked away, shaking off the feeling, afraid it had been only on his part. One thing he would never forget was his station in life. To entertain the thought that a wealthy landowner and he, a poor Indian, could become friends was foolishness and would be opening himself up to heartbreak again.

The moment passed and they began to chat about unimportant matters until the girl reappeared with a tray and set it on the coffee table. She poured the drinks and handed each of them a glass, stepping back to see if they were satisfied. The cola was lukewarm, but tasted good to the thirsty traveler. Carlos and his host emptied the first glasses quickly, and the girl hastened to replenish them, then left the room.

Luis relaxed on the divan and sighed deeply while Carlos longed to question him about the stray horses. Social decorum obliged him to wait until he asked the reason for his presence at the Hacienda Tulcachi.

The subject had turned to the wheat planting in progress when a stout, middle-aged woman bustled through the door projecting a greeting. She wore a scarf that pulled her hair away from a handsome, kindly face prone to laughter and compassion. Luis introduced her as his housekeeper and cook, but Carlos noted a tone of affection in the man's voice. The woman flashed Carlos a motherly smile and disappeared into the shadows of the room. She opened double doors that led to a small balcony and thrust back the shutters of two deep-set windows on each side of the doors, engulfing the room in bright light.

Carlos relaxed as he looked at the high green mountains through the foliage of the eucalyptus trees. A strange emotion settled in him, a tie to this old house, to the confident landlord sitting on the divan, and even to the cheerful cook.

Luis reached out for Carlos' empty glass. The boy was aware that Luis studied him, and was surprised at the emotion he had felt when their eyes had met. He knew this encounter was important and that he would again meet with Luis. As he pondered this, Carlos glanced quickly at the older man only to notice the touch of a smile working across his face. Carlos grinned and turned his head to study the room.

He saw the room had been neglected. Cracks showed mud brick under paint, the floor's wooden planks worn unevenly. A large bureau stood against one wall, and a dish cabinet squatted beside a window. The walls were bare except for a bobcat head trophy, and a perch that balanced a realistic stuffed bird appearing anxious for flight. On the floor a huge stuffed tortoise lay in a lifelike crawling position, compelling Carlos to look more than once at the reptile to see if it was moving..

But the most impressive item in the large room was the dining table set, made of dark polished walnut, gleaming as a mirror. Hand-carved, each leg ended in an eagle's claw, and the table edge gracefully curved to give an exquisite oval effect. The chairs were high-backed. An eagle in flight was carved into the top, the bottom of the chair legs extending its talons. Elegant arm rests extended beyond the tooled leather seat and curved downward.

Carlos was limited in his appreciation for the fine craftsmanship. He noted none of the richly carved features; however he was struck with the contrast of wealth and poverty combined in one room. Smiling, he thought of the wide span separating wealth and poverty...presently deep into conversation just as if the two had been friends for years. Unfortunately, he was the one without worldly goods. If Senor Perez hadn't made him feel at home, just being in his company would be an unbelievable situation. He smiled again, thinking of how his family would thrill to his story this evening.

Luis misinterpreted the smile and beamed with pride. "I bought the table in a town up north. I don't know how much you have traveled, Carlos, but the men of San Antonio produce woodcarvings of the finest quality. Everything from small items to beds, picture frames to amazing chess sets. If you play chess, we must get together for a game." He looked hopefully at the boy, as Carlos nodded, having no idea what a game of chess was.

"Anyway, the table was expensive. It's much too grand for the hacienda, but for some reason I didn't want to put it in my house in Quito. That would be the proper place; however my heart is here in Tulcachi."

Carlos made an appropriate statement, enjoying the way Luis talked. He watched the cook place a linen cloth over one end of the table and add silverware she had removed from the cabinet.

"Please be seated." Luis moved to the far end of the table and motioned Carlos to his left. The cook placed a stained cloth napkin next to the silver, and, perplexed, Carlos eyed it, not understanding its purpose. He watched and imitated Luis as the man opened the napkin and laid it on his lap.

"Have a nice lunch, sirs. I will send two girls with the food, if you are ready." The woman clasped her hands, awaiting the reply.

"Si, senora. We are ready."

Giving Carlos another smile, the cook left the room. Shortly, two young girls brought trays laden with soup bowls and a tureen. They set them on the bureau and filled each bowl, placing them before guest and host. The soup was thick and hot, made from ground corn seasoned with garlic and salt. Leaves of cabbage, potato halves, and pieces of carrot lay on the bottom.

They ate hurriedly and the maids replaced the bowls with large plates piled high with rice, potatoes and meat. Dishes of hot sauce were placed in front of each plate and salads of cooked cauliflower, peas, potatoes and hard-boiled eggs, tossed with mayonnaise were placed to the side. Never having seen so much food at one sitting, Carlos ate to his heart's content, carefully avoiding the salad.

Luis noticed and chuckled. "My cook is from Quito. When I am in Tulcachi, she stays with me and prepares the same type of meals here that she would there. You probably have never eaten this kind of salad, but in Quito we eat a lot of it. My brother brought a few ideas from the United States about salads; however eating fresh vegetables like the rabbits eat isn't my idea of good food. My mother, who is American, has lived in South America for so long she has forgotten her love for stateside salads. It's surprising how many Americans eat raw food. Disgusting. I'd die of starvation. And can you believe many Americans eat their meals without rice?"

Carlos was astonished. "How can anyone live without eating rice? Surely Americans must be hungry all the time."

"Oh, no," Luis laughed. "They have foods you cannot imagine, in an abundance that would cause your head to ache if you had to make a choice. Americans are strange people. They have so much, yet many of them will spend most of their lives complaining they have so little. Of course, I'd complain too, if I had to eat those salads. They are funny, too. They strive and compete to find new and different methods to save time and energy, yet many of them half kill themselves running through the streets in rain and hot sunshine to get sufficient exercise. Strange people. I will never be able to live among them. I'll take the peaceful way of life right here though they would call it backward and primitive."

One of the maids removed the plates and replaced them with bowls of figs cooked in a brown sugar sauce, and two plates of white, salty cheese. Cups of steaming coffee with hot milk and sugar were set beside the bowls. The maids stepped back to wait for their dismissal.

Luis surveyed the table and motioned for the girls to depart, settling back in the chair to sip his coffee.

"Take the cigarette for an example. We have had smokers

in this country for hundreds of years, but certainly not like we do now. I personally believe it was American and West European influence that caused many Ecuadorians to start smoking. It's what is called a 'fad'. You will notice in Quito almost everyone smokes. They believe it's the proper thing to do.

"What makes it complicated is the average Ecuadorian doesn't care for the American, but we want to do the things they do. We want to look like them. You try to understand that. We want to dress like them, style our hair like theirs, entertain ourselves as they do, smoke as they smoke, eat the food they eat. Dios Mio, we have hamburgers and hot dogs in Quito now. You don't know what they are, do you, Carlos? Anyway, on one of my trips to the States, what do I discover? Americans are now spending millions of dollars every year on cures to stop smoking. They diet, starve themselves, run around half nude and have some of the craziest hairdos I've ever seen. In the years to come, Ecuadorians will discover what Americans are doing and will again follow their example. Have you seen some men in Quito with hair to their shoulders? Years ago that was popular in the United States. Next thing you know our young people will want to be too thin and madre mia, if that means we have to start eating raw salads, I might live in Tulcachi for good. Sometimes I wish my brother wouldn't bother me with what goes on in the States. It just confuses me."

Carlos had several questions to ask concerning the man's family, but he remained silent. He knew nothing of the United States. In his imagination Americans lived in another universe. Someone had told him they were all millionaires and had many worldly goods, more than any other people on earth. This was beyond his imagination and now he listened to Luis with fascination and amazement. Moreover, he had heard that all Americans owned homes with dozens of rooms, and a swimming pool for each family. This had occupied his mind for days, knowing each village in Ecuador shared one pool bathing and washing clothes. It was public property and for the families without water the pool became a center of importance. To have a bathing and laundering facility beside each house and a bedroom for each person was more than he could imagine.

Abruptly, Luis interrupted his thoughts. "I've been doing all the talking, Carlos. Tell me something about yourself."

Carlos blinked, startled. "There's nothing to tell you. I've been very interested in what you have been telling me. But, as you know, I work at the Hacienda Hermosa. I live just above Pachuca with my mother, two brothers and a sister. My life is not so interesting. Tell me, does your father live in Quito?"

"My father died several years ago. He lived here in Tulcachi with my mother, my brother and myself, until he became too ill to manage a hacienda. This beautiful old house is about three hundred years old and has been on my papa's side of the family for that long. My mother, as I said, is American, but she was raised in this country, the child of missionaries. Outside of a few years when she attended school in the United States, she has lived here. Her nationality explains my coloring. My only brother is a doctor who lives in New York with his wife and four children.

My life is here in Tulcachi, even though my family has a lovely home in Quito. Because of my mother, I commute each day except during planting and harvesting seasons. Then she lives alone with hired helpers." He sipped coffee and smiled at Carlos. "You are not married, Carlos?"

A hot flush deepened his dark coloring and he adjusted his position on the chair, all the time reluctant to discuss Elena and the embarrassinng emphasis of his poverty. "No, sir, nor do I intend to marry. I have interest only in work and my family. You have not mentioned a wife."

"I've never married, much to the distress of my mother. It is unusual for a man not to marry in Ecuador, but now I'm no longer young, so it's something I'll not plan to do. Many years ago I loved a young lady very much, but just before our marriage she fell ill with a disease that baffled doctors in this country. Back in those days, we kept believing she would regain her strength and by the time we realized its seriousness, we were unable to help her. My family was devastated and I just have not been able to find anyone to compare with her."

He sat, lost in thought, then brightened, looking at his guest.

"The biggest shame of all is there is no one to take the hacienda when I die. That is the only regret I have. But I worry little about this as I feel there are many years yet for me to live and enjoy all that God has given me."

Carlos was fascinated with the man and his conversation, but he was also aware of the lateness of the hour. He didn't want to appear rude, but he needed to find the horses and return to Pachuuca before dark.

Luis must have felt the shift in unspoken communication, because he pushed back his chair. "Well, my friend, this was a pleasure. It's seldom I have guests here in Tulcachi."

Carlos held out his hand. "I apppreciate your invitation to lunch. When I stopped at your hacienda, I didn't realize such an honor was waiting."

Pausing to gaze on Carlos for a moment, Luis smiled and then reached up to rub his tired eyes. For the first time Carlos noticed fatigue on the tall man's face.

"You're a long way from home, son. I haven't asked you why you came this way. Actually, I didn't want you to leave. But now the hour is late and there are many things I must do. Is there anything I can do for you?"

"I'm looking for two horses that escaped from the Hacienda Hermosa. This would be the most likely route they would take, but so far no one has seen them." Carlos gave a general description.

Luis shook his head slowly as if in thought. "No, there have been no reports of stray horses. If they went up the mountain they could be many kilometers from here by now." He looked at the dismay written on Carlos' face and patted his shoulder.

"Why don't you go home? Come back tomorrow if you don't locate them and I'll send a boy with you up the mountain. If I don't see you by noon, I will know all is well. Now you would be wise to return on the road leading to the Pan American highway instead of the way you came. You already know the horses aren't on the back road, since you came that way. It's a longer distance, but much safer."

"They stood and Carlos nodded. "Yes, that's a good idea. Thank you again for the lunch. If there is anything I can do to repay you, please stop by the hacienda. I would be happy to see you again, but now it does seem to be getting late."

"Yes, you must be anxious to be on your way. Sometimes I begin talking and don't know when to stop. Let me show you to your horse."

Luis led him outside. "Your horse will be in the corral, fed and watered." He motioned in the direction of the barn. A small boy ran from the now vacant porch to the corral and soon reappeared with the horse. Again, Carlos held out his hand.

"Thank you, sir."

Taking his hand, the tall man smiled. "I hope we meet again soon. You will always be welcome here. God go with you."

Carlos mounted his horse and trotted to the road, turning toward the road to Quito. Glancing back, he saw that the small boy and Luis had disappeared, giving the hacienda a deserted look.

Chapter 15

The road to Quito turned north through a small community with many huts and side roads. Relieved, Carlos noted the wide lane was laid with cobblestone. Leaving the protection of the trees, the fierce midday sun beat down upon him. It would be another hour before the clouds rolled in from the east, easing his discomfort.

A mile from the hacienda, he met a peon on horseback. Greeting the man, Carlos questioned him concerning the horses. He was shaking his head when another man joined him.

"Do you work in this area or are you visiting the hacienda?" the second man asked Carlos politely.

"I have been to the hacienda searching for two stray horses, but no one seems to have seen them," said Carlos.

"Hmm, I wonder if they are the same two horses my neighbor found in his cornfield last evening. If they are your horses, you'll find them about six kilometers up the mountain, in the first hacienda. You know, if you don't claim them within two weeks, the hacienda owner will be able to claim them."

Carlos began to feel new hope. He thanked the horseman and his friend and contemplated the situation as they moved away. He could travel to the distant hacienda now but that could take three hours round-trip easily with another three hours to travel home, or he could return tomorrow with help. A glance at the sky indicated the late hour and he decided the return to Pachuca to be the more prudent choice.

Now as he walked the mile from Hacienda Hermosa to his home, he considered a plan for the next day. He would send his brothers to the home of a boy who worked with him on occasion, requesting his appearance before dawn. They would travel the longer, but safer, road to Tulcachi, locate the animals and return early in the afternoon.

Satisfied, but exhausted, he arrived home. His mother was stretched out on her bed sleeping, his brothers bent over their homework, straining to catch the light from a flickering candle. Carlos interrupted their concentration to send them to the house of Fausto. Happy for an excuse to leave their studies, the boys grabbed their jackets and ran for the door.

Carlos stripped off his sweat-stained shirt, tossed it on a bench and found a clean, tattered undergarment in a two-drawer end table.

"Do you want dinner, Carlos?" Yolanda asked him.

"Just bring me some soup. Is it still hot? I'm too tired to eat anything else."

Walking into the back room where he slept with his brothers, he climbed into the double bed he had purchased during the past year. Yolanda followed him with a bowl of steaming soup. Gulping the liquid and vegetables, he handed the empty bowl to his sister and rolled over in bed, not realizing another thing until he awoke before dawn.

It was still dark when he descended the crude steps from his house to the road below and found Fausto waiting. The small boy with thick, straight black hair, and slanted dark eyes above broad high cheekbones, stood shaking with cold against the embankment. His face was creased from a constant effort to ease the glare of the sun in his eyes and from the worry that plagues Indian children who never have enough to eat. At age fourteen, he had the build of a ten-year-old and the face of an adult.

The cold was penetrating and Carlos had thoughtfully brought a warm jacket for Fausto. Grabbing it with gratitude, the boy wrapped himself in it.

A quarter moon drifted over Quito and the dense scattering of stars lit the road before them. To take their minds off the cold, Carlos explained his need for the boy's help.

The horses shied away, reluctant to be caught. Desiring to please, Fausto sprang to life and ran after the horses with a rope. Laughing, Carlos followed after the boy until they were able to corner the horses, and slip the ropes over their heads. Pulling the animals to the barn, they saddled them. A peon, roused from his sleep in the back of the building yelled out, "Who's there?"

"Carlos and Fausto." replied Carlos. We're going over to Tulcachi again. We think the horses are in the mountains behind the hacienda. Please tell the rest of the men we'll return this afternoon."

The peon grunted and turned over, snuggling in a blanket.

Carlos checked his gear, strapped a knapsack containing lunch to the back of the saddle. He searched through a pile of old blankets and ponchos until he found a small piece of material for Fausto to place around his head to help keep out the cold. Pulling his knitted cap down over his ears, he grinned at the boy.

"Come on. If we want to be home before dark tonight, we must find the horses quickly."

They followed the Pan American highway for five miles and crossed a large canyon by way of a newly built bridge. Continuing on their way, they reached the partially paved road that took them through the ravines. Despite the tremendous drops in elevation, the young men felt safe and they were struck with a sense of adventure that bordered on gaiety.

A mile from Hacienda Tulcachi, Carlos suggested they stop for mid-morning break near a stream shaded by tall trees. Removing their jackets and other wraps, they ran for the creek, falling on their bellies to drink deeply of the cold water. The horses followed, drank their fill, then wandered, munching on the thick grass.

From the worn knapsack, Carlos pulled a large object wrapped in brown paper. Yolanda had prepared lunch and now he shared cheese, bread, and a banana with the boy. Jars of cola completed the meal and as Carlos watched Fausto eye the package, he rewrapped the remains and gently reminded the boy they would need the rest for lunch later in the day. Stuffing the package and jars back into the knapsack, he felt pity for Fausto, knowing he came from one of the poorest families in Pachuca. He understood the boy's hunger and for that reason invented small chores to put him to work.

They resisted the temptation to remain under the shady trees, and with reluctance interrupted the lazy grazing of the horses to continue their journey.

After an easy mile they reached Tulcachi and Carlos thought of the previous day. In fact, he had thought of little else all morning. Walking the horses past the buildings, he waved to the women on the porch and searched the area with his eyes, hoping for a glimpse of Luis. He was disappointed not to see him.

They passed the small trail that led back to Pachuca and stopped before the entrance to the high mountain range. Carlos smiled at the boy and gently they prodded their horses into a trot. For several meters the road was paved, making the ride easy; however the ascent soon became pronounced, causing the horses to slow. The men let the animals settle into their own pace, knowing the ride ahead would be arduous.

By this time, Carlos had other concerns. He had been filling his mind with thoughts of Luis, ignoring a growing fear they would find the horses at the first hacienda, a farm owned by Hector and Mariana Martinez. He had taken care to avoid Elena's family since the morning of his encounter with Rolando. His agony had been complete and he wondered sometimes if he could live with the hurt and loss. Only the love of his family and hatred for Rolando kept him alive. Never would he give his enemy the satisfaction of running away. In the early days, he had been on constant alert for a glimpse of Rolando's immediate family, but it eventually became evident they were also avoiding him. He knew the day would come he would have no choice but to meet one of them and he desperately hoped it wouldn't happen today. It seemed he never felt ready to face them.

In the past he had fantasized that he and Elena were together again. During the first days of their separation, she filled his thoughts as he created and discarded plans to carry her away from Pachuca. He visualized fighting the entire Martinez family single-handedly to win her. His suffering would be so severe that all would be forgiven and forgotten, but then reality always set in. He had others to consider. This and the painful knowledge that Rolando was correct. He was trapped in a social class from which there was no escape.

Eventually thoughts of Elena ceased to dominate his day. He would always love her, but now there was no desperation to see her or no temptation to run away. Other priorities cropped up and he simply pushed her from his mind until the day came he didn't hurt so much. Long ago he acknowledged she would be better off without him and he rebuked himself for allowing his involvement with Elena to cloud his understanding. Lately, he had begun to put emotional distance between himself and the girl and had even considered dating another young lady. Mercedes lived in an old two-room house a few hundred yards from his own. The front room was used as a small store that carried a variety of dry goods; hard candy, 'chiclets'; and school supplies.

An interest in the girl had been aroused one Saturday afternoon while he was buying a pencil for Joel. Startled, he became aware of the lingering touch of her hand and the look in her eyes as he passed the sucre to her. He had seen that look in Elena's eyes many times. Counting it as foolishness, he ignored her and set his heart on his work. However, he was surprised when frequent thoughts of Mercedes began creeping into his mind. Longings for love and warmth made her more intriguing and as a result Elena was soon lost in a maze of confusion and his unfulfilled need to become a husband and lover.

Now, as he drew nearer to the Martinez hacienda, he decided he would no longer allow his wounded pride to rule him and he would no longer remain alone. He would visit Mercedes this very evening.

They had ridden at a trot the first kilometer, but the steep incline of the road was wearing on the animals so they slowed to an easy plodding pace. The midmorning sun beat down and the winds flung dust in their faces, forcing them to tie handkerchiefs around their noses and mouths.

Two hours passed before they reached the main buildings of the Martinez hacienda. They stopped to pull off their kerchiefs and noticed a large pickup loaded with alfalfa pulling out from the long graveled driveway. Carlos rode to greet the two men inside and asked for the foreman. With waves of their hands they indicated the 'jefe' was in the barn at the end of the long driveway. A barking dog rushed out to Carlos and Fausto, but ran in the opposite direction, tail between his legs, when a large, dark middle-aged man walked rapidly from the barn to meet the riders, yelling at the mutt to retreat.

Carlos glanced quickly around and saw with relief the Martinez' jeep was not there. He wanted to secure the horses and leave as quickly as possible.

"Buenos dias, Carlos. How good to see you. It seems so long since you have been up this way."

Carlos jumped from his horse and grasped the outstretched hand.

"Buenos dias, Manuel. Yes, it's been over a year, I believe."

"You are no longer working with the Martinez', I hear."

"No, I'm with the Hacienda Hermosa. This is my companion, Fausto Tipantiza. We're looking for stray horses." He described the animals.

"Yes, one of our workers brought them up here a couple of days ago. I'll have someone show you where they are. If the two of you wouldn't mind accompanying him, he will be glad to capture the horses." He smiled, his dark face lighting with friendliness. "I will charge only for the feed they consumed." He put out his hand again. "Well, come to see us again, Carlos." Turning, he waved farewell to Fausto, who was shyly hanging back with his horse.

"Thank you, Manuel. You are always welcome at my house," said Carlos as the broad-shouldered man disappeared into the barn.

Shortly, a disgruntled peon pulling a horse walked toward the driveway, motioning them to follow. Carlos smiled to himself, knowing the worker had been denied an early lunch and siesta. He winked at Fausto as the three mounted their horses and trotted to the opposite side of the road. They followed a worn trail down a gentle slope, across a valley, and up one of the many rolling hills. Alfalfa, grass and scrub-brush covered the landscape as far as the eye could see, each small rise dipping into a valley and gradually rising ever higher. Behind them miles to the west, Quito sat small and sparkling in the palm of Mt. Pichincha's hand.

Horses and cows grazed in clumps, feeding off one pasture, allowing other sections of land to rest. Several hundred feet from the road they approached a fenced enclosure, and stopped while the peon dismounted and opened a crude gate. Motioning for them to wait, he prompted his horse into the pasture as Carlos jumped from his mount to shut the gate. The peon spurred his horse into a fast trot as they entered a shallow gully leading to a high plateau. Fausto directed Carlos' attention to two strays grazing in the distance. They watched the peon's careful approach, his lasso ready. Carlos grabbed a rope from his saddle and waited for the man's return with the errant horses in tow.

In a short time both animals were secured and the small party headed toward Pachuca. Anxious to leave, Carlos paid for the feed and added an extra amount for the peon's help. Carlos and Fausto gratefully started down the mountain, towing the two stray horses behind. Moving quickly downhill, they reached the crossroad and the Hacienda Tulcachi in the space of an hour.

Deciding to eat the leftovers for lunch, they returned to the same shady spot they had visited earlier. While the horses drank from the stream and munched grass, the men shared bread, cheese and cola, refreshing themselves. Carlos felt better than he had in days. Now that he was returning with the horses, his heart felt light with remembrances of his visit with Luis Perez the previous day and plans for a possible relationship with Mercedes. He stripped to his waist and washed in the stream, drying himself with his shirt.

Turning, his legs weakened and his heart stopped momentarily. Hector Martinez' jeep passed, heading for the mountain. It happened in a blur, but not before he saw Elena with her family in the back of the vehicle. She hadn't noticed him until they were almost past, but from the jerk of her head and the mixed look of pleasure and surprise, he knew she had seen him. Their eyes met and time froze. A moment later he tried to move, but his limbs were shaking.

"Come on, Carlos. We must start back before it gets too late," yelled Fausto.

He looked at the boy, his mind in a whirl, knowing he didn't have the strength to mount his horse. I've never stopped loving her, he thought. All the emotions he had buried raced to his heart. Passing his hand over his face, he returned to the stream to splash water on himself.

"I must rest a moment," he told a puzzled Fausto as he laid himself down on the grass. "Just let me lie here a moment, please."

"Hey, what's the matter? We've got to get these horses back."

"Yes, okay. I just felt ill for a moment. I'm all right now." He opened his eyes to find Fausto bending over, looking at him strangely.

"Here, help me up."

Walking to the horses the familiar heavy, sick feeling overtook him. "Oh, my God, please don't let me suffer again. I thought my feelings for her were dead."

The rest of the day passed in a fog. Thinking of little else but Elena, his desire for food, the enjoyment of his family, and any thoughts of starting a relationship with another woman dissolved as though they were wispy clouds. Weary from the long day, he retired only to discover he couldn't sleep.Thoughts of a future without Elena pommeled his mind. The wracking pain hadn't died at all. It had been lying dormant, waiting to be revived. "I can't go through this another time. It's unbearable," he cried softly into his pillow.

All through the long night, he tossed and turned debating whether or not he should see her again. In the end, it was his mother who helped him make the decision.

Chapter 16

During the last days of January, the town of Pachuca celebrated its birthday. Town officials hired out-of-town brass and drum bands for street dances and parades. Large collections of firecrackers tied to gigantic wooden frames were carried by brave men through the streets,as drunken bystanders stood and hollered, ducking pieces of flying fire.

Throngs of people came from miles around on foot, buses, trucks and horseback, jamming the streets, sidewalks and door-stoops. Noise from bands, firecrackers, yelling and carrousing filled the air; echoes bounced from the mountainsides casting sounds to the far reaches of the valley.

Carlos joined the celebration wandering with the crowd until he found himself at a street dance. Watching from the top step of a nearby house, he felt disgust at the happy revelings. Unable to find joy as in years past, he wondered what had changed. He was unaware his attitudes had darkened and soured, causing everything to appear ugly and unappealing.

He noticed Mercedes watching him from across the street, a frown replacing her smile as he turned from her without acknowledgement. Knowing he had left her puzzled and hurt, his conscience smote him, but all he wanted to do now was escape to the peace of his home. How could he have considered a relationship with another woman? "Why am I here?" he asked himself as he turned homeward, fighting his way through the thickening throng.

Because of the drunken crowd, heavy traffic, and flying fireworks he had left his brothers and sister home. The thought of returning to them became a refuge for his troubled mind. To his relief the noise in the house was subdued. After shedding his jacket, he sank onto a bench.

"Let's make popcorn," he suggested to the delighted children.

"Oh, yes," they chorused as Joel stoked the fire. Jerman dug a pan from beneath the table and Yolanda opened a small cupboard, searching for a handful of corn wrapped in newspaper.

Within a few minutes, the four gathered around the fire, munching on the popped corn. Begging stories from their brother, the three youngsters crowded close as he related again his visit to the Hacienda Tulcachi, a tale of which they never tired. They talked together until the children became drowsy. Carlos sent the boys to bed and tucked Yolanda into his mother's bed in the front room.

He took off his clothes, knowing there was nothing left to do but retire. He dreaded the long nights when he had to face his thoughts and desires for Elena.

Despite the beat of the drums and booming noise from the fireworks, he dozed. There was silence in the streets when he woke with a start. Listening carefully he heard muffled laughter and talk from outside the house. He heard the front door open.

In horror he realized the loud whispers and strong scent of liquor was emanating from his mother and a companion. Jumping from the bed, he peered into the outer room. Embers from the fire allowed enough light to see his mother leaning against a man. As quickly and quietly as possible, he moved to Yolanda's bed and struggled to pick her up before the drunken couple tumbled on top of her. Placing Yolanda in his own bed, she snuggled down with her brothers, unaware she had been moved.

For an hour Carlos sat in the darkness of his bedroom until all grew quiet in the next room. Lighting a candle, he walked to the door. He wanted to know who was with his mother. There was little doubt, but he wanted to know for sure. Carrying the candle to the bed, he looked down at Rolando for a long while. Even in this condition Rolando was handsome. Handsome, weak and filthy. Dried vomit stained his shirt and the stench was more than Carlos could bear.

"This is the man who said I wasn't good enough for his sister. Well, I'll not stay here to find out if my mother has conceived another child. It's time I find my own happiness."

In that moment he had never felt so low and lost.

Chapter 17

He would plan well. He must meet with Elena. Since seeing Rolando in his mother's bed, he no longer feared him. His concern was the state of Elena's feelings for him. She must despise his cowardice. Why had he submitted to Rolando so quickly without fighting for Elena's love? He had to see her. He had to explain and make her understand. He discarded the idea of walking to her house. During the day chances were she would not be home. If he visited her in the evening, others would be there. He had to see her away from home. His worst enemies would be the people in the plaza. News traveled as fast as a small child could run. No, he would use the utmost caution, knowing a surprise encounter would be the most productive.

He chose the day carefully. During the month of February, the country of Ecuador would celebrate 'Carnaval'. A time of frivolous fun, scores of water-filled balloons would be heaved from passing vehicles onto hapless pedestrians. If in some cases, water didn't create enough havoc, vessels of flour would be showered, or lard and chimney soot smeared on victims. During the final day of the fiesta, the day before Lent commenced, all businesses closed and people gathered in the plaza for dancing and drinking. Carlos decided this was the best time to carry out his plan.

Three weeks after finding his mother and Rolando together, he calmly ate a small dinner and waited until the children were in bed. His mother had left the house earlier using the excuse she was going to visit a friend. Carlos shook his head in disgust at the thought of her probable date with Rolando.

Careful the children were sleeping, he prepared to leave the house. Finding it chilly, he drew his jacket around him and glanced up at the sky. The moon had yet to appear, but the sky was filled with glimmering, glowing stars which dimly showed his way. Standing on the road, he realized soon he would see Elena again and he began to shake violently, his stomach churning from nervousness. He was alarmed at his lack of control now that he was putting the plan into action. He hesitated and considered returning home. No, if he didn't go now, he might never go.

Leaving the main road, Carlos chose the path which led directly ahead. A quarter of a mile later he followed a narrow trail set between mud walls. Most of the pathway was in deep shadows, but the stars lent enough light for him to feel his way. He walked toward the mountains and away from Pachuca until he came to a crossroad. To the right lay a large hacienda, faint lights showing through small windows of the central building. His greatest fear was of dogs guarding their territory. If he remained quiet and stayed close to the wall, they should be no bother. He paused, listening. Tonight's dance was centered in the town proper, leaving the suburbs quiet except for the faint beat of the music echoing off the mountains and the swishing noises of bats and nocturnal birds.

To his left lay a small, deserted building, old and crumbling. The land; however, was in use. Poor families living in the plaza who, unable to afford land of their own, grew crops, claiming half and reliquishing the remaining half to the landowners..

Carlos knew a caretaker would be watching for trespassers and thieves. He had no desire to meet with the man as he didn't have a good explanation for what he was doing. Thankfully, cornstalks were standing tall and he moved easily between the rows. His plan was to follow the mud walls behind Pachuca's properties until he reached Elena's house and wait until she retired, then call her to the window. He walked swiftly into the black shadows until he reached the end of the property. Nearly to the corner; then suddenly, he found himself in the irrigation ditch. Cold water rushed up to his waist and the silent current pulled him off his feet. Startled, he grabbed for the shrubbery growing against the wall. Pausing to catch his breath, he reached for the bank and pulled himself up.

Nursing a sore ankle and ribs, he gritted his teeth in anger.

"What a fool I am. I knew this ditch is here. How could I have forgotten?" He rested for several minutes, shaking with cold. Should he go back or continue on his way?

Covered with mud, his clothes filthy and dripping, he knew he'd have to return home. Sick with disappointment, he stood and limped on feet numb from the cold. The mud and water weighed him down as he plodded dejectedly through the cornfield. Unable to see clearly, he tripped, falling across a large, soft object. Yelping with alarm, he jerked to his knees as the mound groaned. Staring in fright, he was able to make out the form of a body lying face down in the shadows of the cornstalks. His taut nerves snapped and hot tears filled his eyes. Fear and cold beat at him. Then reason crowded out his fear and gathering some composure, he turned the body over. It groaned in protest. Fumes of liquor wafted over Carlos, and with relief he realized it was the old caretaker indulging in his own party. Resisting the temptation to giggle, he saw the man was merely sleeping.

Weakened by his pounding heart, he sat and waited until his strength returned. The bone-numbing cold, overwhelming fatigue and futility of his efforts were more than he could bear. He had no choice but to go home and try another day.

Chapter 18

A ll that night he lay thinking and planning, sick with frustration, but more determined than ever. At dawn, as he heard the first movements of the mountain Indians and the crowing of the rooster behind his house, the idea hit him. What a fool he was. It was so simple. The very tale-bearers who would carry the news of his appearance in town would be the ones who would bring Elena to him. Smiling, he relaxed, knowing all would be well.

Physically, he didn't feel well until Monday. Deciding he could no longer wait to see Elena, he would go into the main plaza today for the first time in almost a year.

To his dismay, three peons did not appear for work, forcing him and Fausto rushed to complete their own chores plus the others' work. He remembered belatedly that most of his workers had celebrated 'Carnaval' and would have continued drinking throughout the weekend, although officially the Lent season had begun.

During the siesta hour Carlos told Fausto of his idea. They must wait until the townspeople were about their duties before they could put their plan into effect. They would need to find an Indian with a horse. His biggest problem would be finding a sober Indian.

He and Fausto sat on a grassy knoll beside the road patiently waiting for a good prospect. Several drunken men passed with their wives and children in tow, crying babies strapped to the mothers' backs.

After an hour's wait they saw a man in the distance leading his horse toward them. Strapped across the animal's back were two burlap bags of corn bound for Pachuca.

Carlos rose slowly and approached the man, holding out his hand. "Buenas tardes, Senor. How are you and your family?"

"Buenas tardes, Carlos. We are getting by. It's been awhile since we have talked. Your family is doing well, God willing?"

They conversed at length an nonessential topics until at last Carlos requested the man's help.

"I will pay you twenty-five sucres."

The Indian's eyes lit up with enthusiasm. Twenty-five sucres would more than pay for the grinding of the corn he was taking to the town miller.

"Yes, I will help you get to the main plaza, if I can."

Carlos counted out and placed silver in the man's extended hand. Then they solemnly discussed the plan until everyone nodded in agreement. Carlos turned and located a paper sack he had placed in the tall grass. Opening it, he pulled out a penknife.

He had worn his oldest pair of pants and without a second thought he jabbed a hole in the material on one leg. Grabbing with both hands, he ripped it to the knee. He paused to look at Fausto and the Indian, but both men had averted their eyes. Gritting his teeth, Carlos laid the blade of the knife on his leg. As if reconsidering, he hesitated a moment, then with purpose pressed the instrument into the side of his calf. A stream of blood oozed down his leg and he involuntarily moaned as drops of sweat formed on his forehead and upper lip. Again he cut; the blood now flowed in a steady stream. Deliberately, he smeared the sticky red substance on his shirt and face.

"Get some rags from the sack," Carlos yelled to the man and Fausto who by now were definitely looking sick.

Fausto fumbled with the bag until he located two clean, faded cloths and bent to wrap the leg. Blood soaked one immediately. Carlos pressed the other rag firmly on the wound, and tied it securely.

"Now, I must get on top of the horse. Can you place the burlap bags back a bit further?" He waved an arm attempting to keep his balance on his one good leg.

The Indian adjusted the bags of corn, looking as if he regretted his part in the scheme, and then reached out to help Carlos onto the horse's back.

"We'd better go or you will really need a doctor."

Fausto tugged at the reins while the horse protested, balking and snorting, nervous with the added weight on her back. Jumping behind, the Indian slapped the animal's rump. "Go! Get going!"

With another loud slap, the horse leaped into action, running in confusion. Fausto hung onto the reins trying to steady her. The Indian took over, calming the mare.

"Now, Fausto, go with the news. Ask for help, do whatever you must do to spread the tale."

The boy grinned and started running, yelling for help. Indians visiting in the street and storefronts turned to look in astonishment at the laden horse being pulled by its worried-looking owner.

As Carlos had predicted, the news reached town before the small procession and people waited in doorways and windows. It was a sight to behold. Slumped on the horse's neck, lay Carlos, his mouth open, blood oozing through the red-soaked rag. His matted hair stood straight out, his torn clothes were saturated with blood. His bandaged, wounded leg was purposely exposed. He looked as though he had fainted.

By the time they reached the main plaza he began to feel faint and had barely enough strength to hang onto the horse. They had been walking for half an hour and, even though the heavy blood flow had almost stopped, he could still feel drops trickling down his leg.

Carlos could not have hoped for more attention. People stood on the restaurant's long porch, store proprietors stepped to the streets and patrons peered from behind. Residents of the mud homes watched from doors and balconies.

Squeezed between the grade school and registrar's office sat the clinic, a long one-story building constructed by the government for the purpose of supplying medical attention to the rural community. The doctor commuted serving her last year of schooling here, completing while an aide remained permanently in residence. To the rear, past a small patio, an addition had been built to house a dentist and assistant working with the same program.

As they approached, Carlos noticed several women with babies sitting on the doorstep in the entrance, awaiting their turn. Through blurred eyes he saw Fausto pacing impatiently on the cracked sidewalk. He knew that people along the way had asked too many questions Fausto would have been unable to answer and the look on the boy's face revealed his fear and doubts.

Apprehensively, Fausto went to the horse's side as it drew to a stop at the curb. Helping the Indian pull Carlos from the animal, the boy steadied his friend as he attempted to walk into the building.

Through a fog of pain, Carlos saw the crowd of women scatter to make room and he tried to understand why there were no men in the group. A terrible thought gained a foothold. There was a flaw in his plan. He had forgotten there was no doctor in attendance on Monday. Sick patients were forced to find rides to the next town, or wait until the doctor was on duty the following day.

Don Eduardo's daughter, Olivia, worked as an aide. A country girl with experience of sorts, but with no official training or schooling, she opened the clinic alone on Mondays solely for the purpose of vaccinating children against common childhood diseases.

What was I thinking of? Carlos thought through a cloud of pain and faintness.

A pathway opened and Carlos, hopping on his good leg, leaned heavily on his accomplices. Entering the waiting room they paused to look for an empty resting place among the benches filled with mothers and babies.

"Please make room for this patient. He is near death," panted the Indian, trying to shift the dead weight lying on his shoulder.

Without a word, the entire population of the room shifted, all cramming against one wall gasping in horror. An inner door opened and the heavy-set doctor's aide appeared in the entrance, her face blanching.

"What happened?" Astonishment held her motionless.

With a leap, Fausto was at her side. "He's been hurt. Someone attacked him in the road up above the hacienda where he works."

The older Indian nodded his head nervously, hat in hand.

"I can't take care of a problem like this. You'll have to find a truck and take him over to Yaruqui."

"I don't think he'll make it that far." A brave mother, a small child clinging to her skirt, moved forward for a better look at Carlos who by this time had slumped over.

Olivia squatted on the floor and studied him, feeling his clammy face. "I could contact the American nurse, but I doubt if she'd do much for us." Sighing in concentration, she bit on a thumbnail. "Perhaps I should clean the wound and give you something for the pain, Carlos."

Standing, she turned to the other patients who chattered with advice and horror stories of past experiences.

"You will all have to wait until I finish with Carlos." She announced in a loud voice.

Guiding him to his feet, she lead Carlos to the office as several of the mothers hurried for the door anxious to relay the news to the waiting crowd on the sidewalk. Fausto and his companion scrambled behind Carlos, helping him to the table in Olivia's office.

"Take off his shoes," she motioned to Fausto, while she cut the rags covering Carlos' wound. "It's not as bad as I expected. And it's clean, surprisingly clean."

The Indian stammered, "I cleaned him before we put on the bandage."

Olivia gave him a questioning look and then set to work, filling a small metal basin with warm water.

By this time, Carlos was a sickly grey color and could hardly remain awake. The loss of blood had been severe and the procedures were taking longer than he had planned. Olivia watched him anxiously and made her decision.

"Actually, I've helped the doctor many times. And I've cleaned wounds for him. I can at least try to sew your wound until you can get to Yaruqui."

Carlos didn't care. Through unfocused eyes he could hardly see her and he knew only that he had made a dreadful mistake and was now dying. His throat contracted and tears welled up in his eyes. He was dying and would never see Elena after all. Feeling a pinprick as Olivia administered a local anesthesia, he felt blackness envelop him.

Chapter 19

Something cool was gently wiped across his face and he drifted upward to consciousness. Struggling to open his eyes, he looked into Elena's face as she bent over him, a damp rag in her hand. Behind her stood a short, bearded man wearing a spotless white coat. A doctor. Through cloudy vision, Carlos saw he was in a large back room of the clinic, an IV strapped to his arm. As his mind cleared, his attention was drawn back to Elena who spoke not a word, but clung to his hand.

"My name is Dr. Rios. I live in Quito, but work in Yaruqui. La Senorita Olivia called me because she felt you were very ill. It's a good thing she did. You could have bled to death. Fortunately you have a common blood type and with the help of a few good people we were able to get blood transfusions for you." Giving them a friendly, quiet smile, he pulled on his beard.

Carlos thanked him and tried to smile as Elena bent over him, continuing to wipe his face.

"Where is Fausto and the senor from Palugo?"

Elena spoke tenderly. "They left last evening after the doctor arrived."

"I've been here all night?" he said, trying to raise himself.

"Yes," she calmed him. "You've been very sick. Your family was here for awhile this morning, but they had to leave."

Olivia entered the room and Dr. Rios walked to meet her.

"Senorita, you will have to keep him here overnight again. As long as someone stays here in case of a problem."

"Our janitor will stay if I ask him. If anything happens, he will call me immediately."

Somewhat satisfied, Dr. Rios re-examined Carlos, patted him on the head, then left the building with Olivia escorting him to his car.

Content that they were alone, Elena leaned down and whispered in his ear. "I'm so glad you are all right. How I worried."

Tears rolled down his cheeks and he tried to wipe his face, but weakness overcame him.

"Elena, before Olivia returns, I must talk to you. I want to go away so we can be married. Do you think we can manage that? I just can't live without you any longer and if you're willing, we can make plans." He searched her face. "Can we meet again, somehow? Can you get a message to me without causing a problem for yourself?"

Watching his face, she hesitated a few moments. "Carlos, I'm only here right now because my brothers are still at school and Rolando hasn't returned from a party he went to on Sunday.

I heard yesterday afternoon that you were injured but because I had to wait until the news had died down and the maid was away, I can only remain for a few minutes. I live in fear someone will find out I still care for you. Things at home have been difficult. Rolando isn't the sweet man he used to be. He is always in a vile humor and I'm afraid of displeasing him. If he knew we were talking now, I'd fear for you and for the misery he can bring to my life." She brushed back his hair and wiped his eyes. "I am miserable. I've not been happy since we parted. I thought you didn't care any longer."

"Oh, my carina, if you only knew how much I care." He grimaced in pain.

Looking concerned, she asked him, "Are you all right? You know, you will have to talk to the magistrate about this."

"No! I will not report this to anyone. We will leave it alone, Elena. I just want to leave Pachuca with you. Please, consider what I say."

She turned to see if Olivia was out of earshot and lowered her voice. "If I can manage, we will meet again and make plans, but only one time. Do you know? Sometimes I think my brother has lost his mind. We will have to plan quietly so no one will suspect."

"How do we know we can trust Olivia?"

"We can't. We will have to take a chance. She has a boyfriend in Quito and she drives to see him almost every evening. Perhaps that will occupy her mind."

He closed his eyes for a long while and in a moment of impatience she reached out to gently shake him.

"What are you doing? I'm not asleep, I'm thinking," he frowned. "How would it work if I leave a note for you with all the plans?" Weakly, he raised his hand against her protest. "Wait a minute, Elena. Remember the mud wall beside your aunt's house on the left side as you leave the front door? Unless they have repaired it, a piece of the mud brick has fallen out and left a hole. I'll have someone pass by the wall and leave a note. When you visit your cousins you can remove it. I'll leave it early next week after my leg is strong and the stitches are removed. I'll figure a plan and write it down."

Groping for her hand, he grabbed it with all the strength he possessed.

"Tell me if you will do it, Elena. If someone else finds the note there may be trouble for my family. They may have trouble anyway."

"Shhh. Here comes Olivia. Pretend you're sleeping. I'll tell her I've been watching you until she returned. Carlos, yes, I'll go with you. I love you."

She turned and stood. "Oh, Senorita. You're here. He's asleep and since you have returned, I will leave. I was concerned because, as you know, Carlos once worked for my family."

The big woman nodded with a touch of a knowing smile on her lips.

"Of course. Well, don't worry, chica. His wound was not as serious as it first appeared. He will be well in a few days."

"Oh, thank God. How terrible this happened. I wonder who attacked Carlos. Was there a chance to question Fausto?"

"No, he and the Indian left as soon as possible saying they had other things to do. The entire incident is puzzling."

Chapter 20

He sealed the envelope and held it in his hand for a moment, thinking back through the past week. Soon he would be leaving his family and the thought made him sad. Oh, he knew they would be all right without him. Yolanda amazed him with her sense of survival. He knew, too, Rolando was more talk than action and the man's bluster and fury were nothing more than a ploy to frighten and dominate him. With a sigh of joy, he quietly acknowledged the fact he and Elena would soon be together.

He had seen Elena only once since that day the previous week. The next morning he had left for home, shaky but able to walk without much difficulty. No one had spent the night caring for him, but Elena had brought food then quickly disappeared. Olivia must have gone to Quito for the evening, as she had not appeared again. Leaving a pile of change on the bed, he had left early in the morning before the clinic opened.

Tapping the envelope, he looked now at Fausto sitting across from him at the family table. A warm glow emanated from the fire curling around a soup pot. An aroma of chicken stew caused the boy to lick his lips and it seemed he made a concentrated effort to turn his attention to Carlos.

"What do you want me to do with the letter?" asked the boy.

Carlos smiled at his friend with affection. "I need your help. I know you've helped me a lot lately but this is the most important favor you have ever been asked to do, and one with more secrecy. You'll have to be careful, but I'll pay you as much as you make in an entire day. Just don't ask a lot of questions, for your own good."

Fausto's eyes brightened at the mention of money.

Carlos saw the look and studied the child who appeared years beyond his age. Hungry, unbathed, with thick, dirty hair—it was no wonder people living a better way of life would look at the neglected, filthy boy, and be repulsed. They would never understand that for his large family to bathe it would be necessary to carry many pails of water. They didn't own a container large enough for a bathtub causing the impoverished Indians to bathe in the streets, fully clothed, shivering in the dusty wind. His heart went out to the boy.

"Does the letter have something to do with Elena?" Fausto squinted his eyes in an attempt to understand the mystery.

Carlos turned to see if they were still alone having purposely sent his three siblings to collect wood.

"Yes, but you don't need to know what. Listen to what you must do."

Hesitating a moment for pride's sake, the boy nodded. "Well, I need the money, but not bad enough to go to Rolando's house. He's wild."

"You don't have to go to Elena's house, just to her aunt's. No one will see you if you go at night. Walk to the house and stay close to the mud wall and when you notice you are alone or when the family is asleep, slip over next to the house. About three meters from the ground and six meters back, there's a spot where part of a brick has fallen from the wall. Feel in there and gouge out a bit more dirt. Fold this envelope and place it inside. No one must be able to see it. Do you understand?

It must be put there tonight. Tomorrow may be too late. After you return I'll give you the money. Are you frightened?"

"No, I guess not," shrugged the boy. "Just so no neighbors see me. Oh, what's the difference? Who would care?"

"Possibly no one, but I still don't want any curious passersby to see this letter. It's only for one person and only she knows it will be there." Carlos sat back, pleased. "Are you hungry?"

He knew the boy was half-starved. "I'll get a bowl of soup for you." He found two metal bowls and spoons on a shelf and limped to the fire. He dipped stew into each bowl and placed them on the table.

"Go on, eat."

Placing a plate of bread and cheese in front of the boy, Carlos stared in amazement as Fausto wolfed it all down and accepted seconds. Swallowing the last bite, Fausto grabbed the envelope, wiped his mouth on his sweater, and headed for the door.

"I want you to come back here tonight when you have finished," said Carlos. "Just knock on the window." He walked to the door favoring his sore leg. He laid a hand on the boy's shoulder.

Grinning up at him, Fausto boasted, "Don't worry. I'll do exactly as you asked and will return in a few hours. I hope your brothers and sister found wood. There was very little this morning."

Carlos lay awake most of the night waiting for the knock that didn't come. In a frenzy the next morning he dressed, preparing to leave the house against his sister's protests.

"Carlos, your leg still hurts you. Stay home with me one more day. I don't want you to leave," she pleaded.

He stooped beside her. "Mi carina, I must get out and walk on this leg or it will never heal. I'm just going down to Fausto's house. If he is there, perhaps we will work for a while today."

Throwing her arms around his neck, Yolanda hugged him tightly. He released her and messed her hair gently.

"I'll be back for lunch."

Walking into town, he tested his leg and found it was more stiff than wounded. Reaching the shack where Fausto's family lived, he knocked on the weather-worn entrance. A small girl opened the door. He shuddered involuntarily and turned his face away as a horrid stench greeted him. Taking a deep breath, he returned his gaze. A fire burned on the floor in the corner, detailing shadowy figures on the ugly mud wall. A scrawny dog with watery, pink eyes sniffed at him as a pig grunted and hens clucked. Animals slept with the family as a prevention against thievery and because they owned no space out-of-doors.

The thin girl looked sick. Sadly undernourished, her bony legs and bare feet added to her look of hopelessness. It seemed her crumpled dress had been slept in. Stringy and thin, her hair was colored the unusual blondish red that accompanies malnutrition. Her skin was blotchy and her lips were parched.

She rubbed her dull eyes against the brightness of the morning sun.

"Dias, Carlos," she muttered unenthusiastically.

"Hola, Lolita. Is Fausto home?"

She turned and peered into the darkness as Carlos stepped out of the glare of the sun and looked over her shoulder. He saw the straw mats lying on the floor. One lone piece of furniture, a bureau, stood in a corner, the top overflowing with various objects. In the middle of the floor sat a large can, the source of the overpowering stench, where the family relieved themselves. Carlos' stomach lurched and he turned back to the street, breathing deeply. He pitied this family. Fausto's father cleaned the streets in the plaza. Each morning he took the village wheelbarrow and a broom to sweep the refuse from the front of each house. A notorious drunk, the few sucres he earned each day paid his way of escape into an alcoholic oblivion.

The child placed one dirty leg across the other and scratched her calf with the heel of her foot as she looked up at him.

"No, I think he's already left for work."

From behind Lolita a woman appeared, wincing against the bright sunlight.

"Buenos dias, Carlos. You are looking for Fausto? I don't think he was here last night. He wasn't with you?"

"Buenos dias, senora. No, I was home all night. You are sure he has not been home?"

"Well, I don't know. I guess he's left for work. Maybe not."

She had lost interest. He watched her, wondering if she still remembered he was there. At times he was puzzled at his people's short attention span. He failed to realize that poor eating and unsanitary habits seriously damaged both body and mind. Almost everyone he knew ate a diet of bread, rice, noodles and potatoes-anything that would fill their stomachs. He and his mother were able to afford meat once or twice a week because both of them worked, but Fausto's family rarely ate protein. The animals that shared their lodging along with eggs their hens produced would be sold to buy more starches to eat.

Fausto's mother yawned, showing a toothless mouth. Her hair had been freshly combed, but obviously had not been washed. A dark skirt caked with dirt hung to her ankles. She, like the other Indian women living in homes without plumbing, purposely wore long, flared skirts in order to squat in the street to relieve herself in a modest manner. Her sagging breasts were partially covered by a frayed sweater and Carlos wondered if perhaps Fausto had failed to mention that he had a new brother or sister. A fat flea hopped from the sweater to the woman's exposed neck and disappeared behind her ear.

Shuddering again, Carlos turned to leave. His own home was never completely clean, but it didn't have the stench and filth of this house. He was proud of the orderly way in which his young sister kept their lodging. He would remember to compliment Yolanda when he returned home.

"I should go to work myself. Thank you."

She stood in the doorway not noticing his departure.

Where had Fausto gone? Hurriedly passing his own house he rushed toward the hacienda. Suddenly, he slowed down. Maybe the note hadn't been delivered. He began to question his decision to leave Pachuca with Elena. Could he bear to live in the big city or in another valley away from the familiar sights he loved? Was a life with Elena worth this? What of Yolanda and his brothers? Or the security of a home and job? And, of course, his mother. True, he seldom saw her because of their work schedules, but he still loved her. With a sudden premonition, he felt perhaps he would never see his family again.

If that were true, was a life with Elena worth it? As he walked the road to Hacienda Hermosa he watched Quito awakening far to his right across the wide expanse of the Tumbaco Valley. Sun rays caressed the mountainside of Pichincha, engulfing the capitol city. From this distance it looked quiet and serene, but he knew even at this hour people were struggling to find room on the hundreds of buses passing through the traffic-choked streets. The mere idea of joining the hordes of people rushing to earn a living repelled him. Passing the first pasture of the hacienda, he breathed in the youth of the morning and looked to the mountains. Perhaps he couldn't leave. A wave of panic engulfed him. Maybe Fausto had encountered trouble delivering the note. If so, he would accept this as a sign he should not marry Elena.

In the distance, he saw Fausto sitting on a fence near the driveway chewing on a bun. Waving, the boy jumped down to wait. Carlos quickened his step.

"Fausto."

"Hola, Carlos. You're late."

"Late? Where have you been? I was almost sick from concern. Why didn't you knock on the window last night? And where were you this morning? I was at your house."

Fausto shrugged. "Sometimes I don't go home. There's not much room."

Carlos stared at him. "What happened to the envelope? Did you deliver it?"

Snorting, Fausto wiped his nose with the sleeve of his dirty, holey sweater and turned, walking up the driveway. Carlos followed with a questioning look.

"Well, What happened?"

"Nothing happened. I sat in the dark against a wall all night. There were people at the Martinez house until late. Lights were on and I was afraid someone would see me and think I was a thief. So, I waited."

"Did you leave the envelope?" Carlos flung out his arms in frustration.

"Yeah, yeah, it's there." Fausto scratched his head. "I'm not sure what time everyone left and the lights went out, but I was sleeping when the cars began to leave. I just stayed all night and I'm tired this morning."

Carlos felt a twinge of conscience and softened his approach. Smiling, he playfully hit the side of the boy's head as they reached the yard.

Recently built of wood and glass windows, the house sat in a grove of eucalyptus trees. A garden of roses surrounded a man-made pond boasting a large family of ducks. Chickens scattered in every direction scolding the thoughtless intruders.

A little brown and white dog ran from the barn dancing about in excitement.

Fausto laughed and patted the mutt. "The note is safe inside the wall. At dawn I passed and couldn't see it."

"Good." An uncontrolled joy flooded through him. He forgot his indecision and knew only that his desire was to be with Elena. "Good work, Fausto. And now I must wait five days. Five long days."

Chapter 21

S unday night, when the villagers of Pachuca were at evening mass or in the crowded saloon, Carlos made his way to Elena's house. He tapped on her bedroom window at the appointed time. It opened quietly and a canvas bag was tossed to the ground. He reached for Elena to help her as she dropped to the high grass lining the house. Within minutes they were running in the direction of the American nurse's compound and the Pan American highway.

Book 4
Elena & Carlos

Chapter 22

"**Y**ou'll have to slow down, Carlos. I can't go any farther," panted Elena, as she stopped in the middle of the road pulling on his arm. "Please, slow down. I'm so tired."

"But if we do, someone might realize you're gone and then we'll have your brothers looking for us."

"No, don't worry. They won't notice anything until tomorrow." Out of breath, she struggled to speak. Wiping her face with the sleeve of her jacket, she refused to move. "Please, Carlos. I can't run any farther."

He placed two ragged canvas bags on the road. "We're only one kilometer from your house. You've got to try."

"It's dark. No one can see us. Please, I'll be ready in a minute, but I've got to rest."

Relenting, he smiled. "All right, carina. Here, let's sit down on the grass. We have to talk anyway."

"I'm sorry. It's just that I'm not accustomed to running in the dark. It's hard to see where we're going."

"Just straight ahead. There aren't any turns until we get down to the unfinished highway."

"It may be straight, but there are a lot of holes in the road and I keep tripping."

"That's why I've been holding your arm."

He made sure she was comfortable, then sat beside her. Reaching for her hand, he laughed.

"What's funny? I can think of a lot of emotions I feel right now, but gaiety is not one." She peered at him through the darkness.

"I guess nothing is really funny, but I was thinking of the look on your brother's face tomorrow when he goes into your room." Solemnly he patted her hand. "I hope you are sure they will wait until then."

"I'm positive. I told our maid not to bother me at all, that I had a headache and needed to sleep. And Rolando and my brothers are out somewhere." Looking at him again, she asked hopefully, "We'll be far away by tomorrow, won't we?"

"Yes, but truthfully, I'm not quite sure what we're going to do now. When I planned this, it was hard deciding which way to go. Perhaps we can walk up to the old highway, but then we'll have to walk through pasture land. Or we can go to the new, uncompleted highway, but it's muddy and difficult to walk on. We could go through town, but we both know that wouldn't be a good idea." He released her hand and put his elbows between his raised knees and pondered the situation a moment. "Of course we could go back up by my house and walk to the old Pan American highway by way of the Tulcachi Hacienda, which would take most of the night. And there's always Yaruqui." He expelled a loud sigh. "We have many choices and none seem too good, so I thought I'd wait until we talked to see what you want to do."

She reached to squeeze his hand. "Let's not worry about it this very minute. I want to enjoy you a little bit, Carlos. This is the first time we've been alone for such a long time. It's so good to be with you." Leaning her head on his shoulder, she sighed as he slipped his arm around her. "You know, I've dreamed many times we would be doing this together."

"Have you, Elena? I thought perhaps you didn't care for me any more. That was my greatest fear."

"I've never stopped loving you. Not for one day. But I have to admit I was beginning to wonder if you hadn't found someone else."

Shaking his head, he said, "I haven't had one girlfriend since we parted. Oh, there was a girl living near my house I considered taking to a dance, but only because I was tired of being alone."

"Do you think that God meant for us to be together?"

"There's never been a doubt." He kissed her lightly. "Now, we must start down toward the new highway."

He lifted her to her feet, then grabbed the bags in one hand. He placed his other arm around her waist as they walked past the maternity clinic owned by the American nurse. Through the main gate they could see lights shining from various buildings.

"That's where I was almost born. Rolando told me he tried to get help from the American when my mother almost delivered me on this very road. Of course you know the story. The whole town remembers. I've wondered just how much my brother has changed from those days."

He released her waist to adjust his hold on the two canvas bags hanging heavily from his shoulder.

"Elena, you're going to have to forget all of that. The moment you decided to go with me, you closed the door on your past. We may never see them again." Stopping, he put the bags down and turned to her. "Mi amor, you don't have to doubt their love for you. I know in his own way Rolando loves you. Perhaps before we go any farther, you should examine your feelings. Can you go through with this? I love you so much that I'm willing to take you back if leaving is too difficult."

"Living with my family was becoming unbearable, or perhaps I was unbearable to live with. One way or the other, I can't live with them any longer, and I can't live without you."

"That's all I need to hear." He reached out in the darkness and touched her cheek. "Let's go."

They reached the highway, which ran north and south, across their path. In the process of being graded, it was strew with piles of dirt. Fearful of tripping, Carlos stopped and pulled a flashlight from his bag.

"I guess we can use this now."

Taking a firmer grip on the bags, he flashed the light ahead as they picked their way across the mounds.

"It's time to make our decision, Elena."

"Could we travel on this unconstructed part until we reach the old Pan American highway? Wouldn't that be better?"

"I don't think so. The heavy rain we had yesterday turned the road to mud. Also, about one-half kilometer from here, there's a large ditch in the middle of the road where they're going to place irrigation tubes. I don't know if they've filled it up yet. It would be too dangerous to try and get past it in the dark."

"Well, we can't go through town. Don Eduardo always stands in his doorway and I'm afraid the neighbors might see us. No matter what area we pass through someone would see us."

"Shall we try running through the pastures?"

"Maybe that is the best way. But when we get up to the old highway, how will we get to Quito?"

"By truck or bus."

"But, Carlos, what if we flag down a truck belonging to a friend and they recognize me?"

"We'll have to be careful we stop a bus or truck from the jungle."

"How will we know the difference?"

"We'll take a chance."

"Do you know how few trucks pass at this time of the night, especially on a Sunday? We may have to wait until morning."

"You're right. Let me think." He shifted the weight of the bags, thinking of each direction they might go and the dangers each presented. All of a sudden he hit his head in exasperation.

"Or course. I'm so stupid. I know what we can do."

"What?" She held his arm tightly. "What?"

"Let's take the road leading west. We'll go to Quito by way of train."

"Train? But the train doesn't pass until tomorrow morning and the station is a long distance from here."

"That's the only way, Elena. We'll just have to walk. No one from Pachuca would travel by train because they are so close to buses and other means of transportation. And the best part is, the station is straight ahead on this old road. We won't have to pass anyone we know."

"Come to think of it, the train might be fun. I've never ridden on one, although friends have told me it is quite uncomfortable." Here, let me carry one of the bags."

"All right." He handed her the lighter of the two bags. "It's not far to Quito. Let's do it."

Stumbling around the mud holes, they searched for the narrow entrance on the opposite side of the new highway. Finally they stood panting on the cobblestone path.

"Do we have everything?"

"Yes." She checked her bag that she had taken from his arm.

On this side of the highway under a canopy of trees, the darkness was denser. Carlos flashed the light occasionally to make certain they had not strayed from the pitted road.

"I would guess that if we rest once in awhile, we will arrive in about two hours."

"How will we know when we get there?"

"Because across the road is a small hacienda and they usually shine a few lights close to the house. When we see that, we'll know we are there."

"Have you thought of how we must spend the night?"

"Do you mean, where will we sleep? I don't think it will be too much of a problem. I doubt it will rain tonight, so we can sleep either under a tree or perhaps close to the station."

"There must be a family living in the station."

"Of course. There would have to be. Someone to guard the building against thieves and vandals. We'll just wait until we get there then we can decide what to do."

In a little over an hour they saw the lights of the hacienda. Across the road, loomed the dark shadows of the train station.

"Wait, Elena. First, I want to talk to the family who lives here."

He left her standing alone as he walked around the side of the building. Carefully, he searched until he found a door with a faint light shining from underneath. Knocking, he heard a small movement and slowly the door opened.

"Who's there?" A short, heavy bosomed woman peeked through the cracked opening.

"I'm from Pachuca and would like to know when the train leaves for Quito."

"It doesn't leave until tomorrow."

"Oh, I didn't realize that," he lied. "What time does it pass?"

"Six o'clock."

"Is there any way I can rest here tonight instead of walking back to Pachuca?"

"I don't care. Sleep on the other side on the porch." She shut the door.

"Elena," he whispered. "Come this way."

She appeared as a shadow and he led her to the vacant cement porch. It was without so much as a bench.

"I'm sorry, amor. We'll just have to make ourselves as comfortable as possible. I'm sorry you have to sleep on a porch tonight in the cold instead of in your bed."

"I would sleep on a cement porch the rest of my life to be with you, Carlos."

He squeezed her hand, and then shined his flashlight the length of the porch, checking for filth. There was none.

"Here, put your things down."

They gathered their belongings and sat on them.

"We have until six o'clock tomorrow morning. Are you tired?"

"A little." She stood. "I'll lay out some clothes. I have a poncho and both of us have jackets." Feeling in the bags, she drew out the clothing. "We'll be comfortable."

Folding sweaters for each of them to use as pillows and improvising a mattress from various pieces of clothing, they were soon huddled under the wide poncho. He found her hand.

"We may have to do this more than once. I don't know what the future holds."

"I'm concerned about what we will do tomorrow," she laughed.

"My mother's brother lives in Quito. I'm sure he will help us. I have saved some money, so I hope he can do something about getting permission for us to marry."

"I'm not eighteen yet. Will there be a problem?"

"Maybe. That's why I want to talk to him. He is a professional man, a lawyer, so he will know."

Silence covered them as they lay without speaking for several minutes. In the distance a dog barked and a baby cried from within the station. Suddenly a low chuckle burst from Carlos and Elena followed with a giggle.

"I'm so happy." She laughed with pure joy.

"Can you believe we finally did it? We did it." He joined in with her laughter.

They talked excitedly for more than an hour, then drifted off to sleep.

Chapter 23

The chattering of two Indians on the other side of the tracks awakened Carlos. Sitting up, he found he was stiff and cold.

Elena opened her eyes and wondered for a moment where she was. "Who's talking?"

"Just two men over there. They haven't seen us yet. It's still pretty dark."

"It must be close to six o'clock, though. You can see daylight above the mountains."

"Yes. Let's get our things together. We can sit here like we've just arrived and are waiting for the train." Elena shivered, snuggling in her jacket.

"There must be a water faucet on the road. Do you want to wash your face?" he asked.

"Yes, just a minute and then you can have your turn."

She wandered to the front of the station and watched the occupants of the road. A few children were straggling by, heading for school. She waited until the way was clear, and satisfied that she recognized no one, ran to the faucet to splash water on her face.

In a few minutes, both were washed and refreshed. They repacked their belongings and were sitting on the edge of the porch as daylight arrived.

A woman appeared at the end of the building and Carlos recognized her as the woman he had spoken with the previous night. With a greeting she thrust a large wooden tray at them. It was piled high with empanadas, a treat made of pie dough filled with sweets, cheese or sometimes meat, and then fried in pork lard. Carlos pulled several silver centavos from his pocket and purchased four empanadas filled with cheese and handed two to Elena.

"We'll drink water until we pass a town where they sell colas."

As the sun rose higher in the sky several new passengers arrived, mingling with friends and acquaintances. A few people gathered at the porch to buy empanadas from the eager vendor, who relied on the few centavos she earned each day to feed her family.

The train arrived with a roar. To Elena's disappointment, it was nothing more than a long bus. The wheels had been replaced with round discs that moved freely on the tracks. The steering wheel controlled the brakes rather than direction; but other than this minor change, it was nothing more than a bus.

Carlos guided Elena inside the train lugging their baggage with him. He found a seat halfway to the back and both of them sat nervously. Slowly they began to move, the driver changing gears until soon they were passing through the familiar, beautiful countryside. Carlos thought he would feel sorrow with his farewell to his past, but failed to sense any remorse. Both of them sat rigidly in hard, lumpy seats, willing the train to hurry from the area where they would be more vulnerable to encounter acquaintances. Eventually they eventually stopped in Cumbaya, a town halfway between Quito and Pachuca. Knowing this was the last stop the train would make in their hometown area, they relaxed with big grins. Carlos forced open the train window and called for two colas. Running to stand below the window, a woman held out warm bottles for him to grab. Sitting back on the hard seat they drank, thirsty from the hot, difficult ride. Polishing off the last sips, they slumped toward each other, dozing.

Despite a long wait in a forest of eucalyptus trees while the conductor carried buckets of water from a stream to feed an overheated radiator, they arrived in the southern section of Quito by midmorning. The quaint city bustled with merchants, beggars, vendors and wandering people; balconies projected above store fronts facing traffic-choked streets.

The streets of the old city crawled up the side of Mt. Pichincha, which has the largest base of any mountain in the Western Hemisphere.

Neither had a desire to live here, but to visit was a pleasure. Elena attended school in the center of town, and was taken aback when she realized they were to pass within a block of the building.

"We can't go this way. My school is down that street. If we walk past with our bags someone may see us."

"Caramba, I didn't think. Let's walk over two blocks. Anyway

I need something to drink."

They stopped, searching the street for a cola sign.

"Walking up these hills takes my breath away." She exaggerated her breathing, holding a hand over her chest. "Let's find some place to sit."

They found an open cafe containing three tables. The entrance was partially barred by a large metal trough filled with hunks of potatoes and pieces of pork which sat on kindled fire. A tired-looking, elderly woman stood inside the door fanning the flames to create more heat.

"Do you want something to eat, Elena? I'm hungry."

"Please."

She chose a table against a wall in the darkened room, hoping no one from school would look in and see them. Carlos soon returned with two large pieces of paper filled with chunks of hot potatoes, meat, and large hava beans. Placing the food on the table, he searched for a cup of salt. Finding one, they pinched enough between their fingers to sprinkle the food liberally. In a bowl they found aji, homemade hot sauce, and began dipping the steaming food in the fiery liquid. The old woman plodded over, two glasses and bottles of cola in hand. In a short time, they felt refreshed and Elena sat back, excitement filling her face.

"It's becoming real to me that we're together and running away. Half of the time I can't believe it. It seemed to happen so fast."

"I'm glad you're not sorry." His eyes softened, watching her. "Yes, we're together, and if we can get to my uncle's house, nothing will separate us again."

"Where does he live?" She sipped at the warm cola.

"Not far from here, but the streets are confusing, so we'll have to find a bus that leaves the main part of town." He was anxious to go. "Do you want anything else to eat?"

"No, I feel satisfied. Perhaps we won't have to worry about meeting someone from school since classes have started, but I still think we should avoid the building. We can catch the bus closer to the Plaza de Independencia, even though it means we must walk farther."

Nodding together in agreement, they gathered their belongings and walked uphill away from the school to the large plaza facing the Presidential Palace. Just as they reached the bus stop, Elena let out a small yelp.

Carlos stopped as she grabbed his arm. "What's the matter?"

"There's Geoff. He just walked down the street where we were. He must have come from Pachuca by bus and now is heading to the school. What if Rolando is here with him? Frozen in fear, hysteria threatened to overcome her. "What if Geoff has already been to the school and is looking around the plaza for us?"

"Why would they think us here?" he asked calmly, though his heart pounded.

"Maybe they're trying to find some of my schoolfriends to see if they know where I have gone. Perhaps they think I confided in some of them."

"Did you?"

"No, of course not. I told no one about this. You asked me not to in the note. Remember?" She answered with a touch of contempt in her voice.

He saw the panic in her eyes and couldn't deny the fear growing in him.

"I'm not going to put up with this. We'll take a taxi. I don't care how much it costs."

It wasn't difficult to find a cab in the traffic-lined streets. It seemed every other car was a yellow taxi cruising, the driver prowling for potential passengers. Without much effort he flagged one down. Helping Elena in, he dumped the bags behind her. He opened the front door, and sat beside the driver to give directions. Within a few minutes they were away from the activity, noise and smells of the old city, entering an area unhampered by the many hills in the older section of Quito. Quickly rolling past a main street, they made a sudden turn and again started uphill, riding toward a suburb built on a ridge overlooking the valley where Carlos and Elena had lived all their lives. The taxi moved along the edge of an immense canyon covered with flimsy, matchbox houses clinging precariously to the sides.

Finally the driver found the sloped street where Carlos' uncle lived and drove down with care, stopping the car at a slant. Paying the man, Carlos and Elena were left standing in front of an old house.

"Which one does he live in?"

"Behind that big door over there."

Carlos pointed toward two large wooden doors drawn together and latched from the inside. Carrying the bags to the other side of the street, he knocked loudly. There was no response.

"Maybe they aren't home," Elena said, shifting her tired feet.

"There's no padlock on the outside of the door so someone has to be here. Anyway, the siesta hour has begun. It's probably difficult to hear from inside."

He pounded until the door vibrated. A minute later they heard running footsteps and the heavy door opened. A teenage boy peered out, pleasantly surprised at the unexpected visitors.

"Hola, Carlos! It's Carlos!" he yelled. "I can't believe it. Come in. Come in. Hey, Momi, Popi, look who's here."

A dark, stout man appeared, running on short legs. He grabbed Carlos in a hug.

Elena stood back, ignored until the excitement of first greetings passed and Carlos stepped back to pull her forward. "This is Elena, Uncle Jose."

The little man reached out to grasp her hand. "Come this way. Come into our house, which is your house. You will always be welcome here."

Beaming with pleasure, he led them behind the double doors into semi-darkness. Carlos waved to his aunt standing in the upper doorway awaiting their arrival.

Elena saw they were standing on an old, worn stairway landing that led up to the entrance of the house. Another stairway behind them led down to an enclosed patio where a cement tub had been built for laundry and gathering water. It was dim, grey, and damp. A light filtered in from a hole in the roof. Climbing the stairway, they walked across a narrow landing until reaching the door of the house.

An attractive middle-aged woman with bright black eyes and pudgy cheeks greeted them with a wide, white smile and a hug. Self-conscious, Elena was overcome with the show of affection from the woman introduced to her as Aunt Carlota.

Elena was offered a place on the davenport as Carlos sat with his uncle on two chairs pulled out from the dining room table.

High, wide windows looked over rows of houses sitting below

them following the ridge of the canyon. In the distance, Elena could see the old city of Quito resting at the base of Mt. Pichincha, white buildings with red tile roofs clinging to their neighbors as if dependent upon each other. A sudden touch of homesickness brought a knot to her throat. She missed her mountains and wide open spaces; the smells of home; her mother; her Momi. There had been no way to explain to her mother why she must leave. Her greatest pain would come later when she allowed herself to think of Aunt Mariana, Uncle Hector and her cousins. Carlos was right when he said that they may never see their families again. Perhaps after this, they would never be welcomed in Pachuca again. Blinking against tears threatening to fall, she looked toward Carlos who was explaining to his uncle the need for temporary hospitality. Carlos. Sweet, gentle, handsome Carlos. Think of it! Here she was, with Carlos. This had been her dream, her fantasy for months. If all worked well, he would be her husband in a few days. Her husband. Now the promises of a home; of babies; of love; of security all lay within reach. Pride dissolved the lump in her throat and dried her tears. There was nothing in Pachuca that could compare to Carlos; nothing that would make her return to that life again. At that moment a spontaneous joy sprouted as from a seed in the center of her emotions, its roots spreading like fire and bursting into a full flowered garden. It was more than she could contain. Her cheeks blazed pink, her eyes shined brightly and her red lips threatened to burst forth with gleeful laughter.

Uncle Jose had been deep in conversation with Carlos, somewhat troubled with the proposition confronting him. Always impressed with the boy and his level headedness despite tremendous problems at home, his feelings were divided, desiring to help the two young people and yet not wanting to betray his sister. He was tempted to offer the comforts of his home for the day and then send them back to Pachuca to think about their future for a few years. Both were so young, and what Carlos was asking bothered him a great deal. Perhaps he, as a businessman, would know how to get them a marriage certificate without much trouble, but first he had to know that he was doing the right thing.

At this moment he turned to look at Elena sitting on the davenport and caught the look of joy and pride on her face.

Quickly all doubts fled and he knew that no matter how many years these children waited, they belonged together. Understanding touched him. He had felt that love long ago. He still dearly loved his wife, but there was nothing more beautiful than unfulfilled love about to be consummated.

"Elena, are you sure this is what you want? Won't you miss your family and home?" Uncle Jose asked merely for the pleasure of being fatherly.

"Oh, yes, this is what I want and yes, I'll miss my home and family in Pachuca. But now Carlos and his family is my family. This is what I want."

Jose sat back in his chair, folding his hands over a protruding belly, and sighed with a feeling of importance.

"You will let me think a little. Mama is in the kitchen preparing a bit of food for you. Then I must get to the office." Turning to Elena again, he explained. "Perhaps Carlos has told you, but if not, I am a lawyer. That is why, if I choose, I leave for work late, early or not at all."

He chuckled, revealing a nice smile. "I'm getting older and don't have the energy I once had. Oh, when I was young like Carlos, I was on my way to work before the sun had a chance to roll over your mountains in Pachuca. Now, I like to stay home and enjoy my beautiful wife."

They looked up as Carlota entered the dining room with a tray of cups and plates of cheese and bread.

Uncle Jose escorted Elena to the dining room and held a chair out for her at the table. Carlos replaced the two chairs he and his uncle had removed from the table. Uncle Jose seated himself to Elena's right and indicated Carlos to sit opposite her. Carlota wandered from the kitchen to the table, puttering with odds and ends, although a place had been set for her. Alfredo, Carlos' cousin had retired to his room after the excitement had died down and Elena could hear boys' voices, laughter and music, and she decided he must have guests.

As they drank hot cinnamon-flavored water and snacked on fresh bread, sweet butter and salty cheese, the conversation turned to matters other than the marriage. A sincere effort was made to include Elena in the talk about family and she spoke freely of her own home, family and schooling.

It was late evening, after Uncle Jose returned from work, before they talked again of the impending marriage.

"How much money have you have saved, Carlos?"

"I have enough to pay someone to marry us without asking questions."

Fatigued from the excitement, Uncle Jose wiped his face with a handkerchief and refolded it, playing with the edges.

"It may take a bit of work, but I think we can do something to pass as Elena's parents."

Standing, Jose placed the handkerchief in his back pocket and walked to a side table. Opening a drawer he pulled out a pad of paper. From a corner of the dining room, he brought a briefcase. Clearing a place on the davenport, he invited Carlos and Elena to join him and for the next hour they made plans. Not one to be left out, Aunt Carlota continued making trips from kitchen to living room, insisting they must be hungry and tempting them with offers of after-dinner snacks.

Uncle Jose would handle the legalities of a civil wedding. Carlos would be responsible for running the many errands to hasten the wedding day. After much pleading on the part of Aunt Carlota, it was decided that Carlos and Elena would spend a few days with the family until they were able to find an apartment of their own.

The busy days flew by and a week later they were married in a civil ceremony.

But the memory of seeing Geoff in Quito bothered Elena and they decided to leave the capital city. Guayaquil became a possibility but tales of the dirty, humid seaport caused them to reject the idea. They had lived in clean, country air all of their lives and they knew they could not abide the filth and smells of the largest city in Ecuador. Even the lesser populated city of Quito was becoming claustrophobic to them.

One night they discussed the possibility of returning home to Pachuca. They were lying in cousin Alfredo's bed, the boy having been expelled from his room to stay at a friend's home until the young married couple found their own apartment.

"We can't go back, Carlos. Not yet. There is a chance we will be welcomed, but I have doubts. As far as they are concerned, what we did was wrong and I fear Rolando will separate us again, especially if he finds out we were married with your uncle's help. He would say it was fraud."

"I will never feel we are married illegally, Elena. No two people love each other more than we do."

"That may be true, but in the eyes of God, I do wonder. And certainly in the eyes of my family, we are not legally married."

"Why? The only thing questionable is the signatures of our aunt and uncle instead of your parents. We were married by an official of the country of Ecuador. He pronounced us husband and wife. Everything is legal. We had to do it this way, don't you see, Carina?"

"Perhaps. Oh, Carlos, please don't think I regret this. I love you so much. It's just that we have been living here for two weeks, causing your cousin to leave home, eating your family's food and taking advantage of their hospitality. I guess I feel guilty."

Slipping his arm under her, Carlos held her close. "Elena, they love you. Can't you see what it means to Aunt Carlota to have a young girl in the house? She has only the one son and taking care of us has made her happy. I know that."

He kissed Elena's cheek. "I know what you mean, though. I cannot live in the city, and living in a part of town that overlooks our valley almost makes me sick. I miss the mountains. Here all you smell are fumes from cars, buses and garbage trucks. How I would love to smell a morning in Pachuca."

"Perhaps we could try living in another valley. There is one on the south side of Quito. Have you been to Conocoto?"

"Yes, once. And all I could think of was getting back to my valley."

Pulling himself up on his elbow he looked down at her. The pale light coming from the window gave her face a faint glow.

"The other night someone suggested we try living in Guayaquil. We could never do that, I know. However it gave me an idea. Have you heard of Salinas?"

"Of course. Some of my friends have gone there for vacations."

"Well, further south and closer to Guayaquil there's a small town named Playas located on a stretch of beach that is quite beautiful, they tell me. Many wealthy vacationers from Guayaquil stay at a hotel located on the beach front. I thought if we could live in Playas for a while I could find a job in the hotel or one of the restaurants."

She sat up and propped a pillow behind her. "Where did you hear about this?"

"Actually my uncle mentioned it by chance. I know they want us here in Quito with them, but he knows we could never live confined in a small apartment in a crowded city. I feel, too, that he doesn't want us going back to Pachuca because of what he did for us. That may cause some problems for him."

She sat thinking for a moment, absently playing with the end of the blanket.

"You're not accustomed to working like that. All you know is farm labor."

"I can learn, amor. Maybe I won't have to work in the kitchens. Perhaps I can find something else more suitable."

"It's close to vacation time from school. What if someone from Quito goes there and sees us?"

"Almost everyone goes to the beaches at Manta or Bahia. Few people will go to Playas from Quito. At least we can hope that."

He rubbed his hands together in anticipation.

"We can't take up room in my Uncle's home any longer. I think we should leave as soon as possible."

"Do we have enough money?"

"Don't worry. I have been saving part of my pay since you were twelve years old—just for this day, Elena. Even when we were separated, I saved. I guess part of me always knew we would be together."

Shaking her head in wonder, she hugged him hard.

"I'll go anywhere with you. I didn't know I would be so happy being married. If someone could have made me believe this sooner, I'd have run away with you when I was twelve."

"Mi chiquita, you think you have family problems now," he laughed, returning her hug.

Chapter 24

Leaving Carlos' family created mixed emotions in Elena. She cared for Aunt Carlota and Uncle Jose and appreciated the help they had given them, but going to Playas with her husband was very exciting. Carlos called a taxi and when it arrived there was a flurry of kisses and hugs, tears and groans.

In no time they arrived at the bus station and bought tickets. Following the barking voices of drivers, they quickly found the bus to Guayaquil. Depositing Elena inside the large vehicle, Carlos checked to see if their bags were tied securely to the racks on top. He then ran off to buy something to eat. Shortly, he returned with a sack full of oranges, tangerines, chirimoyas, and hard-boiled eggs. Leaving these in Elena's lap, he left again in search of empanadas, hot potatoes and pork meat. Despite the breakfast Aunt Carlota had fed them, they settled back in their seats eating the hot food, giggling and licking their fingers like children.

Exiting Quito the road climbed higher than the capital city, passing Mt. Cotapoxi and on to Latacunga, the highest village in Ecuador. From there the road descended and the style of living changed. Thatched roofs adorned small huts, instead of the sunbaked mud tile coverings common in the Tumbaco Valley. As the road took them further from the equator, they noticed the Indians wore thick, heavy ponchos to ward off the chill. The small differences in custom, dress and home styles amused the two young lovers for a time, but soon weariness overtook them and they drifted to sleep. At noon they were awakened as the bus pulled into an area designated for passengers to refresh and relieve themselves.

Stretching, Elena and Carlos made their way to the front of the bus. A low, flimsy building constructed of long, uneven pieces of wood stood open facing the highway. Several benches had been placed under cover. The men gathered around tables laden with bottles of whiskey and beer before finding a place to sit. Several women stood beside metal boxes filled with smoldering kindling. Cooking troughs full of potatoes, beans and meat sat over the embers. One table was laid with several types of colorful fruit and cooked grains, such as havas, a large meaty bean, toasted corn, and chochos, a small white, rich-tasting bean.

"Look, Elena! Tripa! Let's buy some for lunch." Carlos pointed, delighted with his discovery.

"Oh, yes!" cried Elena, pulling on his hand.

At the end of the row of tables, a woman sat on a wooden stool, skirts billowing. Between her legs sat a bucket filled with white and brown objects.

Carlos took a few coins from his pocket and the woman pulled two pieces of brown paper from under a plate. She reached into the bucket and brought out chunks of cooked beef intestines.

"This reminds me of home. I've been hungry for tripa since we left Pachuca." Elena moaned contentedly, savoring every bite. Buying a second helping, they wandered to a vendor selling colas.

Sipping their drinks, they watched their fellow travelers lay aside their heavy ponchos as the strong noontime sun grew warmer.

"Are we far from Playas?" asked Elena, drinking the last of her cola and setting the bottle on a nearby table.

"Oh, Carina, we have a long way to go. We may arrive in the middle of the night." Wiping his mouth with the back of his hand, he shook his head. "If we encounter any problems, it will be sometime tomorrow. I hope you don't become too weary."

"Of course not. This is fun for me. Aren't you glad we came?"

She looked at him and then stood, throwing her arms out as if to capture the beautiful scenery, the warming air and the distant white-capped mountains. Carlos gave her one of his rare, bright smiles that she so loved.

"Yes, I'm glad we decided to do this. I feel we are doing the right thing. Somehow, everything will work out all right. Perhaps we will never want to return, Elena. Perhaps we will be so happy on the coast we will be able to buy a home and raise a family there. Why do we need anyone else? You are the only one I really need."

"And you, my husband, are the only person I will ever need."

Seated on the bus again, Elena handed him a chirimoya, a scaly, green fruit shaped like a large apple. Filled with sections of white meat covering several black pits, it was soft, sweet, and tangy. She giggled and wiped Carlos' chin when he popped too much in his mouth.

As the hours rolled by they lost interest in the scenery, except for the hour it took them to pass Mt. Chimbarozo, the beautiful, lofty mountain of the southern Andes Range. As the sun began to sink, they noticed the road was in a continuous descent and their surroundings were changing. The mountains and their lush, green luster were exchanged by hills and tropical bogs. An occasional village appeared. Houses made of wood sat high on stilts over swamps. A few scraggly trees and thick grass decorated the landscape. The men were wearing the same styled baggy pants and shirts of the mountain Indian, but the women wore lightweight cotton dresses. The children were attired only in shirts, their bottoms uncovered. Bored with the monotony of travel, Elena was happy that darkness was descending and she snuggled close to her husband to sleep.

They arrived in Guayaquil and searched immediately for a bus to Playas. Discovering one would be leaving in a few minutes, they waited for their baggage to be thrown down from the top of the bus. At the same time they noticed nervously that the coastal bus was filling rapidly.

"Elena, you must take these tickets and find two seats. I'll get the baggage."

Hesitantly, she walked to the bus, and found two seats in back. Fearful that Carlos would not arrive before the departure, she decided to return to him. When the bus' motor kicked over, she readied herself to scream, but at the last minute the driver left the bus for last-minute luggage adjustments. She strained her eyes, watching for Carlos. He appeared and the bus driver followed him on board.

"I was scared you'd not be here on time," she sighed with relief.

"They had a hard time finding your bag on the other bus. It was at the front of the rack, but we have it and it's now on this bus." He breathed deeply and gave her a weary smile.

"I'm tired of riding, Carlos. I hope it doesn't take long to get there."

"I know." Looking concerned, he brightened a moment. "Are you hungry?"

They ate hard-boiled eggs, oranges, and finished the cold empanadas.

"We'll probably get there after midnight and will have to look for a cheap hotel." he said.

"We can sleep on the beach. Wouldn't that be fun?"

"We'll see. Since we don't know what to expect, we may have to."

As the bus pulled into Playas, they could see the small town was closed for the night. Locating the big tourist hotel, they found only a solitary light shining in the lobby. After talking with the clerk they knew since the night was almost over that the expense of a room was more than they wanted to pay.

In front of the building flood lights illuminated a sea wall below the flowering gardens. Following the wall until it ended, they found their way behind a long sand dune and laid out their clothing for warmth. Despite the thrill they quickly fell asleep in each other's arms.

In three hours dawn broke over the town behind them and they sat upright, tired but eager to look around. They saw they were lying in front of three wooden houses built high on stilts.

"Look at those houses, Carlos. Why are they sitting on legs?"

"To keep pests, rats and perhaps high tides out."

Elena smoothed her skirt and then gasped. "Rats? What if there were rats here while we slept?"

"There's a chance, I guess, but we have nothing of interest, since we ate all our food."

After shaking the clothes free of sand, and carefully folding them, they replaced them in the bags and moved from behind the dunes to stare in amazement at the ocean. This was the first time they had seen this much water. The beauty and salty smell intrigued them. They strolled for a few minutes enchanted by the shoreline while Elena explained what she knew from reading her school books about the shells and sea animals. Small boats dotted the horizon and a few early risers from the hotel sat on the seawall. Elena and Carlos stared at the white building with red trim for a long while, discussing his approach for a job.

"Before we do anything, we should go into town and eat breakfast." Carlos put his arm around her waist. "Are you sorry yet?"

"I've never been happier. Never."

They found a small, clean restaurant. Using the tiny restroom, they washed and changed clothes. The waitress was friendly and interested in their sierra accents, willing to help them find a place to spend the night. She directed them to a modest hotel off the main street. They decided it was better than the prospect of spending another night on the beach. It was old but clean, and included a dining room where they could take their meals.

After settling in a room, Carlos begged her to take a nap while he walked back to the grand hotel to look for work. He returned an hour later with a job.

When his key sounded in the door Elena sat up and swung her feet to the floor. He ran across the room and picked her up in a hug.

"I got it. It was easy."

"You have a job? Doing what?"

Setting her back on the bed, Carlos kissed her mouth.

"I went to the tourist's hotel. When they heard I'm from Quito, they were very interested. I guess they think someone from Quito has more experience than local folks. Anyway, they were interested, but said they didn't have any positions open. I told them I would do anything, clean the rooms, work on the grounds or help in the kitchen. When I told them I have worked on farms most of my life they changed their minds and I got the job. They had been looking for someone who has worked with plants, trees and in fields of crops. I'll be grooming the grounds and taking care of all their flowering plants." His eyes sparkled. "I'm so happy, Elena."

He jumped up and clapped his hands together as her eyes followed him. He reached down to take her face in his hands and look at her.

"I love you so much. I feel I can't contain any more happiness."

"All we are missing now is a home filled with babies, Carlos. Wouldn't that be wonderful?"

"Babies. Yes, we'll have dozens of babies."

They looked for a room to rent and discovered that one of the three houses they had seen that morning was empty and owned by the hotel. The hotel manager told them if they would invest time and money in repairs, they could have it rent-free for a year. Jubilantly, they walked to the center of town that afternoon and bought nails, boards and paint, carrying them back in several trips. Damaged planks were replaced, holes filled and loosened boards tightened with fresh nails. A saw, paint brushes and small tools were borrowed from the hotel so Carlos could make wooden shutters to cover the windows. Painting would have to wait until another day. The brilliant sun was sinking into a golden sea as the daylight fishermen bearing heavy nets made their way home. Unable to work in the darkness Carlos and Elena walked back to the small hotel. Over dinner, they passed the evening making detailed plans.

The next day, after Carlos' first morning at his new job, they spent the siesta hour scrubbing the inside of the two-room house. They scoured the neglected walls with hot, soapy water carried in borrowed buckets from the grand hotel.

"We're fortunate the roof is in good condition," said Carlos. We'll not be bothered by heavy rains, rats nor pests since we have sealed the house well. The door is old, but heavy enough."

He inspected both rooms carefully. "Now we must worry about mats to sleep on. I hope you won't mind, but it will take a few days before a carpenter can complete a bed for us. Besides I feel we have been spending too much money. We need to keep savings aside so we can buy our own house. Before we start having children, we need a home. Right?"

"I don't mind, Carlos. We can sleep in our clothes until we can afford blankets."

"Blankets are no problem. There's a man who sells them on the street. He traveled here all the way from Otavalo. Can you imagine?" He shook his head in wonder. "We need blankets more than a bed, so I'll buy two before I go back to work."

Standing at the window facing the restless blue ocean, he told her, "We can move in today, Elena, if you can find some other furnishings. I'll go to the hotel and pay our account. Would you like to sleep here tonight?"

Turning, he gave her a mischievous smile, for he already knew the answer.

"Oh, yes, Carlos. Yes. I can have the house ready by this evening."

She danced in the center of the room, her ponytail flying behind. He chuckled contentedly.

She accompanied him to buy the blankets and mats. After

depositing them in the house Carlos left for work and she returned to the center of town to buy a few pots and a bucket.

An old, discarded table that had been placed in a hotel storage room was salvaged and Elena took it home. Lopsided, it sat pathetically under the window. She put a small block of wood under the short leg and pulled a bright scarf out of her bag, covering the scarred top.

A warped bench that had been sitting under an open window in the second room was brought into the front room and placed opposite the table. There, she carefully folded their clothes and put them in small stacks.

Satisfied, she walked down the leaning, wooden steps of the stilted house and went to the beach searching for rocks. Finding several, she placed them on the sand in a circle close to the front door. She lined the shallow well and gathered scraps of paper and pieces of dried driftwood to build a fire.

The head waiter gave her an old grill that had been stored away when modern kitchen equipment had been bought for the grand hotel. Elena now placed the grill on top of the well of rocks as the fire took hold. From a basket she withdrew vegetables and meat bought on one of her visits to town. She simmered the meat with onions and garlic all afternoon. An hour before Carlos returned home from work she would add the potatoes, carrots and bouillon cubes for more flavor.

Since it would be awhile before her husband returned, she decided to walk into town by way of the beach front. She stuffed a few sucres into her skirt pocket in case she found something she needed, and left the house. Gazing down the south beach she saw several people on the shore and decided she wanted to know what they were doing. Since Carlos had suggested she buy spoons and bowls, she wondered if perhaps the crowd was a group of merchants selling wares. But as she drew nearer she saw they were fishermen clad only in swimsuits, sitting on logs, mending their nets. She walked past them, watching and listening to their strange coastal Spanish, the rapid swallowing of words, the small hint of the letter 's'. Beyond the cluster of men and nets she saw an open market sitting on a small rise overlooking the ocean and a slow-moving river. Several long tables had been set side by side and covered with the fish catch of the day. A busy group of men and women stood behind the tables serving the milling patrons as they called out their preferences. The merchants would then grab a fish and deftly chop off its tails and fins. Kept intact were the heads which coastal residents believe is the best meat of the fish for making a delicious, savory soup.

Elena wandered among the tables, not knowing one fish from another, but she decided on a medium-sized white one after being assured it had fewer bones than the others. The merchant cut the tail and fins off, removed the intestines, wrapped the fish in a newspaper and handed her the package. He threw the garbage into a pail which later would be dumped into the passing river or retrieved for use as fish bait.

Elena walked behind the market and up a block to the main part of town. Discovering a store providing a variety of products, she found plates, silverware and a sharp knife. Pulling out a wad of money, she approached the clerk, a thin girl with hair stringing down her back.

"Buenas tardes. May I also purchase a pound of rice, a bunch of bananas, and a chunk of lard?"

"Buenas tardes. Yes, I will help you." Taking a large sheet of brown paper from below the counter, the girl shyly studied Elena. "Are you from Quito?"

"Yes," replied an interested Elena. "I am from a small village east of Quito. But how did you know?"

Folding the brown paper around a mound of rice, the girl smiled slowly. "My sister recently married and moved to Quito."

Elena was immediately drawn to the smiling girl and, hungry for a female's companionship, she decided to do most of her trading in this store. They exchanged names hesitantly, but with the intrigue of new friendship.

Anita spooned pork fat onto butcher paper and put the package alongside the rice while Elena was choosing the ripest bananas. Anita placed the items carefully in Elena's arms, and offered to give Elena an old basket. With a promise to visit soon, Elena stowed her purchases in the receptacle and walked back to her new home. She dropped the vegetables in the soup and placed more wood on the fire. Then she sat down to wait for Carlos to return.

Chapter 25

T he days passed swiftly and soon they had lived in Playas for six months. Any concerns of not adjusting to the culture seemed distant now. Carlos had been accepted by his co-workers as competent and talented, while Elena made herself busy keeping house. Their neighbors were friendly and on occasion she shared light conversation with the women. She never tired of watching the small fishing vessels. The rugged fishermen seemed worldly in a way the men of Pachuca could not. Each day one group paddled out to sea standing on two logs strapped together, gathering fish in small nets. Another form of fishing took place on the shoreline. A band of fishermen walked the beach using the ancient method of throwing a net from the edge of the sea and drawing it back with the captured fish.

Each afternoon Elena walked to the beach with a few coins in her pocket to select a fish. Taking the squirming fish in hand, she ran to the hotel to have the cook kill and clean it for her. At first Carlos and Elena had little taste for seafood, but grew to love it as the friendly neighbors taught Elena different ways to cook fish.

Several varieties of bananas grew plentifully a few miles inland. She learned to fry one variety. She stuffed others with meat; cooked them in soup; or rolled them in a bread mixture to fry with cheese. Their favorite, however, was a small banana called an Orita, three inches in length, that was quite meaty and sweet.

Another treat of the coastal area was coconut milk. One hot afternoon, Carlos and Elena noticed a local native standing on a corner selling the large globes. For a few centavos the man pounded two holes in the top of the coconut with a hammer and nail, placed two straws in the holes, and handed it to Elena. Not fully ripe, the fruit had little meat, but was filled with coconut milk and offering a hearty drink they found refreshing and thirst quenching.

Little by little their house was becoming more homey, much to Elena's delight. Carlos bought another small table and a four-burner kerosene stove. A local carpenter built a simple bed and matching bureau for the inner room, which completed their bedroom suite.

Yellow cotton curtains on the shuttered windows sparked both rooms with color. It became the young couple's delight to pull them aside each morning to watch the sun spread her golden beams on a sparkling sea while eating breakfast.

Elena was happy and thought little of her family. Pachuca was a world away and only when special incidents occurred did her mother and brothers come to mind. Then she would feel a twinge of guilt over her lack of concern. But never did her father enter her mind.

Carlos had written his Uncle Jose, informing him of their location and suggested, with an invented excuse, his Uncle visit Laura and his siblings in Pachuca to see how they fared. Begging him not to let his mother know of their whereabouts, Carlos urged Uncle Jose to write soon with any news. Eight months after they arrived in Playas, Carlos received a letter at the hotel from Uncle Jose. Taking it home, he read it aloud to Elena.

Mi Quieros Ninos,

Our love is yours. It has been such a long time since we have seen one another, but that does not mean you are not in our hearts continually. It hurts that you are so many miles away and we can see no way of leaving our business to visit with you. We pray each day you will soon come back to us. It was with joy that we read you are happy and have a good job. We can see in our hearts the nice house you have created, our little Elena. It is with anticipation that we await news that perhaps a child is on the way. With that we will all rejoice.

At your suggestion, last Sunday afternoon your Aunt Carlota, Cousin Alfredo and I hired a taxi and paid an overdue visit with my sister, your Mama, Carlos. We had a bit of trouble finding the house, but I am pleased it is in better condition than the old house you lived in as a child. We were delighted to see Joel, Jerman and Yolanda. We don't know them very well, but Yolanda is a sweet girl and was willing to kiss us hello. I found your brothers looking well, however, we could not help but feel there are problems. Now, please, do not worry. Before we left we understood what the problem was, but at first we just felt tension. Your mother looks well, but she's aging. Your Aunt Carlota reminds me I am aging too, but, nevertheless, Laura was troubled. She looked as though she had been crying. We had been there about an hour, when, to our great surprise, a man walked in the door. I was shocked, because he acted as if he lived there, and I realized perhaps your Mama is married. It was immediately obvious this man is the problem. The children were no longer friendly. In fact, the boys left the house without explanation. Your mama could not keep her eyes off the man. We soon took our leave as everything had changed. But as we walked out to the waiting taxi, Laura followed, and, for another half hour, she talked with us, crying. She agrees with what you did, Carlos. She knew the only way you would be happy was to leave Pachuca with Elena. She begged us to tell her if we had seen you. She promised to leave you alone and never bother you. I took the liberty of telling her we had helped you and that you live in Playas. I hope you will forgive me, but she seemed so alone and desolate and I felt it was a little bit of good news we could offer. She refused to tell us about the man, saying only he is a friend who is visiting. It is a mystery. Your mama was sad, but we were able to help by putting her mind to rest concerning your whereabouts and your happiness. I pray anyway this is true. We miss you so very much, our darlings. Please write again soon. We await news from you. May God bless you.

Affectionately,
Your Uncle Jose, Aunt Carlota and Cousin Alfredo

A terrified look crossed Elena's face as Carlos finished reading. "What if your mama tells my family?"

"I don't think she will. She's probably worried about us, but satisfied we are happy. Look what Uncle Jose said." He held the letter out.

"I know, Carlos. I heard. But maybe she'll tell someone who will pass it on to Rolando."

"Don't worry, carina. I promise you she won't."

Elena slumped on the bench, deep in thought. "What could be bothering the children? Do you suppose they don't have enough food or clothing? Perhaps your mama cannot afford school supplies."

"Uncle Jose seemed to think everything was all right in that regard. We have never had much money, but mama earns a sufficient amount for food and to pay the seamstress to sew clothes." Carlos stroked his chin. "No. Uncle Jose was probably correct. The problem involves the man. Who could he be?"

Elena leaned to pick up the letter from where he had tossed it and she scanned it quickly.

"I have a feeling the man was more than a visitor. I think he is living there. Who could he be?"

"Probably a young man attending school in Quito who needs a place to stay on occasion. I won't believe he is living there, and I can't imagine she has married."

Elena put her arm around him and snuggled.

"How do you feel now that you have had news of your family?"

"Not as bad as I thought I would. I am still convinced we did the right thing. How do you feel?"

"Happy we came here. I'm so glad we are married and don't live in Pachuca. There seems to be so much unhappiness."

Chapter 26

When they had been married a year, Elena decided to celebrate. She walked into town and found a woman willing to sell a chicken from her small brood. Together, the two women ran through the backyard until finally they were able to corner a young rooster.

"We were going to have to eat him or sell him soon, anyway." The woman gave Elena a toothless grin. "He was getting old enough that the older cock would have killed him."

Expertly, she grabbed the rooster by two feet and tied him with a cord.

"Here, take him."

Elena paid the woman and put him in the gunny sack that she had brought with her.

During the past few months, she had become fast friends with Anita, the young grocery store clerk. Now as she entered the dim coolness of the store, she greeted her friend. Swelling with the approach of childbirth, Anita had put on considerable weight since Elena had first met her. Her hair still remained stringy, offering an unkempt look, however, her cheeks and eyes glowed with health. Cheerfully, Elena inquired after her health, trying to hide the pangs of envy she felt toward her friend's pregancy.

"I'm glad to see you, Elena. There haven't been many customers today. Being a Monday, everyone bought at the open market yesterday."

"We didn't go to the market because Carlos had to work in the morning. Anyway, it gives me a chance to visit with you." She grinned and remarked confidentially, "Today is a special day for us, Anita."

"Oh, what has happened?" With wide eyes and a furtive smile, Anita leaned across the counter to inspect her friend.

"Perhaps you are finally pregnant?"

Elena's face fell, but she kept her composure.

"No. We have been married for one year today. This is our first anniversary."

"That's wonderful." Anita smoothed her dress, touching her belly unconsciously. "And you are going to have a special dinner?"

"Yes, I have a rooster and I need to buy other supplies."

Elena turned toward the cluttered shelves and began searching for bouillon cubes and cornstarch. Unaware of the slight shadow she had cast over Elena's day, Anita continued talking intimately.

"It surprises me that you and Carlos are not thinking of having a baby yet. I didn't realize a whole year had passed already. Surely you will soon think of having one, won't you?"

"Oh, yes. We plan to have one soon. It's just that we need a home of our own before we can think of a family."

Anita laughed, her hands caressing her tummy again. "Babies don't care where they live, Elena. Your son will be as happy in your rented home as he will be in a fine home." Her eyes gleamed with the secret pleasures of motherhood.

"Yes. Any day I will be telling you of my pregnancy." Sighing, she gave Anita a sad smile. "I must get back to the house so I can kill this rooster and prepare dinner."

Returning to the counter, Elena looked at the piles of meat and cheese set in a cool cupboard and she carefully selected fresh pieces. She wandered to a table piled with vegetables and chose tomatoes, carrots, onions and potatoes. Adding a bunch of bananas to her basket, she was about to pay for the items when she noticed a bin that contained raw peanuts. Anita scooped a handful onto an old balance, measuring out the equivalent of a pound.

Taking her money, Anita smiled at Elena. "Do return soon. I enjoy it when you come to visit. There are few I feel close to in Playas. I'm happy you decided to live here. Perhaps we will be friends for many years."

Knowing Anita was attempting to rectify whatever she had done to change her friend's mood, Elena gathered her supplies and smiled again, avoiding the temptation to glance at Anita's bulging abdomen.

"Of course. Now I really must leave. Thank you."

Returning home, Elena decided until she did become pregnant, she would shop closer to home. Was she becoming a spectacle because she wasn't pregnant? The bright, promising morning had turned gloomy. Entering the house, she dropped the basket on the floor and took the gunny sack containing the rooster outside. Finding a strong string, she tied it around the cock's neck until the bird stopped struggling, then she severed it at the neck. Lighting the kerosene stove, she started to heat a pot of water to boiling. She began by peeling potatoes and carrots and setting them in the cold water. When the water boiled, she placed the rooster in the pot and in a few minutes was able to pull out the feathers. Cutting the bird into sections, she boiled it, making broth for soup. She simmered the broth all afternoon adding spices, herbs, and later, vegetables. In a skillet she roasted the peanuts, then ground them on a smooth rock to make a special sauce to pour over the boiled potatoes. Pork pieces were fried and cheese was cut into chunks. Sliced onions were placed in hot water for a moment to remove the strong taste and fresh lemons were squeezed over them. Salt and bits of tomatoes were added to the onions, then set aside in a corner to cool.

Elena waited anxiously until Carlos appeared at the door. Flashing a wide smile, she ran to him, throwing her arms around his waist. His eyes lighted with pleasure as he looked over her shoulder at the prepared table and returned her hug.

"I want to look at this." He released her and walked to the stove. "This looks wonderful, Elena."

"I tried to remember how Aunt Mariana made special dinners."

Walking to the table, she motioned to his chair. "Please sit at your place and see if I cooked everything the right way."

"This is a very special way to celebrate our first year of marriage, Corazon. I am proud of you."

As they ate she watched him closely, noticing his pleasure. When she brought fruit, cheese and coffee, he leaned over to take her hand.

"Wait a minute. Sit down here." He pulled her chair close, still holding her hand. "I want to tell you something. You were a child when I fell in love with you. You were playing with your cousins under the trees at your Aunt's house. Someone had given you a toy for Christmas. I had just started working for your Uncle Hector and had been sent to give corn to the chickens in the hen house. As I walked back out the door and noticed you, you looked up from your toy doll and saw me. Elena, I had never seen such joy, such shiny eyes, such love before. All I could do was stand and look at you. Do you remember? No? Well, you loved that doll and I knew somehow, someday, I wanted to see that same look in your eyes when you saw me." He paused, smiling. "And when I walked in the door tonight, the look was there."

He rubbed his strong thumb across the back of her hand.

"Elena, I love you. I've always loved you. It would be impossible for me to ever desire another woman. And do you know how much you've matured? There was a time every emotion was either high or low for you. You had a tremendous capacity for excitement and pleasure, yet what tantrums! What anger! For a time it bothered me because I felt I had brought you here, away from your family, and somehow destroyed a part of you. But then I saw that look tonight."

He was watching her carefully, searching her face, needing to be reassured.

"Have you been happy this year? Please tell me you have never regretted coming with me."

Tears moistened her eyes at his unexpected outpouring of love. "Oh no, Carlos," she cried fervently, "there have been times I've wondered what was happening in Pachuca, but never have I thought of leaving you to return home. That part of me is dead. It's in the past. My life is with you. I know having me for a wife hasn't always been easy for you. Sometimes I act immature. I cry and yell and you take it without saying a word. But even when I am that way, I love you, Carlos. It's just that sometimes I don't have much to do but walk to town or clean the house. I would like to work. Perhaps in a store."

"No, you can't because you don't have a cedula and to work you must have identification papers. We would have to go through too many procedures. Anyway, I don't want you working, amor." He looked at her closely. "Are you really bored?"

"No, not bored. There's a lot I can do." She stopped, her chin quivering. "That's what I mean. It sounds like I'm complaining and see, you don't become angry with me at all. I have so much and I love you so much. And now I make you think I'm not happy."

Leaning forward, he took her face in his hands and looked at her as tears filled her eyes.

"If I had put in an order for a perfect husband God couldn't have made you any better. You seem to have adjusted easily to our marriage."

"You have to remember how long I wanted to be married to you, Elena. In a way, I feel we've been married all our lives. Can that be possible?"

"I think so, because I feel the same way." Giving him a small smile, she put her head down and fingered her skirt nervously. "Carlos, why do you think I'm not pregnant yet? Does it seem unusual we're not going to have a baby yet? Even my friends wonder."

"A year without getting pregnant isn't unusual. A lot of women don't have a child the first year of marriage."

"Not often. Look around. I'm afraid you'll think I'm not happy, but I really am. I wouldn't trade places with any other woman, but there's a part of me that's empty and I long to have a baby in my arms. Because I am married to you I want to have your child. Do you understand, just a little?"

Nibbling on a chunk of cheese, he sat in thought for a few moments, then took her hand again.

"We'll wait two months and, if nothing happens, we'll take a trip into Guayaquil to visit a doctor."

"A doctor. Of course. That's the answer." She breathed deeply. "I feel better already."

He laughed at her sudden burst of pleasure and as they drank their coffee, Elena felt a great burden lift from her heart.

Chapter 27

Earlier that year, Carlos had requested several helpers to assist him in renovating the hotel grounds. When the project was finally completed, the hotel owners declared that the grounds had never looked so beautiful.

A few days later Carlos was given a promotion. It was decided that the leadership he had displayed could be of use in other areas, as the landscape assistant was trained well enough now to assume the position as head gardener, freeing Carlos to work in the dining room as the day captain. Carlos was responsible for everyone from the chief chef to the bus boys. Dressed in a tuxedo, he greeted people at the door, led them to their tables, handed them menus and then returned to the door, observing the diners from the beginning of their meal until its completion, ever mindful of their every need.

His wages tripled. The owners were jubilant they had found a handsome, ambitious worker who would bring in new business and keep satisfied guests returning.

During this time, Elena had two dreams concerning her family. The dark, realistic dreams began to dominate her thoughts during the day, causing her to brood while Carlos was at work. Fearful he could not understand her sudden concern for those in Pachuca, she refrained from telling Carlos. But her family was fast becoming an obsession with her. The dreams concerned an angry Rolando and her sickly mother. In one, Rolando was raising his arm against a black shape, his mouth forming words of wrath, although no sound fell from his lips. In the other, her mother lay in bed, eyes wide, looking into space, and, except for the movement of an outstretched hand toward someone standing across the room, the only sound was a faint call for help.

The dreams occurred during the space of a few hours, but they created a new thought pattern that dominated her hours alone. She realized Carlos knew she was troubled, but when he questioned her, she was frightened to tell him of her desire to return to Pachuca for a visit. The dreams had come at a bad time. Now that Carlos was making a good salary, he was increasingly impatient to build a new house. She knew she could not disappoint him. But her thoughts of Rolando and her mother were real and the struggle continued.

About the time she was ready to speak with Carlos about a visit to Pachuca she felt certain she was pregnant. The joy of this discovery took priority. With sudden inspiration, she decided she would surprise him. Bursting with exuberance, she set about making plans. She was afraid her suspicions would show on her face, so she decided to approach him that evening under a different pretense. Too eager to wait for his return from work, she donned a sweater and walked through the twilight to the hotel.

The oceanside wall of the dining room was constructed of huge wooden boards hanging on hinges. Each afternoon the wall dropped, revealing a breathtaking view of the Pacific. During the meal, diners were able to watch the tides, the fishermen returning from the sea on balsa wood logs, and the bright fishing tugs making their runs. Trailing lavender-flowered vines wound their way around the wooden posts outside the restaurant. Their fragrance mixed with the salty air and the savory seafoods of the dining room, never failed to please both the patrons and Elena.

When she arrived Carlos was in the midst of the dinner hour and she thought better of interrupting him. At a corner of the building, she stood beside a flowering bush, watching him through the large opening. He was so handsome in his tuxedo. Pride swelled in her heart combined with the joy of her news. She wondered if she had ever been this happy. If only Rolando could see Carlos now. Surely he would change his mind and place his blessings on their marriage.

She waited until his shift was completed and the crowd in the dining room began to thin out. When he went into the back to change clothes, she stepped inside, returning greetings the personnel waved at her. Another surge of warmth spread through her. How could things be any better for them? Everything was perfect and secure.

Carlos found her conversing jovially with his co-workers.

"What a nice surprise. My wife is at home cooking dinner. How about a date?"

Winking, as those standing by laughed, he slipped his hand through her arm and pulled her toward the door amidst loud "hasta mananas."

Arms entwined and happy in love, they walked through a grove of small trees and past manicured gardens to the end of the hotel property. Elena glanced at the ocean to watch the remaining light of the sinking sun and noticed the shadow of a man by the sea wall. She gasped with shock. Her first desire was to run away as fear pounded in her heart. Then she longed to run toward the man.

"What's the matter?" questioned Carlos, stopping suddenly.

"Rolando. That was Rolando by the sea wall."

His head swung toward the bench.

"There's no one by the wall, Elena. See for yourself."

"Someone was there. I saw him. I would know Rolando."

"Cara, it's dark. How could you recognize anyone in this darkness?"

Her shoulders sagged. "Of course. You're right, Carlos." She chuckled uneasily. "He has no way of knowing where we are. Your mama promised not to tell him anything and since you trust her, I must. I'm sorry. It was silly of me to act that way. It's just that I've had Rolando and Mama on my mind lately."

"I understand. I think of my family also." He put his arm around her waist. "Are you all right now?"

"Yes." She laughed, fears gone.

After dinner, Carlos lay on the bed leafing through a Guayaquil newspaper he had picked up at the hotel. Entering the bedroom, she sat beside him, adjusting the candle so he could see her better. He glanced up and pulled her down for a kiss.

"Thanks for the dinner, amor. You are becoming a better cook than our chef. What shall we do if news gets out and the high society of Guayaquil deserts the grand old inn and comes here for dinner? I'd never be alone with you."

Kissing her again, he returned to the newspaper.

"You are so silly sometimes." She hesitated a moment, and

grinned, excitement building in her. "Carlos, what are we going to do on your next two days off?"

"What we always do. Work around the house, go into town and shop, or perhaps we can start looking at lots for sale."

"How would you like to do something special? Maybe we can go somewhere for a while. I'd love to go on a small trip with you."

He sat up, resting on one elbow, and looked at her. "That's a good idea. We've never done that."

"Do we have enough money to go somewhere?"

"We don't have a lot, since we are going to buy property soon, but we haven't been on a honeymoon yet." The idea was catching on. "I don't see why we can't do something special."

"A honeymoon?" she smiled coyly. "I thought we had been on a honeymoon all this time."

Teasing him, she laughed and grabbed at his stomach.

"Oh!" he roared. "Be careful, chica." He seized her arms. They were soon on the floor wrestling and laughing until they could barely breathe.

"You monster. How could anyone love you?" She gasped, laughing and tickling him as he writhed and jerked. She stood weakly and headed for the door. He ran ahead, barring her escape. She attacked him again, tickling his ribs. He howled and she was out the front door in a flash, jumping to the sand. She ran to the beach, dodging him, as the neighbors leaned on their windowsills, amused by their playfulness.

Tripping over a sand dune, she felt her way until she reached a large log and hid behind it, panting heavily for breath.

He acted as if he didn't know where she had gone. With hands on hips and a sigh of resignation, he went to the other side of the dune, then scurried behind her just as she lifted up, uncertain of her next move.

He pounced on her and they rolled in the sand, laughing until tears rolled down their faces.

"Oh, I'm exhausted, you beast," she screamed, fighting for her breath."

"It's not my fault. I was busy reading my paper."

"Oh, now I'm sick," She groaned between giggles.

"Well, I feel fine," he said, kissing her.

She returned the kiss fervently, thinking only of him. Suddenly a cold fear spread through her. Turning her head toward the beach, she tried to see through the darkness. Rolando was there. But how could that be? The feeling passed quickly and she turned her thoughts back to her husband.

Chapter 28

Carlos was able to take off two extra days. A friend suggested they vacation at a small resort owned by New Yorkers on an island across the bay from Bahia. They were advised to call ahead to guarantee a cabin. Informed this was a good time of the year to visit since school was still in session in Quito, they set about making plans for their delayed honeymoon. With four glorious days to look forward to, Elena all but forgot Rolando. She packed a suitcase and a basket of food.

Early one morning a week later, the two stood on the narrow coastal highway awaiting the bus-truck that would take them north. Elena was so excited, all she could do was grasp Carlos' hand and laugh in delight over everything she saw.

The vehicle that stopped to collect them had at one time been a flat-bed truck. The cab was intact, but had no doors. Along the bed, poles had been secured. A tin roof had been placed overhead in a vain effort to shelter passengers from the sun and occasional rains. Narrow benches were bolted to the floor in the center of the truck, so when the vehicle stopped beside Elena and Carlos they merely jumped onto the high step and sat in unoccupied seats. They pushed their suitcase and food basket under the seat and sat back, chattering animatedly.

An old man dressed in casual coastal wear, and a battered conductor's cap atop his head stepped forward, spotted the luggage and shouted at the driver to stop.

"You can't have that suitcase and basket under the seat. It will slide off when we make a sharp turn."

Carlos grabbed the suitcase and passed it over Elena's head, while she placed the basket obediently on her lap. Agilely, the old man took the case and jumped from the truck, running around to the back where a metal ladder hung from the roof. He scrambled up and secured it on a luggage rack that hugged the tin roof. He bounced from the ladder and yelled at the driver to start up again as he leaped back to his seat. Elena and Carlos looked at each other with humor at the conductor's antics. With a chuckle they shrugged their shoulders and turned to view the ugly brown landscape. It was amazing, thought Elena, how different the surrounding terrain appeared only a few short kilometers from the white sands and aqua-blue sea.

They had been warned the trip would take about five hours, and Elena was impatient to arrive. She had so much to tell Carlos and she wanted to give him the news of her pregnancy in a way he would never forget. Somehow, she had made it through the past week without revealing anything, but the closer they came to the island, the more unbearable the wait became.

Carlos was enjoying a conversation with the conductor and another passenger as the bus approached town. The old man informed them they were nearly there so Carlos pulled several bills from his pocket and placed them in the weathered hand. When the bus came to a stop, Carlos jumped down and turned to help Elena. After waiting for the conductor to scramble for their suitcase, they waved good-bye and walked toward the main part of Bahia near the bay. In the distance they saw tall trees waving with the gentle breeze, the open blue sea in the background. Carlos guided her to a freshly painted dock. Wide sidewalks lined with palm trees paralleled the beach. Adjacent to the sidewalks, wooden jetties stretched out over the water were crowded with street vendors, fishermen and vacationers. A long building sat on one jetty, serving as a restroom and the two travelers refreshed themselves before eating. They decided to buy a hot meal and found a lady selling soup along a seawall. Reaching for the only two bowls in evidence, she filled them with the hot liquid, thick with cabbage, potatoes and small pieces of animal skins and fat. Sitting on a wooden bench, they ate their fill while making plans. Handing the bowls back to the vendor, she proceeded to rinse them in a bucket of cold, greasy water and then sat back to wait for her next customer.

Noticing a small group of cars and trucks clustered near one jetty, they walked in that direction. As they drew near to the vehicles, they found that several long, wooden planks had been placed on top of the sand leading from the sidewalk to shoreline. A small assembly of people beside a seawall chatted while watching across the waters. Carlos and Elena approached the first group, asking for information about the ferry that would transport them to the island. They were informed the barge would arrive at any time.

"It must come when the tide is high, hijo. The barge will push itself onto the sand, so the vehicles can drive aboard," explained an aged, toothless fisherman oblivious to the spittle oozing from his mouth.

"Thank you, senor. My wife and I will wait."

"Your wait will be short. The barge is coming now."

A flat, motorized object moved swiftly to the shore. They grabbed their baggage and moved down the sandy beach.

In no time, a loud, resounding honk split the air and the motors of the five waiting vehicles turned over. The big barge hit the sand and by sheer force moved onto the beach, and immediately dropped open a big metal door. Three trucks on the barge backed onto the planks and deftly moved to the street above, making room for the waiting vehicles. Elena and Carlos ran onto the ferry and moved along a walkway, holding low railings. A few stragglers followed them, but the majority of the crowd on the shore continued visiting.

The captain stood at the end of the barge beside a small cabin containing a large motor. He had several levers at his hand and, after checking the security of the vehicles and the closure of the gate, he returned to his position to push a lever forward. Almost immediately they were moving toward an island several miles in the distance.

"Buenas tardes, ninos."

"Buenas tardes, Capitan," they echoed.

"You must be going to the island for a vacation."

"Si, senor. We are going to the motel owned by the Americans. Perhaps you can give us directions when we arrive." Carlos yelled over the roar of the motors.

The short, muscular man smiled cheerfully. "Those cabins are nice." He paused. "What are you niños doing so far from home without a car?"

"We don't live in Quito anymore," explained Carlos, and Elena realized the man recognized their sierra accents. "We're living in Playas and have come here for our honeymoon."

"Honeymoon," the captain echoed thoughtfully. Leaning against the railing, watching for obstacles, he smiled. "Honeymoon. I found out what that word meant a couple months ago. I was watching one of those movies from the United States of America, you know, on television. They talked about a honeymoon. Never heard of such a thing when I got married. We had a church wedding and went to live with her parents. Still live there, behind their house, and we've been married twenty years." He adjusted his captain's hat and looked over the sea and then back to them. "You going back to Quito someday?"

Hesitantly, Elena nodded no, looking to Carlos as he spoke.

"No, we don't think so. We like it a lot on the coast."

"Children are sure independent these days. It was all I could do to say good-bye to my mama and move to the other side of the plaza. Still go over there every Sunday for dinner."

Elena and Carlos laughed with him. Elena liked the engaging captain. He was full of talk and love for his family, like so many Ecuadorians. A momentary wave of longing for a father's love swept over her, but the feeling vanished with the realization they'd be at the island within a few minutes. The captain patted them on the shoulders and pointed into the distance.

"Look over there. Almost to the tip of the island. No, way down at the end. You can see a clump of palm trees and small houses. That's where you're going. About the only thing you'll eat around here is fish. Of course, you already know that, living in Playas. Sometimes we bring other kinds of food over. You'll not find many stores. It's a pretty barren island. The motel has a restaurant and I hear they serve good food." He checked a few gauges and looked out over the sea again. He chuckled good naturedly. "As long as you like fish, you'll never go hungry." Looking at them closely, he asked, "What do you do for a living?"

"I keep house and cook for my husband."

"Elena doesn't have to work outside our home," replied Carlos, slipping his arm around her waist. "I'm one of the captains in the dining room at the big hotel on the beach-front in Playas. I used to work with the trees and plants on the hotel grounds."

"That must have been a difficult job, making something grow in this coastal soil."

"Well, they have the money and I have the skill. We were able to ship a lot of things in, like good topsoil. It's a lovely place."

"I believe it. Well, ninos, I must get to work. We are getting closer and I won't be able to talk any longer."

The captain began collecting fares and by the time he finished they had reached the island. The ferry ran onto the bank of sand and the captain let down the gate. The vehicles disembarked at high speeds, to avoid getting stuck in the sand. Elena and Carlos watched until the barge cleared to hand the captain their fares. Then they ran onto the beach and waved farewell.

"I'll see you on the trip back," yelled the captain.

They had been advised to wait on the beach until low tide when a truck would pass, making a run along the water-line to the cabins. It gave them a chance to look around. A block from the sea was a short main street lined with leaning wooden buildings housing a grocery store, a banana storage room, a mechanic shop and a restaurant-saloon.

Carlos leaned against a palm tree and searched the street. "The people must live in the suburbs. I don't see any houses."

"Maybe they live behind the stores," she offered.

"Probably."

"Let's go back in case the truck leaves early."

"It can't until the tide goes out a little."

They passed an impatient hour, until they saw a truck pull out of a side street and drive down onto the wet sand. From nowhere several people gathered, clambering onto the vehicle. Carlos and Elena thrust themselves forward, holding tightly onto their parcels, hoping to find a seat on the open-sided truck.

"Where did these people come from?" she whispered to him.

"I don't know. I thought we were alone until a minute ago."

They found two seats on a back bench. The truck-bus took off at full speed moving along the beach-front skirting large rocks and logs. Within minutes they were dropped off in front of a row of brown cabins.

After registering in the office, the clerk handed them a key and they ran to their bungalow. Elena stood with open-eyed delight. It was beautiful. The cabin was built of strong wood, with glass windows that could be lifted open. She saw screens on windows for the first time and couldn't get over the fact they were able to keep out insects. Inside, there was a living room, bathroom and kitchenette on the first floor. Upstairs, two large bedrooms overlooked the ocean. Running from one room to the other, from downstairs to the second floor and back, she cried out with delight. Dashing out the front door she stood on the porch, then, turning back into the house, she ran with her arms outstretched, while Carlos stood laughing at her joy.

"I've never been so happy. Oh, Carlos, thank you. This really is the happiest time of my life. I feel so free, like a bird," she cried, sweeping her arms outward. "Aren't you happy, Carlos? You just stand there."

"You cannot imagine how happy I am, carina."

It was late afternoon when they finally settled into their cabin. Since they had eaten soup in Bahia and snacks from their basket, they decided to wait until later for dinner at the resort restaurant. In the meantime, they wanted to explore the beach to the far end of the island. It was a lovely shoreline with high waves of brilliant blue matching the color of the sky. Elena kicked off her shoes and ran close to the warm water.

"Let's wait until tomorrow to swim, Elena. We can walk now."

She caught up with him and slipped her arm around his waist. He hugged her tightly.

"See that white house in the distance? Let's walk that far and come back," she suggested.

Shells and rocks littered the shore in abundance and they gathered them in her skirt.

"Where are we going to put them?" she laughed.

"Let's lay them over here behind this log and later we can come back to get them."

"Okay." She dropped them in a pile and shook the sand from her skirt.

They walked until they were close enough to the white house to see it was abandoned and falling apart. From all appearances, it had at one time been a nice home, with several rooms and windows.

"Isn't that too bad? I wonder why no one lives there now." She stood, perplexed, studying the house shrouded with neglect.

"I don't know. Maybe they moved to Quito and it's too far away for return visits. Or maybe it belonged to someone who died and had no children. Lots of things could have happened." He frowned. "I would never abandon our home. No matter what."

Finding a log bleached white from the sun, they sat down to rest. He took her hand as they stared at the sea birds.

"This beach is almost prettier than Playas," she mused.

"Yes, except it's not home."

"Carlos, I have something to tell you."

"What?" He seemed to stiffen with concern as he turned to her. "Are you all right?"

"I've never been better."

A shy smile crossed her face and Carlos stood, looking down on her.

"From the day you suggested we take a vacation, deep in my heart I thought you might be pregnant. Can it be possible?"

Laughing with relief that the long-kept secret was exposed, she jumped to her feet. "Yes! Yes! I believe I am. Isn't it wonderful?"

"Wonderful? That's not an adequate word." He picked up a stick, threw it with all his might and let out a resounding yell. "Wonderful. The princess asks if it's wonderful!" He sat her gently on the log again and knelt beside her, taking her hand.

"Elena, to me you have always been like a princess. I can't forget all those years I couldn't be near you." Suddenly he laughed. "Imagine a princess from Pachuca. I could not believe I was good enough for you. Your brother told me I was garbage, scum, and I believed him. You see, in my heart I believed you were too worthy and I didn't deserve you." He looked for a moment as though he might cry, but he rushed ahead. "You can't imagine how humble I feel at this moment."

She smoothed his hair and lifted his chin with her hand. "Silly. I am not a princess, but if you must know, all those years I believed you were my prince. Social class has never meant anything to me."

She leaned forward to kiss his cheek. "We'll call our boy, Little Carlos."

"Carlos," he exclaimed with mock disgust, "no. We must name her Little Elena."

With a giggle, she punched his arm playfully.

His reaction was swift. He grabbed her to wrestle in the sand. Stopping suddenly, he looked at her in horror.

"I'm sorry. We can't do that anymore. I'm not going to let you get hurt. We've waited too long for this."

Pulling her up, he held her arms in his strong hands.

"There will never be a baby in Ecuador more loved than this child. Elena, I've heard some of the stories about how some men mistreat their wives and children, but I will never do that. I'm committed to you with a bond of love and I'll commit myself to this child in the same way."

Tears rolled down her face.

They played, swam, ate and slept. Seldom out of their swimsuits, they turned a healthy dark brown from the sun. The four days went too quickly and, on the day they were to leave, Elena stood in the middle of the living room and cried.

"I don't want to leave. It was so much fun."

"We'll come back. I promise you. We have our whole lives, Elena. We'll be back."

"It will never be the same."

"Maybe not. The next time we come, we'll bring Little Elena."

"Little Carlos."

They laughed.

Three months later, she miscarried.

Chapter 29

He had never seen anyone grieve as she did. When she realized something was wrong, she had sent a neighbor to the hotel to find Carlos. The woman put her to bed and he found her there. For a month she stayed in bed. To his dismay there was no communication between them and in his bewilderment, he soon put the straw mat on the floor and slept there.

He was consumed with worry when she didn't touch the food that he brought her from the hotel. He searched for coconuts and Oritas—her favorite treats, and still no response. Then, one day while wandering the streets he found someone who cooked tripa. He took a portion home to her. Still nothing. She lay with her face to the wall refusing to talk with anyone. In a vain attempt to gain her attention, he ordered glass panes and screens for the windows, but even that failed to spark any interest. Finally, he began to believe she was dying. He visited a doctor at the local clinic hoping there was something he could do for her. The doctor informed Carlos that intense depression, caused by the desire to have a child, was normal after a miscarriage.

Carlos had no way of knowing that when he sat on the bed attempting to converse with his wife, that she held herself responsible. She felt a burden of guilt too overwhelming to bear. He realized there was nothing he could do to help her. She needed to have time alone for soul-searching. He stopped trying. The only thing left for him to do was hire a woman to watch Elena and tidy the house.

For a month she lay in bed. And then one day he arrived home to find her washing dishes. A stab of delight shot through him and he approached her with anticipation. But as she turned to greet him, he saw her dull, lifeless eyes, and noticed how much weight she had lost. Her hair hadn't been combed and her nightgown was filthy.

Greeting him without enthusiasm, she made an attempt to draw close, but he averted his head for a quick moment as the smell of her unwashed body repelled and dismayed him. Noting this, she quickly exited to the bedroom and climbed into bed without a word.

He began to dread his time at home and sought more work at the hotel. To his relief, his friends and employers asked few questions. They seemed to know he was suffering.

One night he returned to the house after working a double shift. Walking across the sand, he noticed a light glowing between the curtains. Wondering why Elena would have candles burning, he opened the door quietly and stood in the entrance. Amazement showed on his face. The table was set and decorated with a bouquet of flowers. Dinner was cooking on the stove.

Elena stood in the middle of the room adorned in a clean dress. Her hair was pulled back, and she was scrubbed and shining. He stood quietly, not wanting to frighten her from what he recognized as a return to reality. She rushed to him and he took her gratefully in his arms. Clinging to him, she sobbed until she was spent.

"I was so ashamed, Carlos. I failed you."

"How did you fail me?"

"I lost your baby. It was my fault. After you told me not to lift anything heavy, I did. I carried a big basket of firewood from the beach to the house so I could boil water for washing the pots and some of the small laundry. The next day I lost the baby."

Holding her close he smoothed her hair, feeling a mixture of sadness for her suffering and relief that she was able to speak her heart.

"Elena, in no way do I blame you. It's true a woman must be careful during her pregnancy, but I talked to a doctor here in Playas, and also took a trip to Guayaquil to talk to another. Both told me if you miscarried there was probably a good reason and it was not your fault at all. Sometimes nature causes miscarriages for your own protection."

He wiped her swollen eyes. "The hurt was worse when we couldn't talk to each other. I thought I had lost you."

"I thought I had lost you, Carlos. I wanted our baby so much."

"Of course you did. We both did. But I promised you we would have dozens someday. Remember?"

With great relief they discussed freely what was in their hearts. Slowly, they gained a deeper love and greater appreciation for each other. Each day seemed more precious as they sought to spend every possible moment together.

After she recovered, he took her to look for property as they had finally been able to save enough money to purchase a small lot.

"Where would you like to live, Elena?"

"I don't care. Just so it overlooks the ocean."

Standing back and looking at her with an exaggerated look of appraisal, he smiled. "Chica, for a little mountain girl you have discovered an interesting fascination for the sea."

She flushed at his good-natured teasing. Gazing beyond the

gently sloping, white dunes, the industrious seabirds, and the trolling fishing tugs, she smiled and inhaled the tangy salt air.

"There is something in me that needs the ocean." She shrugged her shoulders and bit her lower lip. "I don't have the ability to tell you how I feel, but sometimes it's as if the sea and I understand each other."

She shrugged again and stopped, embarrassed by her feelings. How could she tell him of the hours spent in the past few weeks by the sea? When Carlos had begun to spend the siesta hours at the hotel, she became convinced he blamed her for the miscarriage. While everyone else was eating the midday meal before napping, she would wander to the jetty below their house. Sitting on the end, among the rocks, she found refuge with her new-found friend. Having never been taught the power of God or the methods of prayer, she poured out her frustrations, angers, fears and hopes to whatever or whomever had created the sea. There she watched the tremendous power of the water rising and falling repetitiously against the huge rocks as if a giant hand was drawing the water back—cradling, pulling, fondling—with quiet strength and then, in a seemingly effortless motion, toss it against the jetty in a great, crashing force creating a tower of cleansing water that swept away the debris, garbage, and the waste that living beings had discarded. She imagined that as she submitted herself to the roaring action, and was one with it, she could release her hurts and disappointments in the cleansing movement. Her mind and emotions were at times jumbled and confused and she acknowledged her own insanity. And yet, when she could pour out her heart, for a short time she would feel better, at peace. At least until Carlos appeared in the door, and the cruel realities of life thrust at her heart as the fear of her husband's disapproval grew. She began to dread his coming home. Only once had she attempted to meet him halfway, but his obvious revulsion for her sent her scurrying into herself again.

When the breakthrough came it was unexpected. One day as she sat alone, she was able to weep for the first time since the miscarriage. Something broke inside and the floods of her torment gushed forth like a burst dam. Her friend, the sea, rushed to her feet and with reaching fingers mixed his salty tears with hers, beginning the healing process. She had risen a different person.

"How I wish I could explain," she said gently.

Carlos stared at her, willing himself to understand what she had been going through and knowing he never would.

"We'll find a place that looks directly over the waves. Would you mind if we aren't too close to the hotel?"

"No. No, not a bit. The only thing I worry about is having to walk from town with groceries."

"Don't think about that. You can catch one of the buses. We'll make sure we're not far from the beach where they make their run."

They found a lot on a small hill twenty meters from the beach. To buy property or build a house on credit was virtually impossible because of high interest rates; therefore they took their savings and paid in cash.

They stood gazing over the wide blue expanse of water. On the horizon, fishing boats appeared as small specks, returning to port after a night of catching fish in huge nets.

"How many rooms do you want in the house, carina?"

"I haven't thought of that yet." She stretched contentedly. "We've just bought the land."

"I figure it took about a year to save for the property, so in six months we should be able to save enough to buy materials and in another six months we can start to build. By that time, we will have enough to pay laborers." He pulled on her ponytail. "In this coming year, do you think you can decide on how many rooms you want?"

"I don't care too much how many rooms we have. Just so there's enough space to put our things away and, of course, I want an extra bedroom, just in case God gives us children." She returned a wistful smile.

"Then we'll have to build several bedrooms."

"You are a sweet man, Carlos."

He took her hand. "Do you know what they did at the hotel? The carpenters built closets into the walls instead of making upright pieces of furniture like your Aunt Mariana has in Pachuca. I'd never heard of such a thing. They are like little rooms. I thought maybe we should do that, and we can hang our clothes instead of folding them on the bench. Perhaps the master carpenter will go with me to the hotel and see how they are built."

"Imagine," she beamed. "All the new things we will soon have."

"Another thing we're going to have is inside plumbing. I'll never have to see you carrying water the way you do now. That, and a real bathroom just like the hotel. We can put a laundry vat outside, and you can wash the clothes out there instead of down at the river. We'll put a sink in the kitchen and you won't have to wash pots outside on a bench. So many things for my amor."

"It will be like living in a palace."

"I told you. You are a princess. Do you remember?" He whispered in her ear affectionately, pinching her cheek. "Anyway, in about a year, we'll start building. Until then, we'll have to watch how we spend our money."

During the year, they talked by the hour of the house's floor plans. She glowed with delight when he promised they would spend an extra amount on large glass windows overlooking the ocean.

They found a wealth of comfort and depth in each other, they had not experienced before. Elena loved Carlos more than a husband. Away from the influence of their families, she knew him also as a father-figure, boyfriend, best friend, companion and lover. The bond between them grew until they became not only one flesh, but one in mind and spirit.

There was no one else. While it was true they had areas to work on in their relationship, both wanted the marriage to succeed, and through the year, each became anxious to satisfy the other.

Elena fought against her independent, stubborn spirit and an insecure nature, but little by little she was able to put Carlos first and to believe he truly loved her. Eventually they were able to reach a point in their marriage when they felt they were united by a common spirit. She wondered if this would have been possible if they still lived in Pachuca surrounded by so many distractions and she felt fortunate.

A construction man was hired and a crew selected. Finally they began laying the foundation. Amidst all this bustle she realized she was pregnant again. Joy, mixed with the fear she could miscarry, had her singing one minute and wringing her hands the next. She waited two weeks to be certain, before telling Carlos. She saw the same fear and joy pour over his face. The next day he made an appointment to visit the doctor in Playas. Taking an hour from his work, they walked to the clinic.

The doctor, a young student working through his last year of school, met them at his office door and shook their hands. He had studied at the university in Quito. During their conversation, they discovered he had once visited Pachuca during an anniversary fiesta, to attend the bullfights behind the marketplace near Elena's home. Despite her attempt, it was difficult to still the stab of homesickness that struck her heart. She glanced at Carlos knowing he must be suffering the same.

However, these emotions passed quickly as the doctor informed them Elena's second pregnancy should be smoother than the last providing she rest, be careful, and eat nutritious food.

In jubilant spirits they returned home full of plans and hopes. Elena bubbled over with excitement as the full impact of what was happening hit her afresh. She counted the minutes as she waited impatiently at the door for Carlos to return from work. When he appeared, it was with flowers from the hotel. Thrusting them into her hands, she buried her face in the fragrant colors, then lifted her eyes to his.

"To think I am going to be a mother, and this time I know our child will be born. It's wonderful, Carlos, that the house will be completed by the time he is born."

He kissed her, her delight contagious.

"Our child will be raised close to the sea, loving it as we do," she said, feeling comfortable and secure.

"She may want to become a fisherwoman."

"A what?" she laughed heartily.

"I want you to rest a lot, Elena," he said, becoming serious. "I cannot bear to see anything happen to you again. Will you stay in bed or, at least, do only light work?"

"How will I do my chores?"

"I'll hire someone."

"But we can't afford it."

"We'll manage somehow. I don't want you to do anything that will endanger your life or that of our baby's."

She had more time to walk to their property. Sitting by the hour, she watched the fishermen paddling out on balsa logs, the activity of the birds, and the people walking along the beach searching for firewood. Much of each day was spent daydreaming of their baby and the new house. As much as she cared for the neighbor women, she felt they didn't share her imagination or understand her deep-rooted love for Carlos and her unborn baby. As a result she clung more and more to him and their life together. She enjoyed being alone and remembered the changes that had transpired because of the miscarriage, Carlos was right. She had matured.

And even though she was careful, in her third month, she again miscarried.

She called Carlos immediately. He telephoned the clinic for help from the hotel and soon she was lying in bed inside the small, white building. A nurse cared for her all afternoon, but toward evening, Elena lost the baby. Her grief was as intense as the previous time, but she handled herself differently. Including Carlos in her sorrow, they bore it together, and her comeback was much swifter.

Still blaming herself, they traveled to Guayaquil solely for the purpose of talking to a well-known doctor. Exuding confidence in his quiet manner, the kindly man took care to explain to them that most likely, the miscarriage had not been her fault and there could still be a chance in the future to bear many children. Carlos and Elena returned to Playas in higher spirits.

When she became pregnant again, Carlos decided he wanted the child born in Quito and would no longer take a chance with the limited medical facilities on the coast. He made arrangements with the laborers to halt the construction work on the new house until he could return to Playas with his wife and child. Believing the doctors and hospitals in Quito were of higher quality, he wanted to give Elena the best chance to go full-term. She agreed reluctantly, consoling herself that their return to Playas would be rapid. But as their thoughts turned to the Andes Mountains, she realized just how anxious she was to see her family. Certainly they would be happy by now to receive her, and the thought tempered the grief of leaving their first home.

Chapter 30

This time Carlos was careful concerning their journey. They had more money and much more at stake. With reluctance, the hotel management accepted his notice of departure and promised a job at his return. He left his property ownership papers with a lawyer in Guayaquil and deposited his savings in a bank. He made reservations with an airline from the port city to Quito and made arrangements with a taxi driver to transport them to the airport. They disposed of the articles in their home, selling a few and giving the rest to neighbors and Anita's family.

Suddenly it was time to exchange farewells and leave the small town, so filled with memories of their first years together. Their sorrow was replaced with anticipation of returning home to the sierras.

Carlos had sent a telegram to his uncle's home stating the time of their arrival in Quito. With crushing hugs and loud exclamations, the two young people were welcomed back. After Carlos explained Elena's need for rest and quiet, Carlota hovered over her like an obsessed mother.

Leaving the airport, the energy of Quito permeated the air as they exited the long, busy airport and entered the fresh mountain breeze. Taxis sat outside in a line while drivers ran to grab passenger's baggage in an effort to secure a fare. Angrily, Uncle Jose pushed them off, looking every bit like a possessive rooster protecting his flock. Vendors hawked their wares, buses honked for passengers, welcome parties greeted guests and families amid screams of delight and tears. Airplanes departed leaving wailing family members and friends scanning the skies for the last glimpse. As Jose ushered his family to a waiting taxi, Elena exchanged a grin with Carlos. They had almost forgotten what home in the sierras meant to them.

From certain vantage points on the northside of Quito they were able to see the Tumbaco Valley and the distant mountain range. The physical features of the mountains helped them pinpoint the location of Pachuca. They strained their eyes for the unusual protruding hump resting on the summit above their home. Pointing and exclaiming excitedly each time they found a break in of trees and houses along the boulevard, they were able to make an eager connection with their past.

An hour later they rested in the familiar surroundings where they had spent the first nights of their marriage. Carlota offered them a refreshing drink created from the combination of taxo fruit, milk and sugar. Sipping on this and eating cheese empanadas, they waited anxiously to hear all the latest news.

"Well, children, we haven't heard anything from Pachuca since the sad news of your family, Elena." Jose gave her a concerned look.

"What news?" they chorused, alert.

"Why, the news we sent by letter several months back." The two older people sat frozen and perplexed.

"We haven't received a letter from you for ever-so-long," replied Carlos, fear in his voice. "Please tell us what you wrote. What is the problem?"

Jose wiped his brow with a handkerchief as Carlota moved her chair alongside Elena.

"You don't know about your parents, ninita?"

"My parents? Oh, no. What has happened to my Momi?" Tears sprang to Elena's eyes.

The short, pudgy man licked his lips nervously. "Elena, mi nina. Let me tell you what we wrote. "Oh dear, the letter must have gone astray. You know how the mail service is."

"Yes, uncle. We know." Carlos looked at Elena with concern.

"Well, one day several months ago we heard pounding at the street door. Alfredo, your cousin, who never seems to be at home now that he has a girlfriend, answered the door." Jose wiped his brow again. "To our great pleasure and surprise, there stood your mama on the doorstep, Carlos. We welcomed her, but truthfully, I was a little concerned because she hasn't been to visit us for years, and it wasn't even a Sunday. She had taken off work to bring news."

Elena, overwrought with fear, felt as though she would scream. Carlota saw this and waved her arms impatiently at her husband.

"Jose, will you please tell them what they need to know?"

"Yes, yes. Well, she was distressed. I could see that. I just don't know how to tell you everything. But, apparently, one evening when she was home, your brother went to her house to tell her about the death of your father, Elena."

Elena breathed more freely. Her papa, not her momi.

"One Sunday night, the week before Laura visited, someone found your papa lying by the side of the road. He had been hit by a vehicle and was badly injured. By the time they found a pickup truck to take him to Quito, he had died." Jose hesitated, averting his eyes from Carlos and Elena, and watched Carlota instead.

"There's more. I can tell by the way you're acting." Elena prodded.

Carlota took her hand. "He had been drinking, Elena. He smelled of liquor. Also, he had been robbed. His pocket purse lay beside him open and empty. Maybe the person who ran him down came back to rob him. We don't know. Whoever killed him has fled. We're not sure whether it was a resident of Pachuca."

Elena sat still, her hands folded in her lap. The news of her father confused her. A thought nagged at her through the haze of shock. Uncle Jose had mentioned her parents. She breathed deeply and looked at him.

"You mentioned my parents. What happened to my momi?"

"Your mama had been in a coma." He slumped in compassion at her startled look. "Oh my ninita, you did not know that either. I'm so sorry." He waited a moment, then plunged ahead. "Apparently she understood more than they thought or perhaps something else took the life from her, but however we can explain it, Elena, three days after your papa's death, your mama passed away."

Somehow Elena had known this from the beginning of the conversation. The dark, oppressive dreams she had dreamt in Playas popped into her mind. Maybe she had known all along. When had she ever known a whole mother? Her birth had been the beginning of a decline that could only have led to her mother's death. And she, Elena, was living at the expense of her mother's passing. There was something else that caught her attention but the shocking news of her mother had buried it. What had it been? Then she remembered.

"Uncle, why did Rolando go to Carlos' mother's house to bring the news of my papa's death? Why would he do that?"

"No, amor. Not your brother Rolando. Your brother Geoff went to the house."

"Geoff! Why would Geoff take the news to Laura unless he suspected she knew where we were. And why wouldn't Rolando go? He is the one who usually takes care of family matters."

"Because Rolando is the man who was living at your house, Carlos."

The muscles in Carlos' jaws moved in a great effort to still himself. He struggled for Elena's sake to remain in control.

Elena swayed in disbelief. "Rolando is living with Laura? Oh, no! Mi dios, no! How can this be? You can't imagine how much my brother hates her. Carlos and I had to run away because of that hatred." She put her head in her hands for a moment and then raised it slowly. A moan escaped her lips and she bowed with the heaviness of grief. Carlos sprang to her side and lifted her up.

"I think Elena should rest in bed. We must be careful of her health. Perhaps it wasn't the right time to tell her."

Carlos guided her to the door of the bedroom with a concerned Carlota following closely behind. Elena collapsed into tears, and leaned on his chest.

"Oh, Momi. I wasn't there for you. Carlos, I shouldn't have gone to Playas. We should have stayed in Pachuca and faced our problems."

"Cara, you need to be in bed resting. Please remember the baby." He tucked her hair back in place and watched her face carefully. Looking back over his shoulder at his aunt, he nodded. She jumped to Elena's side and helped her onto the bed covering her with a light blanket.

Carlos stayed with his wife holding her hand, while Carlota returned to the living room and sat, deep in thought, as her husband ate more empanadas in an attempt to cover his distress.

"We'll let Carlos tell her the rest," she sighed.

Two days after hearing the news of her parents, they lay in bed, resting quietly, Elena's head on Carlos' shoulder. She seemed to have accepted their deaths.

"Carlos, I need to talk to you about something."

"Of course, carina." He laid his cheek on her head. "What is troubling you?"

"I want to go to Pachuca and see my Aunt Mariana and Uncle

Hector. Surely now that Mama and Papa have died, Rolando will be different. I've thought about this a lot and have decided I don't care that my brother has been living with your mama."

Carlos stiffened and released her.

"What's wrong? Oh, Carlos, I'm so sorry. I didn't even stop to think how you would feel." Moaning, she turned from him.

"Elena, I understand. I'd like to see your Uncle and Aunt also. Think of all they did for me. I'll never forget that it was your Uncle who taught me to read. It changed my life. Please don't feel bad. You've had so much on your mind. It's hard for me to make any judgments, because I don't know all the circumstances, but there's something else I must tell you."

"What?" Alarm pulled her into a sitting position.

"We can't go to see your family. If there were problems with Rolando before, things are worse now. Elena, he left my mother, but before he left, he beat her and my sister, Yolanda. My brothers left home for a while. And it happened when they were gone. Rolando is an alcoholic and no one is able to deal with him. No one knows where he is from one day to the next. I won't let you face him now. Elena, listen. Rolando found out that Uncle Jose told my mama where we were. He beat her until she told him we were in Playas. He has known all along."

"He has known?" she smiled in hope. "You see? He knew, but he didn't come after . . . ." she stared at him. "He was in Playas. Remember? Remember, I saw him standing by the seawall."

"Cara, you don't know Rolando was there. Why didn't he step forward?"

Leaning against the pillow, she was thoughtful. "I don't know but, Carlos, I know he was there."

"That I don't know. However, I need you to hear me. We have waited so long for a baby. Please, we cannot endanger it now."

"I could go to see Geoff."

"From what I understand, Geoff would be no problem. He is married now to a nice girl. But Elena, I just can't let you go."

She sat rigidly with defiance. "Why not? I want to see Geoff and his wife. You said Rolando could be anywhere."

"In all the time we have been married, I have never treated you like other husbands treat their wives. I've never been domineering or one to give orders, but now I will. You are not going to Pachuca until the baby is born, Elena."

She burst into tears. Reaching for her, he held her against him.

"Elena, please. I don't want to hurt you further. Can you wait until the baby is born? There's a little over seven months to wait. I promise you, my love, we will visit Pachuca then. But please, tell me you will not go back into that situation until then. If you promise me that, I will give you my word I will not contact my family. Please try to imagine how hard that will be. I have no idea how my mother is or what my brothers and sister are doing. They are much younger than your brothers."

Sobbing even more, she clung to him. "There I go again, forgetting you and your needs. Yes, you're right. The baby is more important than anything else. We'll wait."

They relaxed, feeling better for having talked.

Elena wiped her eyes with the back of her hand.

"I love Uncle Jose and Aunt Carlota, and appreciate the way they are caring for us, but I'm beginning to feel crowded like last time. And we have pushed Alfredo out of his bedroom again. Have you thought about going back to Playas? Quito isn't inviting if we can't go to Pachuca, and since it's best we don't, I would rather be at home. If something happens with the baby, we can hire a taxi to take us to Guayaquil."

He lay thinking for a long moment.

"We have nowhere to go in Playas. I'm sure someone will be living in our rented home, and the construction has been delayed on our new home. We can't live in a hotel because of the cost." He rested his head on hands placed behind his head. "I've been thinking about something for the past few days. Let me see tomorrow if I can find a place for us to stay."

Chapter 31

I n midmorning, he found a telephone book and searched for a Quito number. Dialing, he listened to several rings before a woman answered.

"Perez residence."

Discovering that Luis Perez was downtown for the day, Carlos requested his call be returned as soon as possible. Later that evening Senor Perez returned his call. After Carlos reminded him of their visit almost three years earlier and had told him he needed work, he was invited to accompany Senor Perez to Tulcachi by car. They left by car the next day.

Carlos decided if he was hired, Elena would have to stay in Quito until the baby was born, and he would return on Sundays to be with her. She refused. "I'll not stay here without you. I've not been separated from you since we were married. I won't, Carlos." Eyes flashing, she defied him to challenge her.

"I can't take you away from doctors and hospitals and expose you to the conditions these people live in while you are pregnant. We might as well have stayed in Playas."

"Then you'll have to look for work in Quito."

"Nobody gets good jobs here unless they have a higher education. Have you seen the lines of men looking for work? I should take you there someday. Every Monday morning the men without jobs stand waiting for a landowner or jefe to come along and hire them. I can't do that, cara. Maybe I'm too proud. I'm limited in what I do well. My heart is in the country. You know that."

"I'm going too." She stood firm.

"No, you aren't. Don't you want this baby?"

"If it's between you or him, I will take you."

"You'll not lose this baby if it takes every ounce of strength I possess. Anyway, I'm not sure Senor Perez has work. He may want me to go along with him because we're friends from a previous encounter. Maybe he just wants to talk with me."

She turned away from him toward the window in their bedroom. "If I have to be separated from you, then I want to go back to Playas."

He sighed in exasperation and threw up his hands. "Will you stop acting like a child? You are not going to live in the country and we're not returning to Playas until the baby is born and that is the last word. Do you think I like it anymore than you do? I remember that awful time we were separated before we married. It will drive me crazy too."

She turned to stare at him, unrelenting, until he whirled on his heels and walked out the door, slamming it behind him.

It wasn't difficult for Luis Perez to see the leadership qualities Carlos possessed. After listening to his experiences of the past three years in Playas, Luis hired him to work on the hacienda. The problem with Elena was mentioned but Luis refused to hear of her living in Quito and promised her the best available care at the hacienda. Plus, they would be close to Tumbaco, Pachuca, Yaruqui and not that far from Quito. A car and driver would be available in case of emergency. Luis told Carlos he would see to it personally that Elena received prenatal care in Quito every two weeks until she was closer to delivery and then she would be taken in each week. In addition, she could have the same care in the clinic owned by the American nurse in Pachuca. In case something happened that she would not be able to get to Quito, Senorita Margaret could care for her.

And so, two days later, they moved to Tulcachi. Their minds were at ease with Elena's care assured.

The motherly cook led them to a little room on the first floor of the big house. It was quite a contrast from the home they had grown accustomed to in Playas; nevertheless, Elena was content to be with Carlos. Soon she made their room comfortable. It was constructed of mud blocks two feet wide with a small window set into one wall; the ceiling was low, giving a warm, close feeling. There was enough space for a bureau, bed closet and chair. Happy to be back in the country surrounded by mountains and close to her husband, Elena hardly missed their coastal home.

Within a few weeks, Luis Perez knew his insight had been correct. He had not misjudged Carlos' character. From their first encounter he had perceived Carlos' to be a skillful and capable young man. He was not sorry he had taken Carlos and Elena into his care. He assigned him several small, important tasks the first few days and was happily impressed with jobs well done. In a short time, Luis gave many of his own responsibilities to Carlos leaving him free to be with his mother in Quito while he looked into other business ventures. He found, though, his thoughts returning to Tulcachi. Using the excuse he needed to see how the new wheat crops were progressing, he visited the hacienda several times, returning each day to Quito; finally he began to stay overnight in Tulcachi and visited his mother on weekends. The bond he had felt with Carlos on their first visit was still there and becoming stronger. The young man's pure love for the mountains, his devotion to Elena, his seriousness and pride concerning his work, baffled Luis. He expected any day to find a major flaw in the boy. However, he was impressed that this lad who was from a poverty-stricken, liquor-ridden part of Ecuador had been preserved. His pleasure was intensified as he found Elena, while a bit spoiled and stubborn, a spark of light. In an otherwise drab existence, she added spice to conversations and mealtimes. The young couple took their meals with him upstairs in the dining room and in the evenings they were invited to spend an hour with him, talking over the day's experiences or discussing plans for the next. Elena took a vital interest in the hacienda and her husband's role. The hour soon expanded as they began to include games of checkers, or an occasional card game.

Carlos found a friend in Luis he had lacked most of his life. He took advantage of the wealth of information this man had, feeding on it.

Luis, having no children, found his life enriched by the young couple. When he was with them, he felt ten years younger. A new vitality lit up his bright blue eyes. Most of his cynicism disappeared, replaced with the ever increasing desire to laugh.

Elena seemed to thrive there and after the fourth month of her pregnancy had passed, everyone sighed with relief. Her face shone with health and contentment borne from a sense of security. For the first time she had a father figure she could trust. She adored Luis. She loved to listen to the men talk about Tulcachi and the work that was so dear to each of the them. She treasured the times spent playing games in the living room. Their lives and souls were so closely knit that one unspoken look could provoke either insight or hysterical laughter.

True to his promise, Luis took Elena to Quito every two weeks for prenatal care in the American hospital where she was given encouraging reports and comments on her own health.

On the alternate week, he drove her to Pachuca to have Senorita Margaret check her. They drove the new highway, completed since Carlos and Elena had run away, avoiding the plaza area, going directly to the clinic where Luis parked the car by the patient's entrance where the Indian woman, Lucia Herrera, took Elena inside. Senorita Margaret gave her patient iron pills, took her blood pressure, checked the baby's heartbeat and felt the size of the fetus to see how it was positioned. Each time Elena always returned to the car, she beamed the news that everything was progressing well.

Elena had worried in the beginning that she would meet a member of her family, but the majority of the patients she saw were from Pachuca's small suburbs. Most women in her social class would have delivered their babies in Quito.

Senorita Margaret had been curious about Elena at her first appointment, but Elena had played dumb, putting the nurse off merely by saying she and her husband worked in Tulcachi and would deliver in the clinic, if not at the hacienda. She had no intention of revealing her true plans. Apparently the deception discouraged Margaret from questioning her further. If the nurse had known of Elena's feeling against her, Margaret would have denied her entrance. Elena could never forget that her mother's death could have been a direct result of Margaret's refusal not to help her so many years before. Elena had no intention of delivering her baby in the clinic. She had prenatal care there only as a precaution.

Carlos and Elena were beginning to love the hacienda and almost regretted buying property on the coast. Elena couldn't forget her experiences at the little costal town but she was content in the sierras. The green mountains, fields of corn, potatoes, and wheat were as intoxicating to Carlos as the sea was to Elena.

"Isn't it a shame we can't take Tulcachi to Playas?" she said one day, as they walked to his horse after the siesta hour.

"Or bring the ocean to Tulcachi. That would be more of a challenge, wouldn't it?" Looking at her with a grin, he winked. "Hmmm, you look good enough to eat, mi pequenita."

"Pequenita! I look like a stuffed pig."

"I've always loved pigs," he chuckled.

Laughing, she attacked his ribs, tickling vigorously until he yelled for mercy.

"Stay home with me this afternoon," she cried out, inspired with a bright thought. She grabbed his arm with both hands. "We can walk to the ridge above the house and watch the airplanes flying into Quito or watch the clouds come from the east."

Closing his eyes, he pretended he was making a hard decision. "I can't, Elena," he said, opening his eyes. "How can I keep my wife fed and clothed if we play when I should be working?"

"Please, Carlos," she pouted. "We haven't been up there for at least two weeks. I hate to see you work so hard we can't take a few minutes to go to our special retreat."

"Carina, when the potato crop is harvested I'll have a day off. Neither Luis nor I can take any time from work now." He smoothed her brow. "Perhaps next week. We're almost finished."

Relenting, she looked at him sadly and smiled.

"I do appreciate how hard you work. It's always been important for you to provide for your family. Many men in this world think about themselves first, but you never have."

Slipping her arm around his waist, she hugged him despite her bulk, loving his masculine smell, a combination of sweat, dirt and horse clinging to him.

"Perhaps it's because they don't have you for a wife. I'd probably be like the rest if I didn't have you to come home to."

"Just so you always come home."

"As if you could keep me away." Pushing her back gently, he looked at her seriously. "Cara mia, I promise you I will always come home. Home is where you are and this is the most important place in the world to me. Where else could I go? When you are old, grey and feeble and when I can hardly climb on a saddle, I will come home to you."

He jumped onto the horse, threw her a kiss, and tossed a kiss to her abdomen.

She giggled and threw kisses to him, glowing in his love.

Wearing a broad smile, Luis stood at the kitchen door watching them. He walked to Elena and he put his arm around her thickening waist as Carlos' horse galloped from the yard.

"I noticed you are getting close to the baby's birth, Elena. Do you have difficulty getting around?"

"Some. I feel like one of our ducks that waddle from the feedbox to the pond." She glanced at him. "Luis, I wish you'd let me work with the women on the porch. Sometimes they act as if they resent me."

"Those women have a hard time understanding why Carlos and you have been placed in the position you have." Releasing her, he walked to the corral. A young boy readied Luis' horse. Dismissing the child, Luis rubbed the animal's face affectionately, silent for a moment.

"I don't know how much Carlos has told you about our first meeting, but it is one I'll not forget. I knew then he was special and that we would remain friends. But I almost stopped thinking about that day when he called me in Quito. I wanted to see him again to see if I felt the same way. The bond was still there and I knew I must invite him to come and live at Tulcachi." He smiled gently at her. "Imagine my pleasure when I discovered he had a young wife. There was emptiness in my life, even with all of this." Throwing out his arm as if to encircle his many treasures and holdings, he shook his head. "I thought I was satisfied until I met you two. Now I understand the meaning of family. Sounds strange, doesn't it? Now I know what I missed by not marrying or having children. Since I have only known you for only a few months, Elena, it may seem strange to you that I would consider you as family, but remember, Carlos, in an unusual way, has been a part of me for several years."

She was moved—her eyes misting. "I've never really had a family life. My papa was an alcoholic, who was never at home, while my momi was ill since the day of my birth. My oldest brother tried to raise me and I guess he did a good job, but now that I'm older I can see the way he felt about me wasn't normal. It's nothing I can explain, but it seems he was trying to prove something to everyone. Oh, I'm sure he loved me, but other brothers don't become obsessed about their sisters."

"Maybe he did the best he could, nina. Probably he didn't know any other way. From the little I have heard and the way you have turned out, I would say he did a pretty good job."

"Yes. I sound selfish, don't I? I just wish he would have treated Carlos better so our exit from Pachuca wouldn't have had to be so secretive."

Luis steadied his impatient horse and nodded.

"Maybe we wouldn't have known each other if your brother hadn't been the way he was. Perhaps you wouldn't be here today."

Her eyes opened wide at this new thought.

Luis mounted his horse. "Don't work with the women. I want you to rest. If they don't understand, that's all right. If you and Carlos don't mind, I have plans for your child."

She looked at him questioningly.

Laughing, he patted the horse's neck. "I'll talk to you two soon, I promise. But now I must ride out and check on the men planting corn and then ride over to the northwest ridge to see how the pasture feed is holding up for the cattle. If someone wants to know where I am, they can find me up that way. I'll be back in a couple of hours." Taking off his hat, he rubbed his forehead then replaced the hat on his thatch of grey hair. "Take care, ninita, and don't do any work. I mean it. I promised your husband I'd watch you when he's not around."

"All right. Hasta luego." She waved. "Be careful."

She passed the afternoon sitting in the shade of the tall trees daydreaming of her child, and thinking of her husband, awaiting his return. Isabel, the kindly cook was teaching Elena to knit. The girl was the only bright spot in Isabel's day and the excitement of Elena's pregnancy was catching on.

Isabel joined her outside for some small talk while Elena struggled with a small sweater set she was knitting. When the cook had return to her old-fashioned kitchen to cook dinner for the men, Elena, tired of knitting and nursing a backache followed her inside.

It was dim and chilly in the kitchen after sitting in the warm sunshine outdoors and Elena gladly accepted a cup of hot chocolate. Sitting on the wooden bench along the wall, she sipped the rich liquid.

"Senor Luis and Carlos are working too hard, that's what." Isabel frowned as she banged pans on the crude wooden counter. Dipping water from a barrel, she filled a metal bowl and washed bananas, drying them with an old, clean rag.

Elena nodded her agreement as she finished the hot chocolate and watched as Isabel took a chunk of white cheese from a cabinet and cut it into squares. After placing a few in front of Elena she laid the rest on a plate, covering it with a cloth.

"When was the last time you and your husband spent a few hours together, nina?"

"We have evenings together."

"You two aren't alone enough. You need to take some time alone. I can tell when something is bothering you, and it doesn't take one of those university professors to see why." She banged the pans some more. "I'm not blind. I see a lot of things."

"We will have a day together soon, Isabel. Carlos promised we will when the potatoes are harvested."

"Hmmm."

Chapter 32

They sat close, leaning against the base of a eucalyptus tree, relaxing in the breeze of the late afternoon. She adjusted her bulk and tried to sit comfortably as Carlos tore a long strand of grass, into strips. Out of the clear sky Luis had ordered Carlos to take the afternoon off and after some feeble protests, Carlos had agreed to spend some time with his wife. Their first week at Tulcachi they had discovered a special place and claimed it as their own with the toasting of warm colas. So this day, without debate, they decided to picnic at their favorite spot, a hearty hike away, behind the main house on a short plateau jutting from the side of a hill. Two trees stood at a slight forward angle on the lip of the overhang as if to peer down on the activities of a productive hacienda. Romantically, Elena imagined the trees were protecting them from intruders, allowing them to pretend for a short time they were the only occupants of the world.

"If only I could make myself a little more comfortable," Elena groaned, struggling to straighten a thin blanket under her.

"Just two more months and you can get rid of that load," he grinned, patting her thigh. "How about something to eat. I'm starved."

"Starved? You ate a big dinner two hours ago." She stopped to look at him in surprise.

"That was two hours ago. I'm hungry." Grabbing a small straw basket, he removed a ragged cloth and peered inside, examining the contents.

"Mmmm. Buttered rolls, cheese, bananas, and look! A chocolate bar. Luis must have brought candy from Quito. Wonderful. Do you want some?"

"Maybe a little chocolate, but I'm fat enough."

Looking at her, Carlos' eyes twinkled. "I don't want to eat alone."

Quietness settled between them as they munched on the rolls baked that morning by Isabel. Puzzled, Carlos had told Elena it was strange that Luis mentioned an afternoon off the day after she had spoken with him. Elena insisted she had said nothing to Luis.

High white clouds rolled lazily rolled above them, drifting slowly toward Quito. From their vantage point the city appeared asleep and quiet under the rays of the hot afternoon sun, as if patiently waiting to be cooled by the approaching clouds.

"Look at the airplane circling the valley," Elena pointed.

"It's waiting its turn to land. It seems so long ago we flew into Quito." Brushing the crumbs from his lap, he lay back and put his arms under his head, looking deep into the breaks in the clouds.

"Yes. It's still hard for me to believe we found a home so quickly."

"Do you miss Playas at all?"

Her answer was slow in coming. "A little."

"I'm not sure I want to go back to Playas, Elena. I've had so much pleasure right here in Tulcachi. I've thought many times we should have come here in the first place instead of running south."

"Oh, I wouldn't trade what we had there. Remember our honeymoon? I'm so glad we had that experience."

"Of course I remember. You're right. We have nice memories, but I regret buying land there. We should have saved our money and bought land here. This is where our roots are."

"We could sell the land there and buy here, but I have a feeling Luis plans to give our son the hacienda. He didn't really say that, but he hinted. Has he ever said anything to you?"

"Oh, there have been little comments. I think he's waiting to see if the baby is a girl or a boy.

"Would you mind if he did give it to him, Carlos?"

"He has no heirs and he knows we would take care of the place but, Elena, he'll be living here for years yet, so it's nothing we have to consider today."

Carlos returned to his former position and their talking ceased as they listened to the distant lowing of cattle, the songs of birds and the buzzing of insects. Elena reached over and tousled his hair, content with her life, knowing they were in the right place. As much as she loved Playas and the sea, her place was with her husband here in the mountains of her youth.

His voice broke into her thoughts. "I saw your family today. Mariana and Hector."

Alert, her hand lay motionless on his head. "You did? Where?"

"Going to their property above Tulcachi. I've seen them many times but I didn't want to upset you by mentioning it."

"I haven't seen them once."

"That's because you usually stay inside or at the back of the house."

Her moment of peace having vanished, she shrugged, clasping her hands in her lap.

"Maybe because I haven't wanted to see them. Do they know we've returned to this area?"

"They've known for about six months, carina."

Sadness gripped her. "They don't want to see me. They probably think I've disgraced the family because we married."

"I'm sorry." A hurt look crossed Carlos' face before he could control it.

"Oh, Carlos. I don't mean that. To me, you are the most wonderful, gentle, kind man I have ever known. You are my life, the only reason I want to live."

Reassured, he teased somberly. "What about the baby?"

"To me the baby is you," she said gravely. "I love him because of you."

"Don't you wish sometimes you had stayed in Pachuca instead of running all over the country this way?"

"Never. I would do it again many times. I've never regretted marrying you. Not for a moment. That is the truth, mi esposo."

"I'm glad to hear that because sometimes I worry a little."

"Well, don't." Despite her bulk, she moved to his side and dropped a kiss on his cheek. "The only thing I really wish I'd have is this baby tomorrow. I feel so huge."

"You look beautiful to me." He gathered her to him, placing his face in her hair. "I love you so much, Elena."

"I love you, too."

They slept in each other's arms until the coolness of dusk woke them. Startled, they sat upright, blinking in astonishment.

"We must go." He helped her up. "I don't want you to become ill."

"I'm all right."

"We must hurry down the hill while we can still see our way."

Grabbing the blanket and basket, they laughed at her awkwardness as they trotted down the hill, through a large pasture, and into the warmth of their home.

Luis paced the uneven, worn brick floor of the old kitchen, sipping on a cup of hot, ground corn colada.

"Senor Luis, perhaps you should walk up toward the ledge to see if they are still there." Isabel turned from the stove and folded a damp cloth nervously.

Looking at her absently, he pondered the situation. "No, I think we should wait until dark. Perhaps they wanted to watch the dusk approach. I can't believe Carlos would take any chances with Elena."

Walking to the table, he put the cup down forcefully. He wasn't as concerned as he was lonely for the two young people. The supper hour had been quiet and uneventful, driving home the reality that he had become extremely attached to his two friends. As he walked past the worried cook to peer out the door, voices in the distance made him freeze. Springing into action, he returned to the table and Isabel turned to her chores as the kitchen door burst open. Elena and Carlos rushed through, stopping in the center of the room, their hair mussed, their clothes were dusty and their eyes sparkling. Luis looked up in anger but his heart softened at the sight of them.

"I'm sorry we're late, Luis. We fell asleep on the ledge and didn't awaken until a few minutes ago." Carlos gave Luis an apologetic look.

Elena hurried to Isabel's side. "We missed supper, didn't we? Oh, I hope you didn't worry about us."

Luis gave Isabel a warning look and smiled at Elena. "We did wonder where you were, but certainly it wasn't a worry."

"Would you care for your supper, children?" Isabel bustled past Luis to take the basket and blanket from Carlos.

"Not too much for me, thank you. We ate the rest of the rolls on the way home." Carlos smiled at Elena.

"Perhaps we'll have some hot colada and cheese, thank you," replied Elena, as she peered into Luis' cup. "But, please go to bed, Isabel." She put her hand on the cook's arm. "I'll serve Carlos and myself."

"All right," Isabel nodded, putting two cups on the table. "Now that you are home, I might as well. Please excuse me and have a good night."

"Good night," they chorused, as Elena dipped colada into the cups from a pan. She found the plate of cheese under a cloth in the cupboard.

They washed in a basin, then joined Luis at the table. For an hour the three discussed the past events of the day and plans for the morrow.

Carlos finished his second cup of colada and put his hands on the table. He was concerned with a neglected ridge east of the main buildings that had been ignored due to the steep slope. "I know we can use the new tractor in that area and eventually harvest many hundreds of kilos of corn, Luis,"

"I won't do it, Carlos. It's too dangerous. What would happen if the tractor lost balance?"

"It won't. I rode my horse up there two days ago and walked the length and width of it. We're losing money by not planting there. There's is plenty of room. We can let Raul drive the tractor. He's always careful, and if we measure off his boundaries, I'm sure nothing will happen. I also ran my horse down the slope and found it's really not that steep."

Luis thought for a few moments and scratched his head lazily. "I agree we have been wasting valuable land; I won't however take the tractor in. We'll use men with picks to loosen the earth."

Carlos persevered. "It's time to plant corn now, but if we take men from the potato fields or from tending cattle, they will suffer. The tractor can do in one hour what five men can do in three days. Please. I will be responsible."

Luis threw up his hands in resignation. "All right, Carlos. I don't like the idea, but you're right about wasting time and land. There's a strong market for corn in Quito this year, so we can use the extra yield. I'll go out with you tomorrow and talk things over with Raul myself. If we all agree about his safety, we'll go ahead."

They sat for another hour discussing cows, cheese, and Elena's upcoming prenatal checkup until weariness drove them to their beds.

Carlos was gone by the time the sun appeared over the mountains. This was the time of day she hated. When he left her, it was as if he took part of her with him. She comforted herself with the thought that it was only a few hours until they would spend the siesta and evening hours together. When he left she felt alone and cold until she grew accustomed to the empty place by her side, then she would stretch and sleep for another hour.

Each day she grew more tired and required more rest. After a nice breakfast she sat on the bench behind the house knitting and talking with Isabel. She still felt out of place with the women who worked on the front porch, but she loved the cook and spent hours with her while the men were away.

A week later, Elena was disappointed when news was sent that Luis and Carlos could not return for lunch due to a breakdown on one of the farm trucks. The day seemed unusually long and Elena was not feeling well. After complaining of feeling too hot, Isabel suggested Elena lie down after lunch for a nap. She guided the girl to her room, helped her into bed and bent to feel her flushed face.

"I think you may have a fever. Try to sleep and see if it will pass. We have only about eight weeks to wait until the little one arrives." Isabel smiled tenderly at her.

"I'm fine, really. Perhaps I sat in the sunshine too long. I just feel so tired." Closing her eyes, she took a deep breath. "I will sleep, but if Carlos comes before I wake, please tell him to come in and see me. If Luis arrives, you can also send him. I don't want to sleep if either of them is home. Please."

"I will, ninita. You rest now."

Isabel closed the wooden shutters and shut the double doors behind her, leaving Elena alone.

She hadn't been feeling well. During the night, she had awakened with what she decided was a touch of indigestion, but after a few minutes it had passed. All morning she had been ill due to heavy pressure in her heart region. She was carrying the baby high and it was beginning to cause a great deal of discomfort. Since it was difficult to pinpoint the pressure, she felt queasy and headachy.

Finally, she drifted into a deep sleep. Terrrible and realistic dreams plagued her but she could not wake herself. She heard voices in her room, but she could not speak; no sounds escaped her open, dry mouth. Sweat poured off her body and her heart beat so loudly, she could hear it in her sleep. Faces appeared and dissolved. Then she was in Playas, frolicking in the ocean, until she realized the water was hot and rough. Panicking, she began flailing her arms in the surf. She cried out for Carlos and he appeared on the shore, laughing and waving to her. Luis struggled, swimming out to her, but he was unable to reach her and she didn't have the strength to move toward him. She heard herself screaming and there was a horrible roaring in her ears. Then suddenly she was awake. Sitting up in bed, everything was quiet. She threw off the covers in the unbearable heat. Immediately she was asleep again, peacefully this time.

The door opened slowly and she awakened feeling refreshed. He was there and she turned to smile up at him.

"I heard you were sick," he said, concerned.

"I'm feeling much better."

He knelt by her bed and took her hand, and with a handkerchief wiped her face. A strange feeling suddenly possessed her, and it seemed every fiber in her body tingled.

"Look at me," she ordered.

He turned and the light from the doorway shone on his face. He looked strained and then she noticed his reddened eyes.

"Open the window. Open the window." She cried in a panic. "What's wrong?"

Standing, he went to the shuttered window and opened it, pausing for a moment.

"What's wrong," she repeated, feverishly adjusting her body.

He turned back to her and knelt again. She saw his swollen eyes were full of tears.

A roar started in her ears and she grabbed at the bedding, fighting the feeling she was falling into a dark, black hole.

"Carlos. Where is Carlos?" she screamed.

"He's dead," wept Luis.

Chapter 33

Nothing in her young life prepared her for what she faced now. The agony was unmerciful. The doctor sedated her, but she would awaken in the night, screaming, tearing at her clothing and at her heart, in an attempt to rid herself of the pain, the overwhelming pain. At night she longed for the day. When the day arrived she wept for the night. Above all, she hated her bed, so cold, damp and empty now. They moved her to the living room, but in the dark hours she mourned for the evenings they had spent together in the room. Finally, Luis stayed with her during the nights until exhausted—they both slept as the sun came over the mountains.

Luis was in the depths of despair. Riddled with unnecessary guilt, he grieved for a lost son. None of his friends in Quito had earned his respect as had the degraded, downtrodden Indian from the back mountains of Ecuador. Luis had been taught to expect nothing productive would come from a mountain Indian. He tolerated their drunkenness, and lack of education. They seemed to be interested in nothing beyond satisfying their sex drive and another drink. Could the fault lay with him? Perhaps there were more like Carlos in these mountains. Knowing he was a prejudiced man, Luis was unprepared for the directness and friendliness Carlos had offered him and despite his preconceived ideas, Luis had taken time to listen and learn. Now, he reflected, if he had stubbornly clung to his unyielding bias, perhaps he would never have known his beloved Carlos.

He had loved Carlos as a son and Luis' last will and testament included Carlos' offspring. If the baby was a boy, the hacienda would become his at age twenty-one. If Elena bore a girl, the child would be provided for the rest of her life, her education secured. If he had lived Carlos, would have had a home with Luis for the rest of his life. Carlos and Elena would have been able to live there, if they chose, until they died. The loss was tremendous. Having grown accustomed to sharing his burdens and ideas with Carlos, Luis felt now there was no one to whom he could turn. Elena, as much as he loved her, was suffering so deeply she couldn't see his pain. Having suffered the premature death of his own fiancee' many years ago, he could relate to Elena's heartache. He was helplessly inadequate with words and found by holding Elena he helped soothe her heart.

He considered the thought of marriage to Elena to give the child a father, but he pushed the idea aside. Elena was a mere twenty and in two years, he would be fifty. No, marriage wasn't the answer, but he was determined to be there for her as long as she needed him.

The funeral passed like a dream for Elena. The doctor had sedated her to keep her calm. Onlookers gossiped that she appeared to be without emotion as she passed on her way to the center of Pachuca. It was the first time she had been in the plaza since the day she had run away with Carlos.

Traveling slowly, a truck carried the pallbearers and coffin to the edge of town, while the people of Tulcachi formed a procession, following in farm trucks, tractors and on horses. Elena, Luis, Isabel and Ramon, the driver, rode in Luis' private car until the caravan reached the outskirts of the town proper. The pallbearers pulled the coffin to the ground while the assemblage stood waiting for the Catholic priest and the monks to arrive. The heavy silence was broken by the mournful tolling of distant church bells punctuated by an occasional moan or cough, or the sound of a mother hushing her child. As the small group of church men approached, the priest, attired in white vestments, stepped out to sprinkle holy water over the coffin while softly intoning a prayer. He turned and the entire funeral party followed, with Carlos' fellow workers serving as pallbearers. As they walked into town, members of the procession began to chant in sporadic fashion. Candles were lit and moans and wails mingled synchronistically with the rising volume and intensity of the prayers.

Luis guided Elena as they began the near mile walk to the burial site. She lay against him, finding comfort in his nearness. They passed Carlos' house where Laura, his mother and his brothers joined the cortege. Laura walked to Elena's side and with a sad, tearful smile took her hand. Elena smiled back and nodded her thanks. The road led past the home of Mariana and Hector. As they walked by, they saw the couple with Elena's cousins grouped in the doorway, but Luis noted there was no move toward Elena. Elena felt Luis hold her tighter as if to protect her from this unkindness. Strangely, she felt no pain or tie to them any longer. She had married a man they believed to be socially beneath them and they had been wrong. Eventually their bitterness and loss would eat away at their spirits and defeat them. Elena had made the right choice. She was the victor.

Everything passed in a haze. She recalled various people coming forward to offer their condolences. She hugged Carlos' sister, Yolanda who was overcome with grief. Fausto stood tearfully in the background and her heart went out to him. Because of the Fausto's faithfulness, she and Carlos had been able to run away. She promised herself to return someday to thank him.

Uncle Jose, Aunt Carlota, Alfredo and a girl she presumed to be his fiancee′, in turn hugged Elena. The extracted a promise from her that she visit soon, but Elena knew she would never return to their home in Quito, so full of poignant memories.

The only person she longed to see was Rolando and he wasn't there. That hurt her more than Aunt Mariana's snobbery. Surely after all this time he had forgiven her.

Geoff, with a young woman stepped forward and Elena recalled her brother was now married. Geoff took Elena from Luis and held her closely for a long while, tears brimming in his eyes. He told Elena he loved her and was sorry he had delayed visiting her in Tucachi. She responded with understanding and asked about Rolando. To her sorrow, Rolando was in Quito and had not been able to attend the funeral. Geoff promised he would travel to Tulcachi in two months, after the baby was born.

Contrary to common practice, arrangements were made with the priest to bury the body outside the church plot. Elena was adamant. She wanted Carlos to be buried behind the hacienda under the trees at their special spot. He had loved the mountains more than anyone she knew and was convinced he would be happier there than lying in a neglected churchyard. As the final benediction was offered, the pallbearers returned the coffin to the truck now parked in front of the church. Carlos was buried on the plateau that same day, without Elena in attendance, as she lay in a drug-induced stupor on the living room sofa.

And now, Luis was responsible for Elena. When Carlos lay dying, Luis had promised that he would care for her. It took several days before Elena was able to question the circumstances of Carlos' death, but she did finally, and Luis carefully explained, trying to spare her needless pain.

That fateful day Luis had been having trouble starting one of the farm trucks and had borrowed Raul from Carlos. Raul had spent much of the morning trying to get the truck started. Finally, he was forced to drive a jeep into Tumbaco to find a mechanic. Luis rode his horse up to bring Carlos back for dinner, since the plowing of the ridge could not continue without Raul. He found him frustrated and impatient that his project had suffered setbacks. On the spur of the moment, Luis decided to ride the length of the ridge in order to estimate the amount of time they needed for plowing.

As Luis made his way back down the ridge, his eyes searched for Carlos and then he noticed the tractor was gone. A small fear gathered in his stomach but he pushed it away with a dry chuckle. He was imagining things. But where was the tractor? Perhaps Raul had returned and driven away? No, Raul couldn't have gotten back from Tumbaco this soon.

He could only guess at what happened while he was away. For some unknown reason, Carlos had boarded the new tractor. He had little knowledge, if any, for operating a motorized vehicle, but nevertheless, he had started the motor. Instead of pushing the stick into forward gear, apparently, he had pulled it into reverse and as he let out the clutch, the tractor had jumped backwards down the slope.

The scene that met him as he neared the accident would live with him forever. It froze him to his horse for a full minute before he could manipulate his legs into action. There was no logic to this as he knew Carlos to be a careful, alert individual. The tractor set on its side against a wild hedge at the bottom of the hill. Having been thrown clear, Carlos lay halfway down the slope. He was still alive when Luis reached his side, but he could barely speak. In a labored whisper, he told Luis to care for Elena and the baby. His last words were: "I love you, Luis. Thank you for giving us a home."

And then he died.

Nothing Luis did for Elena seemed to help. Her agony and grief were frightening. They talked by the hour, but sometimes she would become abnormally still. At other times she babbled, describing her pain like waves of the ocean. Luis tried to understand. She complained she felt numb, but he attributed that to the pills she was taking. She described herself as having no feelings, yet the next moment, her emotions hit a high, roaring peak from which there seemed to be no release. Then her head would roll from side to side as desperate moans escaped from her mouth. It was unbearable. She loathed the bulkiness of her pregnancy and depised herself for not being with Carlos when he was in danger. She cured bittersweet memories that produced blinding headaches and spasms of vomiting.

On one occasion as they talked, she suddenly burst into tears and ran to the door, screaming and begging Carlos to come to her. On another day, Luis and Isabel found her in her room packing her suitcase. When they asked where she was going, she replied she had to hurry to Playas for someone had been playing a terrible trick on her. Carlos was waiting in Playas, searching for her. Luis could only take her in his arms as they wept together.

The days passed slowly, but soon she was in her eighth month. Luis wondered if the only reason she continued to live was for the child.

But the suffering wasn't over as Luis became caught in a terrible web of circumstances.

One evening they took a small dinner in the living room and remained at the coffee table to talk. Much to his relief, Luis noted Elena was beginning to rationalize a little, her thoughts turning more to the imminent birth of her child. He felt a spark of hope that this could temper her grief over Carlos. Her sudden fits of weeping and lamenting seemed to be fewer and further apart. He let her talk as much as she desired, knowing it was an outlet. "Would you like to play a game of checkers?" he asked, his blue eyes hopeful.

"Yes, I'd like that," she attempted a smile.

He squeezed her hand, then fetched the checkers set from a bureau. Moving their plates aside, he laid out the game and gave her the choice of color just as the telephone rang. The central office in Pachuca had a call for him from his Quito home. Elena watched him as she listened, her eyes growing large and fearful.

Returning the phone to its base, he sat on the sofa, putting his arm around Elena's shoulders.

"That was my mother's maid. My mama is very ill and they aren't sure what's wrong. You know she's all alone since my papa is dead. She needs my help. They've taken her to the American hospital in Quito." He lifted Elena's trembling chin. "Carina, you understand I must go see what's wrong."

She let loose with a loud wail.

"Do you want to go with me? Of course. I don't want to leave you alone."

It wasn't until the next day that they returned to Tulcachi. Luis was beside himself with concern as his mother needed emergency open heart surgery. With little faith in Quito's medical services, he had already started proceedings on a special visa for himself and his mother. They were to leave the next day for New York, where his brother worked as a doctor. He was equally concerned about Elena. Because she had never obtained a cedula or identification papers, he was unsuccessful in securing a passport for her. It became obvious she would have to remain in Ecuador. He encouraged her to stay at his home in Quito, but she refused to leave Carlos in Tulcachi. She frightened him by showing no emotion after her initial outburst.

"Elena, I'll be gone for a week. Tomorrow, I'll take my mother on the plane and we'll arrive in New York tomorrow evening. My brother is handling everything. My mother will be operated on the next day if she is able, and if there are no complications, I'll leave and come back for you."

She averted her eyes. "I'll probably have my baby while you're gone."

"You still have three weeks to go." He took her hand gently. "Anyway, ninita, I've already talked to Isabel and my mama's chauffeur, Ramon. I'll close up the house in Quito so they'll both be here for you. I've given them instructions to care for your every need. Together, they will see to it that you need nothing."

Her resolve seemed to fall apart. "I can't live without you, Luis."

"I think I know how you feel. I don't want to go , but she's my mother, Elena."

"What if I do have the baby this week?"

"Then Ramon and Isabel will take you directly to Quito. The minute you start to have pains, call Isabel." He pressed her hand. "However, I see little chance of that happening. And I promise you I'll call the central telephone office in Pachuca every night. If they are able to put the call through, we can talk together. If, for some reason I can't contact Pachuca, I'll call a friend in Quito and he will get hold of you. One way or another we will keep in contact, Cara." Shaking his head sadly, he told her, "I would give anything if this hadn't happened right now."

Chapter 34

When Luis left Elena, she wept bitterly. Holding onto him at the airport, she begged him to return quickly. Luis left her reluctantly, promising to see her in a week's time. As the airplane melted to a speck in the sky, Ramon led Elena to the car and drove back to Tulcachi. Meeting them at the door, Isabel comforted her, tried to entice her to eat a good lunch, and then gave her a mild tranquilizer. Elena fell into an exhausted sleep on the sofa.

She slept through supper and into the night, waking at midnight when a sharp pain shot through her middle section. She stumbled to the door and walked the length of the hallway to Isabel's door. Knocking, she heard noises immediately and Isabel appeared, concerned and ready to help. By midmorning, Elena was in labor.

It was Sunday, a poor day for finding doctors, so Isabel and Ramon considered taking Elena to Pachuca.

"I don't know what to do. Shall we take a chance that her doctor will be at the hospital in Quito?" Preparing the suitcase, the stout woman nervously folded and refolded Elena's clothes.

"I think that we should take a chance since Senor Perez left instructions that Quito was first choice."

"What if no doctors are available?"

"There are always doctors in the hospital."

"What if she has the baby before we arrive?"

"Haven't you ever delivered a baby?"

Isabel gave him an incredulous look. "I've had my own babies delivered at the hospital in Quito, but I'm not able to help Elena have one in the car." She shook her head with impatience. "We can't stand here talking. We must get her to the hospital. Let's try to make it to Quito. It will only take an hour."

Within minutes they were settled in the car driving quickly toward the Pan American highway. Elena rested peacefully in the back seat.

At the entrance to the main highway, Ramon slowed the car. Blocking the way were several policemen amongst a crowd of people.

Rolling down the car window, he called to one of the officers.

"What's the matter, Senor?"

"We have a car race today. No one can go to Quito."

"But, we have a lady here in labor. She's going to deliver a baby at any moment."

The officer shrugged his shoulders. "Sorry, I can't help you. The race starts at eleven o'clock and they will be racing through this area in an hour. In a few minutes, we will be closing this highway completely and you'll not go anywhere."

Elena sat forward. "What shall we do?" she asked, anxiety closing her throat.

The policeman leaned toward the window and looked in the back seat.

"You'll have to go toward Pachuca or Yaruqui. Each town has a clinic, but you had better hurry. You have about thirty minutes and no cars will be allowed at all on this highway, even if you have the baby right here."

Ramon turned to the woman. "What shall I do? We can't go to Quito."

"We'll go to the American clinic in Pachuca," Elena said calmly.

They both looked at the girl, who appeared to have taken control.

"Are you sure?" he asked.

"I don't think I have any choice."

Quickly Ramon turned away from Quito and drove rapidly toward Pachuca. Elena's labor pains were about twenty minutes apart. She wished desperately Luis was with her to hold her hand when the cramps overcame her. In a matter of a few minutes they arrived at the clinic and Lucia opened the door. She invited Elena and Isabel inside, instructing the chauffeur to remain in the car.

Leading Elena into the prenatal room, Lucia found that Elena was dilated and would deliver sometime during the night. The Indian told Isabel she was no longer needed and led her to the door.

"Come back on Tuesday to take Elena and the baby home. We will need six hundred sucres, so please be prepared."

Isabel stood nervously at the door. "May I spend the night with Elena? She doesn't like to be alone."

Lucia Herrera gave the woman a hard, cold stare.

"No one spends the night here but patients. Come on Tuesday morning with the money and you can see them then."

Pushing her out the door, she shut it and left Isabel standing on the doorstep, tears in her eyes.

Elena was taken to the showers and bathed, handed a white hospital gown and led to a high bed with the whitest sheets she had ever seen. Lucia worked around her without saying a word. Elena felt an overwhelming sense of loneliness, thinking the woman cold and ugly. Finally, the Indian left her alone and for two hours Elena cried into her pillow. After being fed a nice lunch, she was again left alone, but later in the afternoon the pains became intense. She forgot everything but her need to deliver the burden she had been carrying. She longed to hold Carlos' baby in her arms. How thankful she was she had this much left of him. She and Luis would raise the baby and love it as much as she and Carlos could have. At least she knew the future of the child was secure.

The painful hours that passed were almost welcomed by her. They blotted out the agony and loneliness of her soul. As the contractions came closer together, Lucia appeared more often, until finally Elena was led to the labor room and helped onto a table with two metal stirrups attached. Her legs were placed in these and she was strapped down. A injection was prepared and given and she was prepped. Then she waited for the next thrust of pain.

Margaret Brewer appeared in the doorway. Elena had met with the nurse during prenatal checkups, but had never noticed before the kindness showing on the woman's face today. She radiated love and tenderness. Approaching the table, she took Elena's hand in hers and comforted her.

"Elena, please relax. This will all be over soon." She hesitated a moment. "I'm sorry Carlos can't be with you, my dear."

Tears flowed from Elena's eyes as she absorbed the attention and love. How could she believe this was the same woman who had rejecterd her mother so many years ago on the day of her own delivery? Now she longed to have Margaret sweep away all the hurt and sorrow she had borne these past weeks.

With love and gentle hands, the baby was delivered after a few minutes of hard labor. The last push was almost unbearable, but when Elena heard the lusty cry of her firstborn, she relaxed. Twisting her head to see the baby, she watched Margaret suctioning the infant's mouth.

"Oh, how beautiful she is. It's a girl. Gracias a dios. How we have been waiting for a girl," said Margaret.

"I have a girl? It's not a boy?" Elena asked, disappointed.

"No. It's a beautiful little girl, somewhat premature, but not too much."

Margaret laid the baby in a waiting bassinet and re-examined the child.

"Perhaps we misfigured the due date a little. Oh, she's a beauty."

Elena's first disappointment was being replaced with a spark of excitement. Carlos had wanted a girl.

Through the night she cradled her baby next to her breast, hardly able to sleep. Excitement and unspeakable love toward the infant filled her thoughts. As dawn arrived, Isabel and Ramon appeared at the window, knocking softly. Elena sat up in bed, opened a small door in the glass window, spoke quietly through the screen.

"Buenos dias, Elena. We could not sleep for thinking of you."

Elena beamed, gathering up a small bundle and presenting her daughter to the peering guests. "I have a little girl."

"A girl. How wonderful and isn't she beautiful, Ramon? Isabel exclaimed, turning to the man.

Ramon pressed forward, smiling broadly. "Senor Luis will be happy to hear about the child. His friend in Quito called last night telling us there was no way for the senor to get a line through to Tulcachi. He was very concerned about you, Senora Elena. Wait until the senor hears of the child. He will be delighted."

"Will we be able to come in and visit with you later, Elena?" Isabel struggled to see through the screen.

"I'm sorry, but apparently Senorita Margaret has rules that visitors are not allowed inside. I don't understand, because I would love to have you hold the baby. There are no other patients. I'm all alone."

"Perhaps we can ask, if we see the senorita. Right now, you should rest. If we hear from Senor Luis, we will send the wonderful message of your daughter."

"Thank you, and please send my love." Elena fought a growing desire to leave the clinic. "I can go home tomorrow. Please pick me up as soon as possible."

"We will. We will be here early tomorrow morning. Give our ninita a kiss."

"I will."

Isabel and Ramon backed away from the window and walked to the end of the clinic to watch for movement in the distant house. They waited a moment and then returned to the car. Elena stared in fright when suddenly, she noticed Margaret in the doorway. She hadn't heard the nurse enter the clinic and wondered how long she had been watching.

Without a word, Margaret walked to the patient's door and called to Isabel. "Senora, may I have a word with you?"

"Oh, Buenos dias, senorita," exclaimed Isabel. "We were looking for you. We would love to visit with Elena and the baby for a moment. Would that be possible?"

Margaret glanced toward Elena, whose face was framed in the window. "Visitors are not allowed inside the building until they come to pick up the patient. I'm sure you have seen the baby through the window." Leaning closer, Margaret dropped her voice, and Elena strained to hear her words.

When Margaret turned into the clinic, Elena frantically motioned for Isabel to come to the window. "What did she say to you?"

"That you had a difficult delivery and needed your rest. She said she wants us to leave you alone until we pick you up on Wednesday."

"Wednesday? Do you mean I must stay here until Wednesday? Oh, Isabel. Please come sooner," Elena pleaded.

"Carina, that is the day after tomorrow. We will come very early."

Elena heard a noise and turned. Margaret stood at the end of the bed.

"Tell your guest to leave, Elena. You must rest."

"I must rest, Isabel. I will miss you so." Elena spoke through the window, holding up her baby for one last peek.

Ramon started the motor of the car and the two bid her goodbye with sad waves.

Elean turned and snuggled with her baby before turning her attention to Margaret. "I don't see why Isabel couldn't come in to see the baby," she remarked angrily.

"It's bad enough that we have unclean patients in here, but at least they can shower. Visitors don't bathe, and therefore we are exposed to all kinds of diseases. That's why."

"I admit I don't know much about giving birth, but it didn't seem that my delivery was so difficult that I must stay here until Wednesday."

Margaret's mouth opened in puzzlement. Wednesday? But I told the senora to come on Tuesday. Tomorrow morning."

"Tuesday?" Elena struggled up, pressing her baby close to her bosom. "No, senorita. Isabel said you told her Wednesday morning."

"Then she made an error."

"We must send her a message." Panic filled Elena's eyes.

"Don't worry, Elena." The nurse spoke soothingly. "I'll give them a telephone call and tell them to come tomorrow."

When Margaret departed, Elena buried her homesickness after gathering the baby to her again. "Your popi wanted me to name you Little Elena, but I have been thinking and I have decided I want to call you Angelita, because you are a little angel sent from your popi, wherever he is today."

Elena caressed the infant's soft, downy cheek, ran her fingers over the thin eyebrows and touched the tiny nose. She was astonished that she and her beloved husband had been responsible for the beautiful infant. Reluctantly, she relinquished Angelita only during the time it took for Lucia to give the baby a bath and change the bedding, and for her to take a quick shower. Other than that, they remained together, the bond growing stronger each moment. She prodded the baby to suck until her milk came in a heavy stream. As the tiny mouth sought the source of nourishment, Elena felt a prolonged depth of joy, the first since Carlos death. She knew now she would survive. If for no other reason, she would survive for this child.

Her desire now was to leave for Tulcachi with the baby. She would return and make a home for her daughter. The arrival of Luis would complete her contentment. Remaining at the clinic was beginning to bother her. Her first impression of Margaret was being replaced by a sense of wariness. It seemed the nurse no longer felt concern for Elena, but rather mild hostility. Margaret and Lucia had a violent argument in the kitchen before lunch, which caused the nurse to leave the clinic slamming the door. The Indian aide stomped upstairs to the attic, where Elena heard loud banging for the next hour. Elena thought the clinic was cold and impersonal; she longed for morning.

After supper, Margaret appeared in the doorway.

"Buenas tardes, Elena." She walked to her bedside and glanced at the sleeping baby. "I wonder if I may speak with you."

"Of course," Elena replied, holding the baby close to her side.

Margaret pulled a chair from under the window, sat beside the bed and patted Elena's hand.

"When you first started coming to the clinic for prenatal care, I wasn't sure who you were, since you used your husband's name. However, when I heard of his death, I was able to connect you with the little Elena Martinez from the plaza."

Elena's throat closed with the threat of tears. She looked down at Angelita's curly black locks.

"What are your plans now?" continued Margaret.

"I will return to the hacienda in Tulcachi and raise my daughter there."

"Without a father?"

"No. The hacienda owner plans to help me."

The nurse's face turned scarlet. "Do you mean you will live with Luis Perez alone?"

"We're not exactly alone. But why not? My husband and I lived there with him before...."

"But now you aren't married and neither is Senor Perez."

Elena stared at the red-faced woman, sickened at her implications.

"He's like my father. You will never understand what he has meant to me this past year."

Clearly, Margaret was horrified and Elena became confused.

"What are you saying to me, Senorita Margaret?"

Margaret pressed her lips together and shook her head in wonderment. "Leave it to you people to raise your children in conditions like that."

"Conditions like what?" Elena stared at her with disbelief. "My baby will receive nothing but love and attention."

"Have you thought perhaps I could take her and raise her?"

"No!" Terrified, Elena clutched the baby to her breast. "I wouldn't think of giving this child to you. She is all I have left of my marriage to Carlos. Never!"

"I can give her everything you can't," Margaret continued, undaunted.

"No. Don't talk to me about it. I will never, never give you my baby."

"All right." The nurse stood with a look of disgust on her face. "You don't have to act like I've done something wrong."

That night Elena slept very little, waking every few minutes to see if the baby was by her side. The relief was tremendous when morning came and the threat lessened. Reproaching herself for her needless fear, she began preparing for her trip home. After breakfast Lucia told her to get up, take a shower and change into her street clothes. Shortly, it would be time for her ride to pick her up.

"Is it all right if I wait awhile? I don't have any money with me to pay you, so I would rather wait until my ride comes to start getting ready," she protested timidly, fearful of leaving the baby alone. "You did telephone them to come today, didn't you?"

"They are supposed to be here early this morning. You must take a shower before you leave, so please do that quickly."

Elena did not want to displease Lucia. She disrobed, took a fast shower and dressed in her street clothes. Hoping to find Ramon and Isabel waiting, she left the bathroom and walked to one of the windows. The car was not in sight. She saw Lucia in the labor room and walked to her. Catching her breath sharply, Elena noticed Margaret standing, also, inside the room. She started toward the bassinet, when Margaret stopped her.

"Lucia said you don't have money to pay for the delivery."

Elena's heart began to pound. "No, I don't, but my driver will be here any minute and he'll pay the bill. You were supposed to call them at the hacienda and tell him to come today. Did you?"

"I'm sorry, but we need your bed for other patients, so we have to ask you to leave." Margaret replied, ignoring the question.

A terrible thought struck Elena and she turned again to the big room where she had left the baby. The crib sat in the same spot, with the small bundle inside. Reassured, she returned to Margaret and Lucia.

"I don't understand. Can't I wait or try to call the hacienda?"

"No, you'll have to leave. You can come back later for the baby, but I won't give her to you unless I have the money in full."

"My baby? I'm not leaving without my baby."

"And I'm not going to give her to you unless I have the money."

"Oh, dios, no. Where is my baby?" Panic engulfed her.

She ran into the patient's ward and took up the bundle. Blankets fell through her hands to the floor. Angelita wasn't there. Elena ran from room to room shouting.

Everything went blank; and she fought for her breath. Then the realization that Margaret had taken her baby dawned on her and she rushed at the nurse with a murderous fury.

"Where's my baby?" she shrieked, clawing and scratching.

"Lucia, will you take her outside before someone gets hurt?"

The Indian woman pulled the screaming girl into the hall, opened the patient's door, and put her outside.

Elena stood in shock, not believing what had happened.

"All we need is the money, Elena, and we'll give you the baby. Try to find some money quickly," said Lucia.

In a nightmarish panic, she ran, as if in a dream, to the plaza, pounding on the doors of her own home. No one was there;

the doors were locked. She stumbled, wailing hysterically, pleading for money from door to door. People ran to their windows and entrances to see who was making the commotion. They turned away embarrassed, remembering her state of mind at her husband's funeral. She appeared intoxicated and incoherent. Disgusted, the townspeople retreated behind closed doors.

Elena wandered the streets weeping. An hour later, penniless, she wandered back to the clinic and pounded on the door.

Margaret had been waiting and she opened the door quickly.

"Do you have the money?"

Elena shook her head and the nurse started to shut the door. She pushed against it, until Margaret lost patience, opened the door again and pushed the girl down the steps. Elena fell backwards and lay helplessly on the ground.

"Where are your friends? They've forgotten you, I see."

Noting Elena was dazed and unable to speak coherently, Margaret relaxed a little. "Did you call the hacienda or tell a town official of your need?"

She shook her head dumbly.

"Elena, dear, my mission in life is to rescue children's lives from ungodliness and place them in respectable homes. You'll be able to have other children in the future." She ignored the wild eyes and pathetic form lying on the dirt walkway. "I don't know if you can understand this, Elena, but the truth about your baby is that she is dead. She died after you left the clinic this morning."

The words hit a nerve in the girl's confused mind.

"Died? She didn't die. She's in your house. I want my baby." With a cry, Elena struggled to her feet. "I want my baby."

"No, she really did die." Margaret reached into her pocket and unfolded a paper and thrust it into Elena's face. It was a death certificate. The words blurred, but Elena made out her own name and the words 'Baby Tapia'. She fainted.

When she aroused, she was lying near the road and the door to the clinic was closed. Rising, she walked down to the Pan American highway and wandered slowly home.

Chapter 35

E arly Wednesday morning, Ramon and Isabel arrived at the clinic. Peeking through the window, they saw Elena's bed had been made up. Running to the door, they knocked briskly. Lucia opened it and, seeing who stood there, rang a bell which sounded in the main house several meters away.

Isabel wandered toward the patients' room but Lucia blocked the way.

"Senorita Margaret will be here in a moment. Will you please wait?"she requested coldly.

Isabel gave Lucia a dark stare, but turned back to where Ramon stood. In a matter of moments, a door in the kitchen opened and Margaret approached, acting perturbed.

"Buenos dias," she said roughly. "I'm very busy."

"Buenos dias," they chorused.

"We have come for Elena Martinez Tapia," said Isabel. "She delivered a girl-child on Sunday."

"I told you to come for her on Tuesday. She's not here."

The couple were shocked speechless. Shaking her head, Isabel finally found her voice. "What do you mean? You told us to return on Wednesday, not Tuesday. Here we are. You say Elena is not in the clinic?"

"That's what I said. She left yesterday."

Ramon stepped forward. "I don't understand. How did she leave? Where did she go?"

Disdainfully, Margaret put her hand on her hips.

"I don't know what happened to the girl. How she got home is not my concern."

Isabel and Ramon shrugged their shoulders and turned to each other.

Margaret ushered them out and shut the door.

"I feel funny about this." Ramon shook his head. "The American told us Wednesday, not Tuesday. She made a point of telling us. I am confused."

"Shall we call the United States and tell Senor Luis?"

"No, let's wait. We can check around the plaza. I'm not sure where her family lives. However, if she did stay over she probably found a ride this morning and is right now back at the hacienda. We probably just missed each other."

Isabel wrung her hands. "Yes, no doubt. Poor little girl. To think she had to go through all this by herself."

Ramon chewed on his lower lip and grabbed the wheel tightly, avoiding potholes as they drove up and down the streets, searching.

"I know Senor Perez is going to be upset that we were not with her."

"Yes."

They stopped and asked a few people about Elena, but no one knew where she was.

"We're strangers to them," Isabel complained, after their fourth stop. "But, I feel strongly that Elena isn't here."

"Let's go on to the hacienda," agreed Ramon. "We're wasting time here."

The trip seemed to take forever but upon their arrival they found Elena hadn't been there nor had anyone seen her. They drove to Quito immediately and called the United States. Luis said he would leave for South America very early the next morning and would arrive in Quito just after noon.

Frustrated and frightened, Ramon and Isabel neglected their duties and sat sadly the rest of the day in Tulcachi waiting for Elena. After they had left Quito, they returned to Pachuca and had driven through the plaza asking more questions, but no clear answer was received. No one seemed to know where Elena was.

Luis arrived the next day. He was beyond reasoning when they related the story. Ramon drove quickly back to the hacienda under Luis' instructions, but Elena was nowhere to be found.

Luis decided to visit Margaret. Ramon drove him to Pachuca. Jumping from the car, Luis ran to the door and began banging loudly. Lucia opened it, smiling, as Margaret appeared behind her. The nurse asked him into the kitchen, after he introduced himself, and invited him to take a chair.

"What may I do for you, Senor Perez? I have heard a great deal about your hacienda."

His blue eyes blazed with impatience.

"I'm here about Elena Tapia. I understand she left here with her baby on Tuesday, but I've not been able to locate her."

"Yes, she did leave here, but not with the baby."

"He leaned forward in dismay. "Not with the baby? What do you mean?"

"I mean she didn't have the baby with her."

Sagging backwards, his head pounded. "Why? What happened that she would leave without the baby?"

"Because the baby died."

"Died?" he responded stupidly.

"It was hopelessly premature and didn't survive more than thirty-six hours." Shaking her head sadly, she reached into her pocket. "Here's the death certificate."

Luis studied it. There was Elena's name and Baby Tapia spelled out on the line designated for the child's name. He lost hope. "Oh, dios mio, help her."

He stumbled from the clinic and into the car. Through tears of grief, he explained to Ramon and Isabel.

"Why didn't the Senorita tell us when we were here yesterday?" sobbed Isabel.

They all shook their heads, unable to comprehend the news. "Where could she be?" Luis mumbled.

"Perhaps she went to Carlos' uncle's house in Quito," offered Ramon.

"Of course." Luis sat upright. "We must go to Quito. That's where she is."

They drove off. In his bewilderment, he failed to ask Margaret if he could view the baby, and attend some type of ceremony. That omission struck him several days later; and it would plaque him for the rest of his life.

He and his companions raced to Quito. After an extensive search they located Jose's home, but were stunned to hear Elena had not turned to them for refuge. In an effort to calm Jose and Carlota, Luis promised to call them the minute he learned where Elena was.

They returned to the hacienda. No one had seen her. Luis called his workers together and told them to be ready at dawn to form a search party. They were to walk every route from Tulcachi to Pachuca, searching inch by inch for Elena.

He spent the night in the living room, wringing his hands and pacing the floor. He blamed himself for leaving her. He was angry with Isabel for not insisting on staying with Elena. It was Ramon's fault for not returning Tuesday to check on her. His mind refused to function any longer; in sheer exhaustion, he sat on the sofa. Finally, just before dawn, as he started to fall into a stuporous sleep, he knew where she was. Wrapping his poncho about him, he walked slowly out the back door. Dragging his feet, his heart pounding in his ears, he stumbled through the pasture behind the house and up the steep hillside to the unusual ledge jutting from the edge of the ridge. Under the two eucalyptus trees the earth still appeared fresh where they had buried Carlos. Luis knew he would find her nearby and as he searched in the predawn light, he saw her lying beside one of the trees. Time stood still. He heard the birds singing, announcing the morning's arrival. Roosters crowed in the distant barnyard. Looking down across the valley, it struck him why Carlos had so loved this spot. He watched the tip of Mt. Cotapoxi light up with a blazing orange glow, and in the distance Mt. Pichincha turned from grey to green. He didn't want to look at Elena. Not yet. A thousand memories flooded his mind and each one reflected her laughter and joy. There would be no remembrance of her sorrow. He resolved to keep it that way.

Turning his back on the sunlight that had begun to engulf Quito, he forced himself to walk to her. Exposure in the harsh, cold mountain nights had sapped her life; he was stunned at her condition. In her grief she had torn her clothes; and her long, black hair framed her face widly. But it was her face that captured his attention. In death, it was finally at peace. More so than he had seen it since Carlos' death. He took off his poncho and laid it across her body and from somewhere in the depths of his being, a low moan escaped as he lay beside her and wept.

Book 5   *Margaret*

Chapter 36

Margaret dropped the curtain into place and sighed deeply. She couldn't remember when she had been so badly frightened. Who would have dreamt Luis would have returned so quickly from his mother's bedside in the United States?

"You're lucky he didn't ask to see the baby's body." Lucia spoke in perfect English behind her.

With a startled jump the nurse stomped her right foot and turned. "Will you stop sneaking up behind me?" She glared at the Indian for a moment. "Why would he have asked to see the body? I think I handled things very well."

"I don't like it." Lucia's small, dark eyes closed for a moment. "You should never have taken this baby. There are too many important people involved. Rolando, Luis, Geoff . . . ."

"I need this baby. Did you check on her in my bedroom like I asked you to?"

"Of course."

"Look." The nurse rummaged through a large pocket in her uniform. Transferring a wadded handkerchief to the opposite pocket, she retrieved a piece of notebook paper. Unfolding it, she pushed it toward the Indian.

"A family in Maryland needs a baby girl. And look what they're willing to pay for her. We can have the kid in their home in six weeks."

"I just want to get her out of here. She makes me nervous."

"Why? Both Elena and Luis believe she's dead. Rolando is too drunk to care. Elena's parents are dead and Geoff is certainly no threat. His character is so weak, he'd never do anything about it. Her uncle and aunt were against Elena's marriage to Carlos so they'll never ask about the baby."

"I don't know. I've had a funny feeling about this since Elena started her prenatal care here. She's been like a splinter in my hand."

"Yes, and a thorn in my side. Well, Elena will never find out. I have even made sure the little girl will never know where she's from. My lawyer will extract a promise from the couple in Maryland that they will never tell the child where she was born. They'll just say her family lived in Mexico or some other Latin American country. In that way, even when she is old enough to show interest in her birthplace she will never know it was in Pachuca, Ecuador. You see?"

Lucia shook her head in resignation while Margaret returned the paper to her pocket.

"Now, I should call the lawyer. He'll just have to take care of the baby at his house. I agree, too. I want her out of here as soon as possible."

Book 6   *Rolando*

Chapter 37

Rolando woke with a start, pushing away the hand shaking his shoulder. Opening a bleary eye, he saw the young maid, standing nervously over him.

"What's the matter?" He muttered irritably, the effects of last night's party still clouding his mind.

"Elena's gone."

"Elena? Gone where?" He attempted to rise to his elbow and sank back.

"Her bed hasn't been slept in. I went to wake her for school and she's not here." The young girl apprehensively scratched her head.

Rolando groaned and put his face in the pillow. "She probably went to the store for something."

She pulled at her long hair. "No, I would know that. I think she ran away."

"What?" His head came up. "What did you say?"

"I think she ran away." The girl repeated, stepping back.

Rolando stared at her. "Why would you think that?" He sat up straight.

"I just think so." Her voice trailed to a whisper.

"Where are my brothers?" His eyes swept the unmade empty beds.

"They're getting ready for school."

"Leave me. I'm getting up. We'll see about this." After her exit Roland crawled out of bed, his heart thumping hard. Hurriedly dressing, he headed for the back of the house.

His three brothers were finishing a breakfast of bread and coffee as he entered the kitchen.

"Have you seen Elena?" he demanded.

Geoff set his coffee cup down and shook his head. "Not me. I thought maybe she was at Aunt Mariana's."

Roberto and Pablo shrugged their shoulders and elbowed each other smiling mischievously at their brother's tousled hair.

"She probably is, but Marta says she thinks she ran away," Rolando glared, ignoring their teasing.

The three sat stunned for a moment, then all eyes turned toward Marta who had just appeared out of breath in the doorway.

"I ran up to your Aunt Mariana's. They haven't seen her."

"Madre mia." Roberto exclaimed.

Rolando found a chair and sank onto it. "Roberto, you and Pablo go on to the University. Geoff, before you go to class today, run up to the colegio and see if by chance one of her schoolmates knows anything."

"What are you going to do, Rolando?" asked Geoff, nodding.

With jaw set, the man pounded one fist into the palm of his other hand. "I'm going to find Carlos. I have a terrible feeling that they may have run off together."

"Oh, no," cried Pablo jumping to his feet nearly knocking his cup of coffee to the floor. "I'll help you find him, Rolando."

"The best way to help me is for you to go to school." A terrible look of hatred glazed Rolando's eyes. "I want to find Carlos myself. If it's true they have run away together, I have a feeling they've gone to Quito, and if that be true, I will search every street, every house, and every alley until I find them, even if it takes living there myself."

Chapter 38

T he bus groaned to a halt in a swirl of dust. A dozen children in school uniforms raced for the door, playfully pushing each other aside.

Rolando sat in the rear, watching with a sour expression, resenting their joy.

He and his siblings had ridden to school on this same ancient relic. That had been a precious time. The memories brought quick, hot tears to his eyes and angrily, he brushed them away.

Juan, the slender, travel-worn bus driver rose from his seat to check the aisles for any items left by the children. Looking up, Juan noticed Rolando and gave him a small nod.

"Rolando, you're home. I'm not taking the bus beyond the plaza this trip."

Pulling himself up with a grunt, Rolando returned the nod, handing the driver four sucres he owed for the trip.

"Thank you," he mumbled, descending the steps. Standing on the curb, he looked around with a mixture of disgust and despair. Three small children laughed with delight as they jumped in and out of an empty cement fountain built in the center of the plaza. There was no water in Pachuca at this time of the day. During the rainy season there might be enough to last through midmorning, but without rain, the residents were fortunate if they had running water for one hour in the early morning. It was important to catch and store the precious liquid before dawn. For many years, the same man had bicycled up the mountainside in the hours before daylight in order to open the pipes to release the water stored in the dilapidated reservoir. The water rushed down the mountain, streamed into roadside faucets and into the town proper. He would return later in the morning to stay the flow, leaving Pachuca without water until the following morning. At times, there were problems with the system and water didn't flow for days and finally when it did arrive, it was always cloudy and filled with sediment. Rolando could count the times on his hands that there had been sufficient water to trickle through the rusted pipes into the fountain. Therefore, it had become a recreational habitat for children during the day and a romantic setting for guitar playing serenaders during the chilly, dark evenings.

Rolando watched the children for a time and looked about the brown, scrubby plaza. He was choked with revulsion for this backward town. Quito had water night and day. Quito had class, style and energy. For the past few months he had been living in Quito and working in a downtown hotel, cleaning tables and floors, seizing the opportunity to escape home and memories.

He crossed the dirt road and passed the old grocery story where he had sought refuge so many years ago on the night of Elena's birth. Pain pressed his heart and he feared he would cry again. It was on this very curb he had found Carlos that same night. Now, both were gone. Sorrow and loneliness had long ago been added to the anger he bore. No one could understand the price he had paid for refusing to give permission for his sister's disastrous marriage.

Walking to the saloon, he found a seat in the back and attempted to look uncommunicative.

The saloon keeper approached him.

"Hola, Rolando. I haven't seen you for a long time. Have you been away?"

"Buenas tardes, Raphael. Yes, I've been staying in Quito. Would you please bring me a beer?" Anxious to be left alone, he turned his back slightly and looked away.

Raphael studied him for a moment. "Si, I'll get it."

Rolando snorted inwardly. Everyone in Pachuca knew what had happened with his family. No doubt by the next day, everyone knew that his sister had run away with Carlos.

After he had been served, Rolando sipped his drink carefully. He had no desire to rush home. His mother was very ill, a victim of yet another massive stroke that had left her virtually a vegetable, unable to move, speak or recognize anyone. Geoff still lived in Pachuca in the family home, but everything had changed between the two brothers in the past six months. Rolando could no longer bear to be in the same room with Geoff. Everything he did made Rolando angry. After Geoff graduated from the university, he had married a lovely young girl introduced to him by a friend. Geoff became religious somewhere along the way, attending youth services at a church near the area in Quito called 'Gringaville', a small commune of English-speaking foreigners. There Geoff had met his future wife. After an evangelical wedding, which Rolando had refused to attend, Geoff and Opal moved to Pachuca to care for his mother. It had become unbearable to live in the same house with the do-gooders. Geoff took up the reins of responsibility, driving the family truck and providing for those remaining at home. It seemed to Rolando everything he did was evil in the eyes of Geoff and Opal. Their clean and sacrificial lifestyle, plus their delight in driving to Quito each Sunday to attend church, made Rolando's mode of living look dark and corrupt.

Rolando had left Pachuca a week after Elena's disappearance, escaping to Quito, driven with a desire to find Carlos. Against his family's wishes Roberto had decided to leave his studies and join the military. Pablo might have been a companion to Rolando, but the only thing they had in common was they were both drunks. Pablo had turned to carousing on a scale incomparable to Rolando.

Sipping the warm beer, Rolando looked around the clean, freshly painted room. If nothing else, Raphael took pride in his establishment. Each week, by Monday afternoon the floors and walls had been scrubbed, stripped of the layers of mud and debris left from a busy weekend.

The siesta hour had just ended and the saloon was empty. Small flies darted lazily in the center of the room, forming a misshapen circle, and a cat slept contentedly on a table in the corner. Sometime in the past six months Raphael had purchased an old jukebox which contained only five selections and, except for in the early afternoon, seldom sat quiet.

A shadow of depression settled over Rolando. Why had he come back to this deteriorating town? He had left six months ago to escape the tormenting memories Pachuca offered, hoping a new life in Quito would provide rest for his mind. He had fled, but the peace he sought had always eluded him. Perhaps he had come back to see if by chance, anyone had heard from Elena.

His response at her disappearance had originally been just a burning anger and need to strike back. The energy of his emotional rage cost him; he fought fatigue and physical illness daily. It was costly in other ways, too. His friends began to ignore him. Even his beloved Aunt Mariana thought it best to let this phase run its course. So when the anger passed, he was left exhausted and alone with his guilt and grief.

He blamed himself for Elena's disappearance. It would have been a thousand times better had he permitted Elena's marriage to Carlos and had them living in Pachuca where he could be near her. Dozens of times he had tried to imagine where they had gone and, finally, he decided they had fled either to Quito to hide in a suburb or to the eastern jungles where they would never be found. For his own peace of mind, he preferred to think they lived in Quito. During his six months there he had scanned the crowds, longing to see Elena to tell her she could come home.

Without a word the saloon keeper brought another beer.

Rolando watched moodily out the front door as the entrance of the dry goods store opened across the road and the young, pregnant clerk stepped out to the street, yawning and scratching her belly.

Why had he come back? On a whim, he had walked away from his job at the hotel. In spite of his drinking his employer had liked him. His mother's sister had invited him to live with them in Quito and he had jumped at the opportunity only to find that sharing a room with his cousin, Ricardo, was too confining.

Thinking of Elena caused him to remember the night of her birth and how he had walked through this very room with Senora Ernestina in search of his mother. How the circumstances of that night had changed his life. To his horror he could no longer hold back the tears he had been fighting and quickly turning his head to the wall, he wiped his eyes with the back of his hand. He should never have come back.

He debated where to go. There was no sense in seeking out his parents. They were strangers to him now. He didn't have the emotional strength to begin a relationship with Geoff again. Pablo was so self-centered he couldn't see beyond his own needs. There was no gain in going to his aunt and uncle's home as they tried to hide their disappointment in him, but it was in their eyes, glaring at him in spite of their loving words and touches they gave.

There was only one who really cared, one who would welcome

him with open arms, and one who loved him despite his obsessions and weaknesses. Gulping down another beer, he left several sucres on the table without glancing at Raphael and walked into the sunshine. To avoid passing the home of his aunt and uncle, he walked another route along the outskirts of Pachuca. It took him on a road above the town, where he could look down over it. He was mildly amused to see that nothing had changed. The same potholes decorated the roads, playing havoc with the few vehicles owned by townspeople. Crumbling roofs and missing mud brick would probably never be repaired. The same cheap mementos that had adorned windows a year ago still hung by faded ribbons. Only he had changed. He believed the people of Pachuca merely existed. They lived to eat, breed and die. What a despondent thought. No wonder he was depressed. And after he tried to break away, here he was again. He would grow old and never be able to escape its grasp. Panic rose in him. He was one of them. The thought terrified and sickened him. What had happened to his dreams and his future?

One person had changed all his plans. One assuming, aggressive person named Carlos had twisted his world inside out. Revenge was keeping him alive. Hatred. Even his loneliness, weariness and depression had been fed by this hatred. He was now able to say he hated both of them: Carlos and Elena. The knowledge was sweet; it gave him purpose. He hated his sister. He would destroy her along with her husband. Why hadn't she listened to his words of love and promise? How could she have left her home and loved ones? Or broken her vows of completing her education? Despite his bitter feelings toward her, he acknowledged that because of her young age, it was impossible for Elena to know the meaning of love. Before Carlos seduced her, she had been a sweet, innocent child willing to obey her older brother's simple demands.

Trudging a mile to Pachuca's suburb, he knocked at the door of the hut set upon the small rise.

Joel opened the door, blinked and an involuntary frown crossed his face.

"Buenas tardes, Joel. Is your mama home?"

"Buenas tardes. Si, she is behind the house helping Yolanda with the wash."

"Gracias." Rolando turned, leaving the small, concerned child standing in the doorway.

Rolando was nervous. He knew he could be making a serious error, but there seemed to be no other way. In the distance, he saw two bent figures beating clothes on the rocks. Alternately, they rubbed the clothes with a cake of blue soap until the materials were covered with a heavy lather, then they beat them on same rocks, and rinsed them in the stream. Rolando watched as they hung the clothes on bushes and tree branches to dry.

He walked to the stream where they worked.

Yolanda looked up first and with a quick, disapproving glance, she turned to Laura. "Mama, we have a guest."

Laura raised her head and a flash of happy surprise swept over her face. "Rolando!" She threw the piece of clothing she had been washing on the rock and stood, brushing back stray hairs from her forehead with the back of her wet hand. "Rolando," she repeated. "I've been worried about you. I'm glad you're here."

Smiling, he disregarded Yolanda's scowl. "I hoped we can talk."

"Of course. Yoli, please go to the house and see after the boys and dinner."

The girl stood and walked away without a word.

Laura's rough, red hands again brushed straying hair from her eyes.

Rolando studied her. In her favor, she had warm, hungry eyes, and a presentable though worn, lined face. A shy smile revealed that she still had her own teeth. Strong and wiry, her body showed signs of childbearing and arduous field labor.

For a moment he felt panic and a desire to run, but quickly he pressed back the thought. He needed her. "There is nowhere for me to go, Laura. I am so alone," he confessed.

Exhaling a deep, happy sigh, she smiled and held out her hand. "Oh, Rolando. My home is your home. You will never have to be alone again."

Chapter 39

Sunlight filtered through evaporating clouds and Rolando ventured out from under the canopy of trees where he had tried vainly to stay dry during a torrential rain that had just soaked the earth.

Farmers would rejoice at the relief from the drought that had troubled the Tumbaco Valley for several weeks. The town proper would have water flowing in the pipes for an extra hour tomorrow.

He didn't mind being caught in the rain. In fact he welcomed it. For a short period of time he felt cleaner, and by sheer mind power, he could imagine his soul being cleansed. But it was short-lived. He was a fool. There was no soul-healing in rain. There was no soul-cleansing anywhere. As much as he resisted it, the fact remained that he was slowly beginning to realize he would have to learn to live with guilt and despair the rest of his life. What a fool he had been to think living with Laura would erase his discontentment.

Standing by the stream, watching the birds returning to their flight among the boughs of the trees, he tilted the whiskey bottle. Whiskey was his salvation; his escape; his escape from Carlos. Carlos. Carlos was always with him. He could remember having no problems before Carlos. There was only one emotion greater than his sorrowful depression and that was his hatred toward Carlos, the hatred that had expanded since the day of his return to Pachuca. Now, seldom thinking of Elena, his small world encompassed Carlos. Incredible that he should seek refuge with Carlos' mother. It was almost as though he needed to control something that belonged to his enemy.

At this point, it was almost impossible to analyze his feelings concerning the past three months with Laura. Much of the time, he had been drunk or she had been away working. The woman willingly paid his way and tolerated his habits. With little doubt, she truly loved him, and this only added another layer of guilt on the heavy burden he was bearing.

During the day, he drank whiskey in a saloon close to the house or sat drinking by the stream. Anything to avoid being alone with the children who disliked him. He, in turn, cared little for them.

Throwing the empty bottle into a bush, he looked at his watch. Laura would soon be home. Plodding through the muddy corn field, he felt dulled by the liquor he had and looked forward to the break in monotony that Laura would bring. She could reach his remaining response to tenderness. By no means did he love her or even respect her, but in a twisted way, he needed her.

Scraping the mud from his feet on a piece of rag laying beside the house Rolando pushed open the door and walked to the fire to dry his damp clothes. Yolanda was removing eating utensils from the wooden shelf to ready the table for dinner. The two boys sat on the floor playing with bright colored airplanes. Each child turned to watch him for a moment, then they returned purposely muffling their play.

Rolando glanced at his watch again as he heard the door open behind him. He turned slowly.

Laura entered, her eyes searching for him immediately. She gave him a sweet smile and exhaled a deep sigh, glad to be home.

"Mama, Mama." Yolanda ran to her, taking a tin pail that had contained her mother's midmorning meal.

"Hola, Yoli." Patting her on the arm, she yielded to the show of affection from her daughter.

Rolando surveyed the scene with displeasure at Yolanda's mood swing. Jerman and Joel merely nodded their greetings. He was aware of their love for Laura, but he knew they shunned her as punishment because of her desire for him. Rolando delighted in her struggle trying to satisfy him and yet care for the children.

"What do you have there?" she asked softly, turning in her sons' direction.

"A toy airplane," Jerman said curtly, frowning to cover the look of love in his eyes.

"Oh, a toy airplane," she replied absently, as she glanced Rolando's way.

He smirked at the gleam in her eyes.

"How was your day, Rolando?" Moving to his side, she laid her hand on his arm and looked up at him. Rolando glanced past her at Jerman's downcast face, his eyes twinkling.

He shrugged, ignored her hand, and turned to face the fire. "It was all right. Not much to do when it's raining."

Feeling rebuffed, she walked to the table. "Yoli, is dinner ready? I'm hungry."

"Yes, Mama. Please sit and I'll serve you."

"Joel, Jerman, come. Rolando, are you hungry?" Laura called over her shoulder.

Yolanda placed a plate piled with bread and cheese in the middle of the table, followed by a platter of boiled ears of corn. Rolando watched her under lowered lids, as she watched him. She needed to bring the food that was simmering on the fire, but she refused to move as long as he stood in her way. When he grew tired of the waiting game, he made his way toward the table while, hurriedly, she carried plates to the pots hanging over the flames and filled them with boiled potatoes and rice, and returned them to her family. Quickly placing the skillet on a grill, she fried enough eggs for each of them. Standing to one side, she then waited until everyone had eaten before she took her own plate and joined the group.

Rolando chewed on a cob of corn and reflected on the dinner situation. For him, this was the most uncomfortable time of the day. Laura refused to yield to the one request that the children eat at an earlier time.

If he had only Yolanda to contend with, he felt the situation would improve, but the cold hatred emanating from the boys was, indeed, disconcerting. At first he had felt a fondness for Yolanda simply because she was female. There was little in her physical makeup that reminded him of Elena, but at times when his guard was down, she reminded him of his sister's childhood years. Yolanda's resentment toward him dredged up painful recollection of Elena's hatred when he had driven Carlos away from her.

He recalled one afternoon when he had entered the house quietly and overheard Yolanda and the boys talking together in the inner room. A strange twist of pain had leapt in his heart when Yolanda spoke out against him.

"Everything has changed since Carlos left. There's no more laughter or talking at the dinner table."

Rolando heard the bitter snorts of agreement from the boys as she continued. "Mama even seems different. She's quieter, but do you notice how much she smiles at him?"

Frowning, Rolando was surprised at the disappointment he felt at the contempt in her voice.

The high, reedy voice continued. "At least Mama doesn't go to parties anymore."

"Sure. Because she wants to stay with him." Jerman spewed bitterness.

"I want her to spend more time with us," Joel mourned.

"Carlos was like a father to us. I never thought of him as a brother." Her mature reasoning belied her age. "I am so lonesome. I just wish we knew where he went. I'd go after him."

Rolando relaxed at the closed door. He had questioned Laura and the children at length as to Carlos' whereabouts and received only negative replies. Perhaps they didn't know where he had gone.

"Carlos doesn't want us with him or he would have taken us along," reasoned Joel.

"Maybe he didn't want us to leave Mama alone."

"She's not alone. He's here," grumbled Jerman.

"We never have fun anymore." Yolanda's voice lowered for a moment.

"Remember when Carlos made us popcorn?" said Joel.

"Yes," said Yolanda. "At least Rolando doesn't stay in the house all day. I hate it when I have to cook breakfast for you two and he's still sleeping in Mama's bed. I never know if he's watching me. At least I can go down to the creek and wash the clothes."

"Does he ever bother you, Yoli? I mean, does he try to follow you when you go to the creek?" Jerman's ten-year-old mind was suddenly alert. "Or does he touch you?"

Yolanda puzzled for a moment and replied, "No."

Outside the door, Rolando shook his head in disgust and considered bursting into the room to slap Jerman, but he decided against it in hopes of learning more undisclosed information.

"Do you ever wonder who our real father is?" Yolanda asked hesitantly.

"Why would you want to know that?" Joel asked angrily.

"I've wondered that too," Jerman said. "I think she's worried that Rolando may be our father."

Rolando heard a pounding as Joel jumped to his feet and kicked at the floor. "You make me sick."

"It makes me sick too, but I remember when Mama brought Rolando home many times after her parties."

Uncomfortable, Rolando fidgeted behind the door. He had many times wondered the same thing.

Laura broke into his thoughts.

"Where did you say you found those airplanes?" She looked up from her plate to attempt a conversation.

"We didn't find them. We made them in school," muttered Joel.

"That must be something new they're doing. I don't remember you ever making anything like that before." She sighed. "I guess the school will want money for supplies again."

"No. Senorita Jill comes to the school and brings the paper, paste and scissors. We don't have to pay for anything."

Rolando's hand stopped in midair. "Who is Senorita Jill?"

"An American. She used to work with Senorita Margaret, the nurse," replied the sullen Yolanda.

"You probably mean Lucia. She's not a gringa." He commented, loading his mouth.

"No." Joel retorted, with a hint of disdain. "Senorita Jill is a gringa who lives in the house beside Senorita Olivia. She has a little blue pickup and goes to different schools to work with the children."

"Oh," A light showed in Rolando's eyes. "I've seen her driving the pickup." He felt Laura watching him from behind eyes filled with jealous fears.

"Yes. She has classes after school sometimes," explained Jerman sitting up on the bench. "Mama, we thought you'd let us go someday."

"Perhaps," she replied absently, her mind focused on Rolando.

"Why would Jill live like a poor Indian in Pachuca when she could live in the United States?" The man sat back and watched Jerman with thoughtful eyes.

"I don't know. The people say she loves being here in this country and she cares for us."

A snort of disbelief spurted from the man's mouth. He reached for a roll and chewed off a large piece.

"Well, she does," retorted Jerman, the anger burning in the pit of his stomach.

"Maybe she does," intercepted Laura as she watched an explosive confrontation developing. "It doesn't matter. And we'll see about you children going with her someday."

"It does matter, old woman." Rolando spoke, narrowing his eyes. "No one does anything for a poor, no-good Indian without getting something in return. Don't tell me she's not making money, or should I say, taking money from you poor beggars."

"What do you mean, us poor beggars? What are you?" Jerman rose, fire flashing in his eyes.

Joel sank deeper on the bench. Yolanda watched wide-eyed as Laura half rose.

Rolando stared at the boy for several long moments, then rose to his feet, and stomped to the front door.

Laura was behind him, pulling on his arm. "Rolando, please come back. He didn't mean it."

The man towered over her, sneering. He pushed her back to the floor. "Take your hands from me. I'm sick of you, old woman, and all your bastards. I need room and peace."

Laura lifted herself up from where she had fallen. Tears wet her face as Joel and Yolanda ran to her side. Jerman remained in the same spot, a smile touching his face.

Rolando stormed from the house slamming the door. Bouncing down the muddy, irregular steps, he stopped on the road. A mild afternoon greeted him, the sun was now shining brightly. He stomped to the store, where he counted out several bills that Laura had given him and bought two bottles of whiskey. He started up the mountain, searching for a bush to hide behind while he drank himself to sleep.

He felt pressured and trapped by Laura. She cared too much. How could he be so loved and yet be so lonely? It was the children. Too many insufferable children. Everything would be all right without those unbearable children watching his every move with suspicious eyes.

A large clump of bushes sat off the road beyond a row of houses above the little suburb where they lived. He looked about to see if anyone was watching and then ducked behind the bushes, carefully placing the liquor inside. Making himself comfortable, he opened one bottle and drank deeply from it.

A bit of his anger dissolved and his chin trembled. He had no home; no friends; no family; no one to love him. His only friend was the bottle. Rubbing it affectionately with his thumb, a tear rolled down his cheek.

Again, he was alone. The thought renewed his anger. He was alone and it was Carlos' fault. If it had not been for Carlos, nothing would have changed in his life. He would still be home with his family, with his sister and with his friends. Now because of his enemy, the snake, he sat behind this bush alone, his only companion a bottle. Tears rolled freely down his face as he continued to drink.

A truck traveling toward Pachuca woke him. Daylight was emerged above the towering hills and he could see the moon dipping behind Mt. Pichincha. He sat upright, cramped and wet from the heavy dew, and saw the two empty bottles beside him. Jumping to his feet, his head whirled and stomach lurched as he retched into the bushes.

Dejected, he picked his way to the road and wandered toward Laura's house, stopping only to search for a few pennies to buy bread at the little store. As he drew near, chewing slowly on the bread, he stopped. He couldn't go back to that house, to the cold, hostile feelings, the clutching woman and the disapproving children.

Turning, he retraced his steps to the small grocery store. Sitting on a bench inside the door, he begged a beer and promised to pay later. The store was crowded with people buying drinks and supplies. Suddenly, he remembered it was Sunday. Laura would be home all day. He ordered another drink. Now that his anger had dissolved, he couldn't recall what had happened to make him upset. The only thing he could remember was Laura's pleading eyes. It was just another problem. His life was plagued with problems. Carlos was to blame for it.

Three hours and several begged drinks later, reluctantly, he had decided to return to the house. Surprised, he saw a taxi parked outside, the driver sleeping behind the wheel.

Hating the intrusion of visitors, he climbed the steps and walked into the house without speaking a word. He marched to the fire delighted with the reaction he stirred. The shocked hush that fell over the room told him he had not been spoken of previously. Turning, he saw a brooding teenager obviously not pleased at being there. A man and woman resembling each other returned his stare from the other side of the room. Short, fat and middle-aged, the woman was dressed in a bright yellow blouse trimmed with flounces. Her wide black skirt was long and trimmed with a ruffle. She had black curly hair and wore dark red lipstick. Rolando thought of a carnival he had attended as a child.

The man was also short and fat. He was dressed in a dark suit that looked uncomfortably tight. Perspiration glistened on his forehead.

Rolando saw at once that the man studying him had already formed a negative opinion. Inwardly Rolando shrank. Like a silent signal, Laura's three children moved away from the center of the group and as the boys went outdoors, Yolanda retreated to a corner.

Rolando walked to a shelf and pulled down a bowl, while ignoring Laura's eyes. He walked back to the fire, to ladle out soup. In this simple way, he wanted to show the intruders that he belonged here.

Uncomfortable small talk filtered through the invisible net that had been thrown over the group. Shortly, the man and woman rose and, followed by their eager son, made their way to the door. Laura followed them as Yolanda scurried into her bedroom

As Rolando began eating his second bowl of soup, he sneered with hatred for Laura. Why did he feel jealous when she was with someone else? He hated her. He wished she would go away, yet he wanted her nearby. At the same time he desired her, he was also repelled by her. At least the uninvited guests were leaving. A sense of power swept through him. By his mere appearance he had not only caused the visitors to leave, but he had caused Laura to quake with anxiety and the children to become stiff and silent. His strength and manhood accomplished this. This was his home and when he was present, he was in control. A smile crossed his face and he rubbed the stubble on his chin. What was taking Laura so long? He looked through the high, small window and caught a glimpse of the yellow taxi. They were still here. That meant she was still talking. Resentment grew again. How could she leave him alone without a thought?

Suddenly, a surge of anger rose in him that included Geoff.

Treading the floor, bitterness churned in his heart against the woman who kept him; the child who hid from him in the next room; his father who trusted Geoff more than he trusted his eldest son; his mother who lay in her own cramped world, and against Carlos, always Carlos. His enemy was constantly there to taunt him. These days it seemed Carlos was always on his mind and he was having a hard time remembering Elena. She lived in a former life, a world that existed centuries ago. Her face was a blur, difficult to recall. But not Carlos. He was ever present, with features as clearly defined in his mind as the fat man who had just left the house. Where was Laura? With an energy fed by exasperation, he stomped to the door and flung it open. Walking to the edge of the rise, he peered down just as the fat man looked up. Their eyes met as he leaned forward to kiss Laura on the cheek. After a long moment, he led his companion, the woman, to the taxi, where the bored boy sat waiting.

Rolando and Laura watched the taxi race off in a cloud of dust. Laura turned slowly and climbed the crude mud steps to the house, deep in thought.

She seemed changed, somehow. A sharp fear struck him. He watched carefully as she reached the top step and looked up, seeing him. Her reaction of pleasure set his mind at rest and with renewed dislike, he stomped into the house. Following, she looked for him.

"Where were you last night?" Walking to his side by the fire, she placed her hand hesitantly on his back.

He glared at her but didn't shrug off her hand. He needed her touch as much as he needed to hurt her.

"I do have other friends, you know." He smiled at her involuntary reflex of jealousy. "Who were those people? You didn't tell me we were going to have company."

"I didn't know they were coming. He's my brother, Jose, from Quito. With him were his wife, Carlota, and Alfredo, my nephew."

Rolando threw back his head and laughed. "That fat man is your brother? And the woman who resembles a sow, his wife? What an ugly family you have."

His taunting remarks hit their mark and she moved away without a word. Silence blanketed the room, save for the murmur of the fire and distant Sunday festivities. The need to hurt her was spent and replaced with the more urgent desire for liquor. Realizing that he had just cut off his supply for an afternoon of leisurely drinking, he decided he would have to put aside his pride and ask for money.

The urgency grew stronger each minute. Licking his lips, he turned to the bed where she sat with her eyes locked in a stare. He touched her arm.

"Laura, I'm sorry. Why don't we go out for the afternoon and visit some of our friends at the saloon in the plaza? Perhaps we can dance a little."

He saw her eyes light up, and knew she wouldn't think to question his change in attitude. She never seemed to wonder at his mood swings and certainly didn't have the ability to withstand his desires. From the first day she had drunkenly danced with him in the streets of Pachuca, she had admitted she loved him. Thankfully, she had never mentioned marriage to him, but she readily admitted that his presence in her home was like a dream come true. She had bemoaned the fact that her children didn't care for him, but she voiced her faith that they would someday mature and understand her need for a companion. He was careful not to dampen her hopes, because living with her eliminated his need to wander the streets searching for companionship. Settling himself in with her took care of his physical comforts. She admitted it mattered little to her that he needed her only for these reasons. He had to admire her willingness to work long hours each day in the hot sunshine to provide for him. His guilty conscience was soothed, however, because he seemed to fulfill a need in her.

"Maybe we could stay here. It would be more comfortable." She suggested.

Anger sliced through him. With difficulty he controlled himself, the need for liquor consuming him.

"No. A beer sounds good to me right now. Let's go."

"I'll have Yolanda go for something to drink and then I'll tell her to leave us alone."

He began to protest, then calmed himself. Perhaps it would be better. At least he wouldn't have to appear in public with the old woman.

"All right. If she will hurry." Smiling his charming best, he touched her face. "Perhaps Yolanda can bring whiskey as long as she's going."

"Of course." She returned his look with a knowing smile.

He hated himself. When she smiled like that, it was as if his innermost thoughts lay exposed before her.

Patting his arm, she sat on the edge of the bed and yelled. "Yoli, please go to the store and buy us six beers and one bottle of whiskey."

After a delay of several moments, the child stood in the doorway, blinking sleep from her eyes.

"Yoli?" Laura softly pleaded. "If you go, I'll give you extra to buy a sweet for yourself."

"I'll go. And I'll stay away. Don't worry." Dimness clouded the hurt, tortured eyes. "Just give me the money."

Laura stood and gratefully put her hand inside her blouse to withdraw several bills that had been hidden against her breast. "Hurry, Yoli."

The girl walked stiffly to the door without glancing at Rolando. Laura trailed behind, closing the door after her.

An hour later, with the whiskey bottle half empty and two beers consumed, they were feeling mellow. He liked Laura when she was half drunk for she showed her appreciation willingly. Yolanda had returned only to dump a basket of filled bottles inside the door and run.

Sitting at the table, Rolando sipped a drink and felt the relaxation and warmth of a home, food, drink and a woman who loved him. A smile formed on his lips as he remembered Jose's face when he had filled his bowl with soup. He tried to imagine how Laura's brother and sister-in-law had pondered his place in Laura's life. Perhaps they spoke of it right now with disgust painted on their pious faces. He glanced at Laura and saw she had slumped sideways on the bench, mouth drooping open. Picking up the whiskey bottle, he walked to the bed and swallowed a few more sips. Then he fell into a drunken slumber.

It was dark outside when he awoke. Laura had moved onto the bed with him and was still asleep. He sat up drowsily and felt for the whiskey bottle. It was empty. The warm glow of the fire cast shadowy figures on the wall as he glanced around the room. Yolanda sat on a bench looking into the fire.

"Yolanda, is there more beer on the table?" he asked, as nicely as possible, needing her help.

Turning her head slowly, she cast a haughty look at the table and rose. She found two bottles, opened them and passed the warm beer to him. He gave her his most charming smile and took a long swallow.

Downing the first beer, he sat back against the wall and thought again of the day. Still relishing his effect on Laura's family, he thought again of how no doubt they were still talking about him. The fat little man would return to Quito and tell all of Laura's cousins, her aunts and uncles of the impressive man living in Laura's home. He might even tell Carlos. A dull buzz stirred in his head and he stopped breathing. Carlos. In a flash, his muddled mind was clear and sharp. That's what they were talking about when he arrived and then again outside by the taxi. Carlos.

He had searched each of his own relative's homes and knew Carlos and Elena were not there, but he had not thought of Laura having relatives in Quito. She had never mentioned a family. Of course. It made sense. Carlos and Elena were living in Quito, either with Laura's brother or nearby. Looking over at Laura in her drunken sleep, he felt more hatred for her than he thought possible. Shaking her awake, he leaned close to her face.

"You knew all along that Carlos was in Quito, Laura. Get up and tell me where your deceiving son is."

The woman, startled out of a deep sleep, could not fathom what was happening.

"Wake up, you fool woman! Tell me where your brother lives so I can find your worthless son."

A portentous reality swept over her and she was afraid. She tried to sit up as he pulled her toward him. "Where is he? Do you hear?" he screamed into her face.

"I don't know where he is, Rolando!" she screamed, pleading.

He struck her across the mouth, and she cried out in surprised pain. Yolanda ran from the next room and struck his back in fierce hatred.

"Leave her alone! Don't hit my Mama!"

He heaved an arm backward, and catching the child across the stomach, doubling her over and knocking her to the dirt floor. Rolling in agony, she crawled to a bench and lay her head on the cool wood.

Laura howled with shocked rage and tore at him as he turned back to her to hold her in a firm grip.

"Why didn't you tell me where he was? You know how I looked for him."

"I don't know where Carlos is."

Blood spurted from her nose as he slapped her hard, a spark of delight lighting his eyes. "Where is he? Is he living at your fat brother's house?" he yelled at her silence. "Well?"

She crawled on the bed, tearing away from his grip to wipe her dripping nose. He stared in disgust. "Are you going to answer?"

Silence.

Slowly, he stood on unsteady legs and walked to where Yolanda sat against the bench. Stooping, he took hold of her hair and pulled her up.

"No, no. I'll tell you," cried Laura, jumping into action. "They're living in Playas. Carlos is a groundskeeper at the Hotel Humboldt. They live next door in a cabin."

"Are you lying to me? Playas? Where is Playas?" Letting go of the girl, he turned back to the woman.

"It's south of Guayaquil, on the coast."

He stood, perplexed. Never had he imagined they would run so far. Of course he hadn't been able to find them. An ugly smile curled his lips and he drank from the other beer bottle. Sitting next to the fire, he ignored the sobbing woman behind him. Playas. In the morning, he would find out just where Playas is and go there. He had a score to settle against a man who was responsible for ruining his life. As for Elena, he scarcely thought of her, nor did he have any feeling for her. His hatred for Carlos had erased his love for his sister. A foreign feeling of joy stirred in his emotions and he felt like laughing. The time was fast approaching when he could deal with his enemy. How good it felt.

He heard Yolanda rise to go to her bedroom and Laura leave to clean her face.

He put more wood on the fire. Pangs of hunger made him realize he had eaten only bread and soup that day. He found a bowl to spoon a thick stew from the simmering pot Yolanda had prepared while he slept.

Laura returned to add the bloodied pillow and top blanket

to a pile of clothes in the next room. He heard soft voices coming from inside the room, but for once felt no twinge of jealousy or fear of being left out.

Suddenly, the front door burst open as Joel and Jerman ran into the house. Rolando looked up with mild disapproval and his mouth fell open as he saw Geoff standing behind them.

Rising, he frowned darkly. "What are you doing here? Get out."

The boys walked to a far wall to watch.

"Rolando, I had to see you."

"I can think of no reason why I should see you."

Geoff looked up at his dirty, unshaven, angry brother. "I have news."

Rolando looked down with a shrug and started to turn away as Geoff grabbed his arm.

"It's Papa."

Rolando shrugged again. "You can give me no news about our Papa that would interest me."

"He's dead."

Laura, standing in the doorway, gasped, while Rolando stared for a few minutes at the floor.

"So? What should I do?"

Geoff closed his eyes for a moment and brushed his hand across his hair.

"Rolando, our Papa is dead. He was killed tonight by a person who hit him with a car and fled. Papa was drunk."

"He's always been drunk."

The lines around Rolando's eyes and mouth emphasized his discontentment; his disillusionment; his overall unhappiness. Suddenly, a picture flashed through his mind. He saw himself happy as a boy. He used to laugh a lot, surrounding himself with his family, being loved and appreciated. He remembered how gently he had cared for his mother and sister. For a moment he remembered how much he had loved his father and longed to have him as a friend. What had gone wrong?

"Rolando, won't you come home for a while to see his body before the funeral, or, at least, visit with Mama?"

Rolando shook the childhood scene from his mind and lashed out. "Why? Mama doesn't know me and where was Papa when I needed him?"

"He wasn't there for any of us. For your sake I think you should come home for a while."

To hide the difficulty he had swallowing the lump rising in his throat, Rolando looked absently at Laura and her children, and then back to Geoff. "When is the funeral?"

"The day after tomorrow at the church. Papa will be at our house until then. Please come."

"Don't look for me. I have other things to do."

Geoff nodded and turned to leave. "Hasta manana." He smiled at Laura and the children.

"Hasta manana," they chorused.

Rolando sat on the bed in silence while everyone but Laura slipped into the next room. She moved slowly to his side.

"I'm sorry about your papa."

When he didn't respond, she reached out to touch his shoulder. "Rolando, I'm sorry."

He jumped at her touch and turned toward her. "Why didn't you tell me he was hiding in Playas?"

Her mouth fell open with surprise as he stood. He bent over until they were standing face to face in the dim light.

Stepping back in fright, she whimpered as she put up her hands in defense against his raised arm.

He looked at her cowering before him and dropped his arm to his side. Stomping to the door, he departed, leaving the filth and stench of the house, vowing never again to return.

Chapter 40

He opened the front door of his family home and stepped into the small hallway. The house was brightly lit and he could hear voices coming from the kitchen. It had been several months since he had left, determined to start a new life in Quito. Now, he saw the foolishness in believing he could find peace there or with Laura. By the time he had walked the distance from her house to his home, he was sure the only reason he had moved in with her in the first place was to discover where Carlos was living and it seemed all ties with her had been broken the moment she had told him. The fact that she must have been aware of Carlos' location all these months and failed to reveal his whereabouts had been the last straw. He determined never to see her again.

Now, to endure his family's disapproving stares during their father's funeral.

The funeral would be the last obstacle between him and his meeting with Carlos.

After that, he would be free to leave for Playas and dispose of his enemy and perhaps bring Elena back where they could begin their life again. Now that he knew where Elena was, she was becoming important to him again. He hoped they could recapture their childhood memories and continue where they had left off. If Carlos was cut out of the picture, Rolando was certain Elena would want to return to Pachuca. Then he could begin driving the truck, take up his responsibilities again, and leave his drinking habits behind. Everything would once again be the same. There were so many pleasant memories here. What a thrill it was to be back home.

He would have to shave and wash before visiting his mother. He walked down the hallway to his bedroom hoping to find his old shaving gear. Opening the door, he stopped short. Standing before the bureau, unfastening the belt to her dress, stood a young woman. Shock showed on her face as she gathered the belt tightly to her midriff.

"Who are you?" she echoed.

"I am Rolando and this is my bedroom. Who are you?" he repeated indignantly.

"I'm Raquel and I'm visiting here until after the funeral. Geoff called me on the telephone tonight and I came immediately from Quito."

"Well, I'm afraid you'll not be staying in my bedroom tonight. I have every intention of sleeping here myself."

Amazement crossed Raquel's face. "You certainly are a rude man. It will be no problem for me to leave. I'll just take my things." She grabbed a few pieces of folded clothing that lay on the bed and placed them in a small suitcase. From the bureau she gathered bottles and an overnight case. In stony silence, she left the room.

He dismissed her without another thought and moved to the bureau to search for his shaving gear and some clean underwear.

The bedroom door flew open with a bang and Geoff stood there. Anger erupted on his face. "What are you doing here?"

Rolando gave him a crooked smile. "You're the one who was begging me to come not more than an hour ago. What a surprise. My wonderful brother must be losing his mind." He turned back to the bureau with an exaggerated look of tolerance and shook his head. "You come barging into Laura's house asking me to come home. I come home and find you have put someone else in my bedroom where one would think I have the right to sleep, then you are rude enough to burst in and ask me what I'm doing here."

The younger man closed his mouth tightly and clenched his fists. After a moment's silence, he relaxed and smiled. "You're right. I did invite you home and, of course, you belong here. I'll have Raquel sleep somewhere else. I'm just glad you're here. Mama is sleeping now so perhaps you should wait to visit with her. But you are more than welcome to have some refreshments with us in the kitchen."

"I'll think about it. Right now, I want to shave."

"Of course. I'll find a candle for you."

Geoff left, closing the door softly behind him.

"That's why I hate him," Rolando muttered. Doesn't he ever get upset and yell? No one can be that calm." He banged the top drawer shut, throwing the shaving gear and underwear on the bed. He found an old pair of faded pants and a mended shirt in the bottom of the chest.

Striding out of his room, he found himself standing at the kitchen door. Opal, Geoff and Raquel sat around the table drinking coffee from mugs. Piles of papaya and lemon rinds set on dirtied plates stacked on the counter.

Rolando pushed his way into the small room, though he felt uncomfortable interrupting a group of people in conversation.

Opal rose quickly. "Rolando, we're happy to have you here tonight. Please join us for some coffee and fruit. We would enjoy it very much."

"I don't believe you. I couldn't help but hear you talking about me when I approached the kitchen. What were you saying?"

"Nothing important." Geoff looked embarrassed.

"I'd like to know how you feel about your older brother. Tell me what you were saying."

Geoff swallowed. "I was merely telling the girls what a troubled life you have led, filled with heavy burdens at a very young age. I also feel that you expect too much of yourself, and, due to many disappointments in your life, everything has seemed to fall apart."

Rolando stared levelly at him. "Are you telling them that I drink too much, Geoff? Or of my failure to keep Elena away from that Indian? What are you telling your guest? That I was unable to raise my own sister properly? Opal, give me a candle. I'm going out to shave. Then I'm going to sleep. I will be staying here tonight only." He looked pointedly at Raquel, who stared back at him.

"Never would I speak badly about the way you raised us, Rolando. I'm very thankful to you." Geoff smiled sadly. "Please wait a moment. We must discuss our father's funeral plans. There's very little time and I must go to Quito tomorrow to buy the coffin."

"There's not much more I can do to his body," said Raquel. "The papers are completed and Opal and I will present them to the priest tomorrow."

"Raquel is a doctor, Rolando." Geoff explained Raquel's presence.

Rolando shrugged and made no comment.

Geoff looked at his wife. "Why don't I feel more sad?"

"He never gave you a chance to love him. There are few happy memories."

He nodded, and silence fell over the group until Rolando made a movement in the doorway.

"Do you have a candle for me?" Rolando asked impatiently.

Opal pushed back the chair and hopped to her feet. "I'm sorry, Rolando. My mind is full of other things. Please forgive me."

She rushed to draw back a small curtain covering a cupboard and removed a candle and box of matches.

He took them with a nod of thanks. "Where's Papa?"

"In the back room where he slept when he was home." Geoff pointed toward the hallway.

After shaving, Rolando dropped off his shaving gear in his

room and walked toward his father's room. Quietly, he opened the door. His father lay on a cot, a blanket pulled over his head. Rolando tiptoed to his side and looked down for a long while, debating whether to look at the body. Fear of the unknown made him pause, but the need to see his father won out. Gently and slowly he bent to pull back the blanket. Surprise covered Rolando's face. Although the corpse appeared colorless and grey, the older man was lying peacefully as if in sleep. Rolando noticed an ugly gash at the side of his head, but someone had combed his hair carefully in an attempt to cover it. Dressed in his only suit, he had been shaved and groomed. Pulling a chair from the corner, Rolando sat down and stared at the man for a long time. It was hard for him to believe his father was gone. He tried to remember one time the two of them had held a conversation of any consequence. The regrettable loss brought tears to his eyes. He had needed a father's help and wisdom throughout his life. Now, as if a final door had been slammed, he realized how much he had longed for a relationship with the man. All of the hatred and distaste he had used as a defense against his father for having hurt and neglected him evaporated. Now, in its place was a terrible sense of emptiness.

"I'm sorry about your papa."

Rolando swung around in his chair, a look of impatience crossing his face.

Raquel walked to the end of the bed. "The blow to his head killed him, but actually he would have died soon anyway. The hit-and-run driver just hurried the results a little. Alcohol would have taken a bit longer."

He pressed his lips together and looked at her. "Do you always lurk in other people's bedrooms?"

"I'm not lurking. I've been caring for him."

"Caring for him," he repeated. "What do you mean by 'caring for him'? I would think there was little for anyone to do."

"Geoff called me because I am a friend and because I am a medical student in my last year of studies."

"A medical student," he echoed. "Geoff doesn't use much intelligence, does he?" He looked back to his father. In a clear, measured tone he said, "Now, will you leave? I want to be with my papa."

"I didn't mean to disturb you." She turned.

"Wait!" He held out his arm to stop her. "You really are a doctor and Geoff called you here?"

"Yes."

"What did my papa do? Die in your arms? Geoff was a fool to call on a woman. What are you? A witchdoctor?"

She shook her head in disbelief. "You are an incredibly rude man. No, your papa was dead when I arrived. Geoff thought of me because there was no other doctor in residence on Sunday night. There was nothing I could do but pronounce him dead."

"I've never trusted women doctors or nurses. My mama is sick because of the neglect of a nurse."

Raquel moved to the door.

"Please let me say something," she said.

"Are you still here?" Startled Rolando's gaze remained fixed on his father.

"Yes."

After a moment's hesitation, he reacted angrily. "Well. Say what you will and then leave me alone."

"I am amazed by the nest of negative memories, unresolved bitterness and hatred that dominate you. And apparently you have chosen liquor to forget them. I believe what you are now doing is wise. To sit and think about your papa may bring some of the answers you need."

Rolando's back stiffened with rage.

Raquel continued. "Perhaps you can understand what liquor did to him and how it robbed him of not only his life, but the enjoyment of his family, business, home and friends. Liquor is a destroyer, a thief and a liar. Your papa was a fool not to recognize what he had."

Rolando turned, the fury spreading through him like a forest fire. "Get out of here."

"No." She backed away in alarm. "No, but I wish you would consider what I said." She threw back her shoulders. "All of the bitterness and hatred you are carrying will someday kill you, Rolando, if the liquor doesn't. I would really hate to see that happen. You should resolve some of your problems because coddled, pampered bitternesses are as potentially dangerous as liquor."

For the first time he studied her critically. She looked younger than he had first thought. Perhaps she was about twenty-five years old. Golden glints in the dark brown hair framed her oval face and brought out the green in her eyes. She wore no makeup, but her face and lips were flushed red, giving her a healthy look. She wore a pink dress and high leather boots. He had to admit to himself that she created an attractive sight in the drab surroundings. He felt a check at his reaction and frowned darkly. "I thought you said you were a doctor, not a psychiatrist."

"I'll leave you alone." He watched to make sure she had left. A tiny spark of amusement struck him. He had put her in her place.

Two hours later, he left his father's side and wandered to his room, deep in thought. As much as he disliked Raquel, her words had troubled him. He could and would stop his drinking, as of this night. Meditating on his father's life and death put a desire in his heart to start over. It wouldn't be easy, but perhaps if he filled his days with other activities, he could do it.

He remained at his family's home for a week. His father's funeral passed and he spent time with his mother. He had been sitting with her when she turned to him with clear, bright eyes, and moved her lips. As he sat closer, believing she was calling his name, he pressed his ear to her mouth and with a shock, he heard her whisper his father's name. Then she had died. The notion that his mother may have known of her husband's death surprised him, yet the realization that he was her last thought after all she had endured moved Rolando more than her passing.

With the reuniting of his family, Rolando was quickly accepted back into Uncle Hector's home. After his mother's funeral, he had no desire to remain with Geoff and Opal. With Mariana's enthusiastic invitation he had moved in.

For one week, he had been able to remain sober, strenghtened by love of family that surrounded him. Geoff offered him a job driving the truck and, with mild satisfaction, Rolando sat behind the wheel again. That Geoff would trust him with driving filled him with a sense of pride.

One evening during the second week he wandered behind his uncle's house to stand beneath the fruit trees. It had been a long time since he had been there. Pleased to be alone, he leaned his back against a tree trunk and listened to the chickens settling in the coop and the pigs grunting contentedly in their drowsiness. It would soon be dark. It was strange how it had taken the death of his father and mother to bring him to his senses regarding liquor and his desire to wander. It was good to be back where he belonged.

Glancing over the darkening field, his eyes rested on the bodega, where he had discovered Carlos and Elena. In a rush, it all returned. The forgotten deception. The seduction of his sister. Fool! How could he have forgotten his determination to kill Carlos and bring Elena back? If he had been accepted back into the family, so should she. There was no way for him to have total peace of mind without Elena at his side. He was convinced she wanted to return, but how could she find her way home alone? Perhaps Carlos was keeping her against her will. That was a new thought. Maybe by now she realized what a mistake she had made. The thought straightened his back with new resolve. The grudge was alive again, having been buried beneath the bustle of familial responsibilities.

By the next morning, the joy of driving the family truck was torturous monotony. Geoff's happiness and contentment sickened him again and he saw with clearer vision, unobstructed by sentiment, the deteriorated state of Pachuca. As his discontentment grew, so did his hatred for Carlos.

How could he have been lulled to sleep when his sister was living a full day's journey from him, with a man whom she could only resent? He had to give Carlos credit for moving Elena so far from Pachuca that she could not know how to return. The desire to rescue her and destroy Carlos flowered again in his spirit.

Sharing a room with Francisco, he found little privacy except during school hours when the boy was in Quito with his sisters. A two-month school recess was almost upon them, and he needed to complete plans before his little cousin remained at home all day.

Checking his small earnings from the few days he had worked on the truck, he figured it would take him as far as Guayaquil and house him two nights. He would have to worry later about his passage back to Quito with Elena.

Thinking it better not to mention his plans to the family, he decided to leave his uncle's house with only the clothes on his back. This way, no questions would be asked. Before his departure for Quito, he would pay a visit to the family home to retrieve a few old clothes.

He planned on telling whoever was there that he intended to move all his belongings to his aunt's home, but, much to his delight, he discovered the house was empty. Hurriedly he entered his old bedroom. Pablo still slept there whenever he was in Pachuca.

Both Pablo and Roberto had been home for their mother's funeral. There had not been enough time to return for their father's funeral. It had been easier for Roberto to obtain a pass from the military, than it was for the family to find Pablo, but in the end, all the boys were together for a short time. Nothing had been mentioned concerning Elena, much to Rolando's relief.

He hadn't stepped into the bedroom since his mother's funeral, but now he paused to look at the old mirror above the scarred bureau. Memories crowded his mind. The faded curtains of his youth had been replaced with new, fresh ones, the handiwork of Opal, but everything else had remained the same.

From under the bed, he pulled a battered box and removed some ragged underwear, holey socks and an old school jacket, placing them in a plastic bag. Closing the lid, he pushed the box back, and returned to the hallway, listening carefully. Hearing no one, he succumbed to a persistent urge and knocked lightly on Geoff's bedroom door. There was no answer. Slowly opening it, he stood in Elena's old room, fighting a familiar heartache that choked his throat. Perhaps the memories that hung heavily in the room were the real reasons he could not live in this house.

Turning to leave, he noticed a hand-carved wooden box sitting on a nightstand. Its shiny smoothness stood out from the older objects in the room and he walked over to inspect it. Lifting the top, his eyes grew wide. Several thousand sucres lay in neat stacks. Quickly he closed the lid.

Why would his brother leave money lying around in an unlocked box?

Disgusted, he turned to leave the room and stopped, a thought stirring. That money could guarantee passage to Playas and perhaps a home away from Pachuca for a while.

Why not? reasoned Rolando. After all, it was I who put Geoff through school and cared for him. The money is really mine.

With that, he grabbed the large wads and stuffed them in the plastic bag.

Running from the back door, he sneaked around the side of the house. Instead of turning toward the plaza, he walked down the road that led to the new highway. Marching past the American nurse's compound, he watched over his shoulder for fear his brother might be driving the truck in this area. Reaching the new Pan American highway, which was now leveled, ready for a layer of blacktop, he walked toward Yaruqui. A mile below the exit to Pachuca, he stopped at a pathway leading upward to the Hacienda Chiripa. Climbing the steep hill, he found several bushes where he would be able to watch the road and remain hidden.

Several anxious minutes passed until he saw the familiar Yaruqui bus chugging up the long hill. Slowly walking down to the road, he stepped out in front of the bus and waved. Finding a seat among the residents of Yaruqui, he rode the ten miles to the larger pueblo.

Upon arriving, he stepped from the bus, stood in the large, clean plaza, and glanced around until he spotted the telephone office. Pushing on the door, he stood inside for several moments, as if waiting for someone. He then walked out to the street, his eyes searching. He noticed a group of men standing beside a shiny pickup and, moving swiftly toward them, he scanned their faces as he walked to see if anyone looked familiar. Relieved to note they were all strangers, he approached them. The men acknowledged his presence with short nods of their heads.

"Buenos dias, senores," Rolando smiled.

"Buenos dias," they echoed.

"I have a problem and wondered if there is anyone here who can help me. I came to Yaruqui this morning to see if I could find a small villa to buy for my family as we are interested in a second home. On the spur of the moment, I decided to come from Quito on the bus, so I would be unhampered in seeing the view. When I arrived, I telephoned my wife to tell her of my whereabouts and she informed me one of my little girls has taken ill. I must return home and I wonder if one of you can drive me to Quito quickly. I will pay you well."

"Will you give me 100 sucres?"

"Yes, of course." Reaching into his pocket, Rolando drew out a few bills from his own savings and handed one to the man.

"Thank you," the man said, moving to the pickup and indicating Rolando to climb in on the other side.

They sped toward Quito, cutting travel time in half. Rolando discouraged as much talk as possible, but was forced to continue the lie he had begun in Yaruqui. He put the man off by pleading worry for his daughter.

As they reached the entrance to the capital city, Rolando begged the man to take him to the outskirts of old town.

"I will take you to your home." The young man gave him a concerned look, as they approached the designated corner.

"No. Please. I will be able to walk. It's only a short distance and I must climb some steps. I'll be there in no time. Thank you."

Rolando was out of the pickup and running across the street before the driver could reply. He watched from the shadows of a building until the pickup disappeared, then walked at a fast pace to the CitiBank building three blocks away.

Entering, he moved warily to one of the two tellers and greeted her.

"What may I do for you today?" The girl's eyes batted flirtatiously.

"I wondered if I put my savings into the bank here in Quito, if I could recover it in Guayaquil?"

"Yes, of course. We have branches in Guayaquil. Is that what you would like to do today?"

"Yes. I have money that I saved for several years, working with construction crews here in Quito. I have always dreamed of moving to Guayaquil and investing money there."

"If you are interested in seeing your money grow through investments, that would be the place to go." She smiled professionally. "Now, let me see. How much money would you care to put into savings?"

"Here it is." He set the plastic bag on the counter and opened it. Withdrawing the wads of money, he placed them in front of her.

Her eyes widened at the amount. "You must have been saving a long time."

"Yes, several years." He was growing nervous and impatient. "Is there some way you can deposit this soon? I must get back to work."

"Certainly." She looked at him for a long moment, then gave him a friendly smile.

One-half hour later he was again standing on the street looking in both directions. He was sure there was a tourist shop not far from here and he walked rapidly into the center of town. Stores of all descriptions and sizes were built along the boulevard; shop windows aimed at attracting tourists from Europe and America, displayed colorful Indian goods. Rolando entered a small, dark shop that featured items made of hand-tooled leather. The store was empty of patrons. He walked to the far end of the room and discovered an old Indian sitting behind a tall glass counter.

They exchanged greetings as the old man stood eagerly. "May I help you?"

"Yes. I need two gifts. I have twin brothers and need something for their saint's day. Something that will last for a long time. They're still young and in colegio."

"Twins. Isn't that interesting. I've never seen twins. Heard about them though. Back in my youth, it was impossible for mothers to raise twins. But now, there are so many new products, I guess it can be done."

Impatiently Rolando shifted from one foot to the other.

"What can I show you?"

"I'm interested in a leather purse. One that can strap around the waist and lay against the body without detection."

"Sure. I suppose I can find one here somewhere. I can understand why you would want to give your brother something like that. Everyone should use one. You know, because of the problems we have with thieves." The old man muttered as he opened a glass door behind him, pulling out several boxes of leather goods.

"How's this?" He singled out a wallet that was long and flat with four leather ties, two on each side, that could reach around his waist. Rolando took it in his hand. "Let me see." He put the plastic bag on the floor, and placed the pouch at his side, pulling the ties around him. They were almost too short, but would have to do. Lifting the flap, he saw there would be enough room for a small part of the money when he withdrew it in Guayaquil.

"This is fine. And now I need something for my other brother.

He's a hunter and has a knife to kill small animals for food. Do you have a knife sheath?"

"What size?"

"The trouble is, I couldn't bring the knife, so I will need to see them."

The old man brought out another box and Rolando shuffled through the articles until he found a long, narrow sheath. The straps were thick and had a flat buckle.

He handed the man a bill and took the items, walking rapidly onto the street. Flagging down a taxi, he dropped gratefully onto the back seat.

"Can you take me all the way to Pachuca?"

"Sure, senor," grinned the driver. "It will cost you 100 sucres."

"All right, but drive as fast as you can."

The driver put the old, battered car into gear, and it jumped into action smoking its way out of the city and through the Tumbaco Valley.

He requested that the driver drop him off a mile above Pachuca, a few hundred meters beyond Laura's house. Paying the man, he sent him on his way. Watching the car disappear in a mixture of dust and smoke, he considered which way to go. Having no desire to see any of Laura's children, he started to cross pastureland, stopping only once to dispose of his old clothes. He came out on a road above his aunt's house. He could buy all the clothes he wanted now, he thought. Leisurely, he stopped in a small saloon. Asking for a cola, he downed it in a minute, conversing all the time with the owner. Moving further down the road, he stopped in another store and downed a second cola. Looking at his watch, he discovered he still had an hour before siesta. All the activity of the morning had been accomplished in a little over three hours.

Stopping at a friend's house, he passed fifteen minutes in a casual visit. Then after greeting several people in the street, he purposely walked past his aunt's house and poked his head in the door to announce he had just had lunch at the saloon and would not be home for lunch. Her friendly reply conveyed to him that Geoff had not discovered the loss of the money.

Walking to the plaza, he entered the saloon to spend another half hour eating soup, bread, roasted pork skin and corn on the cob. Exiting before noon, he was not concerned that anyone was conscious of the hour; they wouldn't be before the siesta hour when the children returned from school. No one would remember the time of day he had stopped to establish deliberate alibis.

Returning to his aunt's house, he passed the kitchen where she and the young maid were preparing the noontime meal. Rushing into the bedroom, he pulled the leather wallet from the plastic bag, lifted his shirt, wrapped it around his waist and tied the ends. Sitting on the bed, he lifted his pant leg and strapped the sheath around his calf. He took the bank booklet out of his pocket, and glanced again at the amount. He smiled contentedly. It would be more than enough to keep him for several months in Playas or wherever he chose. Perhaps he and Elena could travel for a while before returning to Pachuca. If Geoff ever discovered he had stolen the money, he was convinced his brother would forgive him when he saw that he had rescued their sister and brought her home. Lifting the flap of the wallet, he placed the booklet inside. Picking up a small mirror, he held it in front of his midriff to search for telltale bulge. Satisfied, he smiled to himself and wandered out the door and into the kitchen. Aunt Mariana looked up, pleased.

"Why did you eat, dear, when you knew I would be preparing dinner?"

Lounging in a chair, he grinned at her. "I ate so long ago I'm already hungry."

"Good. There's plenty for you." She shoved an empty platter at the maid. "Please fill this with potatoes, so we'll be ready when the children arrive."

The girl took the plate and lifted the lid from a steaming pot.

"I'm glad you have the day off, Rolando. Where did Geoff go with the truck?" asked Mariana.

"Up to one of the haciendas, I guess. He said he needed the truck until noon. I think he's hoping to find a job for us up there."

"I thought maybe you'd go with him." She turned from the sink and watched his face hopefully.

"I know what you're thinking, Tia, but you should know things will never be so good between us that we run around together in the truck all day. I'll work this afternoon."

She turned back to the sink, thoughtfully. He stood and walked to her side, leaning over to kiss her cheek.

"I know it disappoints you that we don't get along. I'm just glad to be back home with you."

She turned and embraced him tightly.

"How did you know what I needed?" he grinned.

He and his aunt had spoken only once about Elena and the toll her disappearance had taken on him. He had tried to assure her that he himself had not changed; only his purpose in life had. Mariana expressed her concern that she had watched him evolve from a responsible, caring adult into a hard, embittered man. He was able to convince her that nothing had changed.

Raquel, on the other hand, would not be so easily convinced-not that it mattered-although her insight and insinuations infuriated him. Mariana had been hurt because he had chosen to live with Laura instead of returning to her house. It was probably the fact that he had lived with Laura for a time that turned Mariana and Hector against Carlos for good. For a while they were unable to forget the boy who had been in their care for several years. Now Rolando had been able to make his aunt see what a web of deception Carlos had woven around all of them.

The day would come when God would rightfully punish Carlos and perhaps in His mercy bring Elena back to them. Yes, someday his family would thank him.

He tousled Mariana's hair and turned away as the front door burst open. The voices of Francisco, Susana and Miriam filled the house with announcements of their arrival.

As it was, Rolando need not have worried about establishing alibis. Geoff sent a message by way of a child, that he would not be returning to the house after lunch. He and Opal would be driving the truck into Quito to sign some papers at their lawyer's office. Rolando was advised to take the rest of the afternoon off. This gave Rolando time to plan his next move. He would not be able to do much until Geoff discovered the theft. Once Geoff accused him, Rolando could prove his innocence with the backing of people who could swear they had seen him all morning. Geoff would have no way of finding the money or the bank booklet. In a few days, he would be free to leave Pauchuca with the excuse that he could no longer live with such outrageous accusations and just when he was trying to change his lifestyle.

When Geoff and Opal entered their aunt and uncle's home that night, they were not the angry couple Rolando had expected. Instead, as he looked at Geoff and Opal, he felt they knew he had stolen the money. Inside, he quaked with fear. There were no open accusations, just incredible grief showing in Geoff's eyes. When the theft was mentioned, Rolando acted out his innocence, but no one accused him.

Geoff and Opal sat on the sofa as Mariana and Hector cried out their disbelief.

"I didn't know you had that kind of money lying around, Geoff," puzzled Hector. Shouldn't you have placed it in a safer spot?"

"Uncle, why would we expect thievery in Pachuca, inside our home, and during the day? There is always someone nearby who could spot a suspicious person." Geoff looked directly at Rolando.

"Do you always keep money there?" Mariana frowned her disbelief.

"No, we had it there for a few days, maybe two weeks." Geoff turned to Hector. "Uncle, you know what we had planned. I spoke with you several days ago."

The man folded his hands in his lap and nodded.

Geoff turned toward Rolando. "Much of the money was for you."

Shock waves passed through Rolando, causing his heart to beat faster. "What do you mean?"

"You know the property our family owns north of Oyambarillo? Opal's parents gave her a large sum of money when we married, plus the savings I put aside when I was working alone. Since we pay no rent and the truck is paid for, almost everything I made went into the bank in Quito. I took it out two weeks ago to offer at least part of it to you, Rolando, because Opal and I would like to buy your portion of the land from you. We were going to build a small home over there, inviting Pablo and Roberto to live with us. In that way, our family home would belong to you." He watched his brother with knowing eyes. "The house has always been yours anyway. We thought you might use the money to buy a truck for yourself and start your own business. I'm sorry I can't offer it to you now."

His head pounded. A good portion of the money had been his, after all, and he had no way of letting them know he had it in his possession.

"I wonder who would have entered the house and taken the money?" he asked, trying to sound sincere.

"All eyes were on him and finally Mariana broke the silence.

"It could have been a stranger and someone may have noticed him. It's too bad you were visiting with friends all morning, Rolando. If you had been near the house, you might have seen someone. It's a shame I kept you here all afternoon, visiting with me."

Rolando glanced at Geoff and wondered what he was thinking. Mariana had just given him his needed alibi.

Geoff gave his brother a hard stare and stood, bringing Opal with him. "We must be going. I suppose I will have to report this to the authorities tomorrow. Obviously it was a stranger who broke into our house. He could be as far away as the jungle by now."

Rolando swallowed and lifted his hand from his leg to stop them, then changed his mind as Geoff and Opal walked out the front door.

He sat uncomfortably in the living room, avoiding Mariana's eyes and Hector's questioning face. Stretching, he stood and tried to look as if the incident was over in his mind. "I must get to bed. I'll be driving the truck tomorrow, I suppose." He walked out of the room without kissing his aunt's cheek.

Francisco was asleep when he entered the room. He could hear Miriam and Susana's chatter in the next bedroom as they finished their homework and prepared for bed.

Deciding not to brush his teeth, for fear of meeting his aunt, Rolando lay down beside Francisco and attempted to fall asleep. Leave it to Geoff to turn things around. He had anticipated anger and accusations which would have provided him with an excuse to leave home. Instead his brother used his Christianity to pierce his heart and conscience. No matter how he tried to get back at Geoff and Opal, they were always one step ahead of him. Oh, how he hated them. Never would he believe they were going to give him the money. All of it would have gone to build another house or to buy a new truck. Then they would take both homes for themselves. They wouldn't be satisfied with just the family home. They had to have it all.

He rationalized the theft until he had convinced himself that he had every right to take the money.

Lying awake, he listened to the soft breathing of Francisco. He had to invent a good reason to leave Pachuca and he needed to do it soon. Turning on his side, he knew there would be no sleep for him this night. The minutes passed agonizingly slow.

His heart thumped as he heard the door open slowly. He watched through slitted eyes, while pretending to be asleep. His aunt stood in the doorway, a candle in her hand. Moving to the side of the bed, she sat on the edge.

"Rolando," she whispered, shaking his arm.

Feigning broken sleep, he sat up.

"Shhh. Don't wake Francisco." She set the candle on the nightstand.

"What's the matter, Tia?" asked Rolando, fearful of the reason for her midnight visit.

"I need to know where you were this morning."

"What do you mean?" he asked, his heart hardening.

"Rolando, I love you with all of my heart. My own son could not receive more affection from me. I must know where you were."

"You think I took the money, don't you?"

"Not really, no. But Geoff does, and I need to know where you were so I can persuade him you didn't."

"I don't need your help." He gritted his teeth. "If he doesn't believe what I say, then I don't care. Why should it matter to me?"

"Because he will bring the authorities tomorrow."

"I have nothing to hide. I don't have the money."

She sighed deeply. "All right. I believe you." She leaned forward to kiss his forehead. "I will leave you to sleep. You'll have nothing to worry about." She took the candle, walked to the door, and smiled back at him.

He lay back, trembling from the close call. Part of him was relieved that all would be taken care of by his aunt and the other part of him was torn by his need for her to believe he was innocent. He soothed himself with the thought that once he killed Carlos and after he returned Elena to her proper home all would be forgiven. Then, he would be able to confess.

After Francisco and his sisters left the house for school, Rolando rolled out of bed. He had not slept and now he dragged himself across the room to where he found a piece of notebook paper from Francisco's studies. He sat down to write a note.

After a moments reflection, he wrote:

Dear Tia Mariana,

I have decided I cannot stay in Pachuca with Geoff's feelings so obvious. I did not steal the money, but knowing my brother and his wife, they will never believe me innocent. I am going away for a spell to give you all a rest. It seems all I do is bring grief to my family.

Rolando

Folding it neatly, he placed it on his pillow, expecting the maid to find it when she made the bed. With that, he took the plastic bag from the bureau and put a clean pair of shorts and a T-shirt inside, along with his shaving gear, toothbrush and toothpaste. Pulling his jacket from a hanger in the closet, he laid it over his arm and looked around for anything else he might need. Laying his hand on the wallet against his ribs, he smiled.

That's all he would need.

Moving swiftly down the hallway, he heard Hector and Mariana in the kitchen talking softly. The maid would not arrive for another hour. He closed the front door behind him and hurried down to the plaza.

Chapter 41

A handful of people disembarked, stretched and wandered to the rear of the bus. The conductor slowly climbed the metal ladder attached to the back door, and began tossing baggage to the ground.

Rolando was pleased with the chilly, fresh, tangy air of the coast after the humid, oppressive atmosphere of Guayaquil. He patted his waist for the hundredth time, making sure his money-purse was still strapped around his waist.

A fellow passenger had pointed him toward a small hotel, and now in the early hours of morning, he followed the directions looking for landmarks. Two street lamps attempted to light up the main section of town, which led him to believe he was near the plaza. Off in the distance, he heard the dull roar of an ocean he had never seen. The heavy scents of salt air and flowering bushes escaped his notice. He cared for nothing but to find Carlos. He had almost reached his goal. Soon he would settle a score with the person who had ruined his life. He had purposely boarded the bus that would arrive in Playas after dark, as the element of surprise would place Carlos on the defensive.

Shadowy bats and night birds flew among the trees catching the reflection of street lights. One block beyond the plaza, Rolando stopped before a two-story building with a faint light shining above the door. Knocking loudly, he waited a few moments. He knocked again until he heard an inside door open and shut followed by gentle cough.

A young woman opened the door and peered out. Her long black hair was disheveled, partially hiding a tired, but sweet face. An old cotton dress that had been demoted to sleepwear, hung beneath a hastily donned large sweater. Her feet were bare. Even though she was still under the influence of sleep, her eyes cleared when she saw the tall, handsome man at the door. Unconsciously, she swept her hair from her face and adjusted the sweater.

"Buenas noches. Are you looking for a room for the night?" she inquired.

"Buenas noches. Yes. I'm sorry for waking you. I just arrived on the night bus," he replied smoothly. "Do you have a room available?"

"Yes, of course. Please, come in."

He entered the dim hallway and closed the door behind him, while she led the way to the office. Flipping on a lightswitch, the girl glided to a small desk and chair in the middle of the room. Except for another straight-backed wooden chair and an old worn two-drawer nightstand, the room had no other furniture. A picture of Ecuador's president and one of the Madonna adorned the bare walls.

Sitting at the desk, she removed a pen from the drawer and turned to pluck a register book from the nightstand.

"How long will you be here?" She glanced up at him.

"Maybe just tonight. Maybe two nights."

"You're not from Guayaquil, are you?"

He stared hard at her, until puzzled, she looked away and wrote something in the book. She turned it around and pushed it toward him. He bent to write: Ricardo Hernandez-Ambato, Ecuador.

"I'm sorry. I was only curious about your accent." she mumbled.

He saw she had been properly rebuffed. He was not looking for a romantic encounter. Her reaction to him when he appeared at her door had been immediate. She was attracted to him, as dozens of women were everywhere he went. As a feeling of tiredness swept through him, he hardened his eyes and pressed his mouth closed, accentuating the lines around his mouth.

"The plastic bag is your only piece of luggage?" she asked quizzically, looking around.

Giving her a disapproving look, he nodded yes. "How much do I owe?"

"Seventy-five sucres per night, but you can pay when you check out," she replied cooly.

He noted her response and chuckled inwardly. It boosted his ego to hurt her.

Smiling sweetly, he picked up his bag. "Now, where do I sleep tonight?"

She stood, transfixed, her coolness melting. Returning his bright smile, she motioned for him to follow. Leading him to the second floor, she stopped before a door at the end of the neat, but drab hallway, and opened it. She stepped back to let him pass. He walked through the door, dropped the plastic bag on one of the single beds, and gave a quick look around. Satisfied, he turned back and gave her a curt nod of dismissal. A look of disappointment crossed her face to be quickly replaced by bewilderment. She had been hoping for a chance to talk. But he gave her a forced smile, his eyes remaining cold.

Huddling into her sweater, she quickly left the room, closing the door.

Relieved to see the girl gone, he glanced at his watch and saw he had only two hours until dawn. Slowly opening the door and finding the hallway empty, he padded to a room marked

'Banos'. There, he splashed water on his face and washed as best he could. Back in his room, he bolted the door closed the curtains, and sat on the bed. He laid out his toiletries and the meager articles of underclothing he had brought with him. Laying aside his jacket, he unbuttoned his shirt, removing it. Unknotting the leather cords around his waist, he took the wallet and laid it tenderly on the bed. He lifted his pant leg and unbuckled the leather sheath. Laying everything side by side, he smiled. It was time. He was about to avenge the misery he had endured these past months.

The small room was poorly lighted. It contained only two single beds, a nightstand and bureau. Taking his toothbrush, paste, and shaving gear, he placed them in the top drawer of the bureau. Opening the second, he stacked the underwear neatly inside. He decided against putting his prized possesions in an obvious place so he pulled out the bottom drawer and laid it on the bed, feeling the thin floor of the bureau beneath. There seemed to be sufficient space. Returning to the bed, he removed the knife from the sheath. Narrow and heavy, it fit perfectly in his hand. He held its coolness against his face. Knives were found in abundance in Guayaquil and he had encountered no problem finding someone willing to sell him one. Carefully, he replaced the dagger in the sheath and slid it onto the wooden bottom of the bureau. Then he returned to count the pocketbook of money. The majority of what he had stolen from Geoff was still in the bank in Guayaquil and he was reluctant to touch the part he had withdrawn. As much as he disliked his brother, he didn't want to spend it. He had decided to use it only in case of emergency, so out of necessity he was spending money from wallets he had stolen on city buses and street corners.

He knew tourists were most vulnerable to theft. Their eyes wandered and their attention focused away from their belongings. Purses and pockets bulging with wallets and other valuables were fair game to a thief and he had taken advantage. Now, he had enough money to live on the coast for a long time if Elena chose to do so. Anyway, Carlos would be dead by this time tomorrow. All of his plans now lay with Elena's decision.

He opened the leather wallet and placed all but three bills inside. It was thick, but smooth. He took it to the bureau and laid it beside the knife.

Replacing the drawer, he looked around the room for anything out of place. Putting on his shirt, he rebuttoned it, grabbed the room key left by the girl, and tucked the three bills in his pants pocket.

Picking up his jacket, he moved to the door, and opened it a crack to listen for any noise. All was silent. He closed the door quietly behind him and tiptoed down the stairway. The dim light didn't reach the shadowy corners, but he felt certain he was alone. Releasing the bolt on the street door, he stepped into the night, leaving the door unlocked. Laura had unwillingly revealed that Carlos and Elena lived in a cabin nearby the grand Humboldt Hotel where Carlos worked as a groundskeeper. Rolando was certain Carlos' job would require him to work during daylight hours and for that reason, he wanted to scrutinize the layout of the hotel during the night. It had not been difficult to obtain directions to the hotel. Residents of Playas seemed proud of their landmark.

He walked toward the faint roar of the ocean. Although he had never seen the sea, he held little curiosity for it. Surprisingly, he felt calmer now that he was so close to his goal. When he came face to face with Carlos, he would be nervous, but for now he felt at ease.

Suddenly, he saw the large white building with red trim looming at the end of the street. He walked over and stood on the steps of the hotel.

He watched the lobby through the glass doors. There was no one behind the desk, but he noticed a man lounging in an overstuffed chair, chatting amicably with another man who was leaning on a broom. The night crew. He descended the steps and followed the a walkway around the building. Field lights placed on the eaves of the large building allowed him to see clearly and he had no trouble finding his way to the west end. He would have preferred it to be dark, and he shook for fear Carlos would notice him. Slipping past curtained windows, he reached the oceanside and stopped short at the thunderous roar of the sea. Through the darkness he could see the lights from the hotel reflecting off whitecaps and he caught his breath in wonder.

The seaward side of the hotel had no windows and upon closer inspection he saw it was made up of a series of long, high boards on hinges. Perhaps during the day, they lowered the wall.

He was now certain the night staff was small and Carlos was no doubt at home. Returning to the front steps, he pushed cautiously on the door and found it open. Stepping into the lighted lobby, he walked up to the desk. The clerk came to attention and rose swiftly from the chair.

"Buenas noches. May I help you?"

"Buenas noches," replied Rolando, looking about before answering. "I just came in on the bus from Guayaquil and need information concerning the price of your rooms."

Frowning, the clerk looked beyond Rolando to the janitor and back to the tall man. "I hope you didn't have trouble finding the hotel. The bus stopped here an hour ago with supplies from Guayaquil."

Rolando gave him a black look. "No. I did not have trouble finding the hotel. However, I felt it foolish to pay for a night that was almost over. I have been walking the streets and noticed your gardens. They are beautiful."

A grin lit the dark face of the clerk. "Yes, they are. People from throughout Ecuador and other countries speak of our grounds."

"It must be difficult to grow anything in this soil. Do you have a specialist working for you?" Rolando prodded.

"No." The clerk swelled with pride, nodding his head from side to side. "Actually the group of workers are natives of Playas. They work each day with the trees and plants. Everything they use is imported from other areas."

A horrible thought struck Rolando. Either Laura had lied to him or Carlos had moved on. Had all of this been for nothing?

"All of the workers are natives of Playas?" he questioned, masking his disappointment. He started to turn and the clerk raised his arm to call him back.

"Didn't you want to know our rates? Will you be taking a room later today?"

"I think not," he replied, dejected. "I'll probably be traveling on."

The janitor had moved closer and smiled shyly. "I couldn't help but wonder where you are from. You have a familiar accent."

Rolando returned the smile. "North."

Turning to the clerk, the janitor beamed. "Ah ha. Sure. He means Quito."

Rolando frowned and remained silent, a sense of wariness stiffening his body.

The janitor continued good naturedly. "Sometimes we have a lot of visitors from Quito here. However your accent is slightly different than that. You're not exactly from the city of Quito."

Rolando stared at the janitor in amazement.

"You wonder how I know? It's a game I play sometimes. I try to place dialects. I've worked in this hotel for so many years and have listened to so many tourists from all over South America, the United States and Europe, I can almost tell where each is from. It makes the job more interesting."

He looked up at Rolando, a perplexed frown creasing his brow. "Your accent sounds so familiar to me."

"Really? You may be right. No doubt there have been people here from my area of Ecuador." He again turned away. "Good night. Thank you."

"Thank you, senor," replied the clerk.

Rolando was halfway across the lobby when he heard the janitor remarking to the clerk, "His accent sounds like the one the dining room Captain has."

Rolando let out a small gasp involuntarily, and hesitated for a moment. He continued to the door and stepped out into the night before the janitor could question him further.

A Captain? Could it be possible that Carlos Tapia was in charge of a dining room staff? The janitor had mentioned a sierra accent. Could there be more than one man with a sierra accent here in the hotel? It was a possibility. Laura had said Carlos was here so he needed to fine out for sure. But what would a dumb Indian like Carlos be doing overseeing a restaurant in an exclusive hotel? The idea was so preposterous he almost laughed out loud.

It was time to work out a plan.

Looking at the sky, he noticed the first signs of dawn. A sea bird cried out, as he passed overhead in his early search for food. A cat slinked across his path, hesitating momentarily, alert for potential danger then, increasing his speed, he flashed past, ready for a day's sleep after a long night of prowling. Rolando was also ready for sleep. Weariness prevailed over the stimulation of his encounter with Carlos and he knew he would have to sleep a short time in order to be alert.

The hotel door was still unlocked and he moved swiftly into the hall, pausing to listen. Hearing people stir in the back of the building, he walked quickly up the stairs into his room and bolted the door. He breathed a sigh of relief. After checking the floor of the bureau to assure himself that his money and knife were safe, he fell onto the bed fully clothed and sank into an exhausted sleep.

He was wakened by the sounds intruding upon his dream; the sounds of activity in the streets. Turning over, he shook the sleep from his mind and stared at his watch. Ten o'clock. At once he was alert. Jumping to his feet, he pulled back the curtains and stood at the window. The sun blazed from a bright morning sky on the lazy, drowsy community. Rolando studied the main thoroughfare intently, watching for any sign of his sister or Carlos.

The change in culture made him wonder if he were still in Ecuador. Old, wooden buildings crowded together as if in an attempt had been made to house all the pueblo's businesses into two short blocks. Women in faded cotton dresses wandered by with baskets on their arms, and children trailing behind. Men pedaled past on bicycles with attached wire baskets filled to capacity. Graceful palm trees swayed against the deep blue sky and sleek sea birds swooped over the town, content with the bounty provided by the equatorial sea and the Humboldt Current which flowed past the coastline.

In the distance he could see a corner of the grand hotel and his heart quickened with a mixture of anticipation and excitement. Leaving the window, he took his shaving gear, unbolted the door and walked to the bathroom.

Two cups of coffee and a plate of hard pastries, cheese, and butter in the dining room renewed him physically and he polished them off with another cup of coffee, a thick, black syrupy liquid mixed with hot milk. He walked to the office, knocked and poked his head inside. The room was empty, but he turned quickly when he heard someone walk up behind him. The girl he had met the night before approached him with a questioning look in her eyes.

"Buenos dias, Senor Hernandez. May I help you?"

She caught him off guard temporarily, having forgotten his alias.

"Buenos dias," he hesitated a moment. "May I use your telephone? It will be a local call."

"Certainly," she replied formally, still stung by his attitude of the night before. "Please, come this way."

She walked down the hallway and into a large lounge, filled with sofas, overstuffed chairs, a desk, end tables and reading lamps. Several dreary prints lined the walls, including another large photo of Ecuador's president. A telephone stood on the desk and she pointed to it. "If you make a long-distance call, please let us know."

"Thank you, but it will be local. Do you have a telephone book?"

"A what?"

"A book that lists telephone numbers."

"Oh." She smiled. "Just pick up the speaker and an operator will dial for you."

He was anxious to see her leave and remained motionless until she understood his desire. Again feeling rebuffed, she left the room without a word.

He glanced around. Fortunately, there were no other guests present. He took up the telephone. After several rings, a woman's voice sounded in his ear.

"Buenos dias. This is the operator. May I help you?"

"Will you please let me speak to a clerk behind the desk at the Hotel Humboldt, please."

"One moment."

In a matter of seconds, he heard a masculine voice.

Rolando hesitated a moment, his heart pounding. "I wonder if you can give me some information? My wife and I are traveling along the coast from Manta down to Playas and back up to Guayaquil. We arrived late last night and first discovered the smaller hotel near the plaza. Of course we are interested in nicer accomodations and will be planning to stay with you this evening. However, we are interested right now in your dining hours. Would you be able to tell me when your dining room is open?"

"By all means," the clerk gushed. "Actually, we have two dining areas."

"Two?"

"Yes. There is one we open during the day, a very nice restaurant that overlooks the sea. We begin service at six in the morning and close at sunset, around half-past six. After that our guests may take their meals in our dining room in the hotel. That area closes at two."

"Thank you, senor. My wife and I will be there in a few hours."

Rolando hung up, torn between a feeling of delight and discouragement. Did Carlos work all day? Did he go home for a siesta hour? Did he work a split shift? Was Carlos here at all? Fortunately, the janitor had mentioned a day captain or the confusion would have been greater. He sat, rubbing his chin, pondering what to do next. He could see no problem unless he was spotted or brought attention to himself by loitering. Perhaps this would take longer than one day. Rising, he left the lounge and walked up the steps to his room, bolting the door. Having decided to wait until dusk for another visit to the hotel, he removed his clothing, and laid it on the other bed. He slept until after noon. Rising refreshed, he dressed, and groomed himself and descended the steps, ready to eat a hearty meal.

Several guests sat at the few tables lining the walls of the room, looking more like residents of Playas than guests. He panicked for a moment, wondering if Elena and Carlos would frequent this location. He decided they would no doubt dine at home or at the hotel where Carlos worked.

An elderly, plump woman bustled through a door in the front of the room. She hurried cheerfully to Rolando's side to take his order. His reply was disgruntled. This was always the time of day he fought the urge to drink. It had been several days since he had had any liquor. At times the desire was strong but whenever he thought of yielding to the temptation, a mental picture of his father in death, or of Carlos begging him for mercy rose before him. He must never lose sight of the goal. As soon as he killed Carlos and brought Elena home, he knew the desire to drink would leave him for good. If he could just hold on for a few more days, everything would be back to normal. back to normal.

Having leisurely eaten his meal, he returned to his room and stood by the window until he saw the sun drop below the palm trees. It was time. Going to the bureau, he pulled the bottom drawer from its place and set it on the floor. Taking the sheath with the knife from the plywood bottom, he walked back to the bed and strapped it on his right leg, around the calf. He removed his identification card from his pocket and placed it beside the leather wallet. Replacing the drawer, he checked his pant leg for any bulges. He swayed with the realization that the next time he returned to this room, Carlos would be dead, and Elena would be his again.

Walking to the front door of the hotel, he stood on the steps, looking both ways. Seeing no one familiar, he crossed the street and walked down to the sea.

Fortunately, the grounds were large and abundant with shrubs, trees and flowers. He stood beside a large coconut palm and watched the hotel for a moment. Guests were walking in and out of the lobby and through the grounds, which made him more comfortable. Perhaps if he could mix with some of the groups, he would not be spotted. He moved past some flowering bougainvillea until he was parallel with the end of the hotel. Coming out on the seaward side of the bushes, he saw the ocean for the first time. Never had he seen so much water. Staring at the waves, he could understand the tremendous noise of the night before. The sun was sinking closer to the water and he saw it would soon be dark. Pushing past the bushes, he started to move closer to the open wall of the hotel. He would glance in. If Carlos was actually there, he could continue with his plans and stop him on the way home. He was halfway to the building when he saw a movement beside one of the posts outside the restaurant. He had almost missed the girl standing alone next to the trailing, flowering vines. He ran back to the bushes and watched from there, hoping she would move on. Swiftly she stepped forward and peeked around the corner into the restaurant. A combination of light from the sinking sun and light from inside the building glanced off her face and he gasped aloud. It was Elena. His knees quivered.

Why would she be standing outside the restaurant looking in? Confusion and relief pulled at him. He was relieved he had found them, but she didn't act like a prisoner at all. For several minutes he watched, until, as if at a signal, she hurried into the restaurant, waving her arm. Hearing her laughter above the roar of the sea confused him even more.

After several minutes, he saw Elena and Carlos emerge. In shock he watched them move toward him, arms around each other. In the darkening night, he had to escape before they turned on the floodlights. Running down the dunes, he was level with the ocean. Carlos and Elena were wandering south. He ran parallel with them until he reached a long sea wall. Running up the side of a dune, he stood beside the wall until he saw their shadowy figures passing in front of him.

He saw her glance past Carlos while talking, and suddenly stop, pointing in his direction. He couldn't see her face, but he knew the way she had reacted that she had seen him. In a panic, he ducked behind the wall. By the time Carlos had turned to look in his direction, Rolando was crawling along the wall. He sat in a huddle at the end, waiting until Carlos could reach him. Minutes passed and nothing happened. Perhaps they hadn't seen him after all, or maybe she had merely been commenting on the sunset. His heartbeat slowed to normal. With shaking legs, he stood and walked back to the gardens.

The field lights were on and he could see his way for a few feet. Walking in the same direction as Elena and Carlos, he followed the well-beaten pathway, past the hotel grounds and down onto the sandy walkway. A group of three wooden houses stood near each other and he walked toward them in the darkness. A light was coming from under each door, so he had no way of knowing which house belonged to Elena and Carlos. He knew only, thanks to Laura, that they lived on hotel property.

Boldly, he moved to the first cabin, listening under the high windows for a familiar voice. At the second house, he heard Elena's lively patter and relaxed for the first time since seeing her at the restaurant. Moving back against a log, he decided to sit until an opportunity made itself clear and then he would seize it.

Perhaps he should wait until they slept and then knock on the door. When Carlos answered, he could grab him and plunge the knife into his heart. But what if Elena saw him do it? She may never forgive him. It was obvious Carlos had her under his control. She was still acting silly over him. No, he would have to kill Carlos and then appear on the scene as someone ready to rescue her.

A quiet hour passed, then a scream rent the air from within

the house. He jumped to his feet like a human cannonball. He couldn't imagine what was happening. It sounded like loud pounding and yelling. Perhaps Carlos was beating her. Just as he was ready to rush the door, it opened and Elena ran down the stairs with Carlos following. Rolando began running after them, when the neighbor's window opened. A woman looked out. Rolando started to request her aid, when he saw her lean an arm on the sill. A man joined her and they laughed together, remarking on young love.

A chill grabbed his heart. Could it be they really did love each other? Perhaps Carlos was a good husband. Was he making a mistake? No! He would never accept that. Carlos deserved to die for what he had done to Elena and her family as well as his own. He followed them to the beach listening for movement or voices. Suddenly he heard them. Feeling his way across a high dune, he dropped down behind them, removing the knife from its sheath. Able to see only faint shadows, he crept close enough to grab Carlos. Suddenly a hand covered his mouth, pulling him back, while someone grabbed his arm and took the knife. A heavy object hit him across the base of the head.

The next thing he knew, he was lying on a cot in a brightly lighted room. Two men in business suits sat across the room, watching him. Rolando groaned felt the back of his head, and tried to sit up.

"Don't sit just yet." One man stood and walked up to Rolando.

"Where am I?" Rolando muttered.

"You're in the Hotel Humboldt. I am the manager and this is my assistant manager," replied the man, pointing behind him. "We're interested in why you have been loitering on our property. One of our security guards saw you earlier and thought you were waiting for someone, but when he saw you walk down to Carlos' house, he called me and we followed you to the beach. Our first fear was that you were a thief. When we saw the knife, we feared you were planning to bring misfortune to Carlos. Would you be so kind as to tell us what you were planning to do with this knife?"

Rolando gave them his hard stare, that worked so well with others, however these men seemed undaunted. After a long moment, he looked away and turned toward the wall, fighting nausea.

All night a security guard sat with him in the lighted room, not speaking. Rolando tried to sleep, but terror and a blinding headache kept him awake until he heard the mews of sea birds outside the window.

A door opened and he heard the shuffle of feet. Looking up, he saw Carlos.

"Buenos dias, Rolando."

The hotel manager walked behind Carlos to Rolando's cot and gently pulled him into a sitting position.

"Carlos," Rolando replied curtly.

"Why are you here and how did you find us?"

Rolando snorted. "Your mother, of course. Her brother came running with the news and she was only too willing to tell me where you were." He pressed his lips. "I have come to take Elena home."

The blood drained from Carlos' face. "She doesn't want to go back to Pachuca. I can guarantee that. Why would you want to break up a relationship that is progressing so well? Do you realize what would happen to Elena if you took her from me?" Carlos lifted hands with impatience. "She loves me. Can't you understand that? She has always loved me. And if you love her as you say you do, you wil leave us alone."

Inwardly shrinking, Rolando watched Carlos walk closer and stand above him.

Instead of lashing out, Carlos sighed deeply. "I understand what you're feeling, Rolando. I don't know what I'd do if Elena left me for someone else." Reaching out, Carlos placed his hand on the big man's shoulder. "Listen to me. I understand how much you care for your sister. Believe me. I love her more than anyone else in this world. My whole life revolves around her. Your heartbreak must have been terrible when she left with me. I understand that better now than I did then. I've grown up a lot. Please forgive the way that we left. But, too, try and understand that there was no other way to do it. You would have seen to it that your parents wouldn't have given permission."

"She will never know you were here." he continued. "I have no intention of disturbing her with this kind of news."

The manager spoke from behind Carlos. "What shall we do with him? I can call the police."

Carlos swung around. "Absolutely not. I want him to be free to go."

Rolando's eyes widened as Carlos turned to leave. "Good-bye, Rolando. Please leave Playas. If you really love your sister, you won't bother us again." He left.

Rolando sagged with depression. Standing on shaky feet, he walked to the door and back to his hotel room.

Chapter 42

He opened the door to Aunt Mariana's house and walked in. Hearing noises in the kitchen, he padded through the living room and dining area and stepped into the bright, blue room. His aunt stood at the sink peeling potatoes, and he stood watching her for a moment.

"Hola, Tia," he said softly.

"Oh, oh, Rolando!" she screamed with pleasure, potato and knife flying as she turned to him. He was in her arms in a flash. "Oh, my darling," she exclaimed, "Where have you been? I've been so worried."

"Everywhere and nowhere, Tia, but it's good to be home."

"We didn't know where to look for you. Where have you been living for a whole year?"

Sitting at the table, he sighed. "After leaving here, I went south for a while, then to the jungle. After that, up north, then over to the coast. Like I say, everywhere and nowhere."

"How did you live?"

"I had jobs here and there. Enough to eat and travel."

"Oh, Rolando. Why did you leave?"

"I had to."

"Geoff blames himself for your disappearance."

"He shouldn't do that." A touch of guilt moved his conscience. "I don't blame him."

"Perhaps you should tell him that."

"I will. Right now."

She laughed. "I didn't mean right now. Have something to eat first. He won't be home now anyway."

It was dark when he arrived at his family home. To his surprise, a sedan was parked in front, indicating guests. He decided to find out first who was inside. Walking to the side of the house, he peeked in the living room's small window. Geoff and Opal sat facing him, cheerfully entertaining the couple sitting on the sofa, their backs to Rolando. A pang of jealousy shot through his heart. This was what he wanted. Why was he always on the outside? He wanted to belong. He knew that now. He was tired of being alone and living only for himself. For several minutes he watched, and finally Opal rose from her chair. The man seated beside the woman on the sofa raised his arm from her shoulder, as she stood to join Rolando's sister-in-law, Opal. When Rolando recognized her, he let out a small agonizing cry, not believing what he had just seen. Raquel. He had thought about Raquel during his travels this past year. In the short conversations they had during the week of his parent's funerals, he had found himself reluctantly attracted to her. It was incredible. By the time he had decided to return to Pachuca, he decided to pursue her. But now, it looked as though she had married. It was more than he could bear.

Walking to the back of the house, he sat on the stoop. He would have to wait until Raquel and her husband left before he could let Geoff know he had returned. Placing his head in his hands, he despaired of his life and his failures. Somewhere in the depths of the Ecuadorian jungles, he had decided to return and win Raquel. But nothing seemed to work out for him.

The morning he had left Playas, he had taken a broken dream with him. Elena hadn't wanted to be with him. It hadn't taken long to believe that. Actually, he had realized it the minute he saw her standing outside the restaurant. By the time he had reached Guayaquil, he had surrendered, knowing Elena's marriage was meant to be and that it had been he, Rolando who pushed her out of his life, not Carlos. Because of his misguided hatred for Carlos he had hurt and destroyed all those he loved, almost taking someone's life. Wandering the country of Ecuador, he saw himself as others saw him. It was then he thought of Raquel. Perhaps she would help him change. Because he feared he would also destroy her, he rejected the idea time and time again, until after a year of running, he decided to find her and see if she had any interest in him. Perhaps she would be pleased with the new resolutions he had made.

But tonight, he had seen her with another man. He felt more alone now than ever. A nagging desire to have a drink wormed its way into his belly. Rising, he turned back to the street, but when he heard voices, laughter, and a car's motor, he waited until it had driven off. He debated several minutes whether he should see Geoff tonight or the next day. Walking halfway to the street he hesitated, then turned again, in an agony of indecision. Realizing he could no longer put off seeing his brother, he walked to the back door and came face to face with Raquel.

"Oh!" She jumped with fright. "Oh, Rolando. What are you doing back here? You scared me."

Rolando stood, looking down at her, his mouth hanging open stupidly.

"When did you arrive in town?" she asked, frowning.

"Raquel. I thought you just left for Quito."

"No. I stay in Pachuca during the week and in Quito on my days off." She frowned again. "You haven't answered my question. Geoff doesn't know you're here, does he?"

"No," he replied, delight and dread spreading through his heart. He was afraid to ask about the man he'd seen with her. "Did your husband go back to Quito alone?"

"My husband?"

"Yes, the man who was with you on the sofa."

She put one hand on a hip and gave him a questioning look. "How did you see him? Were you watching through the window?"

"I came earlier to visit with Geoff and saw the car. I didn't want to barge in and disturb you. So I waited out here."

She stood back and looked into his eyes, studying his face. "You've changed, haven't you? Where have you been this past year?"

"No place special. And yes, I guess I have changed a little. Perhaps you had a lot to do with that."

"Why do you say that?"

"Remember how you talked to me the night of my papa's death?"

"Vaguely, but I hardly believe you heard anything I said."

"Oh, but I did." He looked at her carefully, the flickering

candle in her hand changing the color of her eyes as he remembered them. He had traveled many miles trying to remember what she looked like. Taking a step forward, he gave her a small, pleading look. "Raquel, who was that man? Is he your husband?"

She giggled. "No, he's my brother. He came to Pachuca today to help me look for a building to set up a practice. I'm living here during the week and completing my studies while working in the government clinic across the street. I like Pachuca enough that I would like to live here."

But Rolando had not heard a word she said beyond the fact he had no rival for her affection.

"Would you please sit with me a minute. I must talk to you."

She hesitated a moment and then sat beside him.

"Opal will wonder where I am in a minute."

"That's all right. I will tell you quickly what I have on my mind." He rubbed his hand against his knee nervously and turned to look at her. "I have changed. I've done nothing but travel for a year and most of that time, I thought about you."

"About me? You hardly know me."

"I not only know you, but I love you."

Raquel started to stand. "That's impossible."

He put his hand on her arm. "It's the truth. I love you and would like to see if we can develop a relationship."

Fighting off his hand, she stood. "That's impossible," she repeated. "We live worlds apart. I appreciate the fact that you seem to have changed, but, Rolando, our lifestyles are so different. Why start something that we can never continue?"

"Why are our lives different?" A cloud started to settle over his spirit.

"Our goals, priorities, and desires are different. We think differently, our philosophies, theories, and understandings conflict. You must know I'm an evangelical Christian and I believe that before you can ever find yourself, you must make a lot of things right that you have done wrong. There has to be a real change of heart. It's not something that you do to please someone else but because you know it is the only way. There are a lot of people you must ask for forgiveness, and money you have taken that must be returned. It's called restitution."

She had hit the mark. He felt miserable. Again, she had seen past all of his pride, right into his heart. He felt as though all his evil acts and thoughts were exposed before her. The walls he had so carefully built fell at his feet. He stood and walked from her into the night.

The next morning he was gone again, leaving behind him a grieving Raquel.

From now on, thought Rolando, I don't care who I hurt or what I do.

Early the next morning he caught a bus to Quito and disembarked at the bank, withdrawing all of the money he had stolen from Geoff. From this day forward he would steal to live and drink the liquor he had been denying himself for months. His face burned with embarrassment remembering the way he had exposed his feelings for Raquel. Now he detested her.

Months passed in a blur of stolen purses and wallets, with the consumption of liquor, and sleep occupying most of each day in a tiny room on the south side of Quito.

Late, one afternoon he struggled awake, feeling the need for another drink. He realized someone was in his room. A blurry form sat on the end of his bed, and passing his hand over his eyes, he recognized Raquel. Certain he was dreaming, he closed his eyes and opened them again, expecting the illusion to be gone, but she was still there.

"Raquel. Is that you?"

"Yes."

Grabbing the blanket to his waist, he looked around at the cluttered, filthy room and was embarrassed. "What are you doing here?"

"I had to see you. You can't imagine what I have gone through since the last time we talked."

"I've been through a lot, too. How did you find me?"

"Your cousin, Ricardo, found you in a saloon and escorted you to this hotel room. Don't you remember?"

"No," he mumbled. "Why would you want to come here? The room is a mess. I'm a mess."

"Because I can't forget you. I feel I did you an injustice that night in Pachuca."

"You had every right. Look at what you would have been getting into, if we had begun a relationship."

"I feel responsible."

"Everything that has happened to me, I have asked for."

"How can I help you now?" she pleaded.

"There's no help for me. If you weren't here, I'd already be in a saloon drinking. In fact, I need a drink so badly, I can hardly think of anything else."

She sat at a loss for words.

"Raqui, I've always been a drinker. Please don't blame yourself. My real problems started when I allowed hatred and bitterness toward a good friend to ruin my life. I thought I was destroying him, but to my surprise, my hatred had not affected him at all. I ruined myself. While my sister and her husband enjoy their life in Playas, I am an alcoholic living a life in hell. There's no hope for me."

"I will never believe that," she said gently. "There is always hope. I don't understand what you mean by your sister being in Playas, however. They live here in the sierras, in Tulcachi. Your aunt and uncle have seen Carlos several times as they travel to their property in the mountains."

"Tulcachi? How can that be?" His mind whirled with the news. "I saw them in Playas."

"When were you in Playas?"

He sighed deeply and shook his head. "There's so much you don't know about me, Raqui. You were right. It would be a terrible mistake to become involved with me."

She stood and glowered down at him. "Never will I believe there is no way for you to change. It's just as I told you before. You are going to have to want to change. I believe God can help you."

"God?" He laughed. "God wants nothing to do with me."

"I'll never believe that either. Will you come home with me?"

"Home? I can't return home."

"Yes, you can. We all want you there."

"There's so much you don't know," he mumbled. Looking up at her, he smiled. "You go on to Pachuca. Let me spend some time thinking."

"Are you going out to drink? Because if you are, I'll stay with you."

"No, don't stay. I don't know right now what I'll do, but I do need to think about something."

She left reluctantly and he sat on the bed late into the night.

Chapter 43

L ate the next morning, he was on the bus to Pachuca. At the entrance to the hacienda Tulcachi, he descended the bus and began to walk the seven kilometer trek to the large ranch. The siesta hour having just ended, he met a peon on the road returning to the fields. Stopping him, he smiled tiredly.

"Buenos dias, senor. Could you tell me where Carlos Tapia is?"

"Buenos dias, senor. Carlos?" The broad-cheeked, weather-worn face squinted up at him. "I think he's working on a ridge beyond the main buildings and up the road that heads east. If you continue on that road a kilometer you will reach a side road beside a grove of bushes. Take that road for another kilometer and you'll see an odd-looking ridge. It looks like a very long, wide-backed animal lying there. After you get to the top, you can see how wide it is, but from below it looks too narrow to work on. Anyway, they're going to start planting corn today, I think."

Rolando thanked the man and moved on. As he approached the large house which stood beneath a grove of eucalyptus trees, he saw a long porch covered with stuffed burlap bags, piles of corn and a group of women working. Rolando searched their faces for Elena, but she wasn't there. He walked to the bottom of the hill and began climbing upward. He reached the side road and turned to the left, passing several hundred yards of thick brush. He traveled at a slight incline, until, in the distance, he saw a ridge about seventy-five meters high that spread several hundred meters to the east. Sitting on the summit, he saw a tractor and a lone man. Recognizing Carlos even from this distance, he walked rapidly toward him. Carlos sat on the tractor, leaning forward on the steering wheel, deep in meditation. Rolando stepped up the side of the ridge and came out behind him.

His heart quickened. Gently, he called Carlos' name.

Carlos's head snapped around, the fear evident in his eyes. He replied roughly. "Rolando. What are you doing here?"

Rolando shuffled his feet for a moment and put his hands in his pockets. "I'm not sure. I guess I need to talk with you."

He held his breath as Carlos studied him in bewilderment.

"What do we have to talk about?" He looked behind him, as if to search for help in case Rolando had mischief on his mind.

"I'm not here to make trouble. I'm not the blustering, raging, proud individual you have seen in the past. I'm troubled and defeated and I need you to help me."

Nothing could have surprised Carlos more. "What is it you need of me?"

"I need your forgiveness."

Carlos blinked his eyes and sat dumbfounded for several moments. "My forgiveness?"

"Yes, both your forgiveness and Elena's. I thought it best to talk with you first, since I did such a stupid thing last year in Playas." He lifted pleading eyes to the man on the tractor. "You don't know what I've been through. Three years ago I was so blinded that I thought I had everything under control. I thought that because of who I was, I could hold people within my power. I manipulated Elena's life and tried to destroy yours." He smiled without humor. "I thought you could never make anything of your life. A poor, downtrodden Indian, I told myself. You would never get anywhere in this world. Then, you went out and proved me wrong. And here I stand, a poor, downtrodden Indian who made nothing of my life. And I started with everything in my favor."

"I have nothing to forgive, Rolando. Actually you did us a favor. By forcing us to run away, we had only each other. Because of this, our marriage has become cemented in a way that would not have happened if we had been surrounded by a loving family and friends. We wouldn't be here in Tulcachi right now. I have work that I love. Elena is healthy and happy." He smiled. "By the way, did you know your sister is pregnant and will be delivering a baby in a few weeks?"

"A baby?" Rolando's eyes widened and misted. "It's hard to believe my little sister is old enough to care for a child."

"She's not a little girl any longer. She's a fine woman and will make a good mother. Please, come visit with us. If I didn't have to stay here and finish this project, I'd take you with me right now. But we're behind time and short of men." His eyes brightened. "Would you be able to come back tomorrow or the next day?"

"I'd love to."

"Come for the noon hour. I'd like you to meet Luis Perez, the hacienda owner.

"Thank you, Carlos. I can't believe you have accepted me so readily."

"I had no hatred against you, Rolando. I just wanted to protect my wife, your sister."

A great burden lifted from Rolando's heart and he felt a childish desire to yell with delight and run the length of the ridge. Instead he grinned, embarrassed by his feelings. "You have a nice tractor. It looks new."

"Yes, it is," grinned Carlos. "It came through customs just two weeks ago. Would you like to see how it operates?"

"Sure."

"Come sit behind me and I'll show you."

Carlos studied the controls. Rolando looked at Carlos, puzzled. "You act as though you don't know how to run this machine."

Carlos chuckled. "Well, to be truthful, I don't know much about them. We have a man who usually operates the tractors."

Rolando leaned forward and touched the starter. "Here, I can teach you."

Carlos' face brightened with delight. "Please, do."

"Put your left foot on the clutch and push the gearshift forward. Yes, that's right. Now, as you lift your left foot up, press your right foot on the gas pedal."

The tractor lurched forward and stalled.

"That's the idea, but you have to lift your left foot and press your right foot a little slower." With patience, Rolando taught him all the gears, then jumped down from the tractor.

"I guess I'd better leave. I have to get back to Quito."

"You're living in Quito?" He switched off the tractor's motor.

"Not after today. I'm going home. I have some other wrong deeds to make right."

They shook hands, smiling into each other's eyes.

As Rolando walked away, Carlos started up the motor again. Alarmed, Rolando turned, raised his arm, and started running toward Carlos. "Carlos, wait! I don't think you're ready to drive.

The tractor lurched backwards and lost traction. He watched, in horror, as the machine fell, turning over and over until Carlos was thrown free. It finally came to rest against a large bush. The man lay in a broken, crumpled heap. Racing down the hill, Rolando reached Carlos and put his arm under his neck. He patted his cheek and put his ear next to Carlos' lips. He was still breathing.

"Carlos. Carlos. Please wake up. Please. Don't die," he cried. "Please not now." Putting his head down carefully, he jumped up. He must get help.

He ran with all his might toward the road, hoping to find someone. It seemed forever before he covered the kilometer, but soon he saw the intersection. There was no one in sight. Suddenly, he realized he should have carried Carlos with him. Turning back, he ran the distance in a few minutes. Much to his surprise, he saw a tall man bending over Carlos. A stallion remained on the ridge. Rolando started to move toward them, but then he realized he couldn't present himself. There were too many people who knew how much he had hated Carlos. No one would believe it was an accident. He must leave before anyone saw him.

Anxiety and grief accompanied him to Quito. The day had started out with promise. By the time he reached Quito, his mind was in a whirl of conflict. He'd been forgiven. There was no bitterness or hatred left within him against his brother-in-law. Only this recent turn of events saved him because another drinking binge might have kill him. He knew that. He would have to take what had happened this afternoon and build on it. Anyway, there was every chance that Carlos would live. He was thrown clear of the tractor. Perhaps there would be a few broken bones, but Rolando couldn't believe he was dead. When Carlos regained consciousness, he would tell Senor Perez and Elena that he and Rolando have reconciled.

He packed his belongings, paid the landlady with some of the stolen money, and took what remained of Geoff's savings. He resolved that from that moment on the only money he would spend would be the money he earned.

The news of Carlos' death sent shock waves through the town of Pachuca. Rolando learned of it at the breakfast table in his Aunt Mariana's house, where he had been welcomed back with open arms.

"I heard about it when I went down to the corner store to buy bread this morning." said Mariana. "Ernestina was crying. You know how she feels about all you young people who have grown up around here."

Rolando sat stunned, surges of disbelief rippling through him. Dead. He couldn't believe it. Just yesterday, they had parted with a firm shake of hands. It was his fault for trying to teach Carlos to drive that tractor. He had just wanted to show off a little. Oh, God. He should have carried him in his arms down to the hacienda.

"Rolando? Whatever is the matter?"

"I don't feel well. I think I'm going to be sick."

He ran from the room, with Mariana in pursuit. Finding a bucket of water on the back stoop, he leaned over and splashed water on his face. He sat against the wall of the house until the nausea passed.

"Dear, I can't believe Carlos' death would affect you this much. I always thought this is what you wanted."

"I don't want anyone to die, Tia." He leaned his head back. "Please leave me alone. I need to rest a minute."

Tears ran freely and a lump in his throat hampered his breathing. Life is so miserable, he thought. Is there happiness anywhere?

Guilt prevented him from attending Carlos' funeral. He told Geoff he had to go to Quito, but actually he left early in the morning to wander in the mountains above Pachuca. He walked beside deep canyons, climbed small hills, and sat beside tiny streams that flowed through the farmlands. If only he could have told Elena about his new friendship with Carlos. But if he had, Luis would want to know why he left the scene and why he hadn't returned. The foolish mistakes he had made that afternoon in a state of panic would always haunt him. He hadn't been thinking clearly.

The sound of tolling church bells echoed off the mountains behind him, filling the valley with their mournful strains. Rolando grieved. All day he wandered, and meditated, and trying to organize what was left of his life.

At nightfall he returned to town and walked to his family home, hoping to find Geoff. He stepped into the kitchen. Geoff sat at the table, frowning over a book of figures. Looking up, he saw his brother.

"Rolando. Come in. Would you like something hot to drink?"

"No, gracias." He waved Geoff back to his chair, while he pulled one up for himself.

Geoff pushed back the book and smiled at his sibling. "I needed an excuse to stop this torture. I have such a hard time with figures."

"Did you see Elena today?" He turned weary, questioning eyes to Geoff.

"She looked terrible." He shook his head slowly. "She's pregnant. That will make Carlos' death even harder for her to bear. She has good care, however. My heart went out to her, and I approached her for a few moments to give my love and to offer an explanation why you weren't able to be there."

A long silence ensued, until Rolando could no longer bear it.

He thumped his fingers on the table nervously. "Geoff, I took the money. I stole it from your room."

Geoff hesitated a minute. "I know."

"It wasn't that I needed it for myself. I thought I had to have it because somewhere in my crazy, mixed-up mind, I thought I had to go after Elena and bring her home. I wanted to destroy Carlos."

Geoff stared at his brother, and slowly an uncontrolled look of horror crossed his face.

Rolando interpreted the look. "No. I didn't kill Carlos. Actually I did go to Playas. I found out from Laura that Carlos and Elena were living there. I went to bring Elena home and found, much to my dismay and surprise, that Carlos was a wonderful, kind, gentle husband to our Elena, and that she didn't want to come home at all. My hatred against Carlos all these years has been for nothing. I only brought damage to myself and my family. I made a terrible mistake. The money I took from you has been spent on things you won't want to know about, Geoff. It fell like water through a net. I am so ashamed. Will you forgive me? And will you let me work for you again, to pay back what I owe?"

"My dear brother. You never did work for me. You worked with me. This is a family operation and I have needed you very much these past months. We could do twice the work I do if I had proper help." Geoff sat back and thoughtfully played with his ear lobe. "Yes, you can work and pay me back, and when you have earned the amount you took, we'll talk. Until then, it is a subject we'll not speak of again. And, Rolando, you have always been forgiven."

"Why is everyone being so nice to me? I don't deserve it, you know."

"Perhaps not. But your family loves you. You just haven't allowed us to get past the walls you've been putting up around you for years. I've always loved and respected you. The truth of the matter is, I've never despised you, as you have accused me in the past. I've never thought any less of you, nor have I stood in judgment against your livestyle. After I married Opal, my love and appreciation grew for you, Rolando. Much of what I am today is due to your sacrifices while I was a child. Now that I'm responsible for a wife and a growing business, I have nothing but love and respect for you."

The front door opened and shut. The jabber and laughter of Opal and Raquel filled the house. Rolando stood and prepared to leave.

"Where are you going?" questioned Geoff. "Please, stay."

"No, I must get home. Thanks."

"You're not leaving because of us, are you, Rolando?" inquired Opal, walking into the kitchen.

Rolando nodded no and greeted Raquel, who was standing behind Opal.

"I've got a lot of things to do." Turning back to Geoff, he held out his hand. "I'll see you in the morning."

Geoff agreed and stood to hug his brother. Rolando returned the hug affectionately and excused himself, passing by Opal.

As Rolando opened the door to leave, Raquel reached for him.

"Why are you leaving? Can't we talk?"

"There's really nothing for us to talk about, Raquel. Thank you for all your interest and concern, but I think I can handle things now."

Her face fell. "For someone who told me he loved me a few weeks ago, you have certainly changed." She frowned.

"You were right. There is no way we can work things out. Despite the changes that have occurred in my life, we still live in different worlds. I don't need what you have. I have been able to turn my life around on my own these past few days. And I feel so much better. Everything is looking up." He looked down at her crestfallen face and gently touched her cheek. "Oh, Raqui, please don't take this wrong. You're a fine girl and I like you very much. In fact, you helped me turn around. Ever since we met, on the night of my papa's death, you have influenced me. You helped me in Quito, too." He took her hand in his and smiled. "I really do appreciate you."

"Giving her a kiss on the cheek, he walked out the door, leaving her with tear-filled eyes.

Now he had a goal. Working in the truck was pleasurable because he knew each day's work would bring him closer to restoring Geoff's money.

He had gone several weeks without a drink; work was steady, and Geoff was his friend. Even though he still kept his brother at a distance because of his leanings toward the church, he knew they could talk together and that was a far cry from their relationship the year before.

The loss of Carlos hadn't affected him as much as he thought it would. That they had parted friends was sufficient. But, Elena's condition worried him. Geoff's report of the state of her appearance at her husband's funeral surprised him. He understood that she loved Carlos, but he hadn't suspected the extent of her love. Nevertheless, he comforted himself that Luis Perez was there to help her.

If he would have let his true fears be made known, however, he would have admitted that he was afraid to visit Elena at the Hacienda Tulcachi in case someone remembered him walking past the buildings that day. Maybe the peon he had met on the road would recognize him and he would be accused. He would have no excuse. He decided to call on Elena after the baby was born, thereby absolving himself of any feelings of neglect and guilt.

All day he had been driving the truck on the road beyond the pueblo's swimming pool and up into the mountains where there was a large rock quarry. Hauling rocks for the construction workers who were laying a foundation a kilometer west of Pachuca, had kept him busy the entire morning. He had taken a short nap after lunch in his father's bedroom and was now anxious to complete the job.

Turning a bend, he was surprised to see a little blue pickup sitting alongside the road. Since no one was inside the vehicle, he slowed down and looked around for Jillian, the American girl who was now living in the plaza area. Despite the fact he had seen her several times in the pickup carrying children back and forth to school, he had never met her personally. Perhaps this was his chance. Braking the truck, he pulled up behind her pickup. Softly closing the truck's door, he padded across a patch of green grass and around a small rise. Stopping short, he looked down on the girl napping on a large towel.

He smirked with good humor and sat away from her. As if she detected someone's presence, she opened her eyes, squinting against the brightness of the day and peered into his smiling face. Sitting upright, she adjusted her clothes, patted her strawberry blond hair and looked at him sternly. Clearly, she wanted to be alone. Then she smiled and he saw she had a face that wasn't beautiful, but one that would be hard to forget. Her green eyes mellowed and he sensed a compassion and love that made him want to sit with her all afternoon, just to talk. There was no need for introductions.

"You're Rolando Martinez, aren't you?"

"Yes. I'm sorry if I woke you. I only came over to see if you were all right. I saw your pickup and wondered why you would be here." Looking around, he saw a brown paper sack. "What is this, a picnic?"

She laughed. "No. I just wanted to get away for a while. Sometimes my house can get rather crowded. Do you know me?"

"Of course. You're Jillian. I've waited a long time to meet you."

"You may call me Jill." She looked at him steadily. "I guess we had the same desire. I wanted to meet you, too." Turning around, she dragged a thermos from the sack. "Would you like some cookies or coffee?"

"No, thank you. I just had my lunch."

There was a lengthy, but comfortable silence between them. He rubbed the toe of his shoe into the grass, aware she was studying him. He lifted his head and their eyes met.

"How is it that we have lived in the same town so long and haven't met each other?" he asked with a smile.

"I don't know. I guess because I'm never home."

"Yes, I've heard about your classes and have seen you driving into the mountains with your pickup full of children."

She laughed again. "You're right. I'm always going somewhere."

He didn't want to leave, but when she moved to a more comfortable position, he realized maybe she wanted privacy.

"I'm sorry. Am I bothering you?"

"Not at all. It's just that I'll have to return home soon. This was a special time for me. It's not often I can get away."

Making himself more comfortable, he grinned. "Maybe I will take a cookie? They look good."

"Sure." She handed him a clear plastic bag and he took it, pulling out half a dozen.

"Tell me about yourself. I hear you used to work with Senorita Margaret."

"Yes, for a few years."

"How was it living with Lucia and Margaret?"

"It depended. Some days were wonderful, others difficult. The children made it worthwhile."

"I've heard about the children she took in. Did any of them live with you?" He swallowed a cookie.

"Yes. Before I left I had several in my care."

"The nurse is a strange lady. I've had a rather sad experience because of her."

"Oh? How was that?"

"My mother was never the same after my sister, Elena, was born. I blame her illness and death on Senorita Margaret."

"I've heard part of the story from friends. It's hard for the townspeople to forget stories like that." Jillian leaned forward. "I'm aware of the suffering you endured when you were young. I would like to be your friend, Rolando."

His eyes brightened. "I'd like that. It's nice to be able to sit and talk with you." He wiped his mouth with the back of his hand.

"Did you know Elena is at Margaret's clinic with her baby right now?"

Rolando's face fell in astonishment. "No. Why would she be there?"

"Apparently she couldn't make it to Quito. Margaret's maid

stopped by to see me and gave me the news. Her sister-in-law, Yolando, stopped by also. We've become rather good friends." .

His heart missed a beat. Imagine what Yolanda would have told Jillian about his extended stay in her home. Praying that he looked unperturbed, he merely shook his head.

"Have you seen Elena since the funeral?" Jillian noticed his discomfort and changed the subject.

"No." Regaining his composure he replied curtly, covering his uneasiness.

"Why don't you go down to the clinic and visit her?"

"I haven't seen her in such a long time, I don't know if she wants to visit with me."

"Oh, Rolando, that's silly. Of course she wants to see you."

"There's a lot of things you don't know."

"Perhaps, but I can assure you there are a lot of things I do know." She leveled her eyes at him. "Don't miss this opportunity."

Feeling uncomfortable, he stood. "I must leave. I'd like to finish my other haul job today."

"If you ever need to talk, or just need a friend, please come to see me."

"Thank you. He grabbed her hand gratefully. "I will do that."

Sitting inside the truck, his heart beat with excitement. Elena. She was only a few hundred meters from where he was sitting. He could run the truck down to the clinic in just a minute and visit with her. No, not yet. He would wait until tomorrow. As it was, he had sat for two hours this morning waiting until the peons in the quarry showed up for work. He would finish the job today or tomorrow morning and then visit Elena.

He was tempted to tell Geoff that Elena was nearby, but the desire to see his sister and ask for her forgiveness was something he needed to do alone.

Early Tuesday morning he rose, eager to see Elena. Grooming himself carefully, he ate a hurried breakfast, laughingly ignoring his aunt's inquiries. She had not yet forgiven Elena.

By the time he arrived at the clinic it was eight o'clock. Pausing at the bottom of the driveway, it struck him what he was doing. How did he know Elena would be glad to see him? He remembered her temper and the silent treatment he received when she was angry with him. Perhaps Carlos had regained consciousness long enough to tell Luis that Rolando had been there. Maybe they were waiting until after the baby was born to speak with him concerning Carlos' death. Maybe with a baby Elena would have no room for him in her life. He could not bear another rejection from her. After all, Elena had left him in the first place. In agony, he stood on the road. With a final shrug of his shoulders, he turned and walked back to the truck he had parked at Geoff's house. Geoff and Opal had gone by bus into Quito on an errand and Raquel was enjoying two days off with her family. He would wait until after work this evening to talk Geoff into going with him.

Sadly he drove to his next job, his mind heavy with thoughts of Elena.

He would ask for her forgiveness at a later date. Perhaps if Geoff went with him, Elena would be happier to see him.

Chapter 44

Laying his head on the table, he opened one eye to see if Raphael was near. He needed another drink. Rising, he staggered across the room to see if the proprietor had stepped into the back room. In the middle of the filthy floor, among a group of dancers, he collapsed, passing out.

When he came to, he was lying against the wall beside the saloon steps.

It was Saint Pedro's Day and the festivities had begun early that afternoon with the women of Pachuca setting up their food stands. For days they had prepared for this fiesta; walking to local hacienda to purchase potatoes, meat, havas, ears of corn, animal intestines, frankfurters, lettuce, tomatoes, avocados and onions. They had searched the hillsides for firewood and bought charcoal from local families.

The men had built frames ten feet high from sticks of plywood and tied dozens of firecrackers to each frame. Orchestras had been hired from neighboring towns, and dances in several locations were planned. Elderly women had prepared liquors from chewed corn, which had been left to ferment for many days.

Farmers slit the necks of squealing pigs and cleaned their bodies on curbs as scrawny dogs watched, ready to pounce on discarded pieces. Shortly after noon villagers arrived in the plaza and began setting up tables and crude stoves filled with wood and charcoal. Wooden chairs, large pieces of plastic, and buckets of food filled every available space along the curbs. Fires were fanned and great pots of potatoes, ears of corn, and meat were placed on grills. On the tables sat bowls of pork, frankfurters, oranges, tangerines, chirimoyas, bananas, chochos, and havas.

Late in the afternoon the orchestras appeared to begin their marches around the plaza. The people followed. Hundreds of Indians from the surrounding suburbs and mountains converged on the plaza, packing the sidewalks in anticipation of the dances and fireworks.

It was evening when he roused. Men running in the street, holding high the frames of bursting, sparkling firecrackers frightened him as he struggled to a sitting position and leaned back on the saloon wall. He was groggy, but sober. The desires for a drink gripped him and he started to put his hand in his jacket to search for more bills.

Suddenly, as if a curtain had been lifted from his eyes, he saw himself—a young man still in his early thirties, a hopeless alcoholic, alone, miserable and broken. He could not go on this way any longer. If the liquor didn't kill him, someday someone would. An idea that had been rooting in his mind for the past two weeks blossomed: he knew he no longer wanted to live.

Struggling to his feet, he held his head for a moment, then pushed past the Indians packing the sidewalks. Leaning against them, they irritably made way until he reached Ernestina's corner store. He had never been able to pass this corner without a sense of sadness, and now he felt tears on his cheeks. He would never see it again. Since the night she had helped him as a child, Ernestina had always been one of his favorite people. Standing there looking in, he couldn't move for the surge of people passing in and out of the doors. In despair he pushed forward, staggering toward his family home. One man ran the length of the street carrying a frame of rockets and blazing firecrackers. The glow illuminated the street. Stopping to rest a moment, Rolando looked up and saw Jillian standing at the railing of her balcony, watching the scene.

Elbowing aside a family of Indians parked on her front stoop, he fell against the door and pounded with his fists. At first, she could not hear his pounding above the noise of the orchestras and firecrackers. He waited then began to beat upon the door again, until at last the door opened. He fell through onto the cement floor of the entryway.

"Rolando!"

She pulled on his arm until he rested on the floor in a sitting position. His face was covered with dirt, his disheveled hair was filthy.

Groaning he turned and smiled weakly. "You told me I could come when I needed you."

"Yes. Of course." She smiled through a frown. "Just a moment. I'll be right back.

He watched her walk into a room off the entryway where she had a makeshift kitchen. Drawing water from a large plastic container, she filled a pan and laid it over a fire on the stove. When it was warm, she poured it into a basin. Taking a washcloth and a bar of soap from the cupboard, she returned to his side. Placing the basin on the floor, she helped him remove his jacket.

"Here, sit on this bench."

He pulled himself to his feet and sat obediently as she proceeded to wash his face and hands. As if he were a child, he allowed her to cool his flushed face with the tepid water. He began to feel better.

"You were rather dirty," she grinned.

"I guess I'm in terrible condition." Embarrassed, he ran his hand through his hair. "Thank you, Jill. I'm beginning to feel ashamed for being here like this."

"Just rest a minute. I'm going to fix you something to eat."

"Maybe some bread and a little cheese, if you have it. I do feel hungry."

Jillian returned to the kitchen and began to cut bread and cheese. She set the pan of water on the stove again and prepared a tray. She was pouring coffee when something in him snapped.

Tears flowed out of control; tears that had been trapped within his soul for years now gushed forth like a natural spring. Loud sobs racked his body until he fell to the floor in agony, doubled over in pain.

She placed a hand on his shoulder.

"I miss her," he sobbed. "I miss her so much. Oh, Jill, I love her."

"Who?"

Gasping for breath, he collapsed onto the floor again in tears.

"Who, Rolando?"

"Elena. I love Elena so much. Oh, how I miss her." Sobs ripped through him. "I loved her so much. Oh, Elena, Elena, my darling Elena."

He raised his head, the moans of heartbreak tearing from deep within his belly.

"Why did she die before I had a chance to tell her I loved her? Why did I wait?"

He stood, stumbled and grabbed at his head trying to control the spasms racking his body. "Jill, I can't stand this pain. I want to die, but I'm so afraid."

He fell back on the bench in agony, weeping with fresh tears. "I am so foolish. I was at the clinic that Tuesday morning, but fear and pride kept me from going in. I could have helped her. Why did I have to be so proud? Oh, God, help me. I can't stand the pain."

"Rolando." Jillian was fighting back tears. She laid her hand on his arm again. "I'm not sure what I can say or do to take away your pain, but there was no way that you could have known she would be dying. You can't blame yourself. That would only bring more harm to you."

"I want to blame myself. I need to hurt and suffer. This is what will cleanse my soul. I'm so sick of living for myself. I'm so filthy inside. I've done so many terrible things. I need to suffer."

"That is where you're wrong. By suffering, you won't feel any better. Punishing yourself won't gain anything."

"What a miserable life. Why do any of us want to live? I look around me at the distress, the sadness, the ugliness. Why would anyone want to live in this world?" He looked at her with puffy, red eyes. "Jill, I've tried so hard all of my life. In the process,

I've cut off everyone. Just a few weeks ago, I bragged to a girl, who cares very much for me, that I didn't need her, that I could make it on my own. Make it on my own? Look at the mess I'm in. I thought by making restitution to the people I had wronged, I could solve all my problems. It helped for a while, but I don't have the ability or strength to change my own life. I just can't do it. Right now, I feel totally helpless with no desire to live beyond this night."

"I don't think there are too many people who can truthfully say they have changed their lives without some outside help."

"There's no help for me. I've tried everything."

"I'm sure I can offer a suggestion you haven't tried.

Raising his eyebrows skeptically, he waited.

"There is no need to live your life with all these emotions bottled up inside you. There is a way to feel clean."

"Yes?"

"One way is to weep as you have. That certainly can bring a cleansing, but the trouble with that is, in a short time, the results are wiped away by those unresolved problems rising to the surface again. I would like to introduce you to someone who will be willing to have you dump all of your sorrows, problems and emotions on him. I can promise you these same problems won't have to return. In fact, I can guarantee that with the right attitude you will meet this person, tell him what you want, and your visit will bring changes I believe everything will appear better to you."

"Who would that be?" he asked with interest.

"Come with me. I want to take you somewhere." She stood, pulling on his arm. "I'll take you to see him."

He stood, perplexed, and followed her to the door. Pushing their way through the crowds of people, they struggled a few meters from her house to a low stairway leading to a long sidewalk empty of people. Here they were free to walk quickly.

"Jill, where are we going?"

"We're going to see someone you've known about all your life." She smiled up at him. "Well, I know him and he's someone who will be happy to listen to your problems no matter how many times you need to talk with him. If you'll approach him with the right attitude, I promise you you'll leave here tonight a different person."

Approaching the wide, low building, she pushed open the big doors and pulled him in with her. Inside, it was quiet, the muffled noises from without strained through the thick walls. They walked up a long aisle until they stood beneath a picture of Christ on the cross.

"Rolando, you have seen Christ on the cross all of your life. The news I have for you is that He isn't on the cross any longer. He was there just long enough to die, but now He's alive, and He's waiting to listen to even your faintest cry. There is no need too small or no problem too large for Him to handle. You see, that's why He died, so you can live with a soul cleansed from hatred, bitterness and impurities. But the only people who can be totally changed are those who realize they need Him and who come to Him with the faith that He is able to help. Rolando, here lies your answer."

He stood for a long time without speaking, then slowly nodded his head.

"Come, sit with me here." Jillian moved to a front row bench in the quiet church. Rolando followed obediently. "I have been in close contact with Luis Perez. He's visited me a few times since Elena's death, in search of answers because I worked at Margaret's clinic. We have talked of Elena and Carlos. You may not know this about Elena, but according to Luis, she miscarried twice in Playas. They were very happy together, but there was a period of time after her first miscarriage that she had some type of breakdown. She wasn't a stable person under stress. After losing Carlos, Luis had a terrible time with her. With the death of her child, she was unable to survive. No one could have helped her with that under the circumstances. Luis claims the baby died in Margaret's clinic, so, Rolando, you can't carry blame for something that was beyond your control." She gave him a gentle smile. "Perhaps we can go to Tulcachi and visit with Luis someday. Both Elena and Carlos are buried there together in a lovely spot. I think that might help you, too."

Standing, she looked down at him. "I'm going to leave you alone right now. All you have to do is talk to the Lord, just as if He's here, because He is. Don't forget all we've spoken about. I believe you can walk out of here a different person tonight. Then come back to see me. You still haven't eaten your bread and cheese."

He gave her a small smile and nodded his head as she turned to leave.

Book 7
Rolando & Raquel

Chapter 45

S lowly he opened his eyes and squinted against the sun streaming through the window. Automatically he looked at his wife beside him. His beautiful wife. Never did he tire of watching her face, so full of expression and sweetness. In her sleep, she looked like a child, helpless and trusting. They had been married for seven years, and still he tried to awaken before she did, just to watch her sleep. He thought she had the most perfectly formed eyebrows and lovely, long eyelashes. Her nose was tilted and small, in perfect proportion with her face. All of her life she had been spoiled by her father and when Rolando married her, he had happily taken over the privilege. He doted on her.

She moved, coming out of her sleep, and opened her lids revealing brown eyes flecked with yellow and green.

She smiled at him and he leaned to kiss her cheek.

"We've got to get ready for church and volleyball, Raquel. We have our first tournament this afternoon."

"Did you say you're playing against Tababela?" She yawned and stretched.

"Yes, and I believe we can win."

"Of course you can, my love. I wonder if the children are awake yet?"

He grinned. "I've learned to sleep through the noise from the marketplace on Sundays, but there's no way I can sleep when our children are playing in the next room. They're the ones who woke me." Sitting up in bed, he shivered in the cold air and yelled. "Elena, come in here."

The door opened and a laughing, dark-haired, black-eyed child ran into the room, her bright eyes sparkling.

"Hola, my little love." He hoisted her up and kissed her cheek. Raquel leaned over to do the same.

"What is your brother doing?" she asked.

"He's still in bed playing with his toys," replied the child, pointing toward the door.

"All right," said Raquel. "We've got to get up and fix our breakfast. Popi is going to play in the volleyball tournament after church today, before we eat dinner at Aunt Mariana's house. Won't that be fun?"

"Oh, yes." Jumping from the bed, the little girl danced about the room.

"Come and let me comb your hair, then we'll butter some rolls and heat water for some coffee."

Raquel rose from the bed and Rolando leaned back, arms folded behind his head, watching the scene. He would never stop being thankful for what he had. Raquel had opened a clinic a block from the plaza in which she treated patients each afternoon except Sunday. Rolando had bought his own truck, and together with Geoff, operated a lucrative business. Geoff, Opal, and their daughter, Rosa, lived in Oyambarillo in a neat, little house on several acres of land. Rolando had long ago repaid his brother the money he owed, refusing any of it in return. Roberto had remained in the military, choosing it as his career. He had also married and lived in Quito with his wife. Rolando's brother, Pablo, had not been as fortunate as Rolando, having died an alcoholic's death the past year.

Rolando and Raquel had been married a year when Elena was born. Three years later, Raquel had gave birth to a son, affectionately called Pepito.

He waited for a moment to give his wife and daughter a chance to wash themselves and comb their hair at the water vat behind the house. Listening absently to the marketplace noise, he thought excitedly of the activities of the day; the fellowship he would have with the people at church; the volleyball game, and dinner with his beloved Aunt Mariana.

He heard Raquel beckon him to hurry. He got up from the bed and took a towel, his pants and shirt with him. The house was chilly, but the sun outside would warm him. He poked his head in the bedroom across the hall and waved to his son, who was being dressed by Raquel. The little boy giggled and jumped with delight at the sight of his father.

Outside, Rolando stretched and placed his clothes on a table. He put the towel on the familiar branch protruding out from the mud wall. Stopping for a moment, he breathed deeply and looked back at the green mountains and the dark blue sky. He stretched again, absorbing the warmth of the sun.

Excitement stirred in him again. He always looked forward to going to church with his family. The congregation was growing and Rolando was being trained for a possible pastorate. Sunday mornings were the highlight of his week. More and more he was learning to put his priorities in order, and he felt deep in his heart that someday he would be a pastor of a church somewhere in Ecuador. He couldn't help but hope that it would be in the vicinity of Pachuca.

He stopped daydreaming and found a razor on the ledge below the mirror. Lathering a shaving bar, he placed the foam carefully on his face. He drew the razor across his cheek and rinsed it in a bowl of water placed to one side.

"Popi, hurry and come." Elena called to Rolando. "Breakfast is ready and we have to leave for church soon." Elena appeared, fresh and clean in a dress Raquel's mother had given her, wearing her hair braided down her back.

He stared at her for a moment, a thought looming in his mind. He had been here before, watching this scene. He shook his head. He must have dreamed it. But no, it was so real. When? He grabbed at the thought, trying to secure it, but it escaped him.

"I need a hug." He chuckled, holding out his arms.

She laughed delightedly, jumped a little, and ran toward him with outstretched arms. She loved the clean smell of his shaving lather.

Rolando put the razor down and lifted her above him. Drawing her close, he hugged her tightly, careful not to get lather in her hair. Purposefully, she stuck the tip of her nose in his lathered cheek. She withdrew a frosted white nose.

Again, he was aware he had been here before, experiencing this. He shook his head, puzzled.

She giggled and he looked at her.

"I love you, Popi."

"I love you too, Elena."

She disappeared inside the house, returning in a moment, minus the dot of white.

"Popi, Momi says to come right now. Breakfast is ready, and we're going to be late," she exclaimed seriously.

He stared at her. A thought stirred through his mind, but with sense of sadness. Again, it eluded him. Elena, her black hair in braids falling down her back, calling him to breakfast; he grabbed at the thought and it fled.

"Popi, come."

"Elena?" He called softly.

"Did you say something, Popi?"

He shook his head and the mood broke. "No, carina. I just said to tell your Momi I'll be right there."

He rinsed off his face, put on his clothes, looked up at the green mountains and blue sky and thought that it was a perfect day for a volleyball game.

Other Books & Tapes by Starburst Publishers